A WILDERNESS OF STARS

A WILDERNESS OF STARS

SHEA ERNSHAW

SIMON & SCHUSTER BFYR

NEW YORK   LONDON   TORONTO   SYDNEY   NEW DELHI

SIMON & SCHUSTER BFYR

An imprint of Simon & Schuster Children's Publishing Division
1230 Avenue of the Americas, New York, New York 10020
This book is a work of fiction. Any references to historical events, real people, or real places are used
fictitiously. Other names, characters, places, and events are products of the author's imagination,
and any resemblance to actual events or places or persons, living or dead, is entirely coincidental.
Text © 2022 by Shea Ernshaw
Jacket illustration © 2022 by Jim Tierney
Jacket design by Sarah Creech © 2022 by Simon & Schuster, Inc.
All rights reserved, including the right of reproduction in whole or in part in any form.
SIMON & SCHUSTER BOOKS FOR YOUNG READERS
and related marks are trademarks of Simon & Schuster, Inc.
For information about special discounts for bulk purchases, please contact
Simon & Schuster Special Sales at 1-866-506-1949 or business@simonandschuster.com.
The Simon & Schuster Speakers Bureau can bring authors to your live event.
For more information or to book an event, contact the Simon & Schuster Speakers Bureau
at 1-866-248-3049 or visit our website at www.simonspeakers.com.
Interior design by Hilary Zarycky
The text for this book was set in Adobe Garamond.
Manufactured in the United States of America
First Edition
2 4 6 8 10 9 7 5 3 1
CIP data for this book is available from the Library of Congress.
ISBN 9781665900249
ISBN 9781665900263 (ebook)

ORION, *Gamma Ori*
+06° 20' 58"

A hundred years ago, the first Astronomer looked up at the night sky and made note of what she saw: horseshoe nebulas and spiral galaxies and dying star clusters. But she did not yet know what lay hidden in the shadowy darkness between stars. She was not a seer, a fortune-teller, as was common in the old world but rarely talked about now. Instead she used the circular glass rings of her telescope to make sense of the dark; she used physics and chemistry and science. She drafted charts and measured distances and sketched formations like Pleiades and Andromeda onto wax paper.

Maybe if she had believed in fate. If she had listened to her gut—that hollow twisting beneath her lowest ribs—she might have feared what she didn't understand.

She might have known that the shadow concealed more than dust and particles of broken moons.

She would have looked closer.

And seen.

ONE

M om is dying, and we both know it.

She's been sick for almost a month, the consumption shredding apart her insides, clouding her eyes, and making it impossible for her to breathe without an awful rasp.

On the roof of our small house, I lie flat on my back, breathing in the cool, windless spring air—the night sky a riddle of stars above me—but inside the cabin, through the open window, I can hear Mom dozing fitfully: fever making her sweat and toss and mumble in her sleep.

I press my palms against the roof beneath me, as if I could push away the awful sound, push away the sickness inside her. I count the constellations, naming them in my mind—a ritual that Mom insists I repeat night after night so I won't forget—and it calms me, the pattern of unaltered stars, their position always right where they should be. Unlike Mom, who is slipping away. Beyond the row of blue spruce trees on the far side of the summer garden, above the valley wall, I trace Clovis and Andromeda with my fingertip. I find Orion, the hunter from Greek mythology, and Rigel, a bright blue-white supergiant shimmering near the horizon. Each one tells a story.

Each one has some secret to be shared, if I have the patience to look.

I follow the simple line of Aries, the golden-fleeced ram, my finger making a slight arc through the midnight sky. Sometimes I let myself fall asleep on the roof, to be closer to the stars; sometimes I stay awake all night, searching for something up there that might bring me hope.

I search for something that isn't there.

An owl lets out a low, somber cry from the toolshed; the wind slides across the roof, stirring my long, dark hair, curled slightly at the ends, sending gooseflesh across my scarred, copper skin. And I wonder if it's all for nothing. All the knowledge I keep safe inside me—patterns and sequences and the names of constellations—all of it useless if I never leave these valley walls.

Heat rises behind my eyes, but I push it down, counting the stars of Leo, *the lion*, killed by Hercules with his bare hands and placed in the sky. Stories threaded and stitched in the starlight. But I wonder what stories will be told about me: *The girl who stayed safe in her valley. Who never left. Who died like her mother, taking all her knowledge with her.*

I wipe at my eyes, hating the tears, willing the stars to show me something—*begging*. But the sky sits just as it always has—unaltered, unchanged—and I know I've been forgotten by the stars, by the ancient gods. *Abandoned.* They do not see me as I see them.

I press a hand to my ear, a soft ringing in my eardrum, an ache so small that it's hardly there—*scratch, scratch*, like an insect in my skull—but when I swing my gaze back to the sky, blinking away the wetness, a thin, rainless cloud slides along the valley walls, pushing north . . .

And something catches my eye.

Tiny. Flickering.

In the darkness, in the space between stars . . .

A light. *Small at first.* Where none should be.

To the east.

I scramble to my feet, tugging my sweater close across my chest, squinting up at the unusual light. *Light that shouldn't be there.*

It glows a shimmering whiteness, but its position in the sky makes no sense. I blink and recenter my gaze—as Mom taught me—but when I scan the horizon, it's still there. *There.* Only a flicker at first—like a dying ember in a campfire—but after a moment it grows brighter, rising above the treetops.

Not a falling star.

Not a comet.

Something larger. A shiver skips up into my throat—a knowing—like the telltale scent of moisture in the air, hours before a single raindrop has fallen from the sky.

I've stared at this patch of horizon countless times, and seen nothing: only darkness and tiny pine-needle pricks of ordinary starlight. But when I rub my palms against the hollows of my eyes, then look again to the east . . . I find it. *Still there.*

A star . . . where no star had been the night before.

My heart begins to ram against my rib cage, thoughts crashing and tumbling over one another, wanting to be sure. And then I see it: the star isn't alone.

There are *two*.

One fainter than the other, smaller, but they rest side by side: twin stars shivering an amber light from the middle of our galaxy. And as they rise higher above the horizon, they appear so close, it feels as if I can almost reach up and pluck them down, hold them in my palm like an August firefly, golden and pulsing, then carry them inside to show Mom.

Two delicate orbs.

Them.

A hum of excitement and disbelief vibrates up into my chest, behind my eyes, and I swing myself down from the roof, perching my foot against the wood post, then landing on the front porch with a *thud*—something I've done hundreds of times—then dart through the front door into the cabin.

A fire still burns in the stone fireplace, the scent of cloves and rosemary heavy in the air from the herbs drying above the fire, and I drop to the floor beside Mom's bed, taking her skeletal hand in mine. My fingers tremble, and her eyes flit open, damp and bloodshot.

"I saw them," I say softly, voice catching on each letter, as if I might choke on them. "On the eastern horizon . . . two twin stars."

Mom's eyes struggle to blink, her skin the color of sun-bleached bones, but her hair is still long and dark and wavy at the ends. Freckles sit scattered across her nose, and her mouth is the same shape as mine, like a bow tied from rope. I see myself in her—but she has always been braver, fearless, mightier than a winter storm. And I worry that the things that bind me to her, to our ancestors, don't live as strong in my bloodstream.

But now, as I stare down at her, she is half the woman she once was, weak and addled with sickness. And I'm afraid of what's to come.

She tries to push herself up, to crane her head to the window—she wants to see the stars for herself—but her elbows buckle and her dust-thin body falls back to the mattress, teeth rattling. I place a cold cloth, dampened with river water, on her forehead to wipe away the sweat. "Are they—" She coughs, pinches her eyes closed, starts again. "—in alignment with the pole star?"

I nod, tears dripping from my eyes.

"Sister stars," she mutters, a small twitch at the corners of her pale mouth—an almost smile—something she hasn't done in weeks. "It's time." She squeezes my hand and her eyelashes flutter, her sight almost lost completely. She only sees shadows now, waves of dark.

"We can leave in the morning," I answer, my nerves like fire in my veins—*we will finally be leaving the valley.* I will finally be going beyond its sheer cliff walls.

But she shakes her head and swallows. "No."

A small fire burns in the fireplace, but the cold night air still catches at the back of my throat. I already understand what she means: I can see it in the dampness of her eyes, the tight pinch of her mouth. *She* will not be leaving the cabin. Or the valley.

She wants me to go alone.

"I can help you to walk," I urge, feeling the anxiety clotting in my chest like mud. We will go together, like we've always planned. She and I. Venturing beyond the valley walls at last.

But she only blinks, tears rolling down her cheekbones. "I'll be too slow." She coughs and clutches a hand to her trembling mouth, and more tears fall from her chin. "You already know everything," she whispers, eyes straining to see me through the winter fog of her vision. "You don't need me." Her eyes flutter. "Go to the ocean," she instructs, words I already know, that she has told me so many times, they are like a song in my ears, repeating, repeating, without end. "Find the Architect. Don't look back, Vega."

I grip her hand tighter, as if I can already feel the miles, the space widening between us. "I'm not leaving you here." She won't be able to bring up water from the river or even pull herself out of bed. If I leave, she'll die quickly. Of thirst and pain. She'll die alone.

Her jaw clenches along her cheekbones, and I can see the woman she once was: strong, toughened by the land, by the years, some of that fight still left in her. "There's no time," she says forcefully, straining against the words before sinking back against her pillow.

I lift my eyes, wet with tears, to the window, where the twin stars hover against the dark. I knows she's right. Time is already slipping away, hour by hour—the twin stars won't be visible forever. Days from now, they will arch away, out of sight, and it will be too late.

Another hundred years before they come into alignment again.

I think Mom knows I won't leave her, senses I won't let her die alone in the cold of the cabin. She knows I'll stay as long as she's alive.

Because in two days' time, the evening after a rainstorm drenches the valley, she lets the consumption tear apart the last of her lungs, her heart, her eyes. *She stops fighting.* "Leave the valley, Vega . . . ," she sputters near the end, fingers twitching, then mumbles something about black feathers falling from the sky, birds dropping to their death—fevered words.

I brush the dark hair from her face, feeling like my own heart is about to give out, and I watch her features pinch tight, freckles massing together on her forehead while the sunset burns sapphire and pale and colorless through the small cabin windows. At last I hear the air leave her lungs. Feel the slack in her hand.

And just like that, she's gone. *A soundless letting go.*

She gave up. She let herself die.

To make sure I'd leave.

To make sure I'd live.

✳ ✳ ✳

I bury my mother before the morning sunlight breaks through the treetops and sparks across the blades of grass. I do it swiftly, before her body has time to stiffen, wrapping her gently in the cornflower-blue bedsheet, then stitching it closed with a needle and thread. I carry her down the hill from the old cabin and place her in the ground.

For a moment, I feel like I might be sick, the dimmed night sky whirling and tilting above me, but I stumble the five paces from her grave down to the river's edge and wade in up to my knees, feeling the strength of Medicine Bow River carving its slow, ancient path through our protected valley, walled in on two sides.

I know what I have to do.

The stories of my ancestors like a ticking clock against the soft place at my temples.

In the cold river, I scrub away the dirt from my hands, my fingernails, wishing I could strip away the hurt rupturing inside me like a dying star. But it's marrow-deep, cut into me now. I take another step toward the fast-moving center of the river, the water glacier-cold and deep, and I dig my toes into the gravelly river bottom, feeling the weight of the planet beneath me, anchoring me so I don't drift away. *Without gravity, we'd all float up into the stars light as dove feathers,* Mom would say. We'd spend nights out here beside the river, peering through her telescope—the one she built herself with plates of glass fastened at perfectly measured angles. She'd tell me to recite the names of constellations and orbiting moons and comets always breaking through our atmosphere in dazzling trails of light. *You need to know the sky as well as the valley; you need to be able to chart a course using only the stars to navigate,* she'd explain. She taught me the shape and structure of the night sky. She made sure I'd never forget, even after she was gone.

With my shaking hand, I reach toward the moonlight, freckles making a pattern from my thumb all the way up along my forearm, and I try to see her in my own skin—I am made of her, after all. The same cells and atoms, blood of my blood. But it isn't enough. She was brown eyes flecked with green, fingernails always cut short, dirt pressed into the creases of her knuckles. She was both the soil and the sky, a kaleidoscope of parts.

My knees give out and I sink into the icy water, sitting cross-legged on the river bottom, water up to my throat, tears shedding down my cheeks. The cold could kill me; the roaring current could drown me. But I don't feel any of it. I tilt my head back while tears break against my eyelids, and in the pale twilight sky, I find the southern pole star, dim and flickering just above the treetops—the navigational point that will always guide me home, no matter where I am, the star that connects all the others.

"The sky belongs to you now," Mom had whispered right at the end, fighting to keep her eyes open, coughing and then spitting up blood. But even the anatomy of stars are woven with memories of her. *It's all her.* This valley and the cliff walls and the starlight that drapes over me like a ruthless, unmerciful hand. But through the awful blur of tears, I find the twin stars again—Tova and Llitha— sister stars, caught in their own kind of gravity. Bound to each other. The old folklore stories say the sisters were banished to the night sky by their father after they refused to marry two underworld princes. Now they are two points of light hovering in the east. Whispering their ancient words, summoning me closer—to a place beyond the valley where I've never been.

To an ocean, at the edge of everything, across forbidden land.

All my life, Mom had warned of the world outside our valley—*it's dangerous and cruel,* she would say. *But we are safe here, far from it all.* We remained in our isolated valley, studying the sky, marking our charts and maps, where no one knows our names . . . or who we are descended from.

But now she's gone and the twin stars gleam in the night sky.

Now . . . I have to leave, travel to a place where my ancestors have never been. As if it were that easy. As if my legs could carry me beyond this valley when they can barely carry me back up to the cabin from the river.

My body shakes, hands milk-white and numb, and I push myself up from the water—my long cotton nightdress clinging to my skin, the front hem stained with dark, ruddy soil from digging. It will need to be scrubbed, set to soak. Or maybe I'll just burn it, bury it, leave it behind. What use will it be out there, anyway. Beyond the walls.

I stagger back up to the shore, arms hanging wet and limp at my sides, and collapse onto the grass. The night sinks away, and the sun begins to rise, bright and terrible and unforgiving.

I could walk the day's journey to Mr. and Mrs. Horace's place—our closest neighbor, our only neighbor—and tell them Mom has died. I could sit at their kitchen table while Mrs. Horace brings me flattened corn cakes and hot tea, then touches me with her worrying hands, straightening the hem of my shirtsleeves, fussing with my long, coiled hair. Mr. Horace will stand at the door as if there were some way to set this right with nails and hewn boards—the only remedy he knows. But they would not want me to leave the valley. *A girl of only seventeen shouldn't be on her own,* I imagine Mrs. Horace saying. They will insist I stay with them, sleep in the narrow loft of their timber house. They're good people, but I cannot make a life among their stock of goats and cattle and dogs.

I rub my hand across the back of my neck, searching for a reminder—for courage—and I feel the smooth skin that is marked by ink. I can't see it, but I know it's there—Mom had the same mark, a tattoo that assures me of who I am: my mother's daughter. Linked, bound to each other even after her death.

You're descended from brave women, she used to tell me, as if she knew someday it would come to this. I scrub at the corners of my eyes, not wanting to feel the tears, when a flock of starlings tear away from the sagging oaks near the riverbank.

Something's startled them.

They screech angrily, wings beating away toward the west, but in between the sound . . . I hear the distinct thud of hooves against the hard ground of the road.

I turn, gazing up the hill, where the road winds along the valley, and a plume of dust furls into the air.

Someone is coming up the road.

My eyes flash to the cabin, body still shaking from the cold of the river. I could run up the hill and duck inside, feel into the top chest of drawers for the old revolver Mom kept hidden there, load it like she taught me, then wait at the window with the barrel pointed up the road. Or I could hide. The tree line is only a few paces from the river; I could be inside the sparse oaks within a few seconds. I could make my way up the ridge to the Horaces' place and be there by sundown.

But instead my legs don't move. My insides too numb, my chest too heart-shattered.

The sound of a horse, of a wagon, rattles up the road, vibrating at every stone and divot, echoing up across the valley, becoming its own kind of disjointed birdsong.

I lift a hand over my eyes, straining to see, lungs stilled—the cold writhing down my joints—and when the horse appears over the last rise, drawing the old box wagon behind it, I let out a long, shaky breath.

Salty lines of tears spill down my face, the relief sudden and heavy in my chest.

After almost a month away, Pa is home.

* * *

We stand over Mom's grave—my hair dripping with river water.

"I'm sorry I wasn't here," Pa manages, kneeling down to rest a sun-darkened hand against the dirt. His chin dips, reddish-brown beard quivering, and he wipes at the corners of his eyes, catching the tears before they fall. I look away, not wanting to see the pain in his eyes.

"She's been sick since you left," I tell him, biting back the sob waiting at the top of my rib cage, the hurt like floodwaters inside me, almost too big to contain.

Pa nods at the dark soil, the morning wind singing through the cattail reeds beside the river. "Nothing you could have done."

We stand this way for a time—silent, staring at the place where her body now rests—as if each of us is cycling through our own pain.

Finding ways to tuck it away. Pa is a quiet man, more comfortable with uncrowded roads and the silence of an evening spent alone, than with consoling words. An owl lets out a somber cry from the woodshed, just as the sun breaks through the trees, inching higher in the sky. And at last Pa pushes himself up, knees creaking, eyes still damp at the corners, and we start back for the house, each of us silent. I can meet Pa's stride now, nearly as tall as him, legs like reeds and arms swinging at my sides. *Almost as tall as a tree,* Mom liked to say, braiding my oak-brown hair down my back, her fingers brushing the dark ink of the tattoo at my neck—the tattoo she gave me years ago.

At the cabin, Pa lights his pipe and eases himself into one of the porch chairs—chairs he himself made when I was small. I still remember the smell of wood shavings, mottled dust, a sweet nutty scent. Normally, when Pa returns to the valley, I ask him to tell me a story from the *outside*, about distant towns and foreign people and the unusual places he's seen: two-story buildings and deep, calm lakes as warm as bathwater and strangers with eyes as blue as the June sky. They are good stories, tales I sometimes think can't be entirely true—Pa's cheeks grinning, eyes shimmering with some faraway memory. My knowledge of the world has been shaped by Pa's stories. And also by Mom's warnings.

But I don't ask for a story now—I ask something else. "Where will you go, after here?"

It's been nearly a month since he was last in the valley—when the snow still insulated the ground and hung from the eaves of the old cabin—but now spring has crept in over the land, turning it green and soft, the approaching of a gentler season: long, sunlit days, crisp carrots from the ground, frogs singing from the mucky banks of the river in the evening. Something I won't be here to see.

"North," he answers, his tired, creased eyes focused out over the valley, to the slow-moving river winking under the morning sun. "To the market."

"When will you leave?"

"Tomorrow." He releases a puff of tobacco smoke into the air. "I need to be back on the road in the morning."

Beside the porch railing, I run a hand down Odie's neck—Pa's mare, a black-and-white appaloosa who has found a patch of clover sprouting up in the shade of the porch deck. Pa never hobbles her with leather straps around her ankles, or ties her to a tree when he's here. He says she has no reason to wander; all the good pasture is near the house.

"How far away is it?" I knit my fingers through Odie's coarse mane, then down to her black velvet nose.

"A week's journey, maybe a few days more. Depends on the roads." Smoke puffs from Pa's nose, wheeling up into the clear sky, and he touches the wiry strands of his beard, his mustache.

I cut my eyes away to his wagon—sitting near the shed—with its tall wood sides and flat top. Painted along the slats are black, swooping letters—much more elaborate than the straight, perpendicular letters that Mom taught me to write when I was younger. But the words on Pa's wagon are meant to draw people near, to catch their eyes, to entice them to trade a coin or two for what he sells inside.

Pa's Cure-All Tonic Elixir, it reads, and a small blue medicine bottle has been painted beside the words with silver stars erupting from the top. Beneath this is a list of the ailments that Pa's tonic will cure: *headache, heartache, cough, fever, hair loss, tooth loss, arthritis, lethargy, dizziness, sleeplessness, drunkenness, toe aches, warts.*

I shift my gaze back to Pa, his eyes drowsy and distant. I think of summers past when Mom and Pa and I would sit on the porch and watch the sun fade while we peeled baskets of peas and listened to Pa's stories. A time lost to us now. I clear my throat, stuffing down the tears. "I'm coming with you."

But Pa immediately shakes his head, not even considering it. "The road isn't a safe place for you."

I lower my hand from Odie's muzzle. I know Pa doesn't understand why I need to leave. He doesn't know the stories that Mom whispered to me at night when he was away. *The women in our family have kept our secrets for a hundred years,* she would tell me softly, as if she didn't even want the stars to hear. *They are dangerous secrets; they put us at risk. So we keep them to ourselves.* "I'm stronger than I look," I say, shoulders straightening back, my left hand scraping along my neck, fingers tracing the tattoo.

Pa's brow tugs downward as he eyes me, his expression hidden beneath the wiry strands of his overgrown beard. "No," he answers sharply. "You need to stay in the valley, where you're protected."

"Mom wanted me to leave—" I say, clenching my teeth. Mom and I spent most of our life in the valley alone—the two of us with our stories and constellations and a language only we understood—while Pa spent his life out on the road.

He removes the pipe from his mouth, exhaling, a softness to his eyes—a sadness—like he understands the need I feel, but he thinks I'm being foolish. A girl who doesn't know what she's asking for. "Your mother has taught you many things, but she hasn't prepared

16

you for what's out there." He taps the toe of his dusty-brown boot against the worn boards of the deck.

I turn away from him, feeling the threat of tears against my eyelids, and lift my eyes to the sky—to the place in the east where I saw the twin stars, now lost to the morning sunlight. The owl, who had been perched on the woodshed, extends its broad wings, and tears away over the river, beyond the valley walls.

"I'll go on my own," I say.

"You don't have a horse."

"I'll walk." I had planned on walking anyway, marching out of the valley on foot.

He exhales through his nose, eyes clicking up the road. "It'll take you a week just to reach the nearest outpost. And your feet will be raw as hide by then, blistered down to the bone." There is a growl in his voice, a grittiness, as though he's recalling the harsh, unending stretch of roads beyond the valley. Recalling long, hot days when he pushed the wagon on, exhausted, throat coated in dust. And he doesn't wish the same for me.

I kick at a small rock and it skitters under the porch. Odie lifts her head, wide-eyed, before resuming her methodical chewing of the clover and bunchgrass.

Pa rests the stem of the old pipe at the corner of his mouth, mustache twitching, the fragrant smoke—cloves and cinnamon—coiling up into the rafters of the porch roof. "It's easy to think the world beyond what we know is better than what we have, but trust me, Vega, your life here is safer than anything out there." He leans forward to rest his elbows on his knees, gazing out at the road—this day has already worn him thin, down to bone. "She kept you isolated here for a reason." He tamps out the tobacco in his pipe onto the rough boards of the deck, letting the burnt leaves fall between the cracks, then stands up. "I'm sorry, Vega, I can't take you with me." He gives me a quick nod, his shoulders bent forward, bearing the grief of Mom's death heavy in his tired frame, and before I can say anything else, before I can protest, he walks down the porch steps and strides out toward the river, toward Mom's grave.

My heart should sink—I should feel the hard slam of despair and hopelessness landing in my gut. But instead I feel something else: a new story weaving itself together like starlight along the dark night of my skin. The story of what comes next.

What I have to do.

✳ ✸ ✳

Pa is asleep in his wagon, nighttime once again folded over the valley, and Odie stands beside the porch, head dipped low, huge eyelashes twitching softly like reeds of grass.

I press my fingertips to the glass beside Mom's empty bed, nervously counting the constellations out of habit, reciting them in my mind: Crux, Perseus, Leo Minor, and even Cepheus—a broad formation of stars that has always looked like a bow and arrow to me, even though Mom said it was named after the mythical king Cepheus, husband to Cassiopeia, father of Andromeda. My reflection peers back in the glass, the swooped shape of my nose, my ears set low, skin like amber—it's all her. Reminders of Mom everywhere. Through my reflection, I stare out at the twin stars to the east, like lanterns burning in the sky. My ancestors spent their life waiting for them to appear—Tova and Llitha—for a sign that it was time to leave the valley. They watched the sky each night, studied it, and waited. A hundred years have passed since the twin stars last swung this far on their orbit across their galaxy and found themselves close enough for us to see. *A rare event.* One that almost seems impossible—one I started to think might never happen. Only a folktale passed down by the women in my family, a story that had lost all meaning. But the stories were right.

And at last the waiting has ended with me.

I drop my hand from the window, my fingerprints left on the glass—the last part of myself I will leave behind.

I already know what I will do.

I move through the house, gathering a loaf of bread and hard biscuits, preserved blackberries in glass jars that clink and rattle in the burlap sack. I eye the shelf of books near the fireplace: an old book of Scottish poems, a wild foraging cookbook, and several about astronomy. Mom said books were rare, hard to come by. But I know the astronomy books by heart, their pages useless to me now, and I have no need for the others beyond the walls of the house. So I leave them all behind.

I pull my favorite sweater over my head, the color of wheat and flax—the one Mom has mended dozens of times over the years, the one that once belonged to her, and her mother before her—then grab my gray canvas coat from the hook by the door. I fold the quilt from Mom's bed, tucking it under my arm, then pick up the lit candle. My lungs breathe heavy, doubt scratching at my skull. I can still feel her within these walls where I drew my first breath: where I learned to chart the stars, to read while sitting at the small wood table pressed against the corner, where Mom and I have carved our names into the low bench—like the white heron stacks pebbles beside the river to mark its territory, to warn other birds that this is its home. Mom taught me how to survive, to make fire and cut my own hair and mend my own shirts.

But I have to do this—it has to be absolute; otherwise I might change my mind.

I need there to be nothing left to return to.

I lower the candle to one of Mom's pillows, and the flame catches instantly. It springs across the sheets to the curtains, igniting on the pile of stacked firewood beside the stove. It lunges up the log walls, turning hot and ashy in minutes. How voracious fire is. How unstoppable. It destroys without thought.

With the burlap sack over my shoulder, I shove my feet into my boots, not bothering to lace them, and walk out onto the front porch, feeling the flames growing hot and angry behind me. Like something coming alive, devouring my childhood, my entire life in this cabin. Leaving nothing. I fight the urge to run to the river with a pail and bring back buckets of water, dousing the flames.

There's no turning back now.

The sky is still dark, a belt of clustered stars running from north to south. But when I lower my gaze back to the wagon, Pa is awake, a hand held over his brow. Odie has backstepped away from the porch railing, dust rising around her hooves, ears jumping forward and back, frightened of the snapping flames.

"Vega . . ." Pa peers past me at the cabin, at the flames now licking through the doorway. "What did you do?"

Bravery is not summoned overnight; it takes several almost-moments until the one that finally sparks a need bright enough that you're willing to burn your old life to the ground.

"My home is gone—" I say down to him from the edge of the porch. "I should probably go with you now."

* ✳ *

My name—Vega—means *dweller in the meadow.* Mom would say that my name was a reminder that this valley was my home, that I was safe here, like a bird tucked into the cavity of its nest.

But with smoke curling up into the dawn sky behind me, flames chewing apart the cabin where I was born, I leave the valley behind.

For most of my life, I have feared the unnamable longing that has pricked at me like a briar caught in wool—a curiosity about what lay beyond the valley. *The world out there is wild and savage and unkind,* Mom would tell me, eyes trained up the road. *We won't leave until it's time.*

Low, mangy oaks dig their pointed limbs into the side of the wagon, shrieking against the wood, but Pa coaxes Odie on with a soft click of his tongue. In the back of the wagon, the glass jars filled with Pa's tonic rattle a constant chorus of *clink*s and *clang*s—a sweet smell emanating from the wood crates.

The valley walls shrink away around us, and we emerge into the flat rangeland rolling out endlessly into the distance—a stretch of road dotted with bull snakes and dry scrub brush and rocky terrain known to hobble good horses. But this view isn't new—I've seen it before, when Mom and I would make the rare trek to the Horaces'— though this time it's a length of land that I'm not merely seeing from a distance, but that I will be entering into. My chest feels tight, anxious, but I refuse to glance over my shoulder and see the smoldering embers of the cabin behind us. I've made my decision.

Don't look back, Mom told me once. *You're not going that way.*

We slip free of the crowded oaks, and the sun becomes a scowling eye, bright and watchful. I wish we were traveling at night so I could see the stars, the comfort they bring, the reminder that no matter how far I travel, I can always use them to chart my way back to the valley.

We pass the Horaces'—a modest farmhouse set back between four shaded elm trees, with a low creek running through the land behind it. The barn is another forty yards beyond the creek, and the Horaces' livestock of goats and sheep and cattle have gathered near the fence, watching us. Odie slows her gait, head craned toward them, but Pa snaps the reins to prod her forward. My body vibrates, a wave of nausea rising in my belly—I'm now farther beyond the valley than I've ever been.

Pa makes a grumbling sound, low and disapproving: He thinks this is a bad idea, taking me with him, letting me leave the valley. But he stays quiet. Maybe he knows there are reasons tucked inside me that he doesn't understand—the whispered words shared only between Mom and me. Or maybe he can't bear to leave me in the burnt-out remains of the cabin. So we travel in silence across the open plains while the hours tick by, the sound of the creaking wagon becoming an ache in my ears, watching birds fly in slow patterns overhead, crows and ravens out looking for unfortunate field mice and jackrabbits.

It's stark, unwelcoming land, and I push down the knot tightening in my stomach the farther we travel from the valley. From Mom buried in the ground. From everything I've ever known.

Because I don't have a choice.

When we finally leave the long expanse of rangeland and move into the clotted hills, it's well after dark. A coyote lopes through the elms beside us, fur the color of gunmetal, paws thrumming against the soft earth. It follows us for a time, eyes darting at me as if in warning. *Turn back,* it cautions with its golden eyes, before it finally slips back into the briars and woodland.

It must be near midnight when we emerge through the scraggly oaks and Pa slows the wagon. "It's called Soda Creek," he says, nodding ahead at the barren wash, not even a trickle down the center. "It ain't much now, but in a week or so, it'll be flooded from spring rains. Muddy and violent, not safe to cross. We came just in time."

Pa urges Odie through the low, dry channel and up the other side, the wagon cutting back into the trees along a shallow ridge. My eyes have grown heavy, my throat dry from the dust, and I crave sleep with the same sort of immediacy I used to crave the cool river on an unbearably hot summer day. The wagon heaves up the last rise, and we find ourselves atop a ridge, overlooking a long, open prairie. Pa pulls Odie to a halt. "We'll camp here tonight."

"Shouldn't we keep going?" I press, not wanting to stop. Every hour a hammer in my eardrum, knowing there are so few left.

"It's not safe to travel at night." He lumbers down to the ground and begins unhitching Odie from the harness.

Ahead of us, I can see all the way down to the valley beyond—a long stretch of grassland framed by more hills in the distance.

And situated in that prairie landscape is a town.

✳ ✳ ✳

I lie folded in Mom's quilt watching sparks from the campfire pirouette up among the stars, comforted by the unaltered arrangement of the night sky, the placement of the Milky Way and star clusters exactly where they should be—while the dry, sparse land-scape around me feels entirely foreign, smelling of strange plants and far-off winds. Just beyond the firelight, I can hear creatures moving among the dark, the flash of their eyes through the low oak trees. An eerie, ghostly feeling against my skin.

Even though sleep tugs at me, and I crave a long night's rest, I worry that we're traveling too slow. It took us an entire day, and we've only just reached the outskirts of a town in the distance.

How long will it take me to find the Architect? Days? A week? A man I've never met. He could be anywhere. Impossible to find if he's in hiding, if he doesn't want to be found. He might even be dead. But Mom always assured me that if one Architect died, there would be another to take his place. The lineage would never be lost. Just as she taught me the stories of our past to ensure they wouldn't be forgotten, the Architect would do the same.

Somewhere out there is an Architect—and he will know the way to the sea.

I just need to find him.

Briefly I let my fingers stray to the back of my neck, tracing the lines of the tattoo, then drop my hand back to my lap and continue counting the stars above me, marking their names in my mind. "You can see Bellatrix tonight," I say softly to Pa, pointing a finger to the west, just above the treetops. "It's the third-brightest star in the Orion constellation."

Pa lifts his head from the campfire, where he's placed a cast-iron pot filled with water and dried pinto beans to boil, and looks up at the sky.

"*Bellatrix* means *female warrior*," I add, lowering my hand. "Some stars are easier to locate, like Orion's belt or the pole star. But

Mom said you have to observe all the constellations if you want to know the full story." *From a single point in the sky, you should be able to map the rest of the universe.*

Pa makes a paltry sound, like he doesn't want to think about Mom, the grief tucked away in his barrel chest. Maybe he feels guilty he wasn't there when it happened, knelt beside her bed, a hand to her pale, hollowed cheek, a chance to say goodbye. But he has never been a constant in our lives—he is like the wandering coyote, better suited for long, dusty roads than a life within permanent walls, only stopping in the valley every month or so, when his route brings him close. Yet it's also what I admire, envy, about him: his freedom, the ease with which he comes and goes.

His life wasn't built around Mom—not like mine was. He didn't wake each morning to the soft murmur of her recounting the mass and luminosity of stars, or fall asleep to the sound of her laugh, deep and forceful like a man's—that I swear made the slatted roof of the cabin tremble like she was the winter wind itself. She had a gravity about her, and she was more complex—like a series of strange, unending riddles—than Pa will ever know.

He dips his head and resumes stirring the pinto beans, adding a little salt and unknown herbs. Odie wanders among the oaks, nibbling on bunchgrass, tail swishing through the night air. "When we reach the next town," he says, eyes still low, "don't talk about this to anyone else."

"About what?"

"The stars, constellations, all the things your mom taught you."

My eyes trace the carefully stitched seams of Mom's quilt—a blanket that was once her mother's, passed down to her after Grandma died. And now it belongs to me.

"They won't understand," he adds, flashing me a look to be sure I've heard him, that I understand. Like he's still considering taking me back to the valley and leaving me there, letting me sleep in the smoldering ash of the cabin. Where I'd be safe.

"I know." My mouth flattens, a stone rolling around in my chest. I grew up discussing the geography of stars every evening—the row of planets in our solar system, the constellations that spun across the axis of our sky each night—knowledge that Mom was carving into my bones, into my mind, because it needed to be remembered. But out here, she warned, our knowledge means something else. It threatens to unearth a past that some would like to remain hidden—forgotten. While others covet it in a way that makes my very existence dangerous.

Again, the nagging fear creeps up inside me, the old warnings scratching at my insides, telling me that I shouldn't have left the valley, I shouldn't be out here in the wild of this unprotected terrain. But I don't say any of this to Pa—I'll reveal no weakness to him, the doubt that keeps wanting to surface as I peer out into the dark of the forest surrounding us. I keep it tucked inside me. Unspoken.

After we eat, I lie on my side, the quilt tucked up to my chin, and I stare out through the clearing to the small town beyond. There are no lights, no stirring noises in the distance, only the rooflines visible against the dark horizon.

I've never seen a town, but I've imagined the way homes might sit crowded together, people living side by side, neighbors only a few steps away.

The fire sputters beside me as Pa snores, but an anxious knot twists and contorts inside my gut, making it impossible to sleep.

What if I can't find the Architect in time? What if I'm too late.

AQUARIUS, Beta Aquarii
–05° 34' 16"

The first Astronomer slept during the day and woke at night, too eager to map the sky to let a single moment of moonlight be wasted with dreams.

She knotted her copper hair—the color of a red sun, like Capella—at the base of her neck, and she went to work. She created star maps detailed with magnitudes and luminosity and declinations. She watched for the tiny wobbles made by distant stars that revealed the number of planets and moons orbiting around it, yanking its axis this way and that.

While her neighbors planted crops and raised walls for loafing sheds and goat barns, the first Astronomer talked of constellations that did not yet have names, of the far-off Milky Way making a frothy arc across the black sky.

The others thought her notions of the stars were tedious, wasteful, when there was work to be done: sweat on the brow, calloused hands in dry, rain-parched soil, kind of work. The work of making a homestead, trading in the towns, shearing sheep for winter clothes and digging wells to water newly planted spring gardens.

She was largely ignored, left alone, at first.

At first.

But that would change.

TWO

Morning sunlight flashes through the trees, and for a half second I don't know where I am. My eyes search for the walls of the cabin, the low log ceiling, but instead find the border of trees surrounding our campsite, and the copper sun clawing its way above the oaks. I rub at my dry eyes, wince, and think I hear a *whoosh* sound—like air escaping, like the horizon is being sucked away into a void—but when I blink, the sky has settled into a soft blue and the noise is gone.

Beyond the smoldering campfire, Pa is already harnessing Odie, a web of buckles and straps securing her to the wagon. "Ready?" Pa asks. His voice lighter than yesterday—the promise of a town ahead, of tonic to sell and coins to be made.

Quickly I roll up my quilt and kick dirt onto the last of the campfire coals, then climb onto the front bench of the wagon, old metal springs releasing a soft whine. Pa snaps the leather reins and Odie jerks forward, pulling the wagon and us away from our campsite.

The little town draws near, the wagon rattling down the ridge-line. "When we enter the town," Pa says flatly, "you can help me with the jars. Can you count?" He looks over at me, as if for a moment he's forgotten my age, like I might be much younger than my seventeen years and not yet know the basics of arithmetic.

"Of course," I answer, offended that he would think otherwise.

"Good. And keep your hair down." He clicks his tongue, Odie hesitating around a fallen tree, thrashing her head briefly before finally leading us around the upturned oak, roots like fingers sprung free from the soil. "Don't want anyone seeing those marks."

My fingers touch the back of my neck.

"Best to keep it hidden," he adds sternly, nodding at me.

A ripple of unease slips down my spine, and I know he's right—out here, I can't let my mark be seen. By anyone. I unbraid my hair and let it fall in dark, tightly coiled waves over my shoulders, hiding who I am. A girl inked with riddles. A truth that Mom said made me dangerous.

Ahead, the road finally flattens out, and we enter a wide, sweeping grassland—the stalks tall and wavy, licking at the wagon wheels, evenly spaced in long rows—planted by human hands. Crops. "What kind of grass is this?"

"Wheat," Pa answers, as if the expanse of golden-green fields stretching for miles all around us, stalks churning in the wind, is nothing new. But I've only ever known our small garden in the valley, and the rows of potatoes that the Horaces plant every spring. This is something else entirely, though—a crop large enough to feed a whole town. "This town trades in wheat; it's how they survive." Pa briefly presses a hand to his left ear, as if there is a pain there, before he pulls his hat lower over his eyes to shield the morning sun.

I lean forward on the seat, anxious, an indescribable thrill tugging at my chest as the road takes us straight into the center of town. I'm entering a place unlike anything I've ever known. Small, single-story structures line the main street, homes mostly, dust collected in doorways, roofs sagging and sloped from storms or heavy winds. But after several blocks, I notice a wooden sign swinging from the doorway of a squat, low building. POST OFFICE, it reads. A block farther, another sign nailed above a barn with wide double doors advertises a blacksmith.

Dust curls up from the wagon wheels, and I watch as curtains peel back from windows, curious, thirsty eyes staring out at us. I wonder if the people of this town will know of the Architect, if they'll have heard the stories. But as townsfolk appear in doorways, hands over their eyes to block the sun, skin dust-darkened and bodies bent with the hard labor of farming, I feel a growing unease. Mom warned not to trust anyone beyond the valley walls—*they're suspicious, desperate, and most are willing to kill to survive.* Finding the Architect would be a tenuous thing, she'd say. For if he is in hiding, as we have been, then he will not be known by the people in the towns. And if he *is* known, then even saying his name would put my life at risk.

Her words fester inside me as we reach the far end of town, where a corral of horses stand with heads bowed away from the slanted western sun, and Pa pulls Odie to a stop. Ahead of us stands a tall, narrow building, windows shuttered, as if no one has been inside for some time. But it's not the windows or the paint peeling from the walls that catch my eye—it's the long rope suspended from the roof, swaying in the breeze in front of the doorway, with a loop tied at the end.

My throat tightens, and I nod toward it. "What's it for?" I ask.

Pa barely glances at it, like he already knows what I'm asking, like he's seen it before. "For hanging," he answers simply, positioning his hat atop his head and tucking his dark, ruddy hair back behind his ears.

"They hung somebody from that rope?"

"More than a few."

"Why?"

Pa shoots me a look. "Easier than wasting bullets." When I keep staring at him, he adds, "The world is dangerous, Vega," as if to prove what's he's been saying all along: *that I'm better off in the valley.* "You stay in the wagon," he instructs now, securing the reins and swinging himself down to the ground. "You can count the jars we sell, and the money as it comes in, understand?"

I can tell he's anxious—maybe because of me, because I shouldn't be here. So I nod, my legs aching to get down and feel the ground beneath me, but my wariness of the gathering townspeople, the empty rope swinging in the dry air—and the need to keep my tattoo out of sight—outweighs my desire to be free of the wagon. I climb into the back, stepping over the wood crates filled with glass jars, and position myself at the rear opening of the wagon, peering out at the dusty, one-road town.

"Hand me five jars," Pa says, keeping his gaze fixed on the street. I do as he says, pulling out five jars of his tonic, each filled with a golden, syrupy mixture that fills the air with an ever-present sweetness, like the nectar from a lilac flower. He places them on the back edge of the wagon, the golden color gleaming in the morning sunlight.

It doesn't take long for the first customer to make their way up to the wagon.

"Madge." Pa greets the woman, whose right cheek and forehead are marred by a series of scars and pockmarks, as if she was sick once and these are the reminders of the illness she survived. Yet her eyes are a pearlescent green, like looking into a deep pond, and resting against her hip is a young child with ruddy brown hair, squirming to be set down.

My eyes fall to her hands, braced around the child, because Mom told me of something else: a way to identify the Architect.

A symbol.

They would wear a signet ring made of roughly forged silver, with an imprint stamped into the metal: a constellation, *Circinus*. A ring passed through the generations. A way for the Architect to be found.

But the woman wears nothing of the sort. Her fingers are bare. And I doubt the Architect will be so easily found, standing in the open of this out-of-the-way town.

She and Pa talk softly, pleasantries about the road down from the ridge, and if we came across any scavengers on the route, to which Pa shakes his head.

"Jacob has a bad sunburn," she tells him. "Stayed in the fields too long last week."

"The tonic will help with the pain and inflammation." Pa's voice settles into an easy rhythm, words he knows by heart—remedies and old methods to cure and ease and heal. "But you'll need to draw the heat out from the skin with cold cloths, if you can."

The woman nods and places a silver coin in Pa's hand. He, in turn, hands her one of the jars, and she gives him an easy smile before striding back up the road through town, the child waving a chubby hand back at me.

Not a moment later, several children sprint up to the wagon, their fingers gripping the back hatch, eyes round and dewy, marveling at the assortment of jars. But two of them, a small girl with black hair cut just below her ears, and a boy with long arms and knobby, dirt-crusted knees, have eyes that sway toward gray—clouded, mottled. *Sick*.

"Have you brought coins?" Pa asks the children, and several smile, holding up silver pieces in their sticky fingers. It's clear the townspeople have been awaiting Pa's arrival, and they bring not only coins but also empty jars from the last time they bought his cure-all—which I imagine Pa will refill with more tonic later on.

But sometimes, instead of coins, they hand Pa bags of wheat or packaged cheese or other strange items in trade. I count the coins and empty jars, keeping a tally in my mind, while my eyes admire the strangeness and beauty of those who come to the wagon—the shades of their skin, some with hair cropped short at the neck, others long and coiled, nearly reaching the ground. Some have twine and feathers and seeds woven into the braids atop their heads, and their clothes have been dyed the many hues of the earth: bright poppy yellow and rich grass-green. My own muted clothes—dark pants and a ragged sweater—seem dull and colorless in comparison.

But after an hour, through the waves of heat, I notice three men standing in the shade of the nearby barn with the BLACKSMITH sign hanging above their heads. They weren't there when we first arrived in town, and I can't be sure when they appeared, but their hats are pulled low against their brows, eyes hawklike and watchful, and unlike the other townspeople, they do not wander up the street to the wagon. They are uninterested in Pa's tonic. Instead they simply watch, smoking rolled cigarettes—like I've sometimes seen Pa do back in the valley.

But there's something in their sidelong gazes, in the casual way they lean against the wood-framed building, as if they're waiting—in no great hurry—that makes the pulse rise at my neck.

"Did you hear me?" Pa says, louder this time. "One more jar."

I blink up at him, bringing my focus back, then quickly grab a jar from one of the crates. He places it into the hands of a man with bloodshot eyes, not much older than Pa, who unscrews the lid from the jar and immediately takes a long, slow gulp, eyes tipped back. Desperate for it. Before he turns and staggers away into the blinding heat.

But not everyone is able to make the walk up the street to the wagon. Some sit on sagging porches, their eyes shallow and unfocused. Others cough, their wheezing exhales heard even behind doorways, from their beds somewhere inside.

Many of the townspeople are sick.

Consumption. Just like Mom.

It sneaks into the body, causing fever and blindness and a deep, ragged cough. It hollows out the ears, stripping away all sound. And eventually it takes everything else. Blood on the lips, a sputtering breath, and then a body being buried in the dark riverbank soil.

I didn't know how bad it was—that nearly an entire town could be sick. And I feel helpless and anxious all at once. The world is not how I imagined.

The wind stirs up the dust on the road, spitting it against doorways and into the back of the wagon, and I cover my eyes. These people are saturated not only with sickness but with dust—it lives in every crevice of this town. But it doesn't stop a girl from skipping up the road in a yellow dress with white flowers stitched at the collar, then stopping to stand on tiptoes at the back of the wagon. She's a few years younger than me, and utterly unfazed by the wind and dirt. One of her eyes is a paled gray—lost of its sight—and she uncoils her fingers to reveal a coin in her palm, but it looks melted down, half the size it should be. "My brother is sick," she mutters, unable to look Pa in the eyes.

But he hands a jar of tonic down to her, and she takes it cautiously, holding it to her small chest. I think Pa is going to retrieve the half coin, but instead he folds the girl's fingers over it—a gesture for her to keep it—and she jogs back up the street, then ducks into a narrow passage between two dust-scarred homes.

The people here are sun-cracked and weary. You can see the hard-fought existence cut into the deep lines of their faces; living off this land doesn't come easy. There is *want* in their eyes, pain and even desperation. They aren't how I thought they'd be—and I feel a bite of sadness in my chest, realizing that this land has taken something from them. Season by season, it strips them of hope, and eventually it also takes their lives.

The midday sun burns an arc through the sky, a blazing orb, hours and minutes lost to the heat, making beads of sweat rise against my neck. Time is slipping away, *tick, tick, tick.*

I glance up the street, to the blacksmith's shop, but the three men who once stood beside the large doors have slunk away, out of sight. Even the townspeople seem to have settled back into their homes, out of the heat, and I think we will begin the work of closing up the wagon and start out of town, when I see a man making his way up the road, his left leg dragging through the dirt, his creased face bent forward, while a cough rises up from deep within his gut. Pa retrieves a jar and meets the man halfway up the road.

"Afternoon, Liam," Pa remarks, and they shake hands like old friends, speaking quietly while the sun bears down. The man wears no ring, but I wonder, *Could he know where to find the Architect? Could anyone in this town know?* I haven't had a moment away from Pa, where I could dare to ask.

My whole body feels stiff, a dryness in my throat, and I hold a hand over my eyes—a soft ringing in my ears—when a woman appears from the edge of my vision, skulking up to the wagon. Her too-long skirt is dragging through the dirt, the hem frayed, threads unspooling behind her, and with every angled, stiff step, the sound of tiny bells can be heard *tink, tink, tink*ing, as if she has them tucked in her hidden pockets.

She braces a bony, shuddering hand against the back edge of the wagon—no silver signet ring on her fingers—and peers in at me with a sharp pinch between her gray, thornlike eyebrows. Instinctively I sink back away from her—her gaze reminds me of the lone coyote, suspicious, distrustful.

"Do you need to buy a jar?" I ask cautiously.

Her white-gray hair, cut shoulder-length, slides back from her face, eyes like dark clouds, and I wonder if her vision is just as stormy—blurs of silt and gray, like looking through muddy water.

Her head cocks to one side. "Who are you?" she asks pointedly, voice a croak, dust living inside her lungs.

My eyes flash to Pa, several yards away, still talking to the man. I swallow, looking back to the old woman. "Vega," I tell her, my own voice hardly more than a squeak.

"Where have you come from?"

"The valley." Maybe I shouldn't say these things, reveal my name or where I'm from, but the twitchy glint of her eyes, leaning close to see me better, forces the truth from my lips. As if no lie could be uttered to her.

She clicks her tongue, wrinkles puckering at the corners of her jaw, as if she's trying to place me—some memory stored away she's having a hard time locating. "I don't recall the tonic man having a daughter in his wagon before."

"This is the first time I've left home."

At this, the woman releases her hand from the wagon and peers in closer at me, like a bird, a crane on the shores of the river reaching out to pluck a silvery fish was the water. "I believe I knew your mother." Her words are swift, furtive, so they won't carry beyond the wagon. "Many years ago."

I feel my eyes widen. "You knew her?" Mom rarely talked about her life before she had me, before she returned to where she was born, and settled in the valley. She never talked about friends or the places she lived, only that the world out here wasn't meant for us—it was dangerous and cruel.

A cold line dips between the woman's brows, eyes turning darker, long spidery lashes lowering to frame her eyes. "You shouldn't have left."

"What?"

"You should have stayed there, in the valley. Where you were safe."

I feel the workings of something churning in my chest. "How did you know my mom?"

"Go back," she hisses, leaning in so close that I can make out the spots in her eyes that remind me of algae blooms expanding over her retinas. "Before they discover who you are."

Fear carves a straight line from my spine up to my skull, making it hard to breathe, and the woman's jaw shifts forward, clicking her tongue, both of us eyeing the other—trying to discern the secrets hidden behind each of our eyes.

"Do you—" My voice catches and I clear my throat. "Do you know the Architect?" I know the risk in saying the name aloud, my voice trembling on the word, but I lean closer to her, hope itching at my thoughts. If she knew Mom, she might know other things too. Things most won't talk about. Most are afraid to say. "Do you know where I can find him?"

Her eyes dart away, to the rows of swaying wheat outside town, yellow and amber waves. "The Architect?" she asks, face to the wind, as if wading through lost memories. Ones she'd like to forget.

"Do you know him?"

Her gaze swings to the rope hanging from the building ahead of us, and she blinks dryly; then her eyes flatten on me, a strange curl to her upper lip. "You must go back," she insists again, baring her bottom row of angled and broken teeth. Like she's been chewing on rocks. She drops her shoulders, mouth punched into a tight line. "Don't go saying that name aloud. It's much too late to be chasing old, forgotten tales. Leave the past where it is. . . . There's no saving us now."

"Please." I lift both my eyebrows and lean even closer to her. "My mom is dead, and I—" The desperation gnaws at my throat, wishing I could pluck the truth from her mouth. "I need to find him . . ." I drop my voice lower. "I have to find the Architect."

She yanks her hand away from the edge of the wagon, as if I have just bitten her with my words, a snarl tugging at her upper lip. "Foolish girl," she says, clouded eyes spearing through me. "You won't find him here." She steps away from the wagon, as if I am something to fear. Something she never should have gotten this close to. An animal caged in the wagon, too dangerous to touch, or even speak to. "Go back where you belong."

Behind her, up the road, Pa has clapped a hand against the sick man's shoulder, nodding. The man reaches into his pocket for a coin, for some payment, but Pa shakes his head and mutters something only the man can hear. There is a silent exchange of looks, and then, under the watchful eye of the midday sun, Pa ambles back to the wagon.

"Imogene," his voice booms, recognizing the old woman. "Are you well?"

I sink back into the corner of the wagon, out of sight. The woman's clouded, silvery eyes slant away from me and fix themselves to Pa. "The price has gone up," she rasps.

"Again?"

Her head tilts, as if it's on a lever. "Bees aren't producing like they used to." She reaches into some hidden pocket in the folds of her skirt, bells chiming, and produces a jar half the size of Pa's tonic jars. But inside is a thick, golden liquid, the color of a summer sun.

"How much?" Pa asks.

"Double."

Pa makes a sound of irritation, but he reaches into his coat pocket and holds out six coins, handing them to the woman. She takes them in her shaking fingers and lets Pa have the jar.

The woman—Imogene—dips her head, her body like an old piece of wood grown in on itself, depleted of water, and she begins shuffling away up the road. I want to call out to her, beg her to come back, but my throat has gone dry, words strangled. I could see the fear in her eyes, and I knew she wasn't going to tell me anything else. She wanted to get far away from me—far from the girl who should have stayed in the valley. *Foolish, foolish girl.*

A half second later, she has evaporated back into the dusty corridors of the town, only the soft sound of bells hanging in the air.

* * *

We leave the town behind just as the sky turns the color of rust. The air finally cools, and the wagon rattles up the road through the wheat fields. But I keep thinking of the woman, of the hanging rope with a knotted loop at the end—perfect for cinching tight around necks. "How far to the next town?" I ask, a chill in my voice.

"Not far." Pa clicks his tongue at Odie to keep moving when she tries to reach out for the tall stalks of wheat. "I saw you talking to Imogene."

I can still feel the sharpness of her eyes on me, the sound of tiny bells ringing in my ears. "Only for a moment."

"What did she say to you?"

My hands pick at the hem of my sweater, a thread tugging loose, then breaking. "I think she might have known Mom." The words tumble out before I can stop them.

Pa grumbles, fussing with his beard, hands shaking a little. "You shouldn't tell people about your mom, about where you're from. You don't know who to trust."

I don't tell him the other thing that Imogene said, the warning that I should *go back to the valley*. Or he might take her advice and drive me straight back there, leaving me with the Horaces or in the burnt-out shell of the cabin. His willingness to let me come with him is a fragile thing. So I keep my mouth shut, turning my gaze to the wheat fields, where a dozen townspeople are still tending to the crops. It seems they will work until it's good and dark.

I peer over my shoulder, at the buildings fading in the distance, and for a moment I think I see three shadows at the edge of town, seated on horseback. Maybe it's the three men I noticed at the blacksmith's shop. But when I look again, they're gone.

"Her eyes were clouded," I say. "Imogene's."

"She's been sick for a long time." Pa reaches his arm out and plucks a stalk of wheat as we pass, sticking one end in his mouth, chewing lazily. "But she's strong. She'll likely outlive us all."

"Many of the others were sick too."

Pa nods but won't look at me. "Consumption has gotten worse."

Odie snorts, reaching again for a clump of wheat, but Pa urges her straight on. "Doc Holliday died of consumption, you know." His dark, dust-brown eyes squint out at the road, against the setting sun. "They used to call it tuberculosis, or the plague."

"Who's Doc Holliday?"

The side of his mouth lifts, like he's telling one of his stories—a half-true kind of story that grows longer and more absurd over time. "He was a famous gunslinger. He was at the shoot-out at the O.K. Corral."

I shake my head, having no idea what he's talking about.

"Your mom never told you any of the good stories, did she?" he asks.

I raise an eyebrow at him.

"Doc Holliday was a dentist, which is why everyone called him 'Doc.' But he was best known for his fast draw. And he hung around Wyatt Earp in Tombstone, which gave them both quite a reputation."

"How far away is Tombstone?" I ask, liking this story.

Pa laughs this time, a quick, bright sound that rattles his chest. "Too far," he says with a wink, like he's still telling stories, memories from his past.

A storm is swirling against low green hills in the distance, but it's far away, and might not reach us. "How do you know this story?" I ask.

He turns, beard twisting in the wind. "Your mother told me."

A small spark of pain lights behind my eyes, and I wonder if it will always feel this way when I hear her name. It's also hard to imagine Mom telling old stories to Pa, that she never told to me.

The town disappears behind us, and we cross over flat, dry plains where the sky seems bigger than the whole of the land beneath us, bigger than it ever was back in the valley: wide and stormy blue and beautiful. I think of the other thing that Imogene said to me when I asked about the Architect: *You won't find him here.* Which means he's somewhere out there, in a world so big, I wonder if I'll ever find him. Or if I'll run out of time before I do.

"The jar you got from Imogene—" I turn my eyes to Pa. "Is it honey?"

He nods.

Mr. and Mrs. Horace used to have bee boxes, but one summer the bees vanished and never returned. The Horaces never had honey to trade after that.

"Can we have some for dinner?" I ask, remembering the sweet taste on my tongue.

But he shakes his head. "No, we're saving it."

"For what?"

"You'll see."

I rest my head back against the side of the wagon, listening to the jars of tonic rattle in the back. Most of the jars are empty now, only half a dozen still glistening with golden liquid—sweet and marbled and reflecting the evening sun as if the wagon was filled with an amber sunlight.

"How many jars of tonic do you give away?" I ask.

"Too many."

$$* \quad \text{\Large ✳} \quad *$$

Sweat trickles down my temple, my shoulder pressed into the corner of the wagon, my neck stiff. I roll my shoulders back, unknotting my sore muscles, and blink away from the morning sun that looks like the yolk of a fowl egg cracked against the distant hills and smeared across the sky.

"Fell asleep in the wagon," Pa says up to me from where he's harnessing Odie. "Didn't want to wake you." He pats Odie on the shoulder, and dust rises from her mane. "There's dried apples on the seat for breakfast."

"Where are we?"

"Nearly to the halfway bridge." He climbs up to the wagon seat and takes the reins.

I don't know what the *halfway bridge* is, but I hope we'll reach it soon. I hope it means we're close to the next town.

The day is dry and hot, unbearable, same as yesterday, and Pa begins humming a tune as we make our way across the scrubby, barren landscape, his voice deep and wandering, sometimes singing a few words of a song that seem more like stories stitched together. Tales about windstorms and dry summers without rain and lonely roads with only the moon to guide the way. They are *roaming songs*, he tells me. Sung by ranchers and those who travel the outer roads, like Pa. I never knew him to sing in the valley, as if these tunes can only be muttered while on long, dusty roads. Never while staying put.

I rest my head back against the seat, listening to the easy way he slips from one song to another, a rhythm that sways with the teetering wagon.

We pass three solitary homes, all abandoned, windows flung open or boarded up, fence posts leaning sharply, pushed over by heavy winter winds, leaves caught in doorways. In front of a tiny square house with a toppled chimney stands an oak tree with a rope swing hanging from the lowest branch. Idle. No breeze or children pushing it up toward the sky. I had a swing like it once back in the valley—a slab of notched wood and scratchy, fibrous rope—but the rope broke some years back and Mom never fixed it. I was too old for it anyway.

"Where did they all go?" I shake my head as we pass several homes built beside a low-lying pond, but no trace of people, no eyes staring out through dusty windows, no voices behind doorways. Coughing, wheezing. The whole place deserted.

Pa pauses his humming to flash a look at the last empty house we pass, a yellow flowering tree growing through one of the broken windows. "Consumption took them."

I never imagined it would be like this, that so much would be hollowed out—only remnants of those who once lived in these towns. "Other people could live there," I say, craning my head to watch as the small shell of a town fades behind us. "Move into those homes."

Odie takes a half step over a mound of rocks, and the wagon jolts. I grip the side of the seat to keep from toppling to the ground, but Pa doesn't even flinch; he's used to the jarring sway and totter of the wagon—he knows these roads by heart. "People stay away from this area," he says once the wagon has righted itself. "Even scavengers don't come this far."

"Why?"

Pa's eyes seem to twitch, an uncomfortable slant to his mouth. "Because there's nothing left."

My palm finds the mark on my neck; my chest pushes out a long breath of air. "Does your tonic really help them?"

"It gives relief."

"What about all the things it says on the wagon? Heartache and hair loss and tooth loss and warts?"

Pa smiles—actually smiles—and even his eyes take on an unusual, flickering brightness. "It doesn't cure all of those things, but some."

"You lie to people about what it does?"

Pa laughs, a quick, hearty sound, like thunder rolling along the belly of storm clouds—as if it's something he hasn't done in a long time, and the feeling has shook loose something in his rib cage. "They used to call people like me *snake-oil salesmen*. Someone who sells snake oil and makes promises it can't deliver."

"What do they call you now?"

"Someone who brings them hope."

A cold wind whips down from the west, and on up ahead, I can see the wash of gunmetal-gray clouds, the wisps of rain spilling down to the low, grassy hills. It hasn't reached us yet, but we're heading straight for it.

"Pa—" I say, feeling chilled by the sudden cold against my face. "What are scavengers?" One of the women back in the wheat town asked if we'd seen any on our path.

He exhales, the corners of his eyes pinching. "They're people who steal things from others."

"They're dangerous?"

His mustache twitches. "Yes."

"They'd steal from us?"

"Yes."

I rub my palms up my arms, the sky heavy with moisture, turning as dark as the river when it froze in winter.

"Vega," Pa says now, tilting his head to look at me. "You know I'm not your real pa, right?"

I lower my gaze, watching Odie's hooves stamp the ground with each motion forward, the wagon creaking beneath us, the clatter of metal as the harness vibrates. "I know."

* * *

When Pa first came to the valley—I was only seven or eight—he arrived with his tonic, traveling door-to-door, venturing farther than most would ever dare just to reach our valley. At first, Mom was just a customer—buying jars to help with headaches or a throbbing hand after an injury working in the garden or repairing a broken roof slat.

But as the years wore on, Pa started making the long journey to the valley more often, and would stay for days, sometimes a week at a time.

He taught me how to fish in the river, and where to look for wild blueberries near the overgrown thicket. And when I asked him what I should call him, he said *Pa*. Because that's what everyone called him. It was the name painted on the side of his wagon: *Pa's Cure-All Tonic Elixir*. And so he was *my* Pa, and the closest thing to a father I ever had.

Mom loved him, I think. He was someone she could trust. But she was also afraid—our isolation was important to her, more important than anything else—and she worried that allowing anyone into our valley would risk our safety.

The more people who knew where we were, the greater the risk that someday we'd be found.

And now I'm risking everything in search of the Architect.

* ✴ *

At midday, we cross over a low bridge made from roughly hewn logs. I lean over the edge of the wagon to peer down at the river, muddy and thick, flooded from rains upstream—not good for drinking. Odie lifts her legs high, fearful of the swirling water below, and when we reach the far side, a sign has been staked into the ground— hammered in.

WESTERN BOUNDARY CROSSING, it reads, jagged letters cut into old, graying wood.

"It's the halfway bridge," Pa explains, scratching at his eyebrow. "An east and west divider."

I twist around, looking back at the land we are leaving behind:

the western part of the country, where my mother is buried in the fresh soil. The ache in my heart returns, the unsettling feeling—the certainty—that there's no going back. But I knew this was coming. It's what Mom has been preparing me for, teaching me: stories about the sister stars, about an ocean far from here, at the very edge of everything. And an Architect who knows the way.

If I can find him in time.

But there is still a hollowness carved into my heart, and the farther I get from home, the more empty I feel. A tree with no center, only dry, scorched bark holding it together. "Mom said there were states? Boundaries that divided them."

"Someday there will be state lines here. But not yet."

He begins to hum again, a slow, melancholy tune that reminds me of cold winters and frosted ground that not even a shovel can break through. We reach a small creek where we stop to fill our canteens and a large jug that sloshes in the back of the wagon. The trees are tall and lean here, bony fingers reaching up from the flat soil, and Odie lowers her muzzle, patiently gulping up the clear water while I rub a hand through her mane. "Are we almost to the next town?" I'm growing more impatient, anxious. Too many days have passed since we left the valley, time seeping through cracks in my mind. The old woman, Imogene, said I wouldn't find the Architect in the wheat town, but I certainly won't find him out here, in the middle of nothing. I need to reach another town, a place with more people—people who might know something.

"We have to stop somewhere first," Pa says.

I raise an eyebrow at him.

"We need to make more tonic."

My eyes flick back to the wagon while Pa rubs his hands together in the creek, scrubbing away the dust. I don't like the not knowing, feeling like I have no sense of where we are. Only at night can I look up at the stars and place myself roughly in its alignment—knowing that we've traveled east, and a little north. But I do not know our position on a map, or what mountains and plains and towns might lie ahead.

"Where I'm taking you," Pa continues, "no one else has ever been." He casts his eyes over to me, a seriousness in them, unblinking. "You must keep this secret, Vega. Keep its location buried inside you, understand?"

I swallow down a strange, nervous pang, like I'm not sure if I want to know this secret. Knowing things can be a burden—I've felt its weight, and seen the heaviness of it in Mom's eyes. The secrets she carried, like hauling stones up from garden soil. Each one, something that would eventually crush her.

But I nod to Pa, sensing that I don't have a choice. "I understand."

He dips his hands back into the cool stream, rubbing the dirt from his knuckles, when Odie jerks her head up from the water, ears shot forward.

I peer across the creek, up the far slope . . . where a shadow moves.

Something in the trees.

"Pa," I hiss. My heart thuds at my temples, and I flash a look over to him. "Something's there."

He stands up slowly, running a hand along Odie's flank to keep her calm, then glances back at the wagon—maybe he's calculating how quickly we might be able to turn Odie around and head back the way we came. Or maybe he's thinking of the rifle he keeps tucked under his bedroll in the back, where he thinks I can't see it.

My hands begin to twitch, remembering the brown bear who sometimes wandered down into the valley in late winter, hungry and desperate, nosing around the front porch looking for something to eat, and Mom would shove the pistol into my hands, instructing me to wait on the porch, gun barrel aimed at the bear's broad head while Mom shouted at the bear to *move on up the ridge.* I never fired a shot at the bear, but I always sensed it wasn't the bear we feared the most. Mom was preparing me for a time when something else might wander up our road, something more dangerous. *A stranger.* And she wanted me to be ready: to know how to handle the pistol even when my heart was beating wildly in my ears, hands shaking with fear. I had to be able to tune it all out and defend myself when the time came.

Now Pa places a finger to his lips, telling me to be quiet.

Another snap of branches. A shadow shifting just out sight. Something, *someone*, is breathing rapidly in the trees.

I wish Pa'd grab the gun. My eyes pass quickly to the wagon, and I take a slow, careful step toward it—I'll get the gun myself, sink down on the front seat, and aim it across the creek. But Pa shakes his head at me to stay put.

"Is it scavengers?" My voice so quiet, it feels like only air has left my lips. I've never encountered scavengers before; I don't know what they'll look like, how clever or hidden or dangerous they might be. But I know out here, alone, Pa and I don't have a way to defend ourselves—no cabin to protect us—and my heart is now pounding in my ears, dulling all other sound.

But Pa doesn't reply, his eyes trained on the tree line. The bent oaks, the long streaks of sunlight broken by shadow, making it impossible to pick out anything from everything else.

A shape moves. . . . A shadow re-forms itself. I think I see an arm reaching out into a shaft of warm sunlight. But it's not a person at all: It's a deer, picking her way down to the shore of the creek, forked hooves perching easily on the slick rocks, moss hanging between her coiled antlers, ribbons of it, where little white flowers bloom. She's beautiful and also terrifying. I hold my breath, afraid to make a sound. I've never seen anything like her back in the valley, adorned with green from the forest, as if she is made of the land. And when she sees us—head snapping upright, nostrils flared bright pink—I swear she's looking right at me. Eyes the color of a blue river stone— intent, eerie. Her gaze reminds me of the old woman, as if she is giving me a warning in the flutter of her long, dark eyelashes: *Go back the way you came. Danger lives in these woods, beyond the valley. Go home, Vega.*

But just as quickly as she appeared, her ears flick away, and she bolts back into the trees.

I let out an exhale, gripping my hands into fists to stop the trembling.

Pa scrubs a hand across the back of his neck—his own nerves just as frayed. "Let's get moving," he says finally, wiping a hand over his forehead. But his palm briefly touches his temple, and I can see the subtle twitch of his eyebrow—a pain he's trying to hide. And I wonder . . . how long has he been sick? How long has he felt the ache in his eardrums?

But before I can ask, he lowers his hand and starts back toward the wagon. "Still have a long day ahead of us."

I stare one last time across the far side of the creek, wanting to see the deer one last time, but there is only the gentle sway of trees and the memory of her eyes.

* * *

"It's called the Ohavie River," Pa remarks, the wagon bouncing along the rocky path, a cliff wall on one side, a roaring river on the other. "We'll follow it all the way into these hills, to where it bubbles up from the ground." His words are calm, but he keeps glancing behind us like he's worried we might be followed—that someone will track us into these low hills and discover the place he's kept secret.

At last the trees become thin, unable to keep their footing in the slick rock, and the forest opens up into a clearing. It happens so abruptly that I peer up at the steep terrain and the blue gleaming sky, as if the forest had only been a dream.

And ahead, built beside the river, sits a small house.

I lean forward, elbows against my knees. "Does someone live here?"

"It was a miners' camp." Pa secures the reins and removes his hat to wipe at his forehead. "But it's been empty for years."

A sagging porch frames the front of the tiny structure, with a stone chimney on the left side made from rocks likely dredged up from the river bottom. But the river does not roar down the hillside here—as it did along the road—it's a calm pool of clear, cold water that seems to rise up from some deep underground cavern far below.

My legs feel stiff, aching in every joint, and I slide down from the wagon, landing in the dry dirt of the road, and stretch my arms overhead. "What were they mining?"

"They had hoped to find gold—" Pa replaces his hat and eases himself down to the ground, shoulders rolling back. "—but it was silver they uncovered in the surrounding rock."

I try to imagine the rock walls glistening with channels of silver, ribbons catching not just the sunlight but the starlight, too. "Did they get sick? Is that why they left?"

"No. They left once the silver was gone." Pa starts the work of removing the empty jars from the back of the wagon, stacking the crates on the ground. "We can't stay long. . . ." He nods at me to take one of the crates. "We can't risk it. We'll resupply, then head out in the morning."

Dust swirls up from the floor of the cabin when Pa pushes open the door, a blizzard of gray particles, and I cough, wiping at the air. How long has it been since Pa was last here? Months, at least.

I step into the room, where broken clay coffee mugs and metal tools sit cluttered in the corners, along with torn sacks that were once likely filled with flour or grain, but have since been chewed up by mice. I trip over something: an old boot, the laces gone. It's a cabin of artifacts, left behind by the miners. And I feel like we don't belong here—a place of ghosts.

But there are other things in the cabin too, that belong to Pa.

Crates have been stacked three high on the right-hand wall, each filled with empty glass jars—a mismatch assortment, gathered from his customers and then reused. On the left side, beside the fireplace, sit several wooden barrels. And against the back wall are more crates—but these are filled with something I've never seen before.

Pa moves to the empty jars, counting them, but I feel drawn

to the back wall, curious about what lies inside the crates. My eyes adjust to the dark, windowless room, and I reach into one of the full crates and pull out a smaller bottle. They're light, a quarter of the size of the glass jars filled with tonic, and each has a tiny round lid. Letters have been written on the side of every one, but it's a word I've never seen before.

"What is it?" I ask, holding up a bottle and turning to face Pa.

"Aspirin." His voice is matter-of-fact, as if I should already know this.

I turn the bottle over, and the tiny white pills inside spill to one end. "You use them to make your tonic?"

"We'll crush the pills and dilute it in water and honey."

"Where did it come from? All these bottles?" There must be hundreds of them. Each filled with two dozen pills or more.

Pa walks to my side, lifting a bottle into his hand. "My grandfather was a doctor. He used them to treat his patients."

Mom always said that doctors are rare, impossible to find. It's why I never went in search of one when she became sick. It was pointless to try.

Pa shows me how to haul up buckets of water from the river, then pour them into the cast-iron pot hanging over the fireplace. We boil five jars at a time—to sterilize them. And once they've cooled, we fill each one with river water. Pa crushes the pills on the old wood table near the fireplace, then pours a teaspoon's worth into each jar. Next we add the honey that Pa bought from the old woman—Imogene—who stared at me with an itch of fear in her eyes. "We'll put a little in each jar," Pa instructs. "To sweeten it." Now I understand why he wanted to save the jar of honey; it was always meant for the tonic.

We divide the honey into the waiting jars, a dollop in each, and the air instantly smells sweet. By the end, we've filled twenty-five jars, and used only a single bottle of aspirin from the crates. He has enough aspirin in the cabin to make a lifetime's worth of tonic. Two lifetimes' worth.

"Well done," Pa says, surveying our full jars of tonic and giving me an approving look. "We'll have plenty to sell at the market."

I wipe the sweat from my temples, tired, but relieved we were able to refill his supply so quickly. And I wonder suddenly if Pa brought me here not only out of necessity but because he wanted me to know his method, and the location of his supply hidden deep in these hills.

He's teaching me how it's done, in case someday I need to do it on my own. In case someday, like Mom, he's no longer around.

But if I make it to the ocean, as I intend, then I won't ever be coming back here. To these hills and this miners' cabin beside a strange river.

"Let's get them loaded," Pa says, hoisting up a crate and carrying it out through the doorway into the waning daylight. But I hesitate, looking back at the stack of wood crates and the bottles of pills.

I move swiftly, my feet hardly making a sound on the wood floor, and I snatch one of the small bottles, tucking it up into the sleeve of my sweater.

* ✳ *

We camp beside the river, under the stars.

I don't bother asking Pa if we can sleep inside the cabin—I understand now that he prefers to be outside, without walls or a roof to mask the sounds of the trees and the wild creatures who stalk close in the dark. And maybe in case other things creep close as well, more dangerous things.

We eat grilled wheat cakes with slices of hard goat cheese and tomato that Pa traded for back at the wheat town. I eat until I feel so full and round that I sink onto the quilt, hands cupped against my stomach to dull the ache.

My eyes scan the surrounding pines—they feel closer than they did during the day, towering silhouettes that loom and stretch over us—and I feel hemmed in, trapped in a way that makes me nervous. "I don't like these trees," I say aloud.

Pa scrapes out the bottom of the skillet with his knife to clean it. "It doesn't feel safe."

He slides the knife back into the sheath at his ankle, then places the skillet upside down on a rock. "Nothing's safe out here. Best place for you was back in the valley."

I ignore his comment and tug at the collar of my wool sweater, the fibers itching my skin. I feel restless, jittery, and I long for my old bed back at the cabin—now burned to ash. But I long for other things too: the smell of wax candles burning in the evening, Mom and I lying on our backs beside the river, tracing constellations with our fingertips while she told the stories of the sky—of the first Astronomer who mapped the stars and made sure we wouldn't forget. I'd catch glimpses of the tattoo on her neck, dark ink shining in the moonlight.

But I don't allow these memories to pry me open. I close my eyes, watching the sparks against my eyelids, little stars erupting and dying.

Sleep comes in strange fits: I dream of the rope we saw in town, swaying above me while someone hisses in my ear. *Vega, Vega.* But then I see the deer, wandering up the dusty main street of town, its wild, pale blue eyes focused on me, moss sagging between antlers, and then the thundering of its hooves as it darts away back into the woods. It was trying to tell me something, warn me to go back. Danger lurks beyond the valley walls. Danger is close.

Snap, snap. I hear the breaking of limbs. The stirring of leaves. *The deer followed us into these mountains.*

Something breathes in the trees, breathing in the dark.

Footsteps.

Footsteps that don't belong, that are too loud. *Not the deer at all.* The ground beneath me trembles with footsteps.

I shudder awake. The sky is still dark, but there is a shadow standing over me. A figure that isn't Pa.

✳ ✴ ✳

Three men are visible in the circle of light made by the campfire.

They might only be ghosts, remnants of a dream, except one of them grabs my shoulder and shoves me down to the ground to keep me from standing. Dirt in my nostril. Heart thudding in my ears. I blink across the firelight and find Pa standing a few feet away from one of the men, hands rolled into fists.

Not a dream at all.

I recognize them—they're the men I saw back at the wheat town, standing in the shadow of the blacksmith's shop, watching us, watching the wagon.

From the edge of my vision, I catch a shiver of movement in the trees, a shadow slipping just out of sight—there are more men skulking back in the pines, circling the cabin. Hidden. More than just the three I saw back in town. But I can't tell how many. *Too many.*

"I've seen you before," the man closest to Pa says, leaning in like he's trying to make out the features of Pa's face, calculate if Pa's going to put up a fight. The man wears a wool jacket over his pressed collared shirt, a wide belt notched with bullets, and he's the only one of the three who's clean-shaven. But when my eyes fall to his hands, hooked on his belt, I find no ring. The other two men are less civilized in their appearance: dirt in their hair, foreheads slick with sweat. They've been riding these dusty roads for some time and haven't seen a bath in weeks. And none of them wear a silver signet ring with *Circinus* stamped into the metal.

The clean-shaven man tilts his head at Pa, his broad-brimmed hat pulled down to shield his eyes, but I can just make out a scar cut lengthwise beneath his chin, like someone tried to slit his throat but somehow failed to kill him. "Up in Winach, some months back," he says to Pa, his jaw grinding back and forth like a timber saw. "You were selling that tonic." His head flicks to the wagon, and I can hear a smile in his voice, a satisfaction, and it's clear he's in charge—the boss of these road-weary men. "Saw you again a few days ago back in that farming town." He pauses to spit onto the ground, a dark wad of tobacco tucked into his bottom lip. "I've heard people say you're a conman, taking people's money and giving them river water in return."

Pa's eyes click to mine, and I try to read some message in them, if he's trying to tell me to run, but they slip back to the wagon—and I wonder if he's thinking of the rifle tucked inside. But he doesn't make a move for it. He stays firmly planted a few yards away.

"I'd say you're giving people false hope"—a sneer curls across his upper lip, raven-dark eyes blinking, and he walks to the other side of Pa, staring up at the box wagon and the lettering that promises cures from heartache to toothache—"just delaying the inevitable end." He turns back to Pa, hooking both hands against his belt, inches from two holstered guns. His jaw seems to lock in place, puckering the scar along his throat—the flesh wrinkled and jagged, as if it didn't heal right. "People are dying," he says through tight, clenched teeth. "Won't be long until there's nothing left."

Pa's eyes stay on the man, and I can see the tension slipping like water across his brow. This is what he was afraid of—someone tracking us into these hills and discovering his stash of medicine. "They don't need to suffer," he answers, shoulders tucked down, eyes unflinching.

The man laughs, dropping his hands from his belt, and takes a step closer to Pa. My whole body tenses, spine stiff—I know I need to run. Scramble away into the trees. But my mind keeps thinking of the wagon, and the gun waiting inside. How long would it take me to reach for it, drop the lever down to pop a cartridge into the chamber, then aim it at the man facing Pa? It would feel no different than staring down the old brown bear, it's narrow-set eyes watching me, sensing that I was the thing it should fear.

But one of the men is still towering over me, blocking my path—his dark, oiled hair slicked down beneath his hat, nose sunburnt, and a silver bolo tie in the shape of a crow suspended around his neck with two leather straps. In his bottom lip, he chews a wad of tobacco—just like his boss—and I notice something else: a scar on his forearm just visible beneath his filthy gray shirt, rolled up to his elbows. But the scar isn't irregular in shape; it's a perfect starburst, with a circle at the center and several lines unfurling outward.

It's a brand, something normally given to cattle—a way to mark who the cattle belong to.

A hot piece of metal—likely heated on the coals of a campfire—was pressed into his forearm until the flesh bubbled and turned black. And now the scar remains. A symbol that he belongs to someone. Maybe this group of men.

The man notices me watching him, his eyes black and cold and unblinking, and he pushes out his lip to spit onto the ground at my feet, baring his teeth, the color of tar. I sense he's just waiting for the chance to pull his revolver from his waist and shoot me dead right where I sit. If I even twitch or make a move for the wagon, I won't make it more than a foot.

"So you think what you're doing is a mercy?" the clean-shaven man with the scar along his throat asks, leaning toward Pa, jutting out his chin, as if he's challenging Pa to contradict him.

Pa says nothing.

"You're selling them a lie." The man breathes heavy, grit in his throat, and he wipes hastily at his forehead, like he's losing his patience. Still, I catch a quick glimpse of it: the same starburst mark on his forearm as the man standing over me. They both have it, and I suspect all the men hiding in the woods do too. A band of men who brand themselves, maybe for loyalty, duty, but surely for life. This group is not the kind you can leave. I imagine that death is the only way out.

"I'm selling them hope," Pa answers, defiant now, eyes dark in the moonlight. "For some of them, that's all they have."

61

The air changes, a tension pulling tight, and my eyes flash from Pa to the man with the scar at his throat. He looks back at the tree line, nodding at the men who are only shadows and limbs. Then four, no five, figures separate from the trees, forming into human shapes, and under the dim glow of moonlight, they begin moving toward the wagon.

My heart begins to thunder in my chest. Adrenaline pulses at my eardrums, my vision vibrating.

Odie, who had been dozing near the front of the wagon, watches the men with her large brown eyes and stamps a hoof against the ground. She's thinking of bolting, of tearing away into the trees. *Stay put*, I think. *Don't run.*

"You might be right," the man says to Pa, his jaw grinding again, as if he's turning his teeth to dust, an awful sound. "Because there's nothing else left in this godforsaken land."

I breathe, feeling the cold ground beneath my palms, but my eyes flash to the wagon again. *I could reach the gun in time; I'm sure of it.* There is a long, weighted pause, no one saying anything—the silence splitting through my skin. The river bubbles a few feet away, and Odie still looks wild-eyed and afraid, but then the man waves a hand to the others, his mouth sinking back into a straight, ruthless line, his eyes passing briefly over me, then away.

He claps a firm hand on Pa's shoulder, blunt, forceful. "But at least we have law and order," he says. "And in this territory, I am both." More men emerge from the road—some coughing, some staggering just a little, sick with illness—but they take turns leaning into the back of the wagon, lifting out crates of tonic, then hauling them away into the dark, where they must have their own wagon waiting. "And it's about time you pay your tax, Tonic Man."

My eyes swivel to the cabin, where two more men have pushed open the door and are stepping inside. "Boss!" one of them shouts. "Come look at this!"

The man facing Pa turns suddenly and strides up the steps into the cabin. I can hear their voices, a quick succession of words, but not what they're saying.

"Pa," I hiss, my lungs heaving in and out, my voice broken, and I try to stand up, to move toward him, but the man standing over me grabs my arm and yanks me back, shoving me to the ground. I land hard onto my side, hands and face in the dirt. The air sputters from my lungs, and a dull pain shoots through my ribs. I lie for a moment, facedown, trying to breathe. *This is bad,* my mind repeats. *We have to get out of here.*

I see Pa try to move toward me, but the man still looming over me shoots him a look to stay put.

Slowly I push myself upright, but I stay seated on the ground, the breath in my lungs a sharp stab of pain with every exhale. Ribs throbbing. Head pulsing, pulsing. I check my coat pocket—*the bottle of aspirin is still there.* Then I brush my hair across my neck, keeping the tattoo covered. Out of sight.

"You all right, Vega?" Pa asks softly.

I nod, swallowing tightly, and then my eyes click to the cabin, where the man with the scar reappears in the doorway, both hands on his belt. "Well, looks like you've been hiding way more than a few jars of tonic. Where'd you get all those pills?"

Pa looks up at him but refuses to answer.

The man makes a *tsk* sound. "Been years since I've seen a stash like that. I'd guess you either stole it, or your family's been hiding it for generations."

"I didn't steal it." Pa meets the man's gaze, beard twitching.

"It seems luck is on my side today," the man adds, striding down the porch steps, his boots thudding across the dirt, spurs jangling. He moves with a comfortable ease, a man in control—even of himself—who prefers not to lose his temper, although I sense it's always there, just beneath the surface. Waiting. "But I'm not a greedy man, and I'm feeling merciful." He walks to a row of crates sitting on the ground beside the wagon that his men have yet to cart away. He kicks one of the crates. "I'll leave you a few jars of your fool's tonic," he says, as if he's being charitable. "You'll need a way to make a few coins so you can buy a horse."

I can see Pa's face tug together, stiffen. "I already have a horse."

The man smiles again, a menacing arch to his lips, the wad of tobacco pressed to his teeth, and he walks to Odie, running his broad hand along her mane. She blows air from her nostrils—sensing he's not someone she should trust. "No you don't," he answers, looping his hand around her halter. "We're short on horses, and it's difficult to find ones this stout and well trained."

I feel the stone rising in my gut, the fear tasting like bile on my tongue, knowing what's about to happen next.

"We need the horse," Pa says, desperation catching in his voice now. "Without her, we have no way to pull the wagon."

"Seems you won't need a wagon with hardly anything left to trade," the man counters with a dark, raised eyebrow.

"Please." Pa shakes his head, a tremor in the word. The jars of tonic, his supply, Odie—it's all he has.

The man's mouth grinds to one side, like he's chewing over an idea. Then, like a hawk scanning a prairie for mice, his gaze snaps to me, head tilted. "Fine," he says with a snarl, his eyes still on me. "We'll take the girl instead."

With a quick nod from his boss, the bolo-tie man yanks me up, a filthy hand braced around my neck. I wince at the pain in my ribs, at my neck, but I hold down the cry in my throat and tighten my shoulders back. *They haven't seen the tattoo on my neck; they haven't noticed the mark.* But if the man adjusts his hand, if he looks close enough, he'll see it.

"No!" Pa barks, sidestepping closer to me.

"She's worth more than the horse anyway," the man in charge says, pushing the brim of his hat up just slightly, a sinister lilt to his voice, a clicking in his jaw. "We could sell her easily. Or maybe we'll keep her."

No, no, no. I start clawing at the man's hand around my throat, tearing away skin, blood under my fingernails, but he only squeezes tighter, and the air is cut from my lungs.

"Take the horse," Pa says desperately, flashing his terrified eyes from me to the man. "Please. Leave her."

The man with the scar along his throat lets out a small sound, maybe a laugh, maybe a sound of disappointment—I can't be sure with the pain in my lungs and the ringing in my ears. His eyes fall closed, considering, a clicking in his teeth again, before his jaw locks shut. Air hisses from his mouth, eyelids lifting to meet mine. "Fine." He watches me, clicks his tongue against his teeth, then says, "We'll take the horse instead."

The bolo-tie man immediately releases his hand and I drop to the ground, coughing into the dirt, feeling like I might be sick.

I don't know why he's let me go—decided I'm not worth the trouble, maybe—but I turn my head, sucking in the cold night air, fury boiling up in my gut. The man with the scar gives me one last look—a strange glint in his eyes, like he knows he could drag me away too if he wanted, kicking and screaming. He could change his mind. He could take everything—Odie *and* me. He has the power here, not us.

But the fury rises up into my chest now, heat sparking behind my eyes. *I won't let him take Odie.* Without her, we have no way out of here.

I feel my hands pushing me upright before I've even thought it through. I feel my legs catapult me toward the wagon, the adrenaline pounding in my chest, eyes watering, throat still burning where the man dug his fingers into my flesh. Behind me, the bolo-tie man makes a sound, startled by my sudden movement. "Shit!" he says—and I'm certain he's reaching for his gun, but I don't look back. I brush past Pa and sprint toward the wagon. I know where the rifle is hidden, I know exactly where it sits, and I slip my hand into the back of the wagon. Thankfully, my finger locates it on the first try, and I swing it out in front of me, dropping the lever and hearing the cartridge pop into place. My ears ring, my eyes stop watering, and I aim the barrel directly at the man with the scar cut lengthwise across his throat.

And I feel the power shift.

I'm in control now.

His eyes go wide, mouth caught open like a black, bottomless well, and I see for the first time that one of his eyes is blue, the other gray—lost all its color.

I swallow, hardening my stance.

But the man doesn't reach for the pistols at his waist; instead he lifts both palms toward me. "Easy, young lady." His eyes flatten, sharp, ruthless—not the first time he's stared down the barrel of a gun. "No need to be pointing that thing when you don't know how to use it."

"I know how to use it." The words are swift, without hesitation, and I raise the barrel of the rifle so it's leveled at the man's forehead, right between his miscolored eyes—my finger fluttering against the trigger, itching to pull it back and wipe the smile clean from his face.

To my left, I can see the other man with the bolo tie draw his gun—aiming it directly at me. There is no waver in his eyes, no hesitation. He's fired his gun at more than wild animals and an old stump that sat down beside the river in the valley that we used for target practice. He's seen bullets tear through human flesh, rupture lungs and hearts and skulls, and lived to tell stories about it.

But I don't show how frightened I am—adrenaline surging through me—and I steady my eyes on the man with two different-colored eyes. "Leave our horse," I say through clenched teeth, temples thumping.

A wind stirs in the trees, creaking limbs, while behind me, river water bubbles up from the ground, every sound sharp in my ears, and every movement of the man in front of me, shifting his weight from one foot to another, is like thunder. He tips his head toward me, watching me like a fox watches trout jumping at the surface of a river, calculating if it's worth going in to get a meal. "Go ahead and shoot me, little lady. Because even if you're a good shot, which I'm starting to suspect you might be, you'll only get a couple shots off before you'll need to reload." He nods to the rifle, his throat quivering along the scar. "And my men have enough bullets to finish you and your old man off ten times over. I might be dead, but you won't be far behind."

I keep my eyes flattened on him. "You'd give your life for a horse that isn't even yours?" I ask, betting that he wouldn't. That he'd rather leave the horse and spare a bullet in the chest than see how far this standoff will go. What I'm willing to do.

His jaw slides back and forth, his gray eye twitching, before it settles again. "I like this girl." He flashes a look to the man with the bolo tie, one corner of his mouth rising. "She's got more grit than most of you."

The bolo-tie man's eyebrows stuff together—he doesn't like the comment—but he keeps his gun trained on me.

"But that doesn't mean she's smart." He wheels his eyes back and steps closer to me, only a few feet from the barrel of the gun—daring me to pull the trigger. "And I doubt she's ever killed a man." He shakes his head, confident, eyes darkening.

Behind him, several of the men who had been carrying crates of tonic and aspirin up into the trees begin returning from the forest. And when they realize what's happening—when they see the rifle held in my hands—they pull their own pistols, inching closer until I'm encircled, eyes gleaming wild.

No way out of this now.

My heartbeat screams in my ears, finger twitching against the trigger, but I force my breathing to remain steady. *No matter what,* Mom would instruct, *if your breathing stays calm, so will your trigger finger.*

"There's no way out of this where you don't end up dead." His gray eye flutters again, separate from the other eye. Of its own command. "Samuel there"—he nods to the man with the bolo tie—"never misses, and his pistol is trained right at your temple. Your skull will be split clean open before I even hit the ground."

I don't blink; I don't reply. Instead I brace the gun against my shoulder, sliding my finger against the trigger, feeling the tension. Just a subtle squeeze. I know the force will push me back, so I steady my legs beneath me—I'll only have a split second to fire the first shot, then swing the gun to my left and shoot the man with the bolo tie—Samuel. After that, I'll drop to the ground before the other men can fire; I'll crawl back behind the wagon. I'll shout to Pa, and hopefully he'll do the same. From there, I don't know. Maybe we can make it into the trees, lose ourselves in the shadowed dark, and wait for the men to give up. I prepare myself, finger fluttering against the metal curve of the trigger.

This is it . . .

I suck in a breath, clamping down my jaw, but there is a hand on my shoulder—abrupt and quick. I flinch back—but it's Pa, right beside me. "Give me the rifle," he says softly.

My mouth dips open, the adrenaline still surging down every vein, and I shake my head. But he's already reaching for it, pulling it from my hands. "No . . . ," I say to him, my voice a hiss, a rasp, but he's pulled the rifle free from my grip and is placing it on the ground at our feet. The air feels ripped from my ears, my lungs, the blood pumping behind my eyes, making it impossible to blink. Pa lifts his hands in the air so the men can see that he's not going to reach for it again. The rifle is out of my hands.

We're no longer a threat.

I want to scream, to cry, but nothing comes out. I stare at Pa, anger and fear burning up inside me like a campfire out of control.

"Your old man's a lot smarter than you," the man says, a smile creeping across his face, all teeth and sneering upper lip. "He just saved your life."

My arms feel too slack without the weight of the gun, all the power gone, and I watch as the other men slide their pistols back into the holsters, then turn back for the trees. They take Odie by the halter and lead her away, hind legs dragging, wanting to dig into the ground and resist.

No! I want to shout, but still my throat feels lost of all air. Nothing left.

The man with two different eyes tips his hat at me, as if it were a secret parting gesture meant only for me—a recognition that he won. I pointed a rifle at him, finger feathering the trigger, and he walked away without a hole in his gut. Or head.

I should have shot him when I had the chance.

Samuel, the man with the bolo tie, is the last to leave, keeping his pistol trained on us until he steps into the dark of the tree line, out of sight.

I blink. And all at once, my legs feel like they're going to give out—the fear hitting me hard. But I refuse to drop to the ground, to show Pa any weakness. I rub my hands down my face, feeling the tremble from my toes up to the top of my head.

"What the hell were you thinking, Vega?" Pa says, picking up the rifle and carrying it over to the back of the wagon. "You could have gotten yourself killed, or both of us."

I follow Pa with my eyes, my legs still unable to move. "They took Odie," I manage.

Pa leans the rifle against the side of the wagon. "I know. But she's just a horse, Vega. And we're still alive." He climbs up inside the wagon to see what's left.

I look to the trees where the men slipped into the dark. "We can still go after them."

But Pa doesn't reply; he starts hefting out things from inside the wagon. He pitches my quilt onto the ground beside the lone crate of tonic, followed by our jug of water, remaining sacks of beans and flour, the jar of honey, then his own satchel, before climbing out from the back.

"What are we supposed to do now?" I ask.

"We walk."

I shake my head at him, the anger still hot behind my eyes—he took the rifle when it could have at least given us a chance to stop those men, to save Odie.

Pa lifts my quilt and the jug of water, handing them both to me. "Carry what you can."

I stare back down the road, where only darkness and shadows move in the trees, the men out of sight. "Were they scavengers?"

"No," Pa answers, slinging the rifle over one shoulder and hoisting up the last crate of tonic. "They're worse than scavengers."

"They had a mark on their skin." I tuck the quilt under my arm—it smells like campfire smoke and pine. "It looked like a starburst."

Pa heads toward the dense trees beyond the river, away from the road. "It's their brand, their brotherhood."

I move quickly to catch up to him, weighted by the jug of water sloshing at my side, my ribs throbbing with every step as the adrenaline wears off. As everything starts to sink back into focus.

"They're outlaws," he adds, not looking at me. "But some call them *Heretics*, or *Theorists*."

I stare at Pa, my teeth still clamped shut at the back—angry for what he wouldn't let me do. Angry that we have almost nothing left. "Why?"

"Because they believe in something we don't."

I narrow my gaze, not understanding.

He pauses at the edge of the trees, just beyond the river, and turns to look back at me. I sense the irritation in him, the loss of everything he has, and he clears his throat. "They don't think any of us will survive."

ARIES, *Alpha Arietis*
+23° 27' 44"

The first Astronomer charted the constellations that already had names—the oldest ones that had been written about well before her time. But on clear nights, when she gazed toward the western hemisphere, she noted a part of the sky she didn't recognize: stars that had never been observed or mapped or written down.

So she marked them on paper and labeled them: Lorox and Pala, Harebelle and Allium. She used wildflowers and the names of characters in books she read as a child.

But her neighbors—who had often ignored her work, her nighttime vocation of studying the sky—had begun to show signs of something.

An illness: a cough in the lungs and a fluttering in the eyes and ears.

Consumption.

It started slowly, as things like this often do. Tiptoeing up the back of sunburnt necks; a line of sweat on the spine while harvesting crops; a shiver across the vision when raising a hand to block the wavy, setting sun. A shiver that becomes a blur, a cloud, until it becomes something else: blindness. The itch of fear came next, the panicked whispers with neighbors outside barber shops and barn doors; a murmur at kitchen counters that something doesn't feel right, hands shaking while flouring bread for the oven; while tucking toddlers into bed at night, tiny voices complaining of a *crackle* in their ears. A rumble in their chests.

A sickness had emerged, whether from the land or one another, or something else—people were beginning to die.

THREE

The sky is a map, Mom would say, sweeping her hands above our heads to make her point. *It can tell you where you're going, and how to get back.*

She would spin me around in circles, my eyes pinched closed, a dizzying blur of black, then tell me to locate the pole star, the one that marks true south. From there, she would explain, I could navigate my way anywhere.

But tonight, the sky is smudged out by heavy, moisture-rich rainclouds and dense evergreens. We do not follow the road back down along the river—the way we'd come. Pa says the men might camp on the road, so it isn't safe. Instead we trek up into the forest behind the cabin, following a single animal track that cuts a line through the trees and rocky terrain, the earthy scent of moss and pine sap thick in the air, in my nostrils. A dampness to everything.

I can't wait to be free of this dark forest, to once again see the stars, to orient myself against the backdrop of the sky. Without it, I feel dangerously untethered. A restive, fidgety ache knocking behind my eyes.

I tuck my hands into my pockets, feeling for the secret bottle of aspirin—still there. This single bottle, and the crate of tonic that Pa carries, is all that's left. He is quiet while we walk—no more humming his *roaming songs*, and I sense the heavy meaning behind his silence.

He has lost everything: Odie, the wagon, and his entire supply in the miners' cabin. All of it gone. Taken. By men with marks burned into their forearms. Men who almost took me.

Dawn breaks over the horizon just as we finally step free from the forest. But the landscape is still a rugged series of rocky hills rolling out ahead of us, and a light, drizzling rain begins to fall.

"Do you know where we are?" I ask.

Pa's eyes are dim, and he shakes his head.

We reach a wide stretch of prairie where the yellowing grass hisses and thrashes in the morning wind. And we keep walking.

I can't help but think of home, the valley, of what I left behind. *Home.* A word that is so far away, it feels untouchable, lost all its meaning. I had wanted to be brave—the daughter that Mom needed me to be—but the world is sicker than I knew, more cruel than I wanted to believe, and I can't seem to shake the chill that has burrowed into my bones. But there's no turning back now. *Nothing to go back to.* I am the last one, the only one.

If I don't find the Architect, Mom's death will have been for nothing.

I have no choice but to keep going.

Pa and I push on through the meadow, heads down, unprotected from the rain, where fat honeybees retreat from the downpour back to their hive high in the branches of a nearby oak tree, their double rosebud wings beating rhythmically. They make a soft hum while they float through the air, a singsong like a nightingale bird, notes carried up into the downpour. *They didn't always sing,* I remember Mom telling me when I young, when I'd chase the bees up the shore of the river to the far ridge, trying to catch them in my cupped palms. Bees used to buzz silently—but now they warble and chirp like a bird.

Pa looks back at me—my pace slower than his.

My ribs ache, a nagging throb on my right side, and I wince with each step—the pain growing worse, the adrenaline long gone. But I keep peering over my shoulder, listening for the sound of horses—for the men with brands burned into their forearms to appear through the trees. Coming after us. After me.

But there is only the cold rain against my face, and no sign of them.

We need to find a road, a path, a town. Anything.

We drop down from the meadow into a dry creek channel lined with oak trees and sagging willows, limbs like curtains, the air smelling of sage and lichen. An odd scent. We follow the barren creek, and the day peels away into evening, until I catch a flash of something up through the trees . . . a flicker. A wink. Glass reflecting the fading sunlight.

I climb up out of the creek.

"Vega?" Pa calls behind me, but I keep walking, legs taking me through the sparse, water-starved oaks, my eyes afraid to blink, to lose sight of the vibrating light.

My ribs throb in time with each exhale, my ears quake and pulse, but at last I see it: a farmhouse.

And behind it sit rows of blooming trees—an orchard. The sun-ripened scent of apples so rich and thick that I almost drop to my knees.

"Wait here," Pa says, swinging the rifle from his shoulder and holding it out in front of him.

But I don't listen—my legs keep staggering forward, needing to know that it's real. That the farmhouse isn't a trick of the dappling rain and shooting pain in my side.

I reach the back door, left open, and stop to listen for the echo of voices, for children's footsteps racing down a hall. But there is only the wind howling through the doorway, rain pattering against the roof, and the cold hint of ghosts stirring inside.

Pa looks like he's going to tell me to wait again, insist that he go in alone, but I step forward and walk across the threshold into the house, my boots breaking apart the dead leaves that have blown onto the kitchen floor. No one has been here in a while. No broom has swept across this floor in months. The place is abandoned.

Still, I move cautiously from the kitchen into the living room, feeling relieved to be out of the rain, but hesitant of anything that might be hiding in the dark: feral creatures nesting in the shadowed corners. Against the far wall rests a stone fireplace, burnt logs left to rot. My fingers trail along a low wooden couch, carefully stitched cushions, and a wool blanket left folded at the armrest. It smells like rain and rotted leaves, but at least it's dry. Back in the kitchen, wilted flowers sag in a clay vase left on the wood table, summer blooms from last season, and Pa is eyeing a steep set of stairs that must lead down into a cellar. "Hello," he calls into the dark, just to be sure, before he moves down the steps. I follow, and in the damp, cold cellar, we discover shelves filled with dried and canned apples. A stockpile. More than a family could eat in three seasons.

The family who lived here had been orchardists, tending to the crop out back. But they left and never returned—consumption, most likely. Maybe they fled to a town, seeking help, or maybe their bodies are buried somewhere beyond the apple trees. A coldness slides down to my toes. *So much death.* This farmhouse feels like the remains of a life deserted, only a few scraps left behind that tell the story of who they once were.

I climb the stairs out of the cellar two at a time, needing to be free of the dark, and walk to one of the kitchen windows, wiping the dust away to peer out at the falling rain. My breathing slows, calms, and I notice a small creek meandering through the neatly spaced orchard rows, keeping the soil damp and dark. But . . . there's something else.

At first I think it's another deer, like the one we saw in the woods—but a leather halter is cinched over its gray-speckled head. "Pa," I say just as he appears at the top of the cellar. "There's a mule out back." It's wandering untethered through the rain, pulling up the tall grass beside the creek.

Pa steps out through the back door into the orchard, but I don't follow—I stay in the dry house—watching as he carefully picks his way through the trees, and when he reaches the mule, he runs his hand gently down its neck, the rain streaming over them both. The mule nuzzles his hand, unafraid, and Pa begins checking its hooves for cracks or damage, to make sure it hasn't foundered since it's been left on its own.

Whoever had lived here left in such a rush, they didn't even take their mule.

I scan the kitchen, trying to imagine a family seated at the table, eating breakfast, telling stories, and I wonder if they knew what was coming? I wonder if they knew death was knocking on their door, if they left the house knowing they wouldn't return—like when I left the valley. I never truly understood the importance of home; I had never longed for it until I burned it to the ground.

With rainwater still dripping from the ends of my hair, I turn away from the window and walk up the stairwell, everything smelling of dust and the subtle, faraway sweetness of apples. Down the windowless hall, I find three bedrooms with beds still made, quilts tucked into mattresses. No bodies rotting in any of the rooms— *thankfully*.

In the last bedroom on the left, wooden toys are lined up beneath a window in a perfect row, and in the room directly across the hall, hand-sewn dresses sit folded in a closet for a girl half my size. A doll with hand-stitched mouse ears left on the sunlight-yellow quilt folded at the end of the bed. Everything tidy and neat. In its place.

I stay too long in this room, losing myself in a daydream, imagining what a childhood might have been like in a house like this. Summer mornings with the scent of apple jam rising up from the kitchen, hands making shadows against the wall in the moonlight.

A simple life, where the decisions your ancestors made don't haunt you like ghosts hissing in your ear each night before you sink into sleep. Stories that are not bedtime riddles but roadmaps. The echo of my mother's words an itch, a nagging prick, never far away.

A life without ink cut into raw skin.

I leave the room and walk back downstairs—not wanting to imagine it anymore, a different life, because I can't change who I am. Or who my mother was.

I find Pa on the front porch, staring out at the long driveway that disappears into the forest of dark, shadowy oaks. The rain has started to let up, and I wonder how far the driveway stretches before it reaches another road and connects to other towns. Other people.

"The mule is in good shape," Pa says, pulling out the tobacco and pipe from his coat pocket. "It'll help us carry supplies."

I nod and try not to think of Odie, of where those men might have taken her. I tilt my eyes to the sky, the rainclouds pushing north, revealing a few fragments of constellations—reminders of home. "Can we stay the night here?"

Pa tugs at his beard, exhaling deep through his nostrils. He's worried—I can see it in his eyes; he hasn't felt safe since we left the miners' cabin. I don't feel safe either, but I'm craving a soft bed, something that feels like home—and not the cold, wet ground. "This place is well hidden," I point out. "Doesn't seem like anyone knows it's here." The house is untouched, the jars of apples in the cellar unpilfered.

He stares out at the road, like he's waiting for men on horseback to come riding up the drive, looking to finish us off. Or take me with them. "All right," he says, cool and quick, like he might change his mind.

I lean my shoulder into one of the porch posts, my ribs still throbbing. "I'm sorry," I say, "about losing everything."

"Not your fault." He lights his wooden pipe, and the sweet, clove-scented smoke coils up into the starlight. "Time would come eventually, when I either ran out of medicine or someone found it. That day was today." He makes his way down the front steps, legs heavy, tired, and walks out into the softening rain, squinting down the road. He looks older, creases framing his eyes, body bent forward. I wish I could change what's been done, but the past is already written—this I know better than most. "We'll leave first thing in the morning."

"Okay," I agree, not wanting to stay any longer than we have to. Just a few hours' sleep and then we'll keep moving. Always moving. Six nights have already passed since the sister stars appeared in the sky, and I can see their orbit shifting through the sky. Soon they will slip below the horizon, out of sight, and then it'll be too late.

I need to keep moving—get to the next town. Find the Architect. Reach the sea.

Pa turns to look back at me. "You should take two pills from the bottle you took." He gestures toward my ribs, where my hand is clasped, the ache throbbing all the way up to my chest. "I can tell you're in pain from that fall, might have a cracked rib."

I wince against his words, knowing he's right, and I might have injured myself when the bolo-tie man pushed me to the ground. But I had hoped he didn't know about the bottle I took from the cabin. "I—" I didn't mean to steal from him—I was only curious about the bottle, about the tiny white pills inside. I wanted to see them closer, study the words in smaller print on the side of the bottle, then planned to give it back.

"It's okay." He rubs at his neck, muscles sore from the day, from the long walk. "I'm glad you took it—it's the last bottle we have."

"I'm sorry," I say again, wishing I could undo what's been done. First I stole the bottle; then I took his rifle and nearly got us both killed. I feel stupid, and stretched thin, and wrung out, like I haven't slept in days.

"It'll help with the swelling, and pain," he answers, not acknowledging my apology. As if it's not needed. As if things like this come and go in the world beyond the valley, mistakes made, dangers waiting in the dark between trees, and there's no point dwelling on what's already done.

I tilt my eyes back to the horizon, away from the twin stars, to where the night sky is dappled with strange light, particles that hover and crack apart—an anomaly. A part of the sky that is starless, bottomless, where no light lives. It vibrates, as if it's breathing.

A monster always there, growing, like ink spilled onto a floor. Like death.

A thing that has never belonged.

It terrifies me.

I squint my eyes closed, not wanting to see it, the thing hovering in the darkness. The shadow breaking apart the sky.

And I turn away, ducking back into the farmhouse.

✳ ✳ ✳

After a dinner of dried apples and wheat cakes slightly burnt at the edges, and the last of the goat cheese, I climb the stairs of the farmhouse and find myself in the bedroom with the white hand-stitched quilt and lace-trimmed pillows. Whoever once slept in this room collected pinecones along the windowsill and hung a piece of cloth above the bed with tiny flowers printed into the fabric—now faded to pale, watery colors by the sun.

Pa appears in the doorway, his left hand clutching his pipe while his right reaches into his coat pocket for the pouch of tobacco. "If anything happens," he says, eyes clicking to the window, "run past the orchard into the woods, and keep going. If those men come back, you need to get away from here. Don't wait for me."

I touch the window frame lined with dust. The clouds have moved away to the south, revealing a wet, clear sky, and I imagine climbing down the roof, dropping to the porch, then sprinting out into the trees—the breath burning my lungs. Maybe I could make it into the dark unseen. Or maybe those men would catch me and drag me back to the farmhouse.

"If they had seen your mark, if they knew who you were—" Pa shakes his head, eyes lifting to me, and I wonder if he's been thinking about this since we left the miners' cabin. Maybe this is why he took the rifle from me when I was so close to pulling the trigger. It wasn't just about avoiding a gunfight; he was worried what would happen if they saw the tattoo on my neck. He didn't care about Odie, about his supply in the cabin—he only cared about me, making sure they didn't discover who I am. "They would have taken you, Vega. And I'm not sure I'd be able to find you."

His words make me feel instantly cold, an echo across my flesh. My name, my past, the marks on my skin . . . put me in danger. Put everyone near me in danger.

But I wonder if maybe death isn't the worst thing out here. It's being *taken*. Hauled away like Odie and never seen again.

"Okay." I nod at him, but I also know: If those men come riding up the road in the night, guns drawn from their hips, I won't leave Pa behind. I'll stay and fight. It's a feeling inside me I can't explain. A stubbornness maybe—the same part of me that refused to lower the rifle, to accept that they would take Odie and there was nothing we could do.

Because there is a cold desperation in the eyes of every person I've met since leaving the valley, a wild kind of fear hardened into their bones, a thirst that is deeper than the need for water. But a need to survive.

A feeling I didn't know existed, until now.

And if I want to survive in this world, I can't always hide. Tucked away in the valley. Sometimes . . . I will need to fight.

Pa glances down the hall, listening, like he hears something. But it's only the house settling, the last of the rain shedding from the roof. "Get some sleep," he says at last. "We'll leave just after sunup. Fort Bell is still a day-and-a-half walk from here, and we don't want to miss the market, sell what tonic we have left."

I nod. *Another day and a half lost.* Another day and a half ticking closer to the end. He slips away down the hall, and I hear the *thwap* of the front door as he walks out onto the porch.

I slide open the bedroom window and let in the night breeze, listening to Pa puff on his pipe from the front porch. I doubt he'll sleep tonight; instead he'll watch the road, listening for any distant sounds of horses coming up the drive. But right now, only the evening birds chitter from the trees, and the wind sings down the halls of the old house. I like it here, with its sweet-smelling orchard and tall, protective trees and hidden driveway.

But we can't stay.

I watch the horizon, the swirling, spinning universe coming awake above me, feeling a calm in my chest, the night sky familiar to me in a way that no place down here could ever feel.

My thoughts pinwheel back, sifting through all the stories Mom told me about the stars, about a woman who, just like us, looked up at the night sky and *wondered*. She was the first to chart the sky, to measure and make notes of what she saw. And her stories are mine now. Carried in my veins, in the ink tattooed on my skin.

I sink onto the soft, quilted bed, too exhausted to pull the blankets over me, and let my eyes sink closed. It seems strange to sleep in a room without star maps or constellations sketched onto paper hung from the walls. But still, I drift into dreams of stars spinning, *spinning* in that endless dark, galaxies erupting, planets taking shape—green and bottomless blue. I dream of the orchard. Of apples like round moons. But then the men appear, burns on their arms that still smolder and spark, striding up through the orchard, hissing my name. "Vega . . . Vega . . ." Their voices as thin as air, while the man with the slit across his throat reaches out for me, hand cold and wet, rain falling from the red, dying sky. He pulls one of the pistols from his hip and points it to my skull, metal pressing against my soft skin. "Tell me who you really are?" he hisses in my ear, but before I can answer, he pulls the trigger.

I wake, hands grasping for the ceiling, trying to push him back, push the dream away, and almost let out a scream. I sink back onto the bed, gulping down the cold morning air, then force myself to stand, to stagger to the window. Needing to see, to be sure.

But there are no men on the road. No horses. Everything is quiet.

I slide down to the floor, hands pressed to my eyes, then open them again, staring up at the sky.

The sun isn't yet above the horizon, but just above the tree line, the silvery night sky has a sheen to it, a flickering quality—like moisture caught in the air, refusing to turn to rain.

The anomaly.

At night, it is a dark blot in the sky taking up half the horizon, but at dawn and dusk, when the light strikes at just the right angle, it turns shimmery and gleaming—as if it were reaching long tendrils of light down to us, licking at the lower atmosphere over our heads. Mom often stayed up late to chart and measure it, searching for any glimmer of hope.

It's beautiful. But it also sends sharp needles of fear down my spine.

I stare at it a moment longer, blinking, watching, but then it dissipates like dew, and I close the window.

With the sun burning bright against the soft blue sky, the anomaly is gone from view.

But I know it's still there.

Always there.

Getting closer.

* * *

We walk away from the farmhouse, down the drive, the mule plodding behind us with the crate of tonic and jug of water strapped to a harness, jars rattling.

The green of the hills gives way to dry soil and fewer trees, while the sky is still flecked with a few strange particles of light—a grittiness to it, the sunrise a peculiar luster of green.

We travel a full day, the hours flitting away like scraps of paper burning over a campfire, then camp in the open beside an old hemlock that's been split down its center, struck by lightning, the bark turned black and molten. The mule drinks water from the bucket while Pa and I eat canned apples and cold beans. We sleep—

restlessly—and in the morning, before the sun is up, we start down the road again. Always watchful of the road behind us, listening for the sound of horses drawing close.

The taste of dust sticks at the back of my throat.

The sun a wavy, pulsing eye, tracking our path.

But by midday, we reach Fort Bell, a grit-coated town appearing in the flat middle of nothing.

A crush of people is streaming into the town, clogging the main street—some ride on horseback, others in creaking, wobbling carts and wagons, while a few, like us, are on foot—striding into Fort Bell seeking shade and fresh water.

I've never seen so many people in my life, and a strange, bubbling excitement churns inside me. On the outskirts of town, I can see tents and wagons dotting the dry land—campsites. There must be several hundred people, gathered from every direction. All come for the market.

"Remember to keep your neck covered," Pa tells me as we make our way up the main street. "And don't tell anyone where you're from."

"I won't."

But my mind is thinking of something else: *the Architect*. With so many people crowded into one place, surely someone will have heard of him. Will know who he is.

This is my best chance, and I don't intend to waste it.

We make our way up the main street, and I read every sign swaying above doorways and shop windows, advertising hardware stores and apothecaries, bathhouses and blacksmiths and saloons. A sheriff's office, two hotels, and even a bank. Fort Bell is swollen with activity, people passing through doorways and dogs barking and a woman singing from a second-story balcony—a slow, enchanting, dirt-road kind of song. A tune to lure weary travels into the town for the annual market.

My ears thrum with the energy of it. Eyes absorbing in wonder. But there is also a small, nagging fear at the back of my skull. *What if those men are here? Or others like them—scavengers or Theorists. Those who would steal what little we have left.*

Instinctively I brush my fingers down my hair, making sure the mark on my neck is still covered, that no eyes will stray across it by accident . . . when I see it.

Ropes.

Three of them suspended from the awning of a post office.

But these ropes aren't swaying gently in the breeze like back in the wheat town—these are pulled tight. *Stiff.*

Because three bodies hang heavy from the knotted loops at the end.

Two men and one woman. Their clothes covered in dust, muted gray, jackets and cotton shirts hanging from limp arms, boots dangling on feet, but heads covered by cloth sacks. Only the woman's golden hair can be seen draped down her back.

My ears begin to ring as we pass by, but I can't pull my eyes away.

Three dead people hang in the open, beneath the midday sun, while the living pass by around them, hardly paying them any notice. As if their corpses were as common as a dead bird found beside the road. I try to absorb every detail about who they might have been, but with their faces covered, they seem almost like dolls, stuffed with sheep's wool. Not real at all.

"Nothing to be done for it," Pa says under his breath. "Keep your eyes ahead."

But I stare at the three bodies, suspended in a neat row, until they slip from view behind the crowd. "What happened to them?" I ask softly, turning my attention to Pa. "Why were they killed?"

Pa grumbles, like he doesn't like the question. "They're dead now, no point wondering why." His eyes flash to those walking closest to us, as if to see if they might be listening, and I'm surprised by the coldness of his words.

There's something more he isn't saying. A reason for their deaths that he won't say aloud. Like he's afraid to.

And it makes the sharpness at the back of my neck prick even harder. People in the towns are being killed, hung from their necks, and I want to know why. I want to press Pa for answers, but I sense he won't say anything more, not here among all these people. So I keep quiet, for now.

At a cross street, Pa tugs the mule down a narrower road, where wagons are parked in uniform rows, each selling something different: freshly baked corn muffins, a hair tonic meant to keep your hair *slicked out of your eyes*, hand-hewn garden tools, leather saddle straps, hand-dipped beeswax candles, and a particularly wide wagon selling *homemade moonshine from the Laramie River*. A river I've never heard of.

"Wait here," Pa says. We've stopped in front of a squat little building, and I rest my palm against the mule's short mane, rubbing along his ears, while Pa climbs the low wooden steps up to the door and slips inside. A small bell chimes when he enters.

I hold out my palm and the mule's warm breath nuzzles my

hand, large teeth nibbling for something to eat. Around me, vendors and traders and townsfolk move up and down the street, a chorus of voices and horses' hooves, so much noise that it makes my ears vibrate. But a half moment later, Pa reappears, clomping down the steps.

"Mr. Willard says we can sell tonic in front of his shop."

My eyes sway up to the building, and the sign posted above the awning: WILLARD'S BARBER & DENTISTRY. "Is he a barber or a dentist?"

"Both."

* ✳ *

The last crate of tonic sits on the wood bench in front of Mr. Willard's shop. But without a sign, I don't know how customers will know what we're selling.

"I'll go find a stable to keep the mule for the night." Pa pats a firm hand against the mule's neck. "If anyone comes asking about tonic, tell them I'll be back in fifteen minutes. They can either wait or return later." He looks at me, waiting for a response, some assurance that I understand.

"Okay."

I stand beside the bench, peering out at the town. With Pa gone, this is my chance—I can go in search of the Architect. But I can't leave the crate of tonic, can't risk someone taking it. I won't be responsible for the loss of Pa's last remaining crate. So I stay put, fidgety, anxious. Strangers walk past me, moving through the market with desperate, feline looks in their eyes, as if they're willing to steal or lie to get what they want. Some glance at the crate, at me, then continue on. I could meet their eyes, ask if they know of an Architect. I could whisper the word quietly, keeping my voice low. But I remember the way the old woman—Imogene—flicked her eyes at me when I said it: *Architect.* As if the word itself was a curse. A malediction. *Don't go saying that name aloud,* she warned. The word was dangerous. Mom said as much over the years, that to go in search of the Architect would put our lives at risk.

But we have no other choice.

If I can't find the Architect, then nothing matters anyway.

So I scan the hands of those walking past; some wear rings, hand-forged metal of gold and iron and silver. But none contain the constellation Circinus, with its twelve stars running parallel to one another.

Frustrated, I brush my hair across my neck and glance down at my own hands, dirt-packed beneath my short nails. I'm filthy. A layer of dust in my hair, coating both my arms. In the valley, I'd bathe in the river twice a week, even in winter, a bar of castile soap we traded from the Horaces balanced on the rocks. I crave the feeling of clean hair and fingernails, the scent of lavender and mint on my skin. For a moment, I let myself imagine a life lived in a town like this: warm bathwater and store-bought clothes. Strolls down the sidewalk in spring; strangers' faces from distant towns, each with a story to tell. But I'd also know fear with every pair of eyes that passed over me.

The valley hid us from questioning, curious eyes. Allowed us to live with our hair pinned up, skin exposed, never fearing who might see what we were. But here, in the town, every blinking gaze is dangerous.

Across the street, a woman exits the doorway of a bookmaker's shop, her hair wild, loose curls falling across her face as she tilts her head to one side. I watch as her hand searches for the wall of the building, and when her fingertips locate it, she uses the wall to guide her forward, the other hand waving in front of her. She has lost her sight.

Consumption.

I push my hands into my coat pockets, my nerves on edge, and watch a young boy stomping up the street, one hand on his hip, the other holding an assortment of items under his arm. He splashes through a puddle, smiles, then notices me watching him. He changes direction and comes to stand in front of Mr. Willard's shop, peering up at me.

"What are you selling?" His eyebrows part in a gesture of curiosity, his skin pale and unscarred—he hasn't spent as much time outdoors as most of the other people I've met—and his eyes are a clear, bright green.

"We're not open yet," I answer sharply.

"But when you are, what will you sell?"

"It's a cure-all tonic."

His upper lip curls, nose scrunched, tugging together the freckles scattered across his cheekbones. He can't be more than ten or eleven—although I've never known anyone his age, so I can't be certain. "What does the tonic do?"

I think of the pill I took back at the farmhouse, how it dulled the ache in my ribs, and allowed me to sleep. "It relieves pain."

The boy nods, squinting up at me. "I'll take two bottles."

"We're not open," I repeat.

"You'd turn away a customer?" His voice is quick, punctuated, like he has somewhere he needs to be. He wipes at his forehead, at the layer of dirt on his skin.

"Do you even have any coins?" I ask.

"No," he answers plainly, eyebrows lifted. "But I can trade."

"With what?" I'm curious about the stack of items still tucked under his arm. And he sorts through his hoard—no ring visible on his finger—pulling out a long, yellow ribbon the color of a daffodil, and holds it up to me, letting it dangle from his fingertips, smooth as Odie's mane. But the ends are dirty, as if it's been dropped into a horse trough. "It needs to be washed," I point out.

"Nothing a quick scrub won't fix. And it would look lovely in your hair."

I feel a tug in my chest, a desire to reach out and touch it, to feel the smoothness of the fabric. I can imagine it tied in a bow, keeping my thick hair off my shoulders. But I could never wear it in the open and risk exposing the mark on my neck.

"I don't need a ribbon," I say.

The boy pushes it back into his coat pocket, then draws out something else from beneath his arm: a silver-forged spur, meant to slide onto the heel of a boot, to coax a horse onward with the prick of the spiked metal. "You only have the one? Where's its pair?"

"Dunno," the boy answers. "It was gone when I came upon this one."

"Where'd you come upon it?"

"A dead man, up in the alley behind the Buffalo Saloon."

"You took it from a dead man's boot?"

"I took the boots, too," he says with a curved, clever grin. "But I traded those already. Boots are always in high demand."

"You're a scavenger," I say, scowling down at him, trying to imagine this boy sneaking into homes and campsites, taking whatever he finds. A prick of disgust stabs at my insides.

He lowers the spur to his side and laughs. "I ain't that ruthless. I'd never kill a man for his things, but I'll take something if he's already dead."

"I don't want the spur," I say at last. "I think they're cruel. A horse doesn't need pain to drive it forward."

The boy shrugs.

And when he does, I spy something else under his arm, a flattened piece of paper. Like a page torn from a book. "What's that?" I ask, pointing.

He slides it out and peers down at it, like he's unsure what it is. "Can't say. Traded it from a goat farmer outside of town."

He holds it up, sun shining across its printed surface, and lets me take it from his hands. It's a perfect rectangle, the corners of the paper bent a little, a water spot on one edge, but I can still make out the photo. A tall structure is framed at the center of the image, lit with tiny, sparkling lights, wider at its base, then sloping up to a narrow point. It's taller than any building I've ever seen. The bottom of the photo reads: *Paris. La Tour Eiffel.* I run my thumb along the sharp angles of the building, then turn over the photo, where I find a series of numbers, followed by the words *Topeka, KS.* And handwritten beside this are more words, most blurred out, faded with time. *Missed our train . . . took hours to find a hotel that was . . . Versailles completely worth . . . see you in June.* My throat dries up, and my eyes begin to water.

"I'll trade for this," I say before I can stop myself. "But for one jar of tonic, not two."

The freckled boy nods quickly, like he's afraid I'll change my mind. The paper is worthless to him, a curiosity, nothing more. But I've seen others like it—Mom had three of them she kept pressed between the pages of her copy of *Nature, Astronomy, and Black Holes.* They were *postcards*, she said. Photos of places someone visited once—one with a series of snow-peaked mountains called *Glacier National Park*; another with a round, strange-looking building with many doorways, and the words *Colosseum, Rome* in sloped letters in the corner. The last was a dusty-looking landscape with two stone pyramids in the background, and the words: *Cairo—the pyramids.*

This postcard is worthless to me, too, but my heart feels a tugging ache, the sudden, sharp reminder it brings: of Mom, of home. Of all the things I burned to the ground. Every part of her lost. But way out here, in this dry, unfamiliar town, I have found a small thing that reminds me of her.

I retrieve a jar from the crate, then hold it down to the boy.

"Thanks," he says, still nodding, holding the jar close to his face, eye almost pressed to the glass. "Thank you."

He starts to hurry away, up the street, but I call out to him. "Wait."

He pivots around, gazing at me over his narrow shoulder.

"I'm looking for someone," I say, my voice dropped low. Maybe I'm stupid to ask, maybe this is a bad idea, but I suspect this boy knows his way around town, and has heard people talking—knows of things whispered in alleyways and the dark corners of saloons. "I need to find . . ." I look away to the street, to make sure no one else is close enough to hear. "Someone . . . a man, known as the Architect." I say it so softly, the word is quickly lost amid the noisy crush of the town.

But the boy blinks at me, mouth unmoving.

"Have you heard of anyone like that?" I press. And when he still doesn't answer, I say quickly, in a rush, "I'll trade you another bottle of tonic, if you can tell me where he is." I'm desperate, willing to offer up one of Pa's last bottles for any clue about the Architect, and I can feel the tension forming in my chest.

A wagon rattles by, the horse snapping its head against the reins, and the boy turns his head to the sound. My temples begin to ache. *I shouldn't have said anything. I shouldn't have asked this boy.* He swivels his gaze back to me and his mouth dips open, like he's going to speak, some thought hanging at the end of his tongue. But then his mouth clamps shut and he stares at me, a twitch in his eye, a tug of nervousness across his forehead, before he abruptly turns and darts up the wood sidewalk, ducking down an alley out of sight.

Gone.

Foolish girl, I remember Imogene saying to me.

Maybe she was right.

I asked a boy about the Architect, but I have no reason to trust him. And I just bartered a full jar of tonic for a bent postcard.

Foolish, foolish girl.

✳ ✳ ✳

Pa returns without the mule, his hands in the pockets of his tan canvas coat.

When he reaches Willard's Barber & Dentistry, he stares down at the crate on the bench and sees that a jar is missing. "You sold a jar?" he asks. But his voice isn't pleased, it's tight—he told me not to do anything until he returned.

I know I need to tell him the truth. *I won't lie.* "I traded one."

"Traded for what?" His brows drive together, and I pull out the photo from my coat pocket.

"This."

His eyes crease, staring down at the piece of paper with an image on one side, words on the other. "Do you even know what that is?" he asks.

"It's from before."

He blows out a breath and looks out at the street.

I run my fingers across the handwritten letters again. "Mom had three just like it," I say, as if this explains why I traded a whole jar of tonic for something of no use. "But the photos were different."

He doesn't say anything, only swivels his gaze back to the remaining jars in the crate. Now one fewer.

I slide the postcard back into my coat pocket, out of sight. "I'm sorry." Guilt blooms hot in my cheeks; I'm ashamed that I traded one of our last jars of tonic for something that has no value. That we surely won't be able to trade again.

"It's done now," Pa says, voice hoarse. "But don't go making any more trades."

I nod, lowering my eyes to the crate.

For the next two hours, the sick and the half-dead approach our makeshift shop in front of the barber. Most bring coins, holding them out to us in grimy palms, eyes watering with a wretched need for tonic. But some have trades, objects they're willing to part with: silverware and eyeglasses and small sacks of grain. Pa is careful, though, concise about what he's willing to barter for—he knows this is the last of the tonic.

But hidden in my pocket, I still carry the nearly full bottle of aspirin. The last of Pa's stash. He knows I have it, yet strangely, he hasn't asked for it back—he's allowed me to keep it.

I coil my hair down my back, wary of any eyes that might stray over me, while I study the faces of every customer who ambles up the steps, asking about tonic, my gaze always flashing to their hands, looking for the ring. But frustration builds in my chest. Mom said that finding the Architect would be hard—we would need to be patient and swift. But I always imagined she'd be here with me, that her cleverness would lead us to him without much effort. I never thought I'd be searching for him on my own. And I worry I'm not moving fast enough, that I'm doing it all wrong. I think of the boy. . . . Has he run off and told someone that a girl is asking about the Architect? Or like Imogene, did he just want to get as far away from me as possible before my words crept beneath his skin?

I'm wasting too much time. Stuck here with Pa, waiting for him to sell his last crate of tonic.

I chew on my cheek and walk to the edge of the wooden board-walk, a nervous fidget rising up my spine, my fingers tapping against my thighs as the midday sun makes shreds of the shadows, when I notice a man wandering up the street through the crowd, wearing dark overalls, a straw hat, and his left leg dragging behind him with each step. He's ringing a bell, a high-pitched tolling sound, and I walk closer to the street—watching him.

"The cure is near!" he shouts, voice echoing up the busy street. He rings the bell over his head, as if summoning cattle to the trough, but no one seems to pay him any attention. "They will save us!" he shouts. "They will bring the cure, and our sickness will be rid from our bodies."

He makes a sweeping motion with his free hand, from his chest up to the sky, as if something were leaving him—the sickness evaporating. He marches up the street, ringing his bell and continuing to shout. "They are coming!" he calls. "They will save us, the cure is near!"

A few people slow to watch him, but only for a moment or two before continuing on their way. And then I see the brand pressed into the flesh of his upper arm.

The starburst.

Just like the men back at the miners' camp. My stomach knots, sudden and tight, as if a fist has just clenched around my chest and begun to squeeze.

Those men are here.

In this town.

I whip around to Pa, who is sliding a coin into his pocket from a recent sale. "That man," I sputter, voice shaking, eyes starting to water.

He glances to the road, then back to the crate of tonic—only two jars left. But I know he saw the man, heard him shouting up the street. "Don't pay him any mind."

"But he's one of them! He had the brand."

Pa nods, straightening up and placing a palm against his sore back. "Yes, but he's only a messenger. Some in their group travel from town to town, preaching about cures and other nonsense." He grumbles, but I notice a twitch at his temple, a hidden fury he doesn't want me to see. "Most locals don't listen to them."

My hands coil into fists at my sides, anger pulsing behind my eyes. Back at the miners' camp, I had guessed there were a dozen men, at most. But now I wonder if there are men like them in every town. Every outpost.

"We could go after him," I press. "Find Odie."

But Pa shakes his head, eyes glancing up the street. "No, Vega. That horse is long gone, and probably nowhere near Fort Bell."

I stare up the street, where the man slips into the crowd. Simply a *messenger*. A Theorist branded like the others, but not one of the men who was with the group that took Odie and all of Pa's tonic. "He was talking about a cure?" I say, keeping my eyes on the crowd, listening to the last echo of the bell ringing through the air, a pitch that echoes across the buildings and up to the blue, cloudless sky.

Pa leans against the wall of the barbershop, running a hand down his beard, looking exhausted. Like he doesn't have the strength to worry about a horse who he'll never see again. To explain to me all the reasons why it's better to let things be, to not ask questions, to keep quiet and out of trouble. "Lots of people talk about a cure."

A cure. The word plays against my mind.

Do they think there's a cure for the consumption?

Instinctively I touch the back of my neck, my fingers trembling. *A cure.* As if it were that easy. As if a simple tonic, like Pa's, could rid it from our flesh. Herbs and river water. Paste and clay. "I thought you said the Theorists believe everyone will die?"

"They do," he answers, looking away from me. "But nothing is as simple as it seems."

I squint at him, wanting to ask what he means. But a woman walks by, a horse saddle slung over one shoulder, a wad of tobacco in her bottom lip, and she stops to peer into the crate, asking Pa about the tonic. I can hear the low rasp in her breathing, the gravelly exhale. She's sick, just like the others.

Like *all* the others.

I turn back to the street, the man long gone, but a worrying throb pulsing behind my eyes. A scrabbling itch under my skin. *They think there's a cure.*

The sun finally sinks beyond rooftops, and the woman with the saddle buys the last two jars of tonic, just before dark settles over the town. Pa is quiet, peering down into the empty crate—he will never sell another jar of tonic.

I want to tell him I'm sorry again, as if it were somehow my fault, but I keep the words stuffed down. They won't fix anything. And I suspect he doesn't want to hear them.

He hoists the empty crate up into his arms. "I got us two rooms above the Buffalo," he says. "It's a saloon."

The boy who I traded with for the postcard said he stole boots and the spur off a dead man behind the Buffalo Saloon.

"Most of the hotels are full—it was all I could find."

"Okay."

Our rooms are located at the top of a narrow stairwell, in the alley beside the saloon. We climb the steps to a short landing with four doors, each numbered.

"You're room one. I'm in three," Pa says.

I start toward the door, feeling like I've wasted a whole day—a worthless postcard in my pocket, and no closer to finding the Architect.

"In the morning," he says from behind me, "I'll gather supplies and retrieve the mule—then we'll leave."

A stone drops into my stomach. *I can't leave yet.* "Where will we go?" I ask cautiously.

Pa's mustache draws flat, and for a moment he looks away, out at the main street, at the wagons and tents closing up for the night. "I've been thinking maybe we could go back to that farmhouse, and the orchard." His gaze swings back to me. "We could harvest those apples and sell them in the towns. Make a living that way, I suspect." Pa's eyes are watering slightly. Maybe it's the loss of the wagon and Odie and all his tonic. Or maybe it's the sense of responsibility he feels. With Mom gone, he's trying to give me a home. *A real home.* And in truth, the idea of settling in that farmhouse, making one of the bedrooms my own, does stir up a flicker of longing inside me.

But I know I can't have that life. It won't last. None of it.

I am the closest to a daughter that Pa's ever had, and he is the nearest thing to a father, but I can't go back to that farmhouse. I can't waste any more time.

I nod at him—as if in agreement—unable to speak the lie to him directly.

I can't go with him.

I knew it would come to this eventually. He was my way out of the valley, but now, even though my chest aches at the thought of it, a rupturing behind my eyes, I have to go on my own. I can't go back. Only forward. Time is already moving too quickly. But he won't understand this, he won't understand what I must do—he never knew the stories of my ancestors, the women who came before me, the way already marked like starlight on my skin. Mom loved him, but she never trusted anyone to know the whole truth. Even Pa.

I know he will try to stop me—insist that it isn't safe. He won't want me to go on my own. It stings behind my eyes, a mouthful of words and fears I can't say aloud.

I have to leave tonight, or not at all.

I step forward, holding down the bite of tears, not wanting him to see, and I wrap my arms around him—he smells like tobacco and the mule. Like the river in the valley. Like home. He pats his hand gently against my back, not used to affection. "All right, then," he says, not fully understanding the emotion roaring inside me. "Get some sleep—can't have you turning me soft where all these townsfolk can see."

I pull away, wiping at my eyes. This will hurt him, and I hate it. This will break him apart.

But finding the Architect, seeing this through, is more important than the guilt I will carry. The pain that will root between my ribs. And maybe someday I'll be able to tell him why I left, and what I've done. And he will understand. He will see that I had no other choice.

Pa nods finally, swiping at his own eyes, then turns for his door—thinking I'll be here in the morning, waiting in my room, and together we'll travel back to the orchard house. As if a simple life in the apple orchard was something we could have. Something I deserved.

He doesn't know.

In the morning, I'll be long gone.

✷ ✸ ✷

A lantern is lit inside my small rented room, casting dreamlike shadows on the wall above the spare bed and the single wooden chair in the corner. There's no washroom, and it smells like alcohol and smoke from the saloon below.

I wait, wanting to be sure Pa is settled in for the night, before I sneak past his door and down to the alley. I bring the quilt to my nose, breathing deeply, hoping to draw up some memory of Mom, of fresh basil and soap—a scent that seemed to live inside her skin. But those scents are all gone. It smells like campfire now, and dirt.

Can I really do this? I think—leave Pa, the last familiar thing, behind.

But I know, there's no other way.

This is the path that's already been carved into me—a life predestined by the past, by my ancestors. And I will do what Mom never had a chance to: I will find the man who knows the way to the sea.

I will go on my own.

After a good twenty minutes has passed, when I'm certain Pa will think I'm asleep, I tuck the quilt back under my arm, resolve hardened into my bones, and I pull open the door, slipping out into the dark. But before tiptoeing past Pa's room, I stop and rest a hand against the thick wood door. "I'm sorry," I whisper, placing Mom's quilt on the ground next to the door. It's too heavy to carry on my own, and I know he will take care of it—the only reminder of Mom. And in the morning, when he finds it, he will know I wasn't taken, ripped from my room by Theorists or some other shadowed figure—I left on my own. "Goodbye, Pa," I say softly, biting down the hurt and doubt and pain. A million needles of uncertainty stabbing at my thoughts. But it's the cold against my neck, the night sky above, that forces me to lower my hand and turn away.

I was never going to be able to stay with him.

It was always moving toward this. And although I can't see the twin stars through the low layer of clouds, I know they're up there. Tova and

Llitha, spinning wildly in their orbit, closer than they've ever been to our atmosphere. And I can feel time tugging at me, pulling against my chest like a silver-spun thread made of the darkness between stars.

I hurry down the wooden stairway, slipping through the dark to the end of the alley, my heart breaking open, eyes wanting to erupt with tears.

But there's no time for that now.

I'm on my own, and I need to keep moving.

Ahead of me, the town is dark. Lanterns extinguished in windows, shops closed for the night—until tomorrow when the market will open again. In the distance, I can hear people on the outer edge of town, settling into their tents and wagons for the night. The glow of campfires and the smell of food being cooked, filling the air.

I could slip through the shadows to the outskirts of town, wait until the market opens at sunrise . . .

Or . . .

I peer up at the wooden sign suspended above the doorway ahead of me: BUFFALO SALOON.

Voices thrum and echo out from inside, a loud mixture of music and chatter. Whoever is still awake in Fort Bell has gathered inside the Buffalo Saloon. The only thing still open.

Maybe someone inside will know the Architect. Maybe I'll get lucky. But there's also a chance that men with brands burned into their arms will be waiting inside—eyes cold and cruel, talking of cures and saviors and death.

I swallow, steadying myself, when a woman brushes past me, her pale green and white skirts stained with mud from the street. She pauses at the doorway into the saloon. "You coming, young lady?"

she asks with a sly, wicked half-wink. "Won't know what's inside unless you step through the door."

My heart clicks and rubs against my ribs. My eyes gleam, mouth tucking itself into a defiant line. "Yes," I answer, feeling like my mother's daughter—brave, dauntless. Not the girl who once hid in a valley far away from here. "I'm coming in."

She lifts her upper lip, revealing several missing teeth, but her eyes are a water-deep blue, and they urge me to follow her inside, through the doorway, into the Buffalo.

* ✳ *

The saloon is dark, lit by candles burned down to stubs.

I skim the shadowed features of the men seated at the dozen or so tables, some playing cards, some sloshing back the amber drinks in their hands, and I suspect most of them are either traders here for the market or scavengers. And if any of them bear the starburst brand, I can't tell in the dim candlelight.

The saloon is filled with those unafraid to stay up well after the sun has set, and I tell myself that I'm one of them. *That I belong.* But the uneasy patter of my heart in my ears reminds me that I'm definitely not.

In the back corner, a man is seated in a chair, playing a banjo—some slow, wandering song about losing his love in a river and chasing her for *miles and miles, with a broken heart.*

I half hope the round woman will take me by the hand and pull me through the smoky room to a seat in the corner, where she'll explain to me the workings of a saloon, and I can ask her if she knows the Architect, but she saunters off to a series of stairs where she kisses a man full on the lips, and he slides his hands around her broad waist.

I'm on my own, and the beating of my heart in my ears only grows louder.

Most of the seats are taken, except for a few open stools at the bar, built in the center of the room. I feel the eyes pass over me, men lowering their cards to watch me with bloodshot eyes, men with stained teeth who I'm certain can sense that I am not accustomed to places like this. I'm easy prey. I try not to look at them directly, sensing it's best to keep my gaze forward and jaw stiff as I cross the space between the door and the bar.

Mom used to tell me stories about the towns—about taverns and schoolhouses and dentist offices. But to walk through a smoky, candlelit room, with the savage glint of eyes on you, is a different experience entirely.

I reach the bar and slide onto one of the open stools, my heart now stuck in my throat, my jaw aching from clenching it too tightly. But I keep my eyes level, expression unfaltering, as if I frequent places like this in every town I visit. A girl who's seen her fair share of gritty saloons and gritty faces and unwelcome stares.

"Little young, aren't ya?" the man behind the bar asks, voice hoarse and layered in years of smoke, coming to stand in front of me. He squares his gaze on me, his skin pockmarked, muddy-brown hair slicked to one side, with a black mustache trimmed just above his upper lip, while both ears are pierced with silver rings. But no silver signet on either hand.

"No," I reply flatly. Although I have no idea at what age I'm allowed in here—perhaps seventeen *is* too young, and the man will swiftly kick me out.

He raises a thin, pale eyebrow—spots of black rimming his eyes, signs of illness—then rests a palm against the top of the bar. "All right then," he says, chewing over a wad of tobacco. "What do you want?"

I rub my palms together beneath the bar. *I have no idea how to answer this.*

"We have white liquor and dark. That's it." His voice is deep, sensing my hesitation.

I glance down the bar, at the two men nearest me, hands wrapped around glasses filled with an amber-hued alcohol, same as most others in the saloon. The two men watch me from the corners of their eyes. "Dark," I say.

The barman tugs his mouth down at the corner. "You have coin?"

Crap. I touch my coat and feel the bottle of aspirin still in my pocket. Beneath the edge of the bar, I pull it out and open the lid—keeping it out of sight—then pluck a single pill from inside. I lift my palm, holding the white pill up for the man to see. He leans forward and snatches it from me, turning it in his calloused fingers, before quickly clamping his hand closed—like he, too, doesn't want anyone else to see.

"Where'd you get this?" he asks, eyelids flattened on me.

"Found it."

He leans over the counter. He smells like tobacco smoke and something sharp, bitter, like vinegar. "You have any more?"

I shake my head, eyes unblinking. "Just the one."

He tilts his gaze, cracking his neck. "You sure?"

"I'd know if I had more, wouldn't I?" I'm surprised at my tone, the unflinching quality of my voice, as if I've dealt with men like him before.

He straightens back up, an eyebrow still raised, then moves down the counter, retrieving something from beneath it. When he returns, he sets a whole bottle of dark liquor on the bar in front of me, then pockets the pill I gave him.

Apparently, a single aspirin buys me a whole bottle of alcohol. I wonder if Pa knows this, knows how much a whole pill is worth?

The two men seated down the bar glance over at me, at the full bottle, sizing me up, probably trying to guess what I paid the man to get me the bottle, and if I might have more. If I'm worth robbing.

"I'm looking for someone," I say to the barman before he walks away.

He gives me a curious look, like he's still trying to figure out who I am and where I came from. And why the hell I'm in here. "Who's that?"

I touch the bottle, tapping a finger against the glass, then lift my eyes. "A man—" My voice breaks off, unsure if this is a good idea, but if anyone knows the men who come and go into this saloon, who hears the far-off stories from traders who have traveled to the ends of this land and come back to the market to tell their tales, it's this barman. I have to risk it. I have to ask. "An Architect," I continue. "Have you heard of him?"

The barman tips forward and spits into a foul-smelling metal canister resting on the bar top. His eyes narrow to that of a bird's, dark and intent. It makes me uneasy, but I meet his gaze dead-on, refusing to look away.

"Never heard of anyone by that name," he says, squinting, rolling his tongue against the inside of his cheek. But I can't tell if he's lying, if this is a game, and he's waiting to see what I'll say next.

"You're sure?"

His chin lowers, watching me, like he might reach across the bar and take me by the throat for even saying the word aloud in his saloon, for daring to speak such a name, but then he swallows and says simply, "Yep."

We stare at each other a moment more, both of us untrusting, before he turns away and walks back up to the far end of the bar, where he refills the empty glasses in front of the two men who had been eyeing me. Then begins talking to them out of earshot.

Shit, I think.

I need to get out of here.

Whether he knows the Architect or not, lying or not, now he knows *I* was asking about him. A girl he's never seen before, trading a whole white pill for a bottle of booze, is now poking around about the Architect.

And I can feel the eyes of others in the saloon watching me now. A curiosity in their stares, in the words they mumble, nodding at me. I have to get out of this smoke-heavy room.

But if I go now, I'm certain I'll be followed. Pursued out into the dark street, into the quiet, where my screams will be swallowed up by the night. Maybe it's better if I stay put, act like I have nothing to hide. Wait for them all to have a few more glasses of alcohol, let their interest in me wane, and then I'll slip out unnoticed.

I let my eyes skip to my left, to the man still playing his banjo, before sliding my gaze back to the bottle in front of me. The barman didn't give me a glass, so I tip the full bottle to my lips—trying to calm the nerves coiling along my veins—and let a small amount slide into my mouth, along my tongue, then spill down my throat. Instantly I regret it, and a cough rises up from the bottom of my chest. It tastes terrible, and I nearly retch onto the bar, but manage to hold it down.

Now I feel even more eyes on me.

Shit. Shit.

I swallow, wrapping my hands around the bottle to steady myself, feeling a buzzing warmth in my chest, in my head. If I stood right now, I'm not sure I'd be able to keep from tipping to the floor.

A door swings open at the back of the bar, banging against the wall with a loud thud, and several people turn to look. The door must lead out to a back alley, the place where the boy took the boots from a dead body, and I lift my watering eyes to see a girl step into the saloon. She doesn't look much older than me.

However, she's a girl who looks like she *actually* belongs here.

Half her head is shaved, revealing her dark scalp, while her black hair is grown long and knotted down the other side, where I can just make out a line of silver studs along one earlobe. Her pants are rolled up above her boots, and her oversize, pale green coat looks as scuffed and dirt-stained as the men seated around me. The thud of her boots echoes across the floor, and my eyes catch on the knife strapped at her waist, where everyone can see. She doesn't care that every half-drunk man in the saloon is watching her; in fact, I think she prefers it—she wants everyone to know that she's not worth messing with. Try to steal from her, and she'll gut you clean through.

She walks to the far end of the bar, eyes roving the dimly lit room, then perches herself on a stool. She's been here before—she knows the landscape of faces, and she angles herself so her back is to the wall, so there's no chance anyone will be sneaking up behind her. So she'll always have the upper hand.

I watch her, fascinated, as she slides a silver coin across the counter to the barman, which gets her a short glass of dark alcohol. With the glass in her hand, she lifts her gaze, noticing me at the far end of the bar, staring back at her. I want to look away, but my eyes are caught on the striking color of her eyes, a semi-green against her olive skin. She raises her glass in my direction and nods at the bottle in front of me, her eyebrow tugging upward. I lift the bottle and we both drink. But I wince as the sharp liquor slithers down my throat, and when I lower the bottle, she looks like she's holding back a smile.

I turn away, touching the mark on my neck, shifting my hair over it—keeping it out of sight. Maybe I can make my way down the bar, sidle up onto a stool next to her, and ask—quietly, secretly—if she's heard of the Architect. Maybe she's not someone I can trust, but at least she might be someone willing to talk. Unafraid of names like the *Architect*, unafraid of anything.

I brace a hand against the edge of the bar, starting to push myself up, when the front door of the saloon bangs open, and a wind coils in from outside, bringing with it a gust of cold air. And something else—*fear*. The voices in the saloon abruptly fall silent, all eyes turned toward the doorway, where the heavy sounds of boots clomp across the wood floor toward the bar.

I keep my face down, but my eyes flash to my left as several men sidle up to the bar, leaning heavily against it.

"Four glasses," they demand, and the barman moves swiftly, grabbing a bottle and sloshing dark liquid into the glasses, then shoving them across the bar. Even at his size, the barman is clearly on edge, his temples twitching. These men strode into the saloon, and the place is now as silent as the valley at midnight, when nothing dares stir. When a predator is lurking, hungry, searching for a kill.

The four men tip their glasses to their lips, swallowing all the dark liquor in one gulp, then slam the glasses back on the bar. The barman doesn't need any coaxing before refilling them once more. They do the same thing again, but on the third refill, they ease against the edge of the bar, already a little loosened, a little buzzed, and start sipping from their glasses, in no rush.

But everyone else inside the bar keeps their gazes on the men, stiffened in their seats. Afraid to speak. To move.

"You have it?" one of the men finally asks, nodding at the barman. And that's when I see his oil-slicked hair beneath his hat, the gruff jawline, the bolo tie around his neck. And the starburst branded into his forearm.

It's him.

Samuel. The man who stood over me at the miners' camp with an awful, needful glint in his eyes. Like he was waiting for any opportunity to shoot me where I sat. Quickly my eyes skip past him, looking for his boss—the man with the scar along his throat and two different-colored eyes—but there's no sign of him.

A rattling fear scrambles up into my throat and I snap my eyes away, back to the bottle in front of me. They're Theorists. All four of them. A brand burned into their arms.

I press my palms against my knees beneath the bar, to keep them from shaking. From being seen.

I need to get out of here.

I need to stand up from the stool without making a sound, leave the bottle, and escape through the front door. But when I cut my eyes toward the door, I realize that no one else in the saloon has moved an inch since the four men entered. No one has taken a drink from their glasses or stood from their chairs.

And if they're all terrified to move, I should be too.

Only the man at the back continues to play his banjo, strumming slowly, as if he's afraid to remove his fingers from the strings.

So I stay put, face turned slightly away from the men, hoping they don't see me. Don't notice, while anger and fear roil in my gut. From the corner of my eye, I see the barman step forward and slide a pouch across the bar to the bolo-tie man—*Samuel*.

The four men stare down at the pouch, before Samuel scoops it up and tips it over, letting a pile of coins spill out onto the bar. Two dozen at least. He drops the empty pouch, then settles his palms against the bar top. "You know that's not enough."

"I'll have the rest tomorrow," the barman answers. "The market just started today—there'll be more customers tomorrow." I notice that he doesn't offer up the aspirin I gave him. That, he plans on keeping for himself.

Samuel cracks his neck to one side and runs his fingertips along his mustache. "Payment ensures your safety," he says to the barman, as if it were a reminder, a slickness to each word. "You pay, we keep you safe. Simple as that."

The barman nods swiftly, looking as docile as one of the Horaces' newborn kittens.

Samuel blows out an irritated breath, nostrils flaring, then begins scooping up the coins.

But on the far side of him, where the two men who had been eyeing me suspiciously when I first entered the bar still sit, one of them takes a long drink from his glass, then raises his eyebrows to Samuel. "Who the hell are you protecting him from?" he asks, loud enough that the whole saloon can hear. I can also hear the slur in his words, the tipsy sway thick with alcohol. "You're the only thieves in this town. Scavengers don't even bother coming this way."

Samuel slowly finishes collecting his coins, dropping them into the soft pouch and placing it safely into a coat pocket, then takes a drink from his glass. He is careful and unhurried.

"Theorists are the real plague," the man spits now, his words gaining strength. "You rob every business in this town, demanding a tax for protection. You're the scourge, killing us all faster than the sickness." The man stands up, sways beside his stool, but grips the edge of the bar for balance.

"Gil," the man seated beside him says, tugging on Gil's arm. "Sit down and shut up."

But Gil stays put, glaring up at Samuel, who is a good foot and a half taller, and a good ten years younger. "We'd all do good to kill you right here," Gil says, pushing out his jaw, "bury you out in that desert where you won't be missed."

Samuel tips the last of his alcohol to his lips, finishing the glass. But still, he doesn't turn to look at Gil. As if Gil's not even there. And in the slow, languid moment that follows, I even see Samuel sway just a little—the heat of the booze pulsing through him. And I think maybe this is my chance. He's distracted, head thrumming. But right as I flash a look to the front door, I hear the blunt exhale of air leaving lungs, and I turn just in time to see Gil shove Samuel in the chest.

And in an instant, everything changes.

Someone shouts behind me.

Followed by the grinding scrape of chairs being pushed back, clattering to the floor.

The silent, motionless saloon is suddenly thrust into chaos.

I turn, my head pulsing from the alcohol, and see Samuel grab the shorter man by the neck, pushing him against the bar, a large knife pressed to his quivering throat.

My ears begin to ring. My heartbeat thudding at my throat.

Several others in the saloon who had been seated silently only moments ago stand up and rush toward the Theorists, and the room erupts. Glasses break against the blunt edges of tables, then are thrust forward as weapons. Shouts echo along the low ceiling.

I need to move. Need to react. But it's all happening in slow motion, time stuttering through me.

To my left, more shouts erupt; a woman yells something, but it's lost in the din of too many voices.

My eyes flash to the barman and he's reaching for something, a large piece of carved wood, flat on one end, and he wields it like he's about to crack the skull of anyone who attempts to reach across the bar for him.

My heartbeat screams in my ears and I push up from the stool— this is my chance to slip out of the saloon, unseen, unnoticed. But when I try to push away from the bar, the tangle of men is too close, shoulders ramming into mine, shoving me back, crowding the space between the door and me.

Panic rises in my chest. My ears ring even louder. *Too many people. No way out.* The room turns thick with the smell of blood and sweat.

Only a few feet away, the shorter man who started it all—with the knife now against his throat—kicks Samuel in the knee, hard, a loud *crack*, and Samuel staggers back, dropping the knife to the floor and cursing under his breath.

Shit. Too much happening too fast.

I thrust out an elbow, trying to force my way through the crowd, but I'm shoved back, my rib cage slamming into the edge of the bar top. I let out a weakened cry, grabbing my side—the same place where my ribs had just started to heal. But two of the brawling men are now right beside me, throwing punches, growling like feral dogs, and I can no longer tell if the barfight is between locals and Theorists, or just any man against any other.

I try to duck past them, under an arm, but a blow lands against my temple—a fist or an elbow, I can't be sure. I spin around—the liquid-hot pain lancing through my skull—and I try to grab for the edge of the bar, the stool, but instead I'm met with the hard floor, facedown, with a *thud*.

The air is knocked clean out of my lungs. And I stay this way for a half second, gasping.

My vision swirls from the alcohol, from the blow to my skull, from the clot of too many people, the sweat and smoke, and I reach up, trying to hook my fingers around something, to pull myself up before I'm crushed beneath the boots of these men. But one of them steps on my ankle, and I cry out. A shrill, guttural sound.

Then, as if the breathable air has been yanked from the room, everyone falls suddenly, strangely quiet—the entire saloon sunk into a dull, eerie, unnatural hush.

My eyes whip up, searching their faces.

The two men nearest to me have stopped fighting, blood dripping from the nose of one of them, droplets hitting the floor beside me, while the other stands with mouth hanging open, a bruise already expanding in the space between his eyes.

But it's not just the two men gaping down at me; others in the saloon squint at me like insects buzzing toward candlelight. Even the woman who opened the door for me, who ushered me inside, has shuffled close, thin eyebrows driven together in curiosity.

Then, her blue eyes widen in wonder, in shock.

"She has marks on her neck," the woman shrieks, pointing a long, hooked finger at me, mouth stuck open, revealing her row of mangled and missing teeth.

Shit. Shit, shit, shit.

I scramble upright, touching the back of my neck quickly, tugging my hair over the mark. The tattoo. As if I could undo what's been done, pretend there's nothing to see. *But it's too late.* When I hit the ground, my hair fell forward . . . exposing my bare neck.

Shit.

If anyone finds out who we are, Mom would warn, *run!*

But I'm surrounded, caged, eyes piercing me like ravens picking apart a dead rabbit.

"It's a constellation," the woman shouts so everyone in the saloon can hear, her upper lip curling on one side, nostrils flaring.

My eyes dart to the front door, but there's no way through. The crowd is pushing in closer, shoulder to shoulder, trying to get a look at me, pinning me against the edge of the bar.

"Where'd you get that?" one of the men asks, and when I swivel my gaze, I see it's him—Samuel—the bolo-tie man, shuffled close and gaping down at me.

The breath I had been holding in my throat drops into my stomach. Rots there. Turns inside out. Grows into something else: a ticking rage burning at the top of my rib cage.

But he peers at me as if he doesn't recognize me—maybe he's too drunk. Too many glasses of dark liquor swimming behind his eyes, too many punches to the skull.

Fear reworks itself inside me, takes on a new urgent rhythm, and I know I need to get out of here—away from this man before he remembers me. Before his boss appears and decides to finish what he started. I inch back against the bar, my breathing coming quick and panicked now, the pain in my ribs expanding into my chest. My gaze flashes through the crowd, searching for an opening, a way out. But they only move closer. Boots scrape across the wet floor, hands twitching at their sides—calculating.

"I've never seen anything like it. . . ." The woman eyes me like I am something to be gutted, then devoured. Her tongue touching the ends of her broken teeth. Fingers lifting in the air, like she's going to peel me open with her clawed fingernail, see what's inside. "It's beautiful."

To my left, a man with white-gray hair and sun spots dotting his forehead removes the tobacco pipe from his mouth and clears his throat, nodding to me. "I've seen something like it sketched on paper. But never on skin." His voice is a croak, nearly lost with age and the smoke in his lungs.

Samuel lifts an eyebrow at me, staring at me with renewed interest.

My eyes drag across the leering faces, looking for kindness, pity, someone who will help me. But I only find hunger and desperation staring back. *Sickness.* Most have eyes rimmed in black, clouded and dull, lost of their sight. Others with jaws grinding, holding down the constant pain that tears at their insides. There is no sympathy here, not in this town, this saloon. All that's left is *need.* And a rare glimmer of hope . . . that they think they've found in the mark on my neck.

I am what they need.

"Let me see it, girl," the round woman growls, and she reaches her hand forward like she's going to grab my hair and force me down, so she can get a better look. But I swat her hand away. I wish I had Pa's rifle, had it gripped at my side, something to defend myself. Anything. But I'm on my own. I swallow, coiling my hands into fists—I'll fight my way out; I'll claw and kick. I'll make it to the door. *I have to.*

The woman smiles, a slick parting of her full lips, then shouts, "Grab her!" Flashing a look to the men beside her.

And someone does grab me, but it's not any of them—it's the girl from across the bar.

Her strong hand wraps around my wrist, firm and quick, and I let out a small shriek. But her eyes fall to mine, saying nothing, and the knife that had been tucked at her waist is now in her other hand, and for a second, I think she's going to thrust it toward me, at my throat, my gut, and tell me to show her the tattoo. But instead her eyes swivel to the crowd.

"She belongs to me," the girl barks, as if I were her property, the blade of her knife glinting in the candlelight, pointed at the near-toothless woman.

My heart is now screaming in my chest, and I inch closer to the girl. Pressed to her side. *She might be my only way out of here.*

"We just need a closer look," Samuel says, leveling his eyes on me—but somehow still not recognizing me.

"Don't think so," the girl answers, grinning widely, pointing knife at his throat like she's done this before—aimed the blade at a man twice her size and come away with blood on it. "Grab the bottle," she says to me quickly.

"What?" My mind is tumbling forward and back, the terror making it hard to focus on anything for longer than a second.

"The bottle you bought, on the bar. Grab it."

I reach out and swipe it from the bar top, holding it close to my chest—where my heart is a piston against my rib cage, trying to break me open.

With one hand still around my wrist, the girl pulls me backward, through the crowd, toward the far door she entered from. The group follows, steps matched with ours, while the man with the banjo continues to play, undisturbed by the commotion—as if this were as common as any other night in the saloon. We reach the door and she kicks it open with her boot, still holding the knife, and we both duck out into a dark, narrow passage between two buildings. The back alley where that boy found a dead body.

A man is vomiting beside the wall of the building. A woman is singing up at the stars several yards away, arms reaching for the sky.

Before I can blink, the girl has sheathed the knife back into her belt, grabs my hand again, and is pulling me up the alleyway. "Run!" she shouts.

And I do.

FOUR

My heart is beating in time with the pounding of my feet against the well-packed street.

The dark alcohol—the bottle still in my right hand—sloshes onto the ground as we run, and my eyes click to the girl, the wildness of her: coiled black hair streaming out behind her like raven feathers, eyes darting over her shoulder, a wily grin peeled across her lips. As if the thrill of running through the dark streets, voices shouting after us, has awakened something inside her.

We reach the edge of town, and I stop, pressing my hands to my knees, trying to slow my breathing—my heart beating too fast and my lungs scraped open, ribs vibrating like beetles scratching at the bone, breaking it apart. *What happened back there?* What did I do?

The girl grabs the bottle from me and takes a long swig. "We need to keep moving," she urges, wiping at her lips. "They saw the marks on your neck—" She takes another drink, nodding at me.

I straighten up, eyes watering, and scrape a hand across the back of my neck, beneath my hair. I want to tell her that she's wrong, that there aren't any marks. But it's too late for lies now. I have allowed the one thing to happen that Mom always warned of. I was stupid and careless, and now they have seen the tattoo. Now . . . it's only a matter of time until they figure out who I am.

The sound of voices grows in the distance, carried along the narrow streets of town, evaporating in the cold night air. The girl's dark eyes look past me, toward the sound. "They might be good and drunk," she continues, "but they'll sober up quick, and they'll come for you. They've got a tracker with them."

My gaze clicks back to the girl—the hard set of her jaw, the cool calm of her eyes, and the gleam of the studs in her ear. "They won't give up," she adds, snapping her eyes back to me. "So we better get moving." She holds the bottle out to me, but I shake my head. I don't want the amber liquid burning my throat. "Fine by me." She takes another sip, and I watch as her eyes tip back, fluttering like wings as she savors a long drink.

"My pa is above the saloon," I say, a swollen lump in my throat, catching on each word. "I'll go wake him, we'll get out of town before they find me." *Maybe it was a mistake to leave him,* I think. To risk being seen.

But the girl shakes her head. "Too late for that." Her eyes fall on something in the distance, coming up the main road through town. A blur of figures, half a dozen men. "They're already on us—look."

My pulse whispers against my eardrums, growing louder. *No, no.*

I had already said goodbye to Pa, felt the awful sting behind my eyes, but this feels truly final.

No turning back.

The girl touches my hand and flicks her head away, gesturing for me to follow. "Let's go," she snaps, a bite in her voice now. "You have to get far away from this town."

My breathing turns heavy. *I shouldn't go with her,* I think. *This girl I don't even know, who I have no reason to trust.*

But I also don't have a choice.

Her eyes meet mine, she nods, and I let her pull me away from the edge of Fort Bell, from the men who are coming after me—men who peered down at me inside the saloon with a look of crazed desperation: I was something they needed, someone they just might tear apart once they got their hands on me.

So I let this strange girl pull me out into the dark.

Into the wide-open plains of the desert.

✶ ✳ ✶

We run through the night.

Strange, low plants grow up from the prairie floor with spikes sprouting from their green, fleshy exteriors. At the top of each plant, snow-white flowers unfurl their petals to peer up at the waning moon, as if praying to it. They are night bloomers, craving the moonlight instead of the sun.

The girl doesn't slow her pace ahead of me.

She is strong, used to running—accustomed to fleeing on foot. Whenever I stop, buckling over to draw in deep breaths of the dry night air, she turns back to me and says, "We have to keep moving." Her eyes flicking behind us.

If we pause too long, we hear voices echoing over the low valley—the men getting closer. They're slower than us, staggering, stumbling—still drunk—but they're always there. Not far behind.

The sun begins to edge up from the west—the white flower petals shrinking back closed in unison, fearful of the sun—and I know we can't be out here in the heat of the open plains once it's fully risen. We have no water. Only the half-drunk bottle of booze.

"It's not far now," the girl says back to me, picking up her pace.

"Until what?"

She flashes me a look. "The water tower."

Just hearing her say the words makes my tongue feel like clay in my throat, closing up with each dusty breath into my lungs.

"The men will turn back, now that the sun is up," she assures me. "It's too dangerous in the heat. But they'll go back for their horses, and when they sober up, they'll track us again."

I try to dampen my mouth enough to speak. "Or maybe they'll—" I swallow, try again. "Maybe they'll just give up."

She swivels, plants her gaze on me. "They won't. They've been looking for you for too long."

She reaches into the back pocket of her dark pants and pulls out a piece of paper, folded into a square, then holds it out to me.

I blink down at it, and she nods for me to take it.

I have no idea what it is, but I take it from her and begin unfolding the creases, flattening the piece of paper against my palm.

POSTED:

The cure is near!

Any who bear a mark: constellations, star patterns, tattoos of unknown celestial formations, should be reported immediately.

Unharmed, preferable.

Reward to be negotiated.

"These are nailed to saloon doorways in nearly every town west of the halfway bridge," she says as my eyes read over each word twice. "Those three bodies back in town, hanging from the post office . . ." She breathes through her nostrils. "They were killed because Theorists thought they might know something. And they leave the bodies as a reminder to everyone else. *Talk, or lose your life.*"

I remember how Pa refused to tell me why the three people were killed—I sensed he knew more than he was saying. He didn't want to frighten me, because he probably also knew about the flyer that I hold in my hands. He'd surely seen them before, posted at saloons. He knew what they meant.

"They're coming for you," she assures me. "They won't stop."

A wave of dizziness crashes against the curves of my skull. *They're looking for me, for anyone who bears a mark.* And now . . . those in the saloon have seen mine.

They will know who I am.

What I am.

"We have to go now," the girl says, snatching the paper from my hand and quickly refolding it before shoving it back into her pocket. "I saw them knife a man in the alley behind the saloon yesterday. Quick as that, because he refused to say how far east he's traveled, and if he's seen anyone with a mark." She shakes her head, silver studs gleaming along the shape of her ear, and I think of the boy who said he stole boots off a dead body—probably the same one.

My eyes click slowly up to hers. "Why are you helping me?"

She snorts, and I can't tell if it's sarcasm, if she's not actually helping me at all, or if it's something else. But she shoves a hand against my shoulder, nodding out across the plains, the studs along her ear glinting against the rising sun. "If we don't get out of this heat, it won't matter anyway. We'll both be dead."

* * *

The water tower comes into view: a tall, wooden structure casting an insectlike shadow over the desert floor.

But when I bring a hand over my eyes, I see that there are other shadows too—human figures standing like stunted trees around the base of the tower, while others are perched high on the platform that encircles the round, wooden basin. *Dozens of them.* And although my need for water is sharp and desperate at the base of my throat, my fear is greater, and I slow my pace as we approach.

I think of the poster, the offer of a reward, and I wonder if this girl is leading me into a trap. I believed I was in danger in Fort Bell, that this girl with a feral glint in her eyes was helping me escape, but what if I got it wrong, and she has just brought me somewhere far worse? What if she only saved me so she can hand me over and collect the reward herself?

There is nowhere to run. My fingers fidget at my sides and my gaze darts across the darkened faces of those gathered around the water tower—trying to see if there is greed in their eyes, spite and hate. Or sympathy.

But they are too concealed in shadow.

The girl walks ahead of me, her stride swift and agile, as if we haven't just trekked all night into day, as if she isn't feeling the pain in her feet or the dry air in her throat like I am.

Sweat drips down my temples, my spine, and I squint at the faces ahead of us as they come into view. Our arrival is no surprise—the human forms at the tower saw us coming a good distance off—and when we're within a couple yards, I can feel the sharpening of their eyes on us, the shifting of their stances like they're ready for a fight.

I'm an outsider; I don't belong here. And I also might be prey.

"Who the hell is this?" someone shouts, and my eyes flash to a thin, lanky boy stepping out from the shadow of the tower, wearing a gray bandanna tied across his forehead, and a row of tiny hollowed-out seeds suspended from a string around his neck. He looks like the others—coated in a film of reddish dust, their eyes like white pebbles. Most wear hats or strips of fabric tied around their heads to shield the sun. None of them is much older than me, eighteen or nineteen at most, with the youngest around ten. And all of them have a knife or a makeshift blade strapped at their waists, fingers twitching.

"Found her in the Buffalo," the girl says, scanning the group. I try to read her tone, determine if she is still my ally, or if she has brought me to the doorstep of hungry wolves. But she won't look at me, won't even give me a gentle nod to reassure me that everything will be okay. My heart ratchets up into my throat. *I'm on my own.*

"And look," the girl adds, holding out the bottle of dark liquor, spinning it in her hand so the liquid swirls up the sides. The faces of the group change, eyebrows raised, and she hands it to a girl with long, dark braids and a ring through the center of her nose, who takes a drink, winces, then passes it to the shorter, muscular boy beside her. Even the youngest in the group take sips, smiles peeling wide across their faces.

"How'd you get a whole bottle?" the braided-hair girl asks.

"She traded for it." The girl—who could be my ally, could be my enemy—claps me hard on the shoulder, as if to convince the group that I'm okay. That I'm *one of them*. But I know I'm very much not. Everything about this feels wrong: the dryness in my throat, the throbbing at my temples from lack of sleep, the deep painful thirst, and the eyes of so many watching me. Untrusting. I've never felt so far from home.

Above us, three figures begin climbing down the wood ladder of the tower. I try to make out their faces once they reach the ground, but the sun is in my eyes, hot against my forehead. *Thirst, thirst, thirst* screams at me.

Before they've come into view, one of them says, "It's her. She traded with me for a bottle of tonic."

I blink, sweat flicking from my eyelashes, and at last I make out the young boy from the market—the boy who ran off when I asked about the Architect. He's among this group.

"Why'd you bring her here?" another voice asks, words deep and unsettling, like flood water roaring through the valley after it rains. I squint, trying to see him through the blinding sunlight, and when he steps forward through the shaft of golden light, his features come into view—dark-as-night hair swept to one side, eyes lidded against the slanted sun, skin a warm copper. But there is no warmth in his gaze; he is hard-jawed and severe, surveying me coldly, his green, river-deep eyes sliding from my face down to my boots, calculating if I'm a risk—when it's *my* heart beating out of my chest, ready to run, ready to fight. Knowing how quickly this could change.

His eyes skip back to the girl standing next to me, jawline tugging downward, waiting for an explanation.

"You said to find her," the girl answers, lifting both of her dark eyebrows.

Find me? What are they talking about?

"Yes, but not to bring her here."

"I had to," the girl says. "They were chasing us."

The boy rubs a broad hand across his neck. "Shit." Then his eyes flick back to me, peering straight through me, like he could read the truth of who I am in the slope of my mouth, my eyes, as if it were all there, exposed and raw for him to see. I swallow stiffly, holding in a breath, not because his stare is like a cold winter storm—magnetic, hard to look away from—but because he makes me uneasy. Because I sense that whatever comes next, whatever happens to me, is in his hands.

"You're the one who was asking about the Architect, back in Fort Bell?" he asks, as if verifying I'm the *right* girl, while keeping his gaze trained on me, every blink of his eyelashes like a sharp wind, like he's thinking of ways to cut me apart and bury me out here so I'm no longer a problem.

I glance to the younger boy beside him, the one who traded for the postcard, and I realize he must have told them that I was asking about the Architect. Told them about a girl at the market, a stranger, who was asking things she shouldn't be asking.

When the girl beside me strode into the saloon, she was looking for me. She was there for *me*.

But all the words feel tangled in my throat. Too many thoughts slamming together in my mind.

The boy with impossibly green eyes steps closer to me. "Why are you asking about the Architect?" His jaw is locked in place, temple pulsing.

I try to clear my throat but can't; it's too clotted with dust. But I meet his steely eyes—I don't look away, even when a twinge catches in my chest, even when I feel afraid. "Do you know who he is?" My voice a croak.

His eyes only narrow, and he shifts even closer, like I'm a threat, like he will kill me right here for even asking the question. "Who are you?" he asks, tilting his head, mouth still open. My throat quivers in a way that makes no sense, a feeling that is mixed with gut-hard fear.

But before I can sort through the words crashing through my mind, figure out what to say, how to reply with a lie that he will believe, the girl nudges me in the arm. "Show him," she prods, dipping her head toward me. "It's okay."

I frown at her, but then she taps a finger against the back of her own neck.

My eyes flick back to the boy, and I harden my jaw. I won't show him my tattoo. I've already screwed up once tonight back at the saloon—I'm not about to let anyone else see the marks that I should have kept hidden. Protected. Safe. I don't want to see the same hunger in the eyes of this boy, of any of them. "No," I say flatly.

The boy's watchful eyes shiver with something, fury or fascination, and he steps even closer—only a foot away now. But he doesn't reach for me, doesn't touch me; he just stares, like he's trying to read something in my face.

"Trust me," the girl whispers, reaching out to touch my forearm. "We're not going to hurt you. He just needs to see the marks."

I have no reason to trust this girl, or any of them. But my head throbs, I'm in the middle of a barren stretch of uninhabitable land, too exhausted and too desperate for water to turn and run. One way or another, they will find a way to see the tattoo. I don't have much of a choice.

And maybe, *maybe*, they have their own secrets. Maybe . . . they know where to find the Architect. So I drop my eyes to the ground, hands shaking, and I pull my hair forward, letting it fall over my shoulders. I hear the boy inch closer to me, and I swear I can feel his shaded green eyes peering at my skin, the weight of his stare on the exposed part of myself that no one is allowed to see. I feel his soft exhale on my neck, and after a second that feels too long, a flutter and pulse in my rib cage, he finally steps back.

The air slips from my throat. The blood rushes back down my veins.

"Who else saw the marks?" he asks.

I drop my hair and spin back around, every part of me raw, stripped bare. I crave things that are too far away now—the cool river, the safe walls of the cabin, a time when Mom was still alive.

"At the saloon," the girl replies, clenching her jaw. "Theorists—" She gives the boy a look, a silent understanding passing between them. "They saw it."

The boy nods. "They'll be hunting you," he says, turning back to face me. "They're probably not far off. We need to leave now."

I look back across the desert, through the miles of scrub brush and blowing wind, and I wonder if they're still out there. Following our tracks, getting closer. "The Architect," I say, my eyes blurring with thirst, but managing to meet the boy's eyes again, sensing that he knows more than he's saying. "I need to find him."

He looks to the girl, but neither speaks.

"I'm not going with you, unless you tell me where he is."

The boy pushes up his sleeves, the heat of the sun on his skin, and my eyes catch on the black tattoos weaving from his hands up to his elbows. Strange dark markings and shaded lines. Nothing like the delicate marks on my neck, his are broad and deep black and remind me of ash from a campfire. His contain no hidden messages, no secret meanings. They seem like the marks of late nights spent pushing ink into skin to pass the time, marks that are meant to intimidate, to show bravery and fearlessness. To show his grit. "If you want to survive, you'll come with us," he says, revealing nothing. "But we need to go now." Yet in his knife-sharp eyes, I think I see a hint of something. The truth he's hiding. And I know he's my only option. I can't go back to Fort Bell—there's only forward now.

I might not trust him, but I need to go with him.

I swallow dryly, lifting my chin, and I nod.

Quickly he turns to the girl. "Cricket, you'll come with us." *Her name is Cricket.*

She gives me a little wink, like everything's going to be okay.

But as we start off through the desert, away from the water tower and Fort Bell and the men following me, a thought begins tapping on the inside of my skull, a tiny little knocking: What if every moment forward is a step deeper into a place I can't return from? The shadows slipping over my past, making the way home impossible to see, to navigate.

I lift my eyes, squinting through the waves of heat rising up from the desert floor, and again, I remember the words Mom used to say to me, her hands stroking the soft layers of my hair, across the tattoo she branded onto my skin when I was young, her eyes tilted to the evening sky.

Don't look back. You're not going that way.

* ✳ *

Cricket, and the boy whose name I don't yet know, lead me away from the water tower toward a line of trees I can see in the distance: oaks growing stunted and short in the heat.

But soon we'll be in their shade. I can almost feel their shadowed limbs reaching out for me, calling me close into their cool shelter, wind hissing through their limbs. It's all I can think of.

The boy hands Cricket a metal canteen—dented on one side, hanging from a leather strap—and she unscrews the lid, taking a long, messy gulp, water splashing down her chin, before handing it off to me. I drink greedily too, letting it spill down my throat—I've never been so thirsty in all my life—and the cool water plummets into my stomach like a stone, making me shiver.

Cricket takes the empty canteen and slings it over her shoulder, and I hope there's more where we're going, an unending lake of clear, snow-melted water that I can sink down into, mouth open wide. Because my throat still feels as dry and crisp as dead autumn leaves.

With the sun blazing over us, the boy walks several paces ahead, watchful—eyes scanning the desert—but we seem to be the only shadows stupid enough to be out in this heat. No sign of the men behind us. No sign of anything ahead, either.

"The others are staying behind?" I ask Cricket, glancing back at the water tower, where twenty or so figures remain in the shadow cast down by the tower, and about five or six others positioned above on the platform.

"They're guarding it," Cricket answers, her shoulders bent slightly forward, like she's preparing for a long, miserable walk. "We charge a fee for anyone passing through who needs water. During the market, we can make a lot of coin." She scratches at the shaved side of her head, the stubble itchy, then makes a motion with her eyes to the boy ahead of us. "That's Noah."

I let my eyes watch him a moment, the assured pace of each step, the curves of his shoulders, muscular, strong—someone who's no stranger to hard work, of one kind or another. And he carries something in his hands, a thing he keeps turning over and over. A coin maybe, but larger. The dulled metal barely catching the sunlight. "He's in charge?" I ask.

She lifts a shoulder. "More or less. He's been around longer, and can make decisions faster than the rest of us."

The sun makes ripples of the landscape, a trick that almost looks like water, and I wipe at my eyes, sweat dripping from every curve and shallow place of my skin.

"What's your name?" Cricket asks finally, as if it's only just now occurred to her.

I feel the tightness gather at the top of my throat. Telling her the truth feels like giving something up, revealing a part of who I am. *Who I really am.* But they've already seen the tattoo; my name feels trivial now. "Vega."

Ahead of us, Noah turns his head, casting me a sidelong look. Like the name means something to him. But says nothing.

We continue on in silence, my name the last word hanging in the air between us, until at last we reach the shade of the oaks, and the relief is so sudden that I want to press my palms to the cold ground, feel it against my scorched skin, and weep. But Noah and Cricket don't slow their pace.

"How much farther?" I ask, eyes wanting to sink closed, to rest, to dream of places that are anywhere but here.

"Another hour or so," Cricket answers, and her eyes look weary finally, like she, too, is in need of sleep. Like the hours we spent running across the desert are now showing in the steady lines of her face.

We move deeper into the trees, and the landscape becomes uneven, steep in places, and I scramble unbalanced over rocky outcroppings and fallen trees. I'm exhausted and clumsy, my head pounding. But I need more than sleep, more than water. . . . I need someplace that feels safe, where my heart can slow and my eyes can stop flashing over my shoulder, flinching at every shadow that skitters and flashes and moves.

An hour passes, then another.

It begins to rain, lightly at first, but then it falls in great, gasping sheets. Like the rain is being tossed down by the clouds, trying to drown us, carry us away. I tilt my face to the sky and hold out my tongue, letting the drops cool my skin, swallowing what I can. But after another few minutes, my clothes are soaked, my hair dripping, and I wish I was in the wagon, could sink into the back and pull Mom's quilt over my head.

The ground turns muddy, puddles forming in shallow places, but the air is still warm, sticky. After another hour, day becomes evening, and Noah looks back at Cricket and me, rain streaming across his face and eyelashes—he looks even more dark and unsettling in the downpour, and it stirs a knot in my chest. "We're nearly there," he says, his voice a sharp pin drop in my ears.

Cricket doesn't reply, just keeps her head down, away from the rain.

I don't see the place until we're nearly upon it.

A barn.

Tall and rectangular, rainwater streaming from the roof. "What is this place?" I ask.

"It used to be a town called Winnett Springs. But everything burned down. Only the barn is left now," Cricket tells me through chattering teeth, all of us soaked through.

"You live here?"

"For now," Noah answers, moving on up ahead, and pulling open one of the huge barn doors only wide enough for us all to slip inside without letting in the rain.

✴ ✴ ✴

Candles throw light up the wide, slatted walls, and the whole place smells of hay and manure and woodsmoke. It's cavernous, hollow-feeling, with a loft perched high above us, and rain dripping through several holes in the slackened roof. I had hoped for a place that would feel safe, shelter from the rain, but it's barely any drier than standing outside in the storm.

Faces lift when we enter, people gathered in groups along the walls of the barn, huddled around small fires—flames kept low so the light won't be seen from outside—their hands open toward the heat, trying to keep warm.

"Don't worry," Cricket says softly, so close to my ear, I can feel her warm breath. "They're friends."

We walk down the center of the barn, and I eye those gathered against the walls, trying to gauge if I'm truly safe here, or if I need to be ready to run. But nearly everyone inside the barn is younger than me. Just kids really, banded together.

Still, my breathing grows quick in my throat.

We follow Noah to the far back wall of the barn, where another fire has been lit inside a metal barrel, as if to keep the flames hidden. I feel beckoned by its warmth, wanting to sink down to the floor beside it. I crave so many things—shelter, water, sleep—that it's hard to pinpoint what I need most. I'm so focused on the flames, the growing heat, that when we reach it, I almost don't notice the chair positioned beside it—the upholstered back woven with a pattern of yellow daisies, the fabric torn and mice-eaten at the bottom seam. Perhaps it was taken from a nearby house and brought here, the only thing that didn't burn.

As I inch closer, eyes dripping rainwater, I see that there is a man seated in it, waves of snow-gray hair reflecting the firelight.

"You're back early," he says, voice thick with age, a damp rattle in his chest, and he turns in the chair to face us.

"We brought someone with us," Noah answers, eyes clicking over at me. *Eyes that are too green, too wild, too unsettling.*

The old man tightens his hands around the wooden, sculpted arms of the chair, and pivots so he can see me more clearly. His face is marred by wrinkles, deep caverns in his gray, sun-spotted flesh, his mouth thin as a sheet of paper. Yet his eyes are a deep, sad blue, and there is still light in them. The shivering memory of the man he used to be. "Hello," he says warmly, squinting, puckering his eyebrows together. "My eyes don't see as clearly as they used to. You'll need to come closer."

Unsteadily I cross the space to the chair, while Noah turns his gaze to the small fire, warming his hands—like he's no longer interested in me. His job is done, he's brought me here; now he couldn't care less what happens next.

"What's your name?" the old man asks, pale hands folded in his lap, veins raised and distinct like old tree roots. But there is no ring on his hand, no constellation.

"Vega."

I think I see Noah's shoulders twitch slightly.

But the craggy lines of the old man's face lift. "Named after a star," he observes, one side of his mouth trembling in what is either delight or hesitation. I can't be sure.

"Yes," I confirm. But I'm surprised he would know this—Mom always said we were the only ones who carried the names of the stars, who remembered their stories. Hope squeezes my heart. . . .

"I'm looking for someone," I say.

The old man lets out a long, shaky breath, a rasp and clatter, and there is something in his face that tells me he knows more than he's saying, and he's waiting to see what else I offer up. What truth I might reveal.

My eyes flash to those seated around the barn, soft firelight licking up the walls, and I lower my voice so only the man will hear. "He's known as the Architect, and I need to find him," I whisper. "I'm running out of time."

Hearing this, the old man flashes a quick look to Noah, and Noah stuffs the silver thing he had been turning in his fingertips back into his pocket. "She has marks on her neck," Noah says, nodding at me.

"Oh?" The old man's mouth cuts into a strange shape.

I feel the warmth of the fire against my cheeks, my lips, drying the moisture on my skin. *I've come this far,* I think. I've let Noah and Cricket and everyone at the water tower see the tattoo, and if this man can help me, then there's no point wasting any more time by resisting. I hold a breath tight in my lungs, and turn, wrapping my hair over my shoulder, and let the firelight dance across my bared skin.

I hear the creak of the chair as the old man leans forward to inspect the mark—the dark lines dotted with black stars. My ears roar, the sound of the rain against the roof echoing through the barn, and when I drop my hair and turn to look back at the man, I can see the recognition in his eyes. "Do you know what the marks mean?" he asks, his tone changed—serious, deliberate.

My gaze flicks to Noah without intending to, but he looks away, offering no comfort in his eyes. Maybe I shouldn't say, maybe I should keep some things to myself, but I sense that I've landed myself at a place of no return. I either trust this man, and hope he can help me, or I turn and run for the barn doors, heading out into the storm. I run deeper into this forest, away from those men hunting me, and hope I can survive on my own. I decide to give him the truth, and hope I'm not wrong. "Yes," I tell him. "I do."

He leans forward in his chair, old bones creaking, resting his elbows on his knees, and gazes up at me. "Who are you?"

The lump in my throat hardens, air leaving my nostrils in quick bursts. I've never said these words aloud, to anyone. It feels wrong, like walking through the scrubby, overgrown blackberry bushes beside the river, letting the thorns tear at my skin, expose the truth of who I really am. I clear my throat and lift my watery eyes. "My mother was the last Astronomer," I say, clear and sharp, and I swear the entire barn falls silent, a deafening echo of quiet. "But she's dead," I continue, the word barbed and needle-sharp, the hurt trying to resurface. I swallow. "Now—" My eyes fall to my hands, then back to the old man, steadying my focus before I let the words fall from my lips. "Now . . . *I* am the last Astronomer. The last one who can read the stars." I breathe through my nostrils—the words feeling like a spell, an alchemy never spoken before. And from the corner of my eye, I see Noah watching me, intent, an unsettled curve to his mouth. Even Cricket lifts her gaze.

The old man cranes his head to one side, observing me, unblinking, trying to see if there are lies in my words. "And why have you come?"

I understand: He wants me to prove it. He needs to know I'm telling the truth.

"The twin stars appeared in the sky eight days ago," I tell him, my voice strong, swinging over the words like a riddle that was born into my bones. "Tova and Llitha rose above the eastern horizon, and now I need to find the Architect. I have to get to the sea, at the edge of everything, while the sister stars are still visible." I pause, blow out a breath. "I'm running out of time."

The old man is quiet, and then he nods, eyes fluttering as if he's waited a long time to hear these words. A lifetime. His hands shake in his lap, and he curls them into fists to steady them. "You came from the valley?"

I nod, a dizziness sweeping through me, the gravity of everything I've just said, just revealed, to this man. "I've come a long way," I say. "But the days are moving too quickly. If you know where the Architect is, please, I need to find him."

The old man's blue-gray eyes shiver, drawing the wrinkles tight around them like an old tree, and he holds out his hand to me. "I'm

August," he says, leaning forward, and that's when I see it: the thin chain around his neck, the ring suspended from the end, just visible inside the folds of his coat. "It seems we've waited a long time to meet one another," he adds.

I swallow, trying to keep my voice from breaking. "You're—" All the pain and fear and grief I've been carrying around inside me suddenly feels like it's going to rupture. Like I might cry or drop to the floor or vomit. "You're the Architect?" Each word almost breaks in two as they leave my lips, the cold gone from my skin, only heat roaring through my veins now.

He smiles a little, lifting both eyebrows at me, then reaches into his coat, fingers trembling around the chain, then holds the ring up for me to see—proving who he is, knowing it's the thing I've been searching for.

The constellation Circinus, with its two long rows of stars, is stamped into the silver signet ring, generations of stories held within its weight—the ring that was worn by the first Architect. And now the last.

I found him.

And I feel like I might laugh, like my nerves are too wrung out.

The Architect. I step forward, taking his frail hand in mine, peering down at the silver ring that I've tried to imagine many times—an heirloom that has belonged to every Architect before him, worn until the silver has become thin along the band, the indentations of the constellation dulled—the mark of the Architect. His skin is cold, muscles trembling, and I want to weep.

"I keep it hidden," he says, tucking the ring back into his thick coat. "Out of sight."

The walls of the barn rattle against the blowing wind, but before I can say anything else—tell him all the things churning in my mind, all the times I feared I wouldn't find him—he looks to Noah, then Cricket. "Who else has seen the mark?"

Cricket's arms are crossed, the studs in her left ear shimmering in the firelight, and she speaks up for the first time. "A group of Theorists were at the saloon in Fort Bell—they saw it."

"And they're coming after her?" August asks, voice steadier than before.

Cricket nods.

August shifts forward in his chair, hands wobbling against the armrests. He's trying to push himself up, but he's too weak. Noah hurries to his side, taking August by the arm, and helps him to stand—the tattoos along Noah's forearms a sharp contrast of black against August's pale skin.

Once he's upright, he nods at Noah, a gesture that he's okay, and August moves toward me, lungs wheezing against his frail ribs, then grips my hands in his, like he wants to be sure I'm real. "For a time, I wondered if the old stories, told to me by my father, were nothing more than folklore. But here you are." The glow from the flames makes his skin seem even more transparent, every crease and line and furrow like ravines across his water-thin flesh. "Long ago," he continues, "the first Astronomer gazed up at the sky, and knew every point of light, every star beyond our own."

On the other side of the campfire, I see Cricket take a step closer to us, eyes creased, like she's trying to hear—beckoned forward by the cool drawl of August's words.

"The Astronomer passed her knowledge down to her daughter,

and to her daughter after that." His eyes pass up to the ceiling, and he is quiet a moment, breathing heavy. "But many years ago, the first Astronomer disappeared. Some thought she was dead; others said she was merely hiding, afraid of those who were hunting her."

My ribs press in and out, lungs rising, heartbeat rattling. I think of my mother, of the nights we lay on our backs in the tall grass and watched the stars circle in their infinite spirals overhead while she recounted the stories of the first Astronomer—the history of our ancestors, stories that braided themselves into my joints, the fibers of my hair, until they became mine. Stories that didn't just tell of my past but of my future.

August's eyes close briefly, and I see Noah move toward us, like he's ready to catch August in case he collapses. But August clears his throat and continues. "Most think I'm long dead too—only a myth." He looks at me like he's looking straight through me, into the galaxy of my insides, where all my secrets are tucked away, hidden from view. He draws his shoulders back, spine creaking tall. "But my ancestors fled on foot, always moving, never settling anywhere for long, for fear we'd be discovered." His eyes affix themselves to mine. "It's been many generations since our ancestors made an agreement, a pact." He breathes. "They did it to protect us, to protect the truth."

My eyes water, a thousand thoughts swelling inside me at once: these are the same stories Mom told me night after night, and hearing August recite them to me feels like sunlight, like laying down a heavy stone I have carried all on my own.

"But now if the Theorists know who you are, they will track you—they won't stop." He sways a little, releasing his hands from mine, and Noah reaches out for him, helping him to sit back in the yellow-printed chair. His eyes flutter closed, stay that way a moment, before opening again. "They believe there's a cure for the sickness," he says, nodding at me, making sure I understand. That I'm truly listening. "And they think those marks on your neck will tell them where it is."

The wind outside screams through the cracks in the barn walls, and the rain increases its downpour, falling in gusts, violent upheavals from the sky, but there is a storm in my chest. A fury coming alive—this is *my* story now. The last Astronomer who left the valley and found the Architect. Whose real story is about to begin.

August glances up to Noah, and there is a knowing passing between them. "It's time," August says, a strange, shuddering lilt in his voice, as if this were something he's been waiting for his whole life.

My ears begin to ring, a faraway sound that feels like a tolling bell.

"Get some sleep," August says to me at last, each word a pulse along my river-cold veins, a knocking rising in my chest. "Tomorrow we leave for the sea."

✳ ✳ ✳

Noah builds a small fire in one of the back corners of the barn, tucked out of sight, in what was once probably a horse stall.

"Better to sleep away from the others," Cricket says, bedding down in a damp pile of straw. "They'll only ask you questions all night. Especially the younger ones."

Noah kneels beside the fire, adding more hunks of foraged wood, the glow reflecting on a small scar along his chin. He is strong, broad-shouldered, someone who is built to defend himself, to fight back when necessary—his fists have surely been bloodied, his torso able to withstand a punch. He has seen far more of this world than I probably ever will. And he has been made tough by it, muscles worked into stone, dangerous green eyes watchful and quick. He is someone you don't want as an enemy. Someone I'd fear if he pointed a blade at my soft flesh.

I look away, absorbing too much of him. My eyes measuring every detail.

Across the barn, most of the others seem to be asleep, some snoring softly, only a few talking low, their voices hardly more than a whisper.

"Are we safe here?" I ask, feeling uneasy, thinking of the bodies suspended from ropes back in Fort Bell, and I swivel my gaze from Noah to Cricket. But Cricket has already closed her eyes, her mouth hanging open slightly, asleep. I'd guess she can probably sleep anywhere.

"Those men will be slower in the rain, unable to follow our tracks. They've likely stopped for the night." Noah prods the fire with his stick, keeping it alive, sparks peeling away up into the rafters of the barn. "We'll leave just before sunup."

His eyes flash to me, like I am not the girl he first thought I was. Or maybe I am exactly who he suspected, but now he's unsure what to say to the girl whose secrets have been only half revealed.

"Why are you all here?" I ask quietly, not wanting to wake Cricket.

He sinks back onto the straw, leaning against the wall of the barn, arms crossed, like he has no intention of sleeping tonight; instead he'll keep watch, keep the fire alive. And us. "We've all come from different places, different reasons why we don't have a home."

He tilts his gaze out to the barrel fire, where August is still seated. "But August has helped us survive."

I think about Pa, what he must have thought when he woke and found me no longer in the rented room next to his, and the quilt placed beside his door. I hate that I left him like I did, but if I hadn't, I doubt I would be here now. Only steps away from the Architect.

Noah's arms flex, an uneasy slope to his eyes, a hardness I don't quite understand—like I make him uncomfortable—but he reaches out and retrieves a canteen hanging from the wall, suspended from a long, woven strap, and hands it over to me. "Water," he says, nodding, as if knowing the dryness that still scratches at my throat.

I tip the canteen to my mouth, swallowing greedily, but he doesn't tell me to stop, to save what's left. He lets me drink until I'm full. "Thank you," I say, wiping a stray drop from my mouth.

When he retrieves the canteen, his hand brushes over mine, his skin warm—a fire inside him—and he seems to stall there briefly, fingertips against my flesh, a heartbeat of time, before placing the canteen back on the hook, not drinking any himself. His eyes skip back to me—careful, as if he keeps his own secrets, his own untold stories—and my lungs get tight. A feeling I don't like, and don't understand.

He studies my face a moment, a stiffness in his jaw, something he wants to say masked in his eyes, but then he forces his gaze away— as if he's holding something back. I let my eyes fall to my hands, rubbing them together, trying to keep out the cold. I can't believe Cricket is able to sleep with rain streaming through the roof, forming puddles in the straw.

I sink back against the wall beside Noah, hands pulled up into the sleeves of my coat. He is a boy who smells like pine trees and wind, who looks at me like he doesn't know *what* I am.

A girl or a riddle.

Rain streams through the sagging roof, the storm howls against the trees outside, and Noah tips his head back against the wall, turning something over in his palm—the round piece of metal he held when we walked from the water tower to the barn—it busies his hands, his mind, helping to keep him awake.

Hunger gnaws at me, a deep pain in my gut, but I force my eyes closed, trying to ignore the sounds of so many people—strangers—breathing inside the barn, the sound of Cricket fidgeting, a soft sputter from her lips, and the nerves bouncing along my thoughts—the jittery fear of what comes next. Time scratching at my mind like a beetle in soft wood.

I wish I could see the night sky, count the stars, name them until I fell asleep. I wish I could see Tova and Llitha—the stars that brought me here. But I will have to settle for the dark. Because I need the sleep. . . . I need to be ready.

Tomorrow we leave for the sea.

CASSIOPEIA, *Alpha Cas*
+56° 32' 14"

The oldest settlers began getting sick first. A crackle in the ears, a gasp for air.

The consumption came on quick, before the first crops had even bloomed. Before the first snow of a long winter had fallen over the newly built towns.

The first of the dead were buried in the ground well before the soil froze. Shovels in hard-packed dirt, the cold licking at fingertips, as if it were an omen of what was to come.

Death had found them, even here. Even after they fled the old world.

Disease came anyway.

Found its way into their homes. Into their small, scraped-out towns.

And it broke their bodies apart, bit by bit. Limb by limb. Blood at the surface, where it didn't belong.

FIVE

I wake to a loud *crack*.

My eyes spring open, blood roaring in my ears, one side of my body damp from the rainwater that had been dripping onto my coat through the barn roof.

Bang, bang, bang.

I don't even have time to blink, to focus, before Noah is on top of me, hoisting me up. His hands against my ribs, the air gusting from my lungs. "What's happening?" My voice rattles into not-quite-awake pieces while my eyes snap to Cricket, who's kicking ash onto the fire, sending smudgy smoke up into the rafters.

But Noah holds a finger to his lips, only a few inches from mine, his green eyes too wide. Too white.

Another loud *bang* reverberates through the barn, followed by a series of muffled shouts.

I clench my teeth, my heartbeat too loud at my throat. *Someone's outside.* It's still dark, no light through the cracks in the barn walls—but it's stopped raining.

Noah grabs my hand—warm palm to my cold skin—and pulls me out of the stall into the main part of the barn. Cricket quickly unsheathes her knife, licking her lips like she's ready for a fight, and follows Noah at his side.

I blink, trying to see, to understand what's happening. The others in the barn are scrambling through the dark, some standing at the barn doors, open just a crack, rifles pointed out into the dark; while the rest are huddled together near the back. I spot August, standing over a group of younger kids, as if he could protect them—his thin, aging frame shaking in the cold. His eyes meet mine, then Noah's.

Noah nods, as if understanding some silent meaning, words not spoken, and then he's pulling me toward the back of the barn, panic cracking through me, lungs gasping, as Cricket waves an arm at someone to our left, a small girl with summer-wheat hair and a wild, terror-struck look on her face, standing in the middle of the barn. *"Get down!"* Cricket half screams, half whispers; and the girl drops to her stomach.

But there's no door here, at the back of the barn, *no way out.*

Shit, shit. We're hemmed in. An acrid taste claws up my throat, fear tapping at my skull. *We're going to die in here.*

More screams erupt from outside, bullets explode against the walls of the barn, splintering the old wood, and several older kids dart out through the opening in the doors. Some have weapons: crude, rusty knives, long pieces of wood with nails poking through the ends—I think I even see one with a gun. But whatever is out there, I suspect, is more than they can handle.

Another *crack*, but this one sounds closer. I pinwheel my gaze back to Noah, and he's kicked free one of the old boards at the back of the barn, now mottled with bullet holes, then yanks it away, creating an opening in the wall. "Go," he hisses at me.

I hesitate, afraid of what I'll meet on the other side. My eyes cut over to the far side of the barn, thinking we might be safer in here. Hidden in straw and darkness.

But Cricket yells, "What the hell are you waiting for?" Pointing her knife at the low, narrow opening.

I choke on the fear, swallowing it down, then drop to my knees, knowing: *Whatever is outside will find its way in eventually.* With my hands first, I wriggle through the gap in the wood, spilling out into the dark night, gasping, eyes tearing to my left and then right. But there are no figures moving through the dark on this side of the barn. They're distracted, intent on breaking through the massive double doors on the other side, gunshots echoing through the air.

I scramble to my feet, wiping the hair back from my face, hands muddy. I was wrong about the rain—it's still falling but only lightly, a soft patter against my adrenaline-hot skin.

Cricket is next, appearing through the tight space in the barn wall, the knife still clutched in her hand. "Run," she shouts when she gets to her feet.

But I hesitate, looking back at the opening. "Where's Noah?"

"He'll be right behind us," she barks, reaching out for me and fisting the sleeve of my coat, trying to tug me toward the tree line. Away from the gunfire. But I pull against her, my eyes snapping back down at the hole. "Come on!" she hisses, impatient.

More bangs, someone smashing through the front doors of the barn, followed by several gunshots and a long, awful scream. The air is punched from my lungs. I blink. *He's taking too long.* More gunshots echo up the walls. I wipe the rain from my face, staring at the dark opening. *No,* my mind repeats. *They're inside the barn.*

155

A second passes and Cricket tugs on my sleeve again, urging me to move, to follow her, but then I see it. An arm reaches through the opening in the wall, followed by another, and then he's crawling through—*Noah*—the space hardly large enough for his wide shoulders.

"What are you doing?" he barks, dragging himself to his feet. "Run!"

He grabs my hand, wet from the rain, squeezing tight like he's not about to let me go, and we sprint toward the tree line, my heart a hammer, slamming against my ribs with each breath.

We're almost to the pines when the whiz of a bullet rips through the air only a foot or so from my left ear, then explodes against a tree trunk. Noah's eyes swing over to me, panicked, looking to see if I'm hit. I shake my head, letting him know I'm okay, even though my ears ring with adrenaline and fear.

"Shit," Cricket shouts, ducking, then making a half dive into the crowded evergreens, into the cover of darkness. "They're fucking shooting at us."

In the half shadows of the trees, Noah releases my hand and I buckle over, breathing gasping, rain dripping on me from the overhead branches, but his gaze stays on me a moment more. "You okay?" he asks, touching a hand to my forearm.

I nod up at him, feeling the warmth of his palm, not wanting him to let go. "Fine." The word is a wheeze, lost of all sound.

Finally he releases his hand and turns to survey the barn behind us, the shadowed forms sprinting through the dark—some staggering, then dropping to the ground. Injured, wounded, crying out. His friends are dying. But then I see them: men on horseback, appearing through the gray wash of rain, rifles balanced on their thighs, scanning the perimeter of the barn.

They tracked us from Fort Bell, just like Cricket said they would.

"They really want her," she whispers now, out of breath, eyes darting over at me. But I don't like the sharp, serrated way her gaze cuts through me, like maybe I'm not worth the fight, not worth their lives, and maybe they'd be better off just handing me over to those men.

But Noah ignores her comment. "We need to get moving. These trees aren't safe."

I straighten up, sucking in the damp air, panic itching at my skin, but Cricket doesn't move. She taps the knife against her hip, rhythmic, in time with her heartbeat—and the motion makes me nervous. I don't like the way her eyes keep skipping over me. "We should go to the water tower," she says to Noah. "Tell the others, bring back help."

Noah is quiet for half a breath, the seconds ticking in my skull, and I wish I could read the thoughts stirring inside him, masked behind his steady eyes. But finally he shakes his head, dark hair dripping with rainwater. "It's too late," he answers, wiping the mud from his palms onto his pants. "We have to go now."

But Cricket lifts both hands toward the edge of the trees, to the barn. "We can't just abandon them. We need to warn the others at the tower."

I sense the disquiet in Noah, something he doesn't want to say—eyes colder than the dark, wet sky. "If those men made it here—" His gaze scrapes over to Cricket, his mouth flat. "Then they've already been to the water tower."

Cricket ceases to tap the blade against her thigh, but I already understand Noah's meaning. "No," she says, eyes cut to slits, anger spurring up inside her. *"No."*

"Everyone at the tower is gone." Noah's voice breaks a little, eyes vibrating, trying to stuff down the part of him he doesn't want us—or maybe just me—to see.

I keep my mouth shut . . . because I know this is my fault. I don't say a word.

Another bullet screams through the trees, just past our heads. *We need to run.* It's only a matter of time until they search the barn, realize I'm gone, and come looking for us in the line of trees. I take a step back, deeper into the forest.

"It's too late, Cricket," Noah says, quickly touching a hand to her shoulder. "We need to go now."

She shoves him away, refusing to look at him, heat in her cheeks. I wonder if it's always like this between them—bitter, short-fused. Like brother and sister. Or like something else.

Noah gives me a look, quick, and I nod in return.

We don't have time to argue—we have to get away from the barn. *Now.*

Together, we break away from the tree line, cutting a jagged path into the dark, into the woods. Noah leads, but Cricket lags behind, glancing over her shoulder—hating that we're running away when she wants to stay and fight.

The farther we go, the sound of bullets shattering tree trunks and barn walls and bone, of footsteps and screams, fades away into the soft rain. As if it was only a dream, a wretched, unspeakable nightmare we are slowing waking from. Mile by mile.

But it doesn't wipe away the sour, rotting ache in my stomach, the knots binding themselves tighter with each exhale from my lungs. The hard ground rising up to meet me, thudding in my ears. We run . . . while others die.

Because of me.

But my legs keep pumping, I keep breathing, I don't look back—because more will die if I don't keep going. Those men tracked me all the way from Fort Bell, across a dry, scrubby desert, because they're willing to kill to get to me.

And I have to be willing to let others die, to save what's left.

It's a story that's already been written, etched into the stars, in the ink on my skin, in the blood that runs through me from my ancestors. I don't have a choice. *Get to the sea, or die trying.*

That's all there is now.

So I keep running: wet air and night sky and a boy named Noah who I follow, and a girl named Cricket whose eyes have gone cold, who glances at me as we scramble down into a gully and up the other side, feet slapping against the muddy ground. She looks at me like I've taken something from her—everything.

But we keep going. We don't slow.

We run through a maze of dense forest—hemlocks and firs and spiky plants that run their thorns along our clothes, searching for bare skin. Drawing blood. Plants that didn't grow in the valley, that Mom never pointed out and made me memorize—like stinging sage, and honey manzanita that bloomed twice a year with sweet, sticky pollen. These are foreign plants, in a foreign land. A place farther than I've ever been.

Dawn creeps through the trees, making everything soft and colorless.

The sky flares against the horizon, the sun catching through the atmosphere at just the right angle—the anomaly showing itself in this brief moment before sunrise. A strange preternatural sight. Like the sky has come alive. But Noah and Cricket don't pause to stare up at it—they've witnessed it countless times before. And likely never wondered at its origin. Never gaped up at the horizon and thought that something might be wrong. We grow used to things—even if they don't belong.

We all tell stories to ourselves, Mom would say. *We ignore what's right in front of us. And the obvious is often hardest to see.*

A moment later, the sun burns away the atmosphere, sending the shivering light back into the dark, leaving only a pale blue sky and a hint of storm clouds. We keep moving, traveling through the hottest part of day, until at last a ravine opens up ahead, the sheer, granite rock falling away. We inch closer, keeping our bodies low so we won't tumble over. Far below, a river cuts through the land, violent and crashing, a river that could sweep you away and carry you down several miles in a matter of minutes.

"There's a cave down there," Cricket says, nodding below. In the light of day, her features are soft, eyes cool and watery from running. "I've camped in it before."

But before we start down the ravine, Noah walks several yards back the way we came, to a broad oak, where he snaps one of the lower limbs, then moves deeper into the trees, out of sight.

"What's he doing?" I ask.

Cricket is silent, not looking at me—and I know she's still thinking of the barn, the water tower, all her friends who we left behind. But finally she says, "It's a diversion." She runs a hand along the shaved side of her head. "Giving their tracker something to follow."

"Will it work?"

"It'll send them in the wrong direction for a little while. But not forever. Once they realize we're not in the barn, they'll need to reassemble. Hopefully they lost some of their men and they'll need to bury the dead. If that trail works"—she nods to where Noah disappeared into the trees—"we should have a day or so ahead of them. Maybe a little more, if we're lucky."

I should tell Cricket that I'm sorry, that I know she lost people she loved because those men tracked me to the barn, but the hard cut of her mouth, her eyes staring down the ravine, makes me think that she doesn't want to hear it. It won't undo what's been done. But I wonder: *Is August still alive?* If he died back there, along with too many others, then I am a girl with all the knowledge of the stars but with no way to reach the ocean—no way to set anything right.

And the thought threatens to break me open. Drop me to the ground.

But Noah returns, wiping the back of his hand across his forehead. "Found a deer trail heading north, merged my trail with it— hopefully their tracker will follow it for a while."

Cricket nods, swift, not meeting his eyes either.

Without another word, we start down a shallow point into the ravine. There might have been a path here once, an animal track that's been washed away with the rain. But we follow it where we can, holding on to trees growing along the sheer wall, sliding across loose shale, sending rocks down to the water below. Cricket scrambles down the slope, sure-footed, while I slip and lose my balance, uncertain of the steep ground. Noah stops, holding a hand out to me, but

I shake my head. Back in the valley, I scaled the steep walls picking wild blackberries and yarrow; I would skip across the slick rocks over the river, never missing a stone, never losing my balance. But out here, in this strange terrain, I feel clumsy and heavy-limbed, like I'm not in my own body. Maybe it's the steep drop below us, down to nothing but foaming water and pointed rocks. *A quick death.*

Or maybe it's the adrenaline, the lack of sleep, the thirst and hunger, the fear that those men might not be far behind. All of it. But I keep scrambling down the wall, following Cricket's path, refusing to slow down.

The sun is high overhead when we finally reach the bottom of the ravine. And Cricket was right: A cave slopes back into the rock wall. It's not large, no taller than our heads, and as wide as two arms stretched out. We explore the inside and find signs that Cricket—and maybe others—have been here recently. A ring of burnt logs from a campfire sits near the opening of the cave; a half-singed wool blanket lies crumpled at the back corner, along with a single shoe, left behind for reasons unknown.

Cricket sinks onto the ground at the mouth of the cave, rubbing at her eyes, her temples. The last couple of days finally catching up to her.

Noah stares down at the river below, listening. But it's hard to hear anything over the roaring flow of water. If those men came down the ravine, we might not hear them until they were too close. But the sound of the river will mask our voices too. And the cave is tucked back enough—I doubt they'd be able to see us from above. It's as good a place as any to rest. For now.

Cricket closes her eyes, resting her forehead on her knees.

"You okay?" I ask.

"Fine," she answers sharply, turning away from me. "Just a head-ache."

We haven't eaten in a whole day, and only managed a few hours of sleep in the barn. We're all exhausted. Nerves rattled, fear and grief and anger stewing inside us, and even now, we can't rest for long. We have to be ready to leave, to climb down to the river and keep going if we hear even a hint of those men.

Inside the pocket of my coat, I feel for the bottle and pull it out. "Here," I say, unscrewing the cap and shaking out two pills.

Her head lifts from her knees, eyes gaping at my palm. "Where did you get those?" She takes them from me quickly, as if I might change my mind.

"From my pa," I answer truthfully.

"Does he have more?" Her voice is anxious now, an edge to it that I don't like.

I stare down at the nearly full bottle in my hand, with *Aspirin* printed on the side. "Not anymore. This is the last one."

Her mouth tugs up into a smile. "That's how you bought that bottle of booze back at the Buffalo."

I nod at her, sliding the bottle back into my pocket, beside the worthless, creased postcard I still carry.

But then her eyes dim; she shakes her head and looks up at Noah. "We could buy a lot with these pills."

"It'll also take away your pain," I say.

She closes her eyes, rubbing a hand across her ear, as though a pulsing ache is battering her eardrums, then swallows down both pills without any water.

✶ ✸ ✶

The sun settles low on the horizon, turning the air cool in the shadow of the cave.

Cricket folds herself into a small coil, like a woodland animal tucked into the leaves and dirt, and she sleeps. Deep and twitching. Mumbling from time to time.

I hope it's just exhaustion, and not something else.

"We need supplies," Noah says, still standing at the entrance to the cave, turning over the unknown silver object in his hand—something he does when he's thinking, considering, making a plan. We fled the barn with nothing, no food, no way to carry water, no blankets. He runs a hand through his short, dark hair, then turns to looks at me. Again there is something in his gaze—like he doesn't know what to make of me. Like he doesn't trust me, not yet. His temples pull tight, jaw tensed. "I'm going to hike up the far ridge, see what's over there." He nods at the steep, uneven ridgeline across the river.

"I'll go with you." I move to the edge of the cave, hunger swelling in my stomach, needing something to eat. But also—not wanting him to go alone. To risk being separated.

But his eyes swing back to Cricket, a small form in the dark of the cave. "No, stay with Cricket." He turns, peering down at the river, his eyes reflecting a cool bottle-green in the waning light. A softness in him I haven't seen until now. Maybe it's worry I see in the shape of his mouth—he's worried about Cricket, worried we don't have enough supplies to survive, worried that *I* might not be worth it. Any of it. But he settles his shoulders back, clenching his jaw, the softness gone. "If I don't return," he tells me, his breathing heavy, "don't come after me."

I lift both eyebrows. "What if those men find us?"

"Then run. Get into the river if you have to. It'll carry you out of the ravine, and almost all the way to Mill City."

I hesitate, anxiety threading though my chest. But when he looks at me, there is strength in them, resolve, and I take some of it for myself. He looks at me like he knows I'm stronger than I might seem. That I'm capable of taking care of myself. And at last I nod, because he needs to know that I'll do it—that I won't go looking for him. That Cricket and I will leave without him, if it comes to that. I'll make sure she's safe. That I'm safe. But then what? Will we make our way back to the barn eventually? Look for August? Time is running out. But before I can tell him any of this, Noah has turned away, and I watch as he makes his way down to the river, a dark silhouette in the wet, rain-soaked trees, picking a path easily over rocks, then up the far side of the ravine.

And I hope that he'll—I need him to—come back.

* ✳ *

Hours pass. The sky turns dull again, the sun falling to the west, and the walls of the ravine cast long shadows over the river and the cave before the sun has fully set. The air becomes dark, cold. Bitter, teeth-clenching cold.

I pace along the opening to the cave, watching the far side of the river for Noah to appear through the trees. But he doesn't return.

How long do we wait?

My nerves bounce along my thoughts—imagining all the things

that might have happened to him. He could be hurt, injured in the trees on the far side. Or he could have come across Theorists or even scavengers. My mind won't settle, won't stop conjuring up reasons I need to cross over the river and look for him. This boy I hardly know.

I pull the postcard from my pocket, tracing the shape of the tall, glittering tower with my fingertip, *Paris. La Tour Eiffel*, and I think of Mom, of the cabin, the valley. Wishing she was here. Wishing I was safe back in my bed, just for a night, listening to the river outside my window and the stalks of corn in the garden swaying in the wind.

I long for something familiar.

Anything.

But then Cricket's eyes flutter open and she moans, a pain still inside her, eyes glancing around the cave. "Where's Noah?" she asks, voice thick with sleep.

I slide the postcard quickly back into my pocket, out of sight. "He went up the far ridge to look for supplies."

Cricket turns on her side, face pinching as she pushes herself up to sitting. "How long's he been gone?" She looks pale, chilled, and I retrieve the old, burnt blanket at the back of the cave, shaking out pine needles, dead leaves, and a small orange beetle that falls to the cave floor, then skitters away back into the dark. "Here," I say, folding it over her. It smells like ash, like rot, but she doesn't argue. I'm surprised by how unwell she seems—I wonder if she felt this bad when I met her at the saloon, but she's been hiding it? Or if maybe it's getting worse, a thing that's come on quick. Something that's taken root now, and she won't be able to shake.

"He's been gone all day," I tell her, looking back to the river, reflecting silvery white in the moonlight.

"I'm guessing he told you not to go after him?" She shakes her head, not expecting me to answer, because she already knows. "No point looking for him anyway. We'll be too slow. Better to wait here."

But I don't want to wait. *We need to keep moving.* Yet, Cricket still looks too weak—she needs more rest. And I can't carry her. We'll wait another hour, maybe two. "I can start a fire," I say. Mom taught me to build fires with a smooth rock and a stick split down the middle. I can even use the charcoal remnants from the last campfire that was burned here.

But Cricket frowns. "We can't risk the flames being seen."

So we wait in the dark of the cave, watching the river, the far side of the ravine, for a shadow slinking down through the trees. For Noah to return.

Cricket asks for more pills, and I give her two. She falls asleep beside me, head on the hard ground. With my index finger, I trace the constellation on my neck into the ash near the old campfire. It comforts me, the dark straight lines, each star cluster. The mark of an Astronomer.

I lie on my back next to Cricket, staring up through the pines. Tova and Llitha are just visible above the treetops, twin stars that started it all. But they've shifted a little to the south since I first saw them. They're moving away. Not long now until they'll be gone, swung wide on their orbit, away from us. To the north lies the dark half of the sky—a black patch empty of stars, where light cannot exist.

It's the shadow, Mom would say, gesturing with her palm to the place where there are no constellations to memorize or name. No nebulas or Milky Way. Only darkness and nothing else.

167

I let my eyes sink closed, not wanting to count the stars, not wanting to think about what's been lost or what comes next. I rest my head against the hard ground of the cave, my rib aching a little— but not nearly as bad as it was—feeling the cold night air against my face, and listening to Cricket's fevered, restless dreams.

* ✳ *

Someone is in the cave with us.

A shadow grows long across the walls; a boot steps beside my ear. I turn my head, slowly, eyes scanning the dark—afraid to move, afraid to make a sound.

But when the shadow comes into view, and my eyes adjust, I see: it's Noah.

"Tried not to wake you," he whispers.

I push myself up, relief swelling in my chest. I had thought the worst, feared he wouldn't come back, and seeing him standing a few feet away, I resist the urge to reach out and touch him to be sure he's real. Not just a dream. Beside me, Cricket is still passed out, sunk into a deep, wincing sleep. "You were gone a long time."

He nods softly. "Found an abandoned house up on the other side. Grabbed what I could." He holds up a crudely made metal canteen for carrying water, dented on one side, and a bit of rope, too short to be useful. He didn't find much.

"Did you see anyone over there?" I ask.

He kneels down beside the unlit campfire, only a few feet from me, mouth cut into a sharp line. "No one." Then his eyes lift, and I can see the exhaustion, a burden he carries that he doesn't want me to see. But there is even more in his bone-weary eyes: a hint of who he really is, a gentleness he tries to keep hidden. Yet, it's there all the same. A boy who knows sadness as well as danger. Who perhaps has even known love, who has touched another and felt himself sinking into the comfort of their arms. Who has whispered words in the coldest hours of night and placed his lips on the soft places of someone he's afraid to lose. He is a boy who looks at me unlike I've ever known, like *I* am the riddle, not him. Like I am something to be unwound like a spool of thread—something he both fears and longs to be closer to, to peer beneath my skin and see the starlight etched onto my bones. I swallow, and at last he says gently, "Get some sleep. The sun will be up soon, and we'll need to keep moving."

Still, he won't take his eyes away from mine, and for a moment I think he's going to say something else, his lips parted just a little. But the air between us feels too thin, like it's about to break, and I pull my gaze away, crossing my arms over my chest.

Noah stands and walks to the edge of the cave, looking out into the dark. I lie beside Cricket, folded beneath the burnt blanket while her breathing is a rasp in my ear, but I watch Noah. Wishing I understood. Wishing I knew the secrets he keeps, wishing I knew what waits for us out in the dark.

When sleep finally pulls me under, I dream of the market, of running down the streets under a revolving night sky that spins and jolts above me, until everything splinters apart—the stars erupting, turning dark, until a great shadow sinks down from above and swallows me up.

My eyes flash open, and Noah is touching my shoulder, knelt over me, face only a few inches from mine. "Bad dream," he says, like he already knows. Like he's no stranger to them.

The morning sun is casting warm cords of light into the cave, and sweat beads across my forehead. Cricket is already awake—apparently feeling better—and she's seated in front of the old campfire, poking at it with a short stick. "We have to go back," she's saying. "See if anyone is still alive."

"No." Noah releases his hand from me, and stands up, shaking his head.

I've woken up in the middle of an argument already underway.

"We can't leave August behind," she retorts.

Noah walks out of the cave, several paces down the rocks, as if he is going to the river, but then he stops, turning the circular object in his hand—the one I still haven't gotten a good look at. "August is dead."

Cricket drops the stick into the coals, sending a puff of ash up into the air.

No, no, I think, quickly pushing myself up. *He has to be wrong.*

"You don't know that," Cricket says for the both of us.

Noah slides the object back into his pocket, his gaze dipped to his feet. "I saw him."

I feel my brows puckering together, and I stand up. "You're sure?" I ask, my chest starting to rattle, an unnamable weight sinking over me. *If August is dead, then this was all for nothing. I'll never reach the sea, I'll never do what I was meant to, and I won't save anyone.* I scrape my fingers back through my knotted hair, tugging against my scalp.

"Those men broke into the barn right after you made it through the wall. They shot him clean in the chest—" Noah swallows tightly, cutting his eyes away from Cricket and me, a wetness gathering at his eyelids. "I ran to him, but he was already gone." A long exhale leaves his lips.

"No." Cricket's voice sounds like a whimper, her breathing shallow, and for a moment I want to reach out and touch her shoulder, but I sense that I shouldn't. None of this would have happened if they hadn't brought me to the barn—those men came looking for *me*, and August died because of it. *This is my fault.* And now that August is dead . . .

It's all over.

It's too late.

Cricket turns away, but I can hear the soft exhale of tears streaming down her cheeks, and she places the heels of her hands against her eyes as if she could quell the surge.

I feel myself sink to the ground—the hollowness of my heart dropping into my empty stomach, the ache in the very center of my bones making it hard to breathe. *It's over.* The sister stars will arch farther and farther to the south, day by day, and soon they will blink out completely. I've come all this way, burned my house in the valley to the ground, and for what? *I failed.* Every Astronomer before me, who stayed in the valley, who marked their skin—they sacrificed themselves. For this. For me. So I could finally reach the sea. And now . . . it's over.

All of it, for nothing.

I want to cry, a deep, unearthing sob, but my body is too weak, too dehydrated, and I only feel the weight behind my eyes, the pulsing pain.

I did this . . . I ruined everything, and now—

"We have to go on our own, without him—" Noah says firmly, swallowing down his own grief, stealing himself against the pain. But I can see the dampness at the edge of his eyes, a quiver at his temples. "We have to finish this. We don't have a choice."

My thoughts are broken by his words, cutting down to bone. "What?"

"We keep going," he continues, as if it were obvious, his eyes flicking to me briefly, a cool taciturn green, before they fall to Cricket. "We can't stop now."

My lips tremble. "You know the way to the sea?" The sun shivers higher through the trees, warming my skin, but I'm shaking now, confusion and doubt pushing down every vein.

"Maybe we do have a choice," Cricket interrupts before Noah can answer me. She drops her hands from her face, and I can see the slope of her mouth, the awful, grimacing frown, and the idea forming behind her eyes. "We could let those men take her." Her voice is hoarse, low, like she doesn't want me to hear even though I'm only a few yards away. "That's what they want, Noah—they just want her. And they'll stop hunting us." She points a finger at me, but won't turn her head in my direction. I'm not worth her cutting stare, not after what's happened—not now that she knows August is dead, and it's all my fault. *She wants me to pay for what's happened.* She helped me escape the saloon, kept me alive as we crossed the desert plains to the water tower, and she came with me to the barn. But now I suspect she regrets it all. And although her words race up my spine, sending needles of fear along my skin, I also don't blame her. I understand her anger, her fury—I blame myself too.

Still, I push myself up to my feet and take a step back into the cave, away from them both.

Noah moves closer to her, a hardness in his eyes, and he stares down at her, daring her to look away. "You don't have to come with us," he says bluntly. "You can go back to the barn, back to the water tower if you want. But I'm staying with her."

I blink at him, a deep, broken part of me surprised that he still wants to help me—after everything.

"Why?" Cricket lifts a hand in the air, her mouth turned down in disbelief.

But Noah's jaw sets in place, letting his gaze slip over me, like he's trying to remember the reasons, trying to recall why he won't just hand me over to those men. "You know why," he says to her, breathing deep through his nose, a thousand hidden thoughts behind his eyes.

"You're going to get yourself killed."

His mouth stays flat, formless, as if her words mean nothing, unimportant. As if death is not the worst thing waiting for us out there.

A fattened bee swerves past my shoulder, doubled wings slow and lazy, searching for pollen it won't find in the cave, before it veers away up into the sky. "Do you know where it is?" I risk to ask, stepping out from the shadow of the cave. "Do you know how to get to the sea?" I direct my eyes on Noah, but it's Cricket who answers.

"Of course he does," she snaps, giving me a cutting look. "Now that August is dead . . ." Her voice falters, then finds itself again. ". . . Noah is the last Architect."

The blood in my ears begins to thunder like a storm, sparks of lightning breaking across my eyes. I suck in a shaky breath, and watch as Noah reaches into his dark coat and pulls something out. Something that just barely catches the moonlight.

The silver signet ring. *August's ring.*

It hangs from the chain around his neck.

He had kept it hidden, maybe because he didn't want Cricket to see, because the ring means that August is truly dead—taken from around his lifeless neck. And now he tucks it back beneath his coat, against his chest—as if it's right where it belongs. Where it was always destined to be, eventually. But his eyes falter a moment, like the weight of the ring is greater than its actual size.

The duty and responsibility it brings.

It's no simple thing to take over the role that's been handed to you, that's been passed down for generations. The weight heavier each time. *I would know.*

But now: Noah is the last Architect.

Mom always said that if the Architect died, there would be another to take his place—someone who would know the *way*. To the edge of everything. And now . . . my eyes scrape over to Noah, feeling as if my mind is a storm of stars, reconfiguring, settling into a whole new pattern—*Noah is the Architect*—but he won't look at me. A heaviness in his shaded eyes. A hundred years of waiting in them. He looks raw, vulnerable—*different*. A boy splintered by grief, then reassembled with the sliding of a ring around his neck.

August's life, his purpose, held in the palm of Noah's hand.

He is the last one. Just like me.

I want to speak, say something to him to ease whatever he feels, but all the words are tangled up in my chest like a bird's nest destroyed by the wind.

Cricket paces to one side of the cave, bringing her hands behind her neck, looking down the ravine to the river. "If she's really her," Cricket says now, speaking only to Noah, "if she's the last Astronomer, it won't just be the Theorists looking for her, it'll be everyone."

She drops her arms, eyes unblinking. "She's dangerous, Noah. If word gets out that the Astronomer has really been found, just being with her puts our lives at risk. Are you willing to die for her?" She says *her* like I am not even worth the word.

Noah breathes, and I suddenly feel afraid, my ears starting to ring, the breath becoming short and quick in my lungs—maybe he will think she's right, that I'm not worth dying for. Maybe it's not duty he feels but doubt.

This is the fear that Mom spoke about on nights when she couldn't sleep, when she watched the ridge above the river for signs of someone coming. She was terrified that someday we'd be found. I never truly understood the panic she felt—the sharpness at the back of the neck when you know you're being hunted. But now I do.

I clear my throat, and Cricket's eyes drag over to me. "Death is coming for all of us—" I say, keeping my voice level, a sureness in each word. "Sooner for some, if we don't reach the sea . . ." I need them to know, to understand that there's no turning back now. If Noah can take me to the sea, I can't allow him to give up. *I need him.* And in ways he doesn't yet understand, he also needs me.

Cricket snorts, blowing out a gust of air. Like she doesn't believe me . . . and doesn't want to.

But Noah's eyes flatten, deep and fervent, his head tilting, jaw tensed, like he's trying to see the truth in my face. See if he trusts me. It reminds me of the *need* I saw in the faces of those crowded around me at the saloon. But there is no fear in my gut when Noah looks at me; the *need* in his gaze is different, tenuous, near breaking, like he wants to step closer, fold his fingers through mine, tightly, desperately, like he won't ever let go. But he keeps himself planted where he stands.

Still, it sends a shiver, knife-sharp, down to my tailbone.

"I won't leave her," he says to Cricket, his eyes still on me. "I've spent most of my life waiting for her—" He blinks, mouth parted, caught on a thought, then breathes before continuing. "August said there was nothing more important than this, than protecting the Astronomer . . ." He blinks. ". . . than protecting *her*. And if she asked me to, I would take her to the sea." His eyes are lit from within, jaw contracting in little pulses. "Is that what you want?" he asks, shadows strung across his face, lidded eyes and half-open mouth.

My body is trembling, the light through the trees seeming to sway outward. He's offering himself to me. He's giving me a choice. A promise. *A vow.* If I ask him to, he will stay with me until the end. And something in me wants to cry. *I'm no longer alone.* I have found the Architect, as Mom said I would, and I'm starting to believe—I need to believe—that we will make it to the sea. That we will get there in time, and we will survive. "Yes," I say, a lightness in my voice, suspended in my eyes.

Noah looks at me like he sees every thought strumming through me, like he understands what lies before us, but he feels the fullness of our story weaving itself together. He blinks once, twice, then nods back at me—like the pact has been made. And it can't be undone.

But Cricket shakes her head, eyebrows stuffed together, shadows beneath both her aqua eyes, like Noah has betrayed her in some way. Like she wants to grab him by the throat and drag him back to the barn, far away from me. "Dammit, Noah," she mutters.

At last he pulls eyes away from me to glance at Cricket. "It's what August wanted—" he says, then turns to walk back to the edge of the cave, the morning light winking through the trees across his determined face. "And you know it."

Cricket's mouth pinches flat, but there is a change in her eyes, in her tilted chin. "Fine," she answers brusquely. "But you'll need someone who's better with a knife than your clumsy ass." She flashes Noah a look.

Maybe because it's what August wanted, maybe because she won't leave Noah on his own, or maybe simply because she's stubborn . . . but she's staying with us.

"We should be able to reach Mill City by nightfall," she says, tapping a finger against her sheathed knife. "If we leave now."

✳ ✳ ✳

We follow the river downstream, moving quickly, keeping to the shadows cast over us by the steep ravine walls and thick trees. Noah plucks berries from the thorn-covered bushes as we pass, then hands them back to Cricket and me. "Crowberries," he says, not slowing his pace. He knows we need to keep moving, put more miles between us and those men.

But I'm so hungry, I nearly cry when the tart sweetness explodes between my teeth, tasting unlike anything I've ever had before. Near the roots of an upturned tree, Noah kneels down, quickly digging into the dark soil with his hands, then uses the knife sheathed at his ankle to cut away a deep red root.

"Wild carrot root," he says, handing me a thickly sliced piece. I bite into the knobby root—it's hard on the outside but soft in the middle, and has a sweet, earthy taste. I prefer it over the berries. Noah cuts out several more pieces, tucking them into his coat pocket for later, then glances up the river behind us, listening for men on horseback, for voices, but when he hears nothing, he falls into a steady stride beside me, letting Cricket march ahead—thrashing her way through a wall of reeds down to the river, creating a detour for a tracker to follow—to confuse them, and hopefully send them in the wrong direction. She's seemed stronger all morning; maybe the few hours of sleep has fortified her, or the pills have simply dulled the pain. And it'll wear off eventually.

"I know she seems tough," he says, nodding up to Cricket, who turns from the riverbank, back up to the trail. "But it's not that she doesn't want to help you—she's just afraid."

"Of what?" I slide my hands into my coat pockets, feeling the bottle of pills, wondering if I should have given her more before we set out. "Dying?" *Because of me.*

One side of his mouth twitches up. "If there's one thing she's not afraid of, it's dying."

Some distance ahead, Cricket climbs up the lower limbs of a dead tree, peering upriver to be sure we're going the right way, before dropping back to the ground and continuing on.

"Cricket's parents died of consumption when she was young," he says, voice settling into a low, unbreakable rhythm. "No one really wanted her—they worried she would die soon after, that she wasn't strong."

I shake my head, finding it hard to imagine anyone thinking Cricket was anything but sturdy and resilient and tough.

"She was only eight when she started living on her own, scavenging for food," Noah goes on. "She joined August's group from time to time, but she never stayed long—she always preferred to live alone. I think it's because she's afraid of getting too close, making a family she might lose." He swallows, looking ahead to where Cricket has wedged her way through two large boulders that must have fallen from the top of the ravine, nearly blocking the path, but leaving a slim, narrow channel just large enough to squeeze through. "But even when we don't see her for weeks, she always comes back to August's camp, usually with something she stole. And this time—" He looks at me, pauses, like he's trying to see something reflected back in my eyes. "She came back with you."

The wind slides up from the river, brushing through his dark hair, and he lifts one of his eyebrows at me—a sincere look of curiosity. Maybe he never thought he'd really find me, like I feared I wouldn't find him. Both of us hoping for something that seemed impossible. Both of us moving toward each other, like hands feeling into the dark, unsure of what we'd find.

I let my eyes fall over him: the heavy slope of his eyelids like peering into a forest of green, and the dark, sun-drenched hue of his skin. He seems so guarded, a toughness that has surely kept him alive. Yet I've caught glimpses of something else: sadness, but softness, too, cracks where the light peeks through his armor.

"We need to move faster!" Cricket calls back to us before ducking into a patch of thin elm trees, probably to create another diversion—a path to nowhere.

Noah picks up his pace, sidestepping around a spiky bitterbrush. "She's just scared of what will happen," he says softly so she won't hear. "She knows you're a risk."

And yet she's still here, I think. She hasn't turned back; she hasn't fled to those men and handed me over. If Noah is right, and she isn't afraid to die, then maybe it's him she doesn't want to lose—she's afraid for Noah's life, more than her own.

We move through a clot of tall cattail reeds, the same kind that grew back in the valley, and my fingers touch their soft stalks before letting them sway back into place. "Are you afraid?" I ask, squinting away from the sunlight that flashes through the giant trees.

"I'm scared shitless," he answers, lifting the corner of his mouth and skipping his eyes over to me, the same reticent warmth in his stare I noticed moments ago. The part of him he keeps tucked away beneath hard glances and steely eyes and a deep, commanding voice. He has the presence of someone who leads, who others will follow.

But I give him a quick smile, then look away. Because my mind is a mess of too many thoughts. Too little sleep. Too many reasons why we need to move faster.

The walls of the canyon begin to retreat, becoming shallow, and the path ahead rises up out of the ravine into a flatland, the river trailing away in the distance.

Cricket stops, a hand held over her eyes to survey the expansive terrain, heat rising in waves from the dry prairie. "Haven't heard anyone tracking us," she says. "No horses."

"They haven't given up," Noah answers, his voice sure, like he knows they won't just turn back—they'll follow us to the very edge of this land, until there's nowhere else to go and nowhere to hide. These men won't stop. He pulls out the circular thing from his pocket and holds it in his palm. For the first time, I see an arrow balanced in the center beneath a small round piece of glass. The arrow hovers, then turns slightly to our left. Then he places it quickly back into his pocket, like he doesn't want me to see.

But ahead of us lies a bleak stretch of prairie, no forest to travel through, nothing taller than bunchgrass and a few scattered heaps of dry brush. Beyond it, I can see a string of low, rolling hills. But it's a day's journey from here, at least. As soon as we step out from the cover of the few oaks along the riverbank, there's nowhere to hide.

"Which way is Mill City?" I ask.

"Straight ahead," Noah answers. *Straight into the open rangeland.*

He kneels down beside the river and fills the canteen. Then he runs his hands through his dark hair, letting the water stream over his face, down his neck. I don't let my eyes linger on him: flushed cheeks and unsaid thoughts. "The river turns west a half mile up, the opposite way we're headed," he says, water dripping from his lashes. "This is the last time we'll see water for a while."

Cricket bends down, splashing water onto her face, cooling her skin, and I do the same, sinking my arms in up to my elbows—goose bumps prickling my flesh. But I know it won't last. Soon we'll be out in the open, in the midday heat with no shade. Soon my skin will burn.

"Ready?" Noah asks, wiping the last of the water from his forehead.

Cricket brushes past him, away from the river and into the open—without a word, as if to prove her grit. To prove she's unafraid.

But my eyes flare with sparks, little prisms slicing through my vision. I squeeze them closed, pushing the flickering light down, forcing it away—hating the way it feels—and I follow Cricket out across the plains, with Noah behind me.

✳ ✳ ✳

It doesn't take long for regret to sink over me—to wish for the ravine and the cool river and the shade of elm trees.

The sun bakes my skin, makes dust of my throat. Sweat down my spine and cracked lips. It's worse than I thought it'd be—hotter and dustier, with a nipping wind at my back and the sun in my eyes, making waves of my vision.

Noah's eyes sweep across the parched, open landscape, watching for figures on horseback emerging through the heat, coming after us. I squint, trying to be watchful like him, but it's all searing heatwaves and blinding sunlight. I feel useless. I open my mouth to suggest we turn back, that we find another way, but only dry air leaves my throat. *No point wasting the words.* I know we can't go back. If those men are behind us, we have to keep moving forward.

Always forward.

Sweat streams into my eyes, and Noah hands me the canteen. I take a small sip, afraid we'll run out. Afraid to take more than my share.

The ground changes: Where it had been acres of brittle scrub brush in every direction, I can now make out the remnants of farmland, a great endless patchwork that once grew crops, but now is only sideways wind and cyclones of dust. I wonder if the dust came first, then drove the farmers away, or if they got sick with consumption and abandoned their farms, leaving the soil to wither under the relentless sun.

I try to keep pace with Cricket ahead of me, but her gait is longer than mine, more assured—like a thin-legged deer—and I start to feel light-headed, feet dragging. In the echo of my ears, I hear a wordless hissing, but it's only the wind growing louder.

"How much farther?" I manage, my voice a wobble against my eardrums, making loops in my stomach.

But if Noah or Cricket answers, I don't hear it. Only the wind now, a warm breeze always tugging at my neck. Coiling through my hair. Waves of heat cutting through my vision.

Time passes, the sun high above, burning, blistering, never slipping beyond the horizon. But I suspect the night will be cold and cruel, perhaps worse than the heat.

"There," I hear Cricket say.

I lift my eyes. They burn, stinging with each blink. I look for the outline of buildings, a town rising up from the scrubland. Rooflines and manmade angles. But there is nothing.

"There!" Cricket shouts, urgent this time. Perhaps she's seeing things, her eyes conjuring phantoms in the heat. "Run!" she screams, an echo across the desert floor. "We need to run!"

I swivel to face her, my legs weak, unbalanced, feet sinking into the sand. "What?" I say, wiping at my eyes.

"I said run!" She grabs me roughly by the shoulder. And then I *see*.

A wall of something, a broad swath of particles rising up into the sky.

"What is it?" I sputter through cracked lips, legs staggering, unable to orient myself. Cricket releases me, and I pivot my head up, gulping down the dry air, a cough at the back of my throat.

"Dust storm!" Noah says. His hands are on me now, fingers through mine, tugging, while my eyes continue to blink. "We have to move!" he yells.

Cricket is already running, a good distance away. And when I swivel to look behind me, I see the wall of dust—a plume of awful darkness churning across the barren farmland. I've never seen anything like it, and for a moment I feel mesmerized, watching it grow taller, wider, meaner. It's heading straight for us.

"Vega!" Noah shouts, his face a few inches from mine. "We have to run. Now!"

And then my legs are moving, pumping beneath me, dust rising up around my face, filling my lungs. I can't breathe, but I keep moving, the ground soft, my heart hammering. *Run, run*, my mind repeats, the only command, narrowed down to a single thought.

Beside me, Noah's eyes flash over to me.

But where are we going?

There's no escape out here. No shelter. The sky turns from chalky blue to brown, like Medicine Bow River after a storm, mud and silt clouding it over. Only seconds now, moments, until it reaches us. I suck in a breath—maybe the last one—and I clamp my eyelids closed.

The wall of dust slams into our backs. A force that yanks me free of Noah's grasp, our fingers separating, and nearly drops me to the ground.

Shit, I think. It's too late.

I lose sight of Cricket; of Noah, who had been right beside me. I lose all sense of direction, of my own hands, my own feet beneath me. I try to touch my face, to clear my eyes of dust, but it's useless—there's too much wind and dirt. It's everywhere. In my ears. My nostrils. I feel like I'm suffocating.

I try to yell for Noah—he had been right there—but only a cough comes out. I need water. I need the river.

I'll turn back, I think. I'll return to the ravine and the river. *No,* my mind screams. *That's too far. Hours behind us now.*

My hands slash the air in front of me, hoping to see some outline, some feature, of the land ahead of me. But my legs give out and I drop to my knees, wheezing, coughing. *Choking.*

Too much dust.

The sun is gone, blotted out by the thick, brown cloud. Only darkness now.

I can't see where I am, can't see what happened to Cricket and Noah. I press my hands to my eyes—I'll wait it out, wait for it to end. I'll sit here, lay my head on the ground, and wait for it to pass. But fear weaves through my thoughts, blood pounding in my ears, so I recite the names of stars in my head: *Bellatrix, Alhena, Caster, and Pollux.* I imagine their formation, their placement in the sky. I count the constellations, number them. I let their patterns become the only thought in my mind.

I lose myself in them.

I disappear.

But then, without warning, through the blur of sand and wind . . . a hand touches my shoulder. It yanks me upward.

A voice in my ear, steady, firm. *Noah.*

"This way," he says. "Stay close."

Relief spikes in my chest, and his hand slips through mine—a tether I refuse to lose again. My legs take a few staggering steps until I find my balance. I still can't see, but Noah squeezes my palm and pulls me with him, as if he knows where he's going. Two phantoms pushing through the wall of dust.

Something appears ahead of us.

My feet collide with a series of wooden steps, and we're moving up them, onto a porch. Cricket is there, ahead of us, her fist pounding against a door. She's shouting, pleading.

The door swings open and we stumble inside.

The howling of the wind becomes dull, quiet.

I'm on a floor, Noah beside me. Cricket a couple of feet away. We cough, heave up deep exhales of dust, lungs burning with it.

"Don't move," someone says. I try to push back, thinking the order to stay put is a hostile one. But then there is a cup in front of my face, and water against my lips. "Drink," the voice says.

I gulp it down greedily, desperately, choking on it. And then there is water streaming over my eyes onto the floor, washing away the layer of dust.

"Shouldn't have been out in that," the voice says. A man's voice—gravelly, hoarse. "Could have killed you all."

Beside me, Noah pushes himself up, then reaches a hand down to me.

Cricket is already in a chair, coughing, eyes pinched closed.

"I'll bring more water," the man says.

I try to see, to focus on where we are, the features of the house around me, but my eyes burn each time I blink. Like gravel caught beneath my eyelids.

We're in a stranger's house.

And I worry we've just fled one danger and staggered into another.

Time passes—maybe I fell asleep. Noah and I are on a couch now, heads lolled back, breathing, *breathing*.

I hear footsteps across the floor; then another cup with water is placed in my hands. I drink, then give it to Noah, his hands clasped briefly around mine. Familiar.

"Eat," the man says, a voice moving around us that slips in and out. A bowl of something is set on my lap.

I touch the spoon; smell the dull scent. "Rice," I say to Noah. I eat from the bowl, several bites of the salted grain, then hand it to him.

"You can sleep here tonight," the man says.

I lift my chin, squinting, trying to make him out—this man who let us in out of the dust storm. "What time is it?" I ask.

"After dark."

How long have we been here? I think. *Hours?* Wasn't it daylight when we ran from the wall of dust, when Cricket led us to this house? Have I slept, passed out? *We've been here too long, wasted too much time.* We need to leave.

But the man starts a fire near us in a woodstove—I can hear the metal hinges of the iron door, the rustle of kindling, of a fire crackling and warming our faces. "Thank you," I say to him, the words like dirt under my tongue.

He makes a sound, an acknowledgment, and then his footsteps fade.

I hope this house we're in, this man, is truly helping us. That he isn't a man of another sort.

I try to push myself up while my eyes remain closed—too painful to open—but my head swims, ears throbbing, so I sink back down to the couch. I touch my hair, keeping it draped along my neck.

Whatever happens, I need to keep the tattoo covered. If he doesn't see it, then he won't have reason to question who I am.

✳ ✳ ✳

"Vega." Noah's voice is in my dreams, in my skull. "Wake up."

I peel my eyelids back, the motion throbbing and painful, the grit not fully gone. "What's wrong?" I croak, dragging myself upright on the small, dusty couch. *I fell asleep again.*

Noah's standing over me, tall and broad, eyes flashing around the house. "We need to go," he hisses quietly.

I nod. Too many hours have passed—time we won't get back. "Where's the man who helped us?" I ask.

"Don't know." He shakes his head, eyes still scanning the dark interior of the house. "But I'd like to get out of here before he realizes we're awake." He walks to a chair beside the front door, where Cricket is slumped back, still asleep. I watch—my head still clotted and drowsy—as he touches Cricket's shoulder and her eyes bolt wide. She coughs, then buckles over, hands on her knees, eyes watering, tears hitting the wood floor beneath her—her eyes still caked in dust.

I struggle to push myself up from the couch, lungs wheezing with each breath, and I survey the tiny, single-story house: the kitchen is to our left, where a small porcelain vase of withered, dead flowers sits on the windowsill; the front door is to the right, framed by two windows; and at the back is a short hallway that must lead to a bedroom.

"He helped us," I whisper to Noah.

"And let's leave it at that, not give him reason to do anything else." Noah moves silently to one of the windows beside the front door, pulls back the cornflower-blue curtain—also coated in dust—and looks out.

"Morning," a voice says behind me.

I startle at the man's voice, the air sinking to my stomach. Noah drops the curtain and jerks around.

The man appears from the short hallway, a mug in his hand, steam rising up around his face. He's tall, slight, with an angled face and a flattened nose, like he was crushed at some point in his life. Most of the bones in his face broken.

"Didn't want to wake you all," he says, moving into the kitchen, swinging his hip awkwardly, gingerly—perhaps the same accident that flattened his features also injured the joints in his leg. "Got some coffee brewing, if you're interested."

Noah steps back into the living room, positioning himself between the man and me. "Think we'd better get going; we've burdened you long enough."

The man's gaze flutters a moment, like he understands the true meaning behind Noah's words: *We don't trust him, even after he helped us.*

"Dust storms have been getting worse lately," the man says, turning to the cast-iron pot of coffee and pouring more of the dark liquid into his mug. His eyes are sloped, soft, and there is a gentleness in them. But also something else—a twinge of nervousness. Like there's something he's hiding.

"It's been a while since I've been up this way," Noah replies, and I can hear the tightness in his words, like he's trying not to give anything away.

"Seems they come almost every week now. It rains less too." The man brings the mug to his mouth and takes a drink, the creases of his weatherworn face pulling together, nose like a bent piece of old wood.

I think of the rain that fell the night we arrived at the barn, the steady downpour. That was only a couple days' walk from here, and yet the storm never made it this far. The land has a way of changing quickly—moisture gets trapped against mountain peaks and never reaches the dusty territory beyond.

"Rarely see anyone crossing the plains this time of year, especially on foot." The man's face turns toward the front windows, but his eyes seem unable to focus, like he's just staring at the wall. "Gets pretty hot out there during the day."

Noah is quiet, and I wonder if he's considering how much he should say, how much to reveal to this man we don't know. "We're headed to Mill City," he says truthfully.

The man raises a quick eyebrow. "You don't want to be going that way." He sets his mug back on the counter, a seriousness in the line of his bent mouth.

"Why's that?" Cricket asks. She's seated upright in the chair now, but there's a pained look between her eyebrows, teeth mashed together—like her head is pounding again, ears ringing, and she's trying not to pass out or vomit. I touch the bottle of aspirin still in the pocket of my coat. Once we leave, I'll give her two more, enough to get her through the day. But I need to be careful, ration what I have left.

"Whole place is boarded up. Nothing left there anymore," the man says, eyes focused just beyond his coffee mug.

I see Noah's posture change, shoulders dropping, the scar on his temple drawing tight. "What happened?"

"Same as everywhere else." The man shakes his head. "Consumption swept through there. They quarantined the place, wouldn't let outsiders in. That was three months ago." He lifts the mug to his mouth but doesn't take a drink. "Now the place is deserted. Nothing for you that way."

190

Noah shifts uneasily, glances over at me. This isn't what he wanted to hear.

"You know someone in Mill City?" the man asks.

"No," Noah answers, looking to the door, then back to the man. "Was hoping to trade for a few horses, though."

A cough echoes through the house, and I snap my gaze to Cricket. But her eyes are just as wide, scanning the room for who might have made the sound. Noah backsteps toward me. "Is someone else in the house?" Noah asks, directing his stare at the man, his dark eyebrows cut close.

The man's expression dips, tensed at the corners of his mouth. "Just my wife, Della."

Cricket rises from the chair, her breathing suddenly heavy.

"Is she sick?" I ask.

The man blinks, clears his throat. "Yes."

Noah touches my arm, protective, eyes cutting over to the door, and starts pulling me back. "Time to go," he says, his breath warm against my ear.

"Wait," the man says, shifting his clouded gaze to me, stepping around the kitchen counter. "You don't have to leave just yet." But there is a slickness to his words, oily and hoarse all at once. A glint in his eyes I don't like, a serpent coiling around a thought, a motivation. There's something else he wants to say, and he taps his front teeth together, *tap tap*, before finally uttering, "I saw the mark." His teeth fall still, and he nods to me, his gray, thick eyebrows pulled together. "On your neck while you were asleep."

My lungs stop pulling in air.

Noah's arm flexes, still holding on to me, and his expression hardens—like he's preparing for a fight. "Move toward the door, Vega," he hisses.

"Please," the man insists, stepping closer, a hand held toward me. "Are you her?"

I feel my mouth dip open, my heart a hammer, clapping, *clapping* against my ribs.

"The old stories say the Astronomer knows how to stop the illness, how to save us."

My fingers start to tremble. "I'm sorry, I—" But my voice stops short.

"Cricket," Noah says now, not even needing to look at her. But I catch sight of her moving to the door, touching the handle. She's quick, reactive, even when pain mars every feature of her face.

"You could help us—" the man pleads, and I don't like the way his voice sounds, strained, clawing up from some grave place inside his chest. The place where desperation grows. *Rots.* Until it's all that's left. Becoming the most inhuman part of you.

"She can't help you," Noah answers, his hand squeezing me tighter—not about to let me go, not for anything.

"But she knows something," the man counters, eyelids peeled back too wide. Lower jaw pushed out. *He's thinking of grabbing me, reaching out and yanking me from Noah's hands.*

Another cough echoes from the hallway—his wife gasping for breath.

"The Theorists were right," he says now, teeth clamped down. "The Astronomer is still alive—" His breathing turns quick, abrasive. "And you're her, aren't you?" He says it with certainty, a thing he needs to believe, and he starts moving toward us.

Noah folds his arm around me and pushes me behind him—putting himself between the man and me while we backstep toward the door.

"Go," he says urgently to Cricket.

She pulls the door wide and slips outside, the wind howling through the doorway.

But there is a heaviness in my chest, meeting the old man's unblinking, uncaged eyes. The desperation is rimmed by something else: loss and pain. Just like the people who strode up to Pa's wagon, grief tucked in their eyes. This man is searching for the same thing: any last remnant of hope. Anything I can give.

I touch Noah's hand against my arm, looking into his eyes. "It's okay," I whisper, then slide free of his grasp.

"Vega," he says, reaching for me again and shaking his head.

I smile up at him softly. "Trust me." I squeeze his hand, meeting his eyes, and he lets me go.

The air around me softens, a humming quality against my ears, and I can feel Noah's eyes on me, the breath held in his lungs as he watches me cross the room.

"If your wife is sick, then she's in pain," I say to the man, reaching into my coat pocket and finding the bottle. The man's expression is fixed, like he might reach forward and rip my hand from my arm just to get at the bottle—to get at me. But slowly I open the cap and shake out a handful of pills, half a dozen at least, then reach forward to grasp the man's hand—calloused and rough—and place the pills gently in his palm. "To ease her discomfort," I say, offering him a tiny smile. "They won't cure her, but they'll dull the pain."

The man's eyes are like a serpent, flicking from me to his open hand. And I see the flecks in them, the spots of black—like he, too, might be sick with consumption. He brings his other hand to his palm, struggling to locate the pills—eyelids squinting—feeling each one, then rolling them against his palm. *He's lost most of his sight,* I realize. But not all of it, since he was still able to see the mark on my neck. "Thank you," he manages, and his voice sounds level again, the fevered thoughts, the panic, subsiding.

"I wish I could offer more," I say, knowing it won't be long until he's just as sick as his wife.

I place the bottle back into my pocket, my ears crackling, and walk to Noah's side. He looks at me, mouth tense, then lets out a deep breath, as if he's been holding it in since I slipped from his grasp.

The wind howls through the open door, and Cricket is already standing on the front porch, leaning against the railing, waiting for us.

"If you're her," the man says before I can slip out the doorway, "you can save us all." He coughs once, clears his throat, then says louder, "We're dying. And soon they'll be no one left."

I look back at him, my heart aching, and part of me wants to tell him the truth: that I *am* her. Give him some small, dying ember of hope. But if those men come asking about us, he might tell them that the Astronomer stayed in his house. It's not worth the risk. So I only offer a tight smile. "Keep your wife alive as long as you can," I say. Because time is slipping like sand through cracks in rotted wood, and it might already be too late for him, and his wife. For everyone.

I give him one last look—knowing we can't waste another minute more in this house, in this dry, dusty landscape—and Noah wraps his hand through mine, pulling me out into the dawn light.

GEMINI, Beta Gem
+28° 01' 34"

The sickness was only getting worse.

Season after season, settlers lost their eyesight, their hearing, and more graves were dug in untilled soil, in pastures where cattle once roamed, on the outer edges of towns.

Even the first Astronomer was not immune: she heard the low *hiss* in her ears and felt the burning rush behind her retinas.

She woke each evening and walked out onto her simple porch—feeling the sickness inside her, cells splitting apart—and she stared up at the sky. She could offer no remedy or relief to dull the pain in others, or herself.

All she had now were the stars.

She lay on her back in the tall meadow grass behind her house, listening to the crickets wail their sad, lonesome tune, while she blinked up at the sky and wondered what was there.

She wondered . . . what she had missed.

SIX

"You shouldn't have done that," Noah says, once we're a good distance from the lone house. "He could have grabbed you, hurt you."

I breathe, letting my eyes stray to the hard lines of Noah's face, tension cut into the space between his eyes. "But he didn't," I answer. And I suspect Noah never would have let that man hurt me. He would have been at my side in an instant if the man reached for me; he would have protected me no matter what. I sense it now more than ever. That Noah will do whatever it takes to keep me safe, to get me to the sea.

No turning back.

Still, he grumbles under his breath, clenching his jaw—not liking the risk I took. But I couldn't let that man and his wife suffer. Even if he knew who I was.

"We need to find water, a creek, somewhere we can bathe," Cricket says, glancing back at us. Dust still clings to our clothes, our eyelashes, packed inside our ears.

"There's a lake to the east of here," Noah replies.

I lift both eyebrows. "We're not going to Mill City?"

"Hell no," Cricket answers. "We ain't going near that place."

We walk for a full day under the monstrous sun, burning our necks, the tops of our skulls, until the land begins to change. At first, a few trees rise up around us, and then the ground becomes hard-packed like clay, then a stubble of green. Little white flowers poke their heads up through the soil, and we move into a series of low hills crisscrossed by dry creek beds, the water long ago soaked into the thirsty ground.

We follow one of these channels down into a gravel wash, among tall fir trees.

And then, at last it appears: a lake.

Cricket strips out of her clothes down to her underwear, unabashed that we can see her dark, perfect skin, muscles like ropes, arms just as strong as any boy. She wades out into the lake, then sinks below the water line. Even her hair vanishes.

A few feet away, Noah kicks out of his boots and pulls his shirt over his head. For the first time, I see that the tattoos covering his arms trail all the way up to his chest and back, blotting out nearly every inch of his skin. He scrapes a hand along his neck, rubbing at the sore muscles; then his eyes sway to me, and I snap my focus away—embarrassed to be caught staring.

"I have a few more than you," he says with a half smirk.

"What?" I don't want to look at him, so I keep my eyes settled firmly on the water, where Cricket has emerged and is swimming out toward the center of the lake, arms casting perfect crescent strokes over her head.

"Tattoos," he answers. "Although mine won't cause a rebellion."

Rebellion, I think. Is that what will happen if those men find me?

Is that what's already happening? How long will it take before word spreads among the towns, rumors that the Astronomer has been seen inside a saloon in Fort Bell? And soon enough, everyone will be looking for me, and there will be nowhere I'm safe. Except out here, under the cover of the stars, in this unfamiliar, unmapped stretch of wilderness.

I allow my gaze to settle back on him, on the broad outline of his shoulders, his inked chest, the chain with the silver signet ring around his neck. Most of his tattoos are nondescript, lines and arched shapes cut across his skin in solid black. "I had a friend once, who I grew up with," he says, rubbing a hand over his shoulder, over the ink. "And we would mark our bodies."

With my eyes, I trace the dark lines along his shoulder blades, ink spreading over the muscles of his back and down his spine. My heart hitches. "Why?" I ask, the word cracking a little.

He releases his hand from his shoulder. "It was a sign of our brotherhood, that we were banded together. And that we would die for each other."

"Where is he now? Your friend?" I ask, easing myself onto a rock, and begin unlacing my boots, but moving slowly—unsure if I want to strip out of my clothes in front of him—let him see the rest of me, feel his eyes on my bared, *bare* flesh.

His mouth pulls down, a quiet, unnamable sorrow in the curve of his eyes. "Dead."

I swallow tightly. "Was it the consumption?"

But he shakes his head, looking out at the lake.

I stand up and move closer to him. I want to touch his arm, his hand, offer some comfort—I know what it's like to lose someone—

but I'm also afraid to let my fingers rest against his warm skin. Afraid of what I'll feel stirring in the emptiness of my stomach. He scrapes a hand across his eyes, at the tears taking shape, and that's when I see it.

Something I hadn't noticed before . . . something I missed.

Hidden under the sleeves of his shirt.

Quickly I take a step back from him—my heart crashing up into my throat, my vision narrowed to pinpricks, to a single point. *He's one of them.*

Burned onto the inside of his forearm, into his flesh . . . is a starburst.

The brand of a Theorist.

I take another step back across the beach, through the sand, moving toward the tree line.

"You're one of them," I say, fighting to find the breath in my lungs, to steady my racing, cracking thoughts. "A Theorist." I flick my eyes out to Cricket, remembering the paper she showed me when we crossed the desert, the reward for anyone who has a tattoo like the one on my neck—for the Astronomer. And now I wonder, does she have the same mark as Noah? Something I've missed? Both of them branded as Theorists. Have they tricked me into coming this far with them—tricked me so that I would trust them?

My breathing turns quick and hot, panic welling up in my chest. *I need to run.* Again, my eyes dart to the trees, only a few paces away. I could vanish into the dark, make my way through the dense forest. I'll be fast, silent, and they won't catch me. I'll hide. I'll wait.

My eyes swivel back to Noah, sensing his movement, his hand reaching out for me, but I jerk back. "Don't touch me," I snap, taking several more steps toward the trees, my heart a club against my chest, my hands shaking, ready to fight him if I have to, ready to claw my way free.

But he pauses, deceitful eyes leveled on me, his own breathing quick.

"You lied," I sputter, backstepping away from him, swallowing down the hurt and pain and deceit. "You're a Theorist."

He breathes, keeping his gaze on me. "Yes," he admits. *The truth.* The awful, burning truth that tears me apart, splinters me into a thousand little pieces of broken bone and muscle. I wanted to believe he was good, that beneath the hard wall he had built, he was protecting me, keeping me safe. But I was wrong and I want to cry, I want to scream. To run.

I take another step back, more distance between us, and Noah blows out a long breath, turning his forearm so the scar catches in the moonlight—a perfect star at the center with rays of scarred skin branching outward. He runs his thumb over it. "I'm not proud of it," he says coolly, eyes half-lidded and dark. "I wish I could undo it."

My lungs tighten and I want to recoil, but my eyes are focused on the brand. A mark I should have seen, should have noticed before now. But his tattoos wind around it, through it, blurring its edges. Making it harder to spot.

He is quiet a moment, remembering . . . and then his eyes lift back to me, shoulders relaxed, like he wants me to see that he's not a threat. That none of it is what I think it is. "My friend's name was Wells, and he didn't die of the sickness—he was a Theorist too." He shakes his head, as if the memory is still razor-sharp. "He tried to leave, escape the group . . . and he was killed." He places his palm over the mark on his forearm, like he can still feel the heat burning his flesh, the memory right at the surface, just as painful as the day it was branded into him.

"You were escaping together?" I ask, my chest still coiled tight like a rope near breaking.

He winces, then lowers his forearm so I can no longer see the brand. "Yes," he says, barely getting the word out.

"Why?" I need to see the truth in his eyes—I need to believe him. My legs fidgeting beneath me, still ready to run, my lungs drawing in short bursts of air, while my mind tries to slow my thoughts.

Darkness rims his eyes, the burden of too many things inside him. Words he's never said aloud. "Theorists will do anything to get what they want," he says. "And they only wanted one thing." His dangerous, sorrow-scorched eyes lift, squared on me, a subtle twitch in his shoulders. "They wanted you. The Astronomer."

My vision sways a little, my heart pressing, pounding, against my ribs.

"They'd kill anyone to get to you," he continues. "Anyone who they thought might know something. They didn't care who died. They were cruel and inhuman, even when they claimed they were looking for a cure, a way to save everyone. But they weren't saving a single person—they were killing." I feel desperate to say something, a feeling in my throat like I'm holding back all the night sky, and yet not a single word forms. My thoughts too tangled up.

"We couldn't watch anyone else die," he continues. "Couldn't help them murder innocent people." His expression falls to the ground, and I can't deny the sadness I see in the weary slant of his eyes. "I knew I couldn't stay. I couldn't let Holt—" His voice breaks off again, then re-forms, a firmness to his words now. "We thought we could sneak away after dark and we wouldn't be seen. We were camped outside a farming town called Lohaw, and we tried to leave on foot, but one of the men on night watch spotted us." He breathes, like he's trying to keep the memory from overtaking him. "He shot Wells first. It happened so fast, I barely heard it. And he just dropped to the ground. Just—" Noah pinches his eyes shut, a twitch in his hands, and it takes a moment before he looks at me again. "I managed to get the rifle free before he could fire another shot . . . but then Holt was there—" He looks away, out to the flat, blue lake, tears alight in his eyes, the long-buried pain and fury finding him. He crosses his arms over his chest, as if he's suddenly cold. "I had a knife and we fought, Holt tried to stop me, but I—" A part of me wants to tell him that he doesn't need to finish, but I need to hear it all. I need to believe him. "I dug the knife along his throat. . . . I tried to kill him." He shakes his head, then grates both hands behind his skull before letting his arms fall back to his sides. "I got away into the trees. But Wells was dead, and I thought maybe Holt was too. I didn't even look back—" His shoulders flinch, just barely, but I catch it. And I know, I sense, he's leaving something out, something he doesn't want to say. Maybe only because it hurts too bad. Or maybe it's something else.

"I want to believe you," I say, because I do, more than anything. "But I don't know how."

Noah's eyes are weighted against mine, like there is a new, raw hurt inside his rib cage. "I can't prove any of it," he says, tears starting to wet the edges of his eyelids, emotion caught on each word, and he lifts his arm so I can see the brand—the mark he can't erase. "But this is not who I am." He swallows, unblinking. "It never was, not really. And now I'm a traitor. If they found me, they'd kill me." His eyebrows tug down, mouth parted only a little—the place where he hides all his sadness. All his hurt. His mouth that I want to touch for reasons I don't understand, his face that I'm not sure I can trust.

If he's lying, if he betrays me, if he leads me to the sea and then reveals who he truly is, if he hands me over to those men—then it will all be for nothing.

"Vega," he says, and my name sounds like desperation on his lips, like need and forgiveness and a part of him that just might break. "Please." The hurt reaches his eyes, watering at the edges, pain tucked into the shape of his mouth. It's *me* who's causing him pain. *Me*. Because he needs me to believe him. Needs me to not slip away into the trees and leave.

Because he needs me as much as I need him.

We are bound to each other, whether I trust him or not. I won't reach the sea without him. He's leaving something out in his story, some part he won't say. But for now, I have to trust that there is more truth in his words than lies.

"You made a promise to August," I remind him. "To protect me, to bring me to the sea."

His gaze doesn't break from mine, and I let myself stare back at the dangerous, uncommon green of his eyes, tracing the form of his mouth.

"Will you keep that promise?" I ask, my body still tensed, chin lifted, observing every flicker and twitch of his eyelashes, looking for any hint of a mistruth.

His jaw hardens, but his eyes are still soft, damp, fearful even— afraid I'll slip away. His mouth falls open. "Yes. I will get you to the sea, no matter what it takes. I promise."

My shoulders begin to relax. A settling in my rib cage. I want to fight it, resist, but I can see the honesty in his eyes—mostly—and we each have our own secrets, mine monstrous and bottomless. And likely far more dangerous. I can't leave him now. I exhale the breath I had been holding in, my hands unclenching. "I trust you," I say, my voice almost breaking, and it feels like my own promise. An agreement between us. A pact. We will reach the sea, together. Or maybe not at all.

He is my map, my way there. I need him.

For now, I will trust him.

A moment passes, I step closer to Noah, and my mind reorganizes itself, spins forward and back. Recalling the story he told, of escaping the Theorists, and the name he said, the man who he fought. "Holt is their leader?" I ask.

Noah's eyes flick to the lake, prisms of light dancing across the surface of the water under the late-afternoon sun. "Yes."

I think of the man who took Odie back at the miners' cabin. The scar cut lengthwise along his throat, how he stared back at me when I pointed the rifle at his chest—like he was used to getting what he wanted and he wouldn't be dying that day. Not by my bullet. "Does he have two different-colored eyes?"

Noah flinches—a look of unease sweeping over him as he turns back to face me—and he nods.

"I met him," I say. "He stole Pa's horse, and all his tonic." *I could have killed him,* I think. I had a chance to take his life, but I didn't.

"If you met him," Noah says, "then you're lucky you're still alive."

I feel a crackling, indescribable ache in my ears, like the rubbing together of two autumn leaves. And when I look into the star-flecked, impossible galaxy of Noah's eyes, I see only the boy I need him to be. Not the Theorist brand on his skin. But a boy who has come this far with me, who feels more like a cool summer breeze in the valley than a dagger against my throat.

His mouth parts, eyes damp, and he says, "There's nothing I wouldn't do to keep you safe." He breathes, like the words are a firestorm inside him, burning his throat. "I won't let anyone hurt you, not even Holt. They'll have to kill me first."

The air feels trapped in my ribs like a lost bird.

I bend forward and pull off my boots, feeling the warm sand against the soles of my feet—while Noah's eyes watch me. If I'm going to trust him, I have to show him who I am.

He was wrong when he said he has more tattoos than me.

I can see he's about to speak, his eyes caught on the tattoo weaving its way across my right foot, out to my big toe, but I shrug out of my coat, letting it fall to the ground, then pull my shirt over my head. His eyes widen even more—but not because I've bared more of my skin—it's the black trail of ink that his eyes are following. I stand up and unbutton my canvas pants, letting them slip down my legs to the sand, where I step free of them. Standing in only my underwear.

I lift my gaze to Noah, letting him look at me, letting his eyes trail across the marks making patterns along my soft flesh. Because the tattoo he has seen on my neck is only the beginning—only the first mark that Mom inked into my skin.

My tattoo is not a single constellation; it's many, woven together like a wandering vine in the garden.

The first point of starlight begins at the nape of my neck, where it spirals out to several other stars, then weaves down my spine, across the left side of my ribs like it's tiptoeing along each crescent bone. It widens across my hip, a starburst of several suns, and then it meanders across my stomach just below my navel, where it begins its zigzag path down my right thigh, across my kneecap, over my shin to my ankle. Finally ending on my right foot, at the end of my pinkie toe.

An interwoven network of stars and constellations.

My entire body is braided with ink.

The only person who has ever seen it in its entirety was Mom—the one who branded it. But now I allow Noah's eyes to trace every curve and line. The only break, where it passes under my soft cotton bra and the fabric of my underwear.

I trust him, I think, I tell myself. *I need to.*

He told me the story of being branded by the Theorists, of escaping with only his life. And now . . . I show him a part of me that no one has seen. And I feel both raw—with his eyes grating over my flesh—and also a strange quiet, a settling in the deep cavity of my chest.

If I trust him, then he needs to trust me too.

"What is it?" he asks, voice hardly more than a whisper.

"It's many constellations, woven into one."

He swallows, like he's having a hard time tracking his own thoughts. Like maybe it's not just the tattoo that's a distraction but something else. The nearly naked girl standing only a few feet from him.

I dig my toes into the sand, and finally he clicks his eyes away from me, like he can't bear it anymore. Like his head is screaming against his heart. And I feel both relief and a hollow unmooring. As if his gaze was holding me up, and now he's left me teetering.

"I'm sorry about August," I say at last, the first time I've apologized for what happened back at the barn.

He nods slowly, thoughtfully, touching the silver chain around his neck, the signet ring against his chest that once belonged to August. And I want to tell him that I know what it feels like to have your heart split wide in a way that you're certain will never heal. But instead I cross the space dividing us, and stand beside him, silent—our hands so close, they almost touch—looking out at the lake. The Architect and the Astronomer.

Side by side.

Just as we were always meant to be. Both of us marked by our pasts. *His* brand makes him a target, a traitor. While mine makes me someone others would kill to find.

We are both bound by a future handed to us.

I listen to the sound of his breathing, the slow in and out, and he reminds me of the river back in the valley. Cold, violent at times, breaking apart rock and soil and anything in its path. But beneath the surface, there is calm, a gentleness that can only be seen if you're willing to risk drowning.

He is familiar in ways I can't explain.

And I know, I will follow him to the sea. To the edge of everything. I will follow him anywhere.

Out at the lake, Cricket flops onto her back, floating on the surface, arms wide, staring up at the big blue skyline. "You guys coming in?" she shouts, her thumping skull momentarily forgotten.

Noah's hand drifts closer to mine, his fingers grazing my skin, stalling there. Warm flesh to warm flesh. I hold my breath, the feeling inside me too massive to contain. Fathomless and terrifying. His fingers slide through mine, slow, careful, and my eyelids flutter closed. I want to look at him, stare into his eyes and see what's waiting there. But I'm afraid. I'm afraid I'll shatter like a star made of too-thin glass.

"Hurry up!" Cricket shouts.

I draw in a breath; I open my eyes.

Noah is looking at me, and I nod, swallowing down the stone in my chest, not wanting him to let me go. And he doesn't. His fingers squeeze mine, a soft, glimmering light in his eyes, and he pulls me down toward the shore. We wade into the water, up to our knees, our waists, until he finally releases my hand as he slips into the deep.

I do the same, sinking below the surface, feeling the cold wrap itself over me, ridding my skin of a layer of filth. And when I come back up, Cricket is still on her back, near the middle of the lake, staring up at the sky.

But Noah is only a few feet away, his mouth just above the water line, eyelashes dotted with drops of lake water.

He watches me, a cool, clement stare, and I feel light-headed. The water brings us closer, drifting, and I want to touch him again. But it's his hand that leaves the surface, his fingers that lift to my chin, the soft place behind my ear. My eyelids blink; my lips draw in air. My skin shivers. His fingertips slide around to the back of my neck, tracing the lines of my tattoo, as if he's making a map, bread crumbs he will be able to follow later. A way back.

To my skin, to me.

Air sputters from my lungs, and his fingers graze around to my throat, my lips, wiping away the lake water. Something unspools inside me, my thoughts stripped away . . . a feeling that almost hurts. Wishing he would come closer.

Wanting his eyes to never look away.

And for a single half second, I see a pain in his eyes—as if waves were stirring in the deepest part of his chest, an ache at the top of his solar plexus—just like I feel in mine.

His mouth parts a little, like he's going to speak, words hanging on his tongue.

But the uncertain weight in my chest is too much, the questions too many. *What about the secrets we both keep? What about Cricket?* Has he loved her in this way? Deep and dizzying. Has he touched her and made maps of her golden skin? Is she watching us now?

I swallow down the knot in my throat, and I turn away, slipping from beneath his fingers.

It hurts. Looking away from him, severing the feeling of his hand on me.

But I dip my head beneath the surface, feeling the cold against my skull, my too-warm skin . . .

And I swim back to shore.

We build a fire. A small one, up in the trees overlooking the lake, out of sight. We don't want to be spotted, but we also can't eat our dinner raw—a glistening fish that Noah speared at the far side of the lake where the water was deep and dark.

He places the fish on a pronged elm stick in the middle of the fire to cook, while Cricket and I sit side by side, warming ourselves beside the flames, our hair still dripping with lake water. She looks pale, worse than an hour ago, and I can see the pain hiding beneath her sallow skin when she blinks, when she presses a palm to her ear. And I'm starting to wonder how much farther she can travel.

"You should take another pill," I tell her.

But she shakes her head, bending closer to the fire, shivering. She doesn't want to admit what's happening to her body, that something is wrong. She reaches for the knife at her waist, touching the blade to her thumb to test its sharpness. I watch her, unsure what she's doing, but then she brings the blade to the side of her head, and using her other hand as a guide, she begins scraping the blade along the shaved side of her scalp. The hair has started to grow long, and she wants to shear it close again. But her fingers tremble as the blade slides close to her ear, and she almost drops it.

I stand up, fearing she's going to cut herself, and touch her shaking hands. "I'll do it."

She makes a muttering sound, like she's going to protest, but she must know she's too weak to wield the blade, and maybe she doesn't have the strength to argue, so she lets me take the knife, her hands sinking helplessly to her lap. It's strange seeing her like this, every exhale a tremor in her lungs, all her toughness gone, as if she is only a shell now, all her insides scraped out.

Carefully I begin gliding the blade across her scalp, watching the dark hairs come away, flitting through the air like pollen in spring.

"They might have lost our tracks in that dust storm," Cricket says softly, her eyes focused on the fire, sparks leaping out into the sand. I wonder if she's thinking about turning back, the pain in her skull enough to make her second-guess her decision to come with us. "We haven't seen any sign of them."

"It probably slowed them down," Noah answers, sliding more scraps of wood onto the campfire, hands unfazed by the heat. "But if they have a good tracker, a dust storm won't be enough to lose us."

Cricket falls quiet, and Noah's eyes watch me for a time, the slow movement of my hands across Cricket's scalp, the firelight sparking along the blade. A smile ghosts across his lips, there and then gone.

When I've cleaned away the last of the stray hairs, one side of her scalp cut clean, she lets out a sigh. "Shave the rest."

I lift the knife away, staring down at her. "Are you sure?"

She nods. "It's all knotted anyway—it'll be easier without it."

My eyes cut over to Noah, his mouth flat, tensed—I'm unsure if I should do it, if it's really what she wants, or if it's just the exhaustion talking. But Noah exhales, looking up at me, and nods gently.

It feels like a letting go, like a sacrifice to once-worshipped star gods. I slide the blade across the uncut side of her skull, peeling away the long, beautiful black layers of her hair. I watch them drift to the ground, feeling like I want to cry. Like some part of me knows that this has meaning greater than this moment. A tenderness in it, a ritual, that my hands have found themselves anointing.

She breathes, her posture relaxes, and Noah sits on the far side of the fire, elbows resting against his bent knees, watching us—a quiet, mournful glint in his eyes. And at last, with the fire snapping and sparking, I scrape away the last of her hair against the nape of her neck, the strands smelling like campfire smoke, until there is only a pile at my feet.

"It's done," I say, and she runs both her palms over her shorn head, pale and a little red from the blade.

"Good," she answers, bending to gather up the long strands

from the sand around her feet. On shaking legs, she pushes herself up, and makes her way down to the shore, bare feet dragging across the sand. Noah and I watch her, her silhouette wading in up to her shins and then stopping to peer across the lake, before she lets the long lengths of her hair fall from her fingertips. Some catch in the wind, lifting up to the sky, carried toward the trees; the rest scatter across the calm water. An offering. A surrender, maybe. And it feels like goodbye—to the old us. Who we were before we all found one another.

And I get the sense, Cricket won't ever turn back. She won't abandon us or hand me over to those men. She'll stay until the end.

Until there's nothing left of her.

Bare scalp and raw feet and gasping lungs.

It's the three of us now, for as long as possible.

We eat the fish cooked over the flames, picking around the tiny bones, and then Cricket falls into a fitful sleep. Feet twitching, breathing heavy and sputtering, like she's dreaming of the barn, of wriggling through the wood slats while bullets screamed past us. Or maybe it's the dust storm that plagues her sleeping mind, the memory of wind and sand biting at our skin.

She needs rest—for longer than just one night—but I also know she won't take my advice. If she wakes up in the morning, if there's breath in her lungs, she'll want to keep moving.

Noah places more wood on the fire, and the tattoos on his arms look like serpents in the flickering light. Monsters with cruel eyes.

"Are you cold?" he asks me.

I shake my head, but in truth, the fire is barely enough to keep my skin from trembling. I wish we had brought the blanket from the cave, anything to keep out the night's chill. But Noah sinks onto the sand beside me, eyes focused on the fire.

"She's not well," I say, glancing to Cricket.

He nods knowingly.

"It's not good for her, sleeping outside like this."

"She's tough," he answers, but I can hear the doubt in his voice. He's worried. "And I don't think we could convince her to sleep anywhere else."

I smile only a little. "You're probably right."

Our small campfire shivers in a gust of wind blowing up off the lake, threatening to put it out completely. Noah rubs both hands over his eyes and yawns.

"You've hardly slept in days," I point out. "I can keep watch so you can sleep." I know we're running out of time—soon the twin stars will be out of sight—but he needs to rest. If we don't sleep, then we'll be too slow. Clumsy and more likely to make mistakes.

"I'm okay," he says, eyes skimming over me. Furtive, drowsy. I feel the knot inside my chest, the swimming in my solar plexus, like waves crashing against my rib cage—a feeling that's only growing worse.

A flock of bats darts out from the trees behind us, skimming over the calm surface of the lake, quick and precise, devouring the night insects. In the summer, we sometimes saw bats in the valley, but they'd vanish again when the air turned cold.

"Have you been this way before?" I ask. "To this lake?"

He shakes his head. "August was always too weak to make the journey, so he only told me the way." Noah slides his hand into his pocket and pulls out the circular thing. In the firelight, it looks like brass, and he places it flat on his palm, watching as the little arrow beneath the glass swivels to point out across the lake. "It's a compass," he explains for the first time. "August gave it to me the first night he recounted the way to the sea. I would follow it north until I reached the mountains, then turn east."

His eyes cast out to the water, where the last of the sunset reflects gold and amber against the surface, the air speckled with strange light. *The anomaly.*

Time is moving too quickly.

"Do you know what's at the sea?" I ask, curious how much August told him.

He closes his fingers over the compass. "August was careful about what he said—he knew there were those who would kill to know the things he did, to know the way to the sea. Telling me everything would put my life at risk."

I press my hands together, thinking of all the nights I sat with Mom and she made me recite the names of stars, then point to them in the night sky. If I got one wrong, she'd keep coming back to it, over and over, night after night, until it was burned into my memory. She made sure I knew the night sky as well as I knew the valley. She made sure I knew what our ancestors gave, what was at stake.

But maybe Noah's right, and *knowing* is the worst part. The heaviest stones to carry.

He knows the way to the sea. That's all.

But I know the rest. The stories and sacrifice and the death. And it tears at my thoughts, cutting me apart. This story was born into my flesh.

Noah's shoulders draw down, the black marks of his tattoos

peeking above the collar of his shirt. I sink back on the sand beside him, hands on my stomach, staring up at the clear geography of stars. A sudden rupture of light tears across the sky, spearing the upper atmosphere and peeling away the dark before it burns up just above the tree line. A falling star, cutting across the darkest part of the sky—the place where no stars shimmer from the depth of the universe, a swath of black filling up half the horizon. Always there. "People used to make wishes on falling stars," I say. "They believed it brought luck. They even wrote songs about it."

Noah follows my gaze, his breathing low, relaxed. "Did it work? Did their wishes come true?"

"Doubt it. Otherwise we'd still cast our wishes up to the sky." I think about what I'd wish for now, the words I'd whisper to the stars, but I can't say them aloud. They are things I won't let myself feel. Things I can't allow myself to want. With Noah beside me, there is a roar in my chest, a riddle in the thump of my heartbeat I want to ignore but can't. So I bite the inside of my cheek, pushing the feeling away. "The Greeks believed the gods put the stars in the sky," I go on. "Each one is meant to be a lesson, a warning of mistakes made. Like Orion, who was killed by Artemis, who he loved. Or Princess Callisto, who was accidentally killed by her son, then became Ursa Major, the cursed bear. Or the constellation Corvus—the crow— in honor of the princess Coronis, who slept with a mortal warrior, betraying Apollo, so he had her killed."

Noah lifts an eyebrow. "The gods sure did a lot of killing."

"It was a dangerous time to befriend a god," I admit with a smirk. "You were likely to end up dead and immortalized in the night sky."

A smile steals across his lips, and his eyes relax at the corners, looking more gray than green in the darkness. With his gaze still on me, he asks, "What else do you see in the sky?" His voice is so quiet, it feels like summer air against my skin. Like an exhale.

"I see my own stories," I admit, letting myself smile a little. Liking the feeling of his eyes on me, the comfort they bring, as if I am lost in a dream. And I never want to wake.

"What kind of stories?"

"About the past," I tell him, pulling in my bottom lip, deciding what to say, how much I should reveal. "About the first Astronomer— the stories told by my ancestors, and the story I'm living now."

His face relaxes even more, a small crease forming between his dark eyebrows. "You think of your life as a story?"

"Every life is a story." I breathe, filling my lungs with the dry night air. "And our story will belong to someone else someday. They will tell it, write it down, maybe even name stars after us."

Light finds its way into his eyes, and he exhales. Like my words have nested a feeling of calm in his chest, his eyelids heavy.

I turn back to the sky, finding Tova and Llitha—the stars I don't point out to him. The ones I keep secret. But their alignment has shifted, inching away, night by night. I try to recall how many days it's been since they first appeared in the valley. How long have I been traveling? I've lost track of time; the hours we slept in the old man's house feel like a dream. It might have been a full day, a full night, or longer. I can't be sure.

But time is moving too quickly now.

"How many more days to the sea?" I ask.

He is still, and I wonder if he's fallen asleep, but when I tilt my gaze, his eyes are open, scanning the stars. "Two or three at most. We should be close."

I study his eyes, looking for what I saw in them when we floated in the lake. I look for something to hold on to, a sturdiness, an assurance that we will reach the sea in time. And when he turns to look back at me, I find it.

"I'll get you there," he says, voice deep. And his hand strays to mine again, barely touching, his chest rising with air, with determination. And I believe him.

The sand makes tiny indents into my flesh, and I count the constellations I can see, naming them silently. But the dark half of the sky has swallowed the rest—the atmosphere infused with a vibration, snapping and shivering, nearly imperceptible. *The anomaly always there.*

Something my ancestors—the Astronomers before me—could never identify.

Until Mom discovered what it was.

Until the night she pointed up at the sky and named it aloud, a shiver in her throat, full of excitement—the rush of knowing a thing that previously had been a mystery. *It's beautiful,* I thought then, briefly. The expanding darkness. A soft gleaming in our night skies.

But now, when I look up at it . . . I feel only fear.

✷ ✷ ✷

I stand on the shore, the lake a calm, placid blue eye, reflecting the starlight.

I told Noah to sleep, promising to wake him when Taurus dips below the horizon—signaling midnight—then he'd take the next shift until sunrise.

He fell asleep quickly, so exhausted that he could hardly keep his eyes open, and I watched him for a moment, his chest rising softly with each dreamlike breath, before I stood and walked down to the lake's edge.

I consider leaving them, stealing the compass Noah keeps in his pocket, and heading off on my own. Traveling north, like he said, then east when I reach mountains. I would be saving them—keeping them alive from the Theorists hunting me. I'd be saving myself from this feeling blooming inside me whenever Noah looks at me. But they've sacrificed too much for me to abandon them like that. And I can't leave *him*. The Architect was always meant to take me to the sea—it's in the stories Mom told. Already written.

He will take me to the edge of this land. The edge of everything. Together.

It can't be any other way.

I let my legs carry me along the shore, needing the cool air and the night sky to keep me awake—so I won't doze off beside the warmth of the fire, beside Noah.

A hush sings between the trees, frogs bellow from the shallow pools of water as I walk along the narrow shore, but there is also a crackle in my ears, a hum, and I wonder how long before I'll be just as sick as Cricket. Before it starts to peel apart my insides. Before it takes my hearing, my sight. Everything.

Time, time, crumbling away beneath me.

The twin stars are already drifting farther on the horizon, becoming less bright, their glow dulled.

I need to get to the sea before then—while there's still something left of me.

At the farthest end of the lake, where the beach starts to bend back around, I pause, looking up into the trees and the perimeter of oaks like a wall sheltering us from whatever lurks beyond.

I start to turn back, when the wind stirs, releasing the scent of pine and dead leaves, and also a voice.

A *voice*.

Distant and echoey, up beyond the tree line.

I swivel to look back across the lake, where I can still see our small campfire, and two bodies sleeping beside it. It's not Noah and Cricket I heard.

I tilt my gaze toward the trees, listening for the sound of horses' hooves thundering against the hard ground, their hot breath in the cold air. But there is only a voice. And then another.

Someone is camping nearby.

I move away from the lake, up into the dense oaks.

The campfire vanishes behind me, and so does the quiet lake, until I'm surrounded by only the cold shade of evergreens.

I know I should go back to camp, wake Noah and Cricket, tell them what I heard. But my legs don't slow, curiosity edging me deeper and deeper into the trees. It's likely only ranchers, travelers passing through these hills and bedding down for the night. *Nothing to fear*. No reason for us to pack up and leave.

Dry pine needles crunch underfoot and I slow my pace, not wanting to be heard. But the forest is dark, no moonlight peeking through the branches, and I stumble over a tangle of roots, cursing.

The voices grow louder—several of them—and I move up the ridgeline crowded with pines and hemlocks. There is laughter, too, late-evening chatter. The amber glow of a fire appears ahead—the flames much larger than our own back at the lake.

Through the trees, five distinct figures come into view. Five men—seated around a campfire.

Five horses tied to nearby trees.

I crouch down behind a thicket of saltbush, knees in the dirt. Their voices are deep, rolling up into the low branches and down the ridge to the lake where I first heard them. They're talking about tobacco, about a bullsnake that was found in one of their bedrolls the other morning. They laugh, several of them leaning close to the fire, while something cooks on a skillet over the flames.

They are eating, drinking from a shared canteen, telling stories. *Harmless enough.* I watch them a moment, careful not to make a sound. One of the men leans toward the fire, tossing a spent corncob onto the flames, and for the briefest of moments, the skin of his forearm catches in the firelight, and I see it: a starburst branded into his flesh, red and scarred. New—like it had just been burned into his skin within the last day or two.

I jerk my face back, dropping down behind the saltbush.

Them.

They're here, in the trees, not far from our camp. They found me.

I steady my breathing, the fear expanding in my chest, getting larger. *I need to get away from here.* But one of the men laughs, loud and forceful, and I snap my gaze back toward the campfire. Another man—with his back to me—shifts on the log where he's seated, tossing out a brown liquid in his cup toward the line of bushes—coffee maybe, the gritty dredges.

But for the briefest moment, his face comes into view, and it's *him.*

The man from the saloon with the silver-crow bolo tie, the man who stood over me at the miners' camp, who pointed his pistol at me and would have pulled the trigger if his boss—Holt—had given him the okay.

Samuel.

Shit. I shift my weight back, to slink away into the dark, into the trees—soft and quiet and unseen—but the adrenaline is swimming in my veins, my entire body a coil of nervous sparks. I take a step back, then another. I swear I don't hear my foot catch on the dead limb—only the feel of it cracking underfoot—but one of the horses, tied to a branch only a few yards away, snaps its head upward, eyes roving the tree line.

I pause, suck in a breath.

Shit.

Shit.

One of the men I don't recognize stands up, walks to the horse, and runs a hand down its neck. He turns in a circle, looking for the cause of the horse's nervousness.

My throat narrows on the fear. Tightens.

Then closes up completely when the man's eyes find me.

I scramble back.

Back back back.

Feet catching on the underbrush, lungs heaving in and out, but I push myself up. And I run. My heart crashes in my ears, screaming at me not to slow down.

Run!

The ground rises up to meet me, legs tearing through the pines, through the brush and briars that grab at my skin, cutting me open. But I don't feel any of it.

My hands tear through the trees, pulling me forward. I was stupid to come here. My ears are ringing now, but I can still hear the men behind me, their footsteps, their shouts of pursuit. There is a pressure in my chest, my body like a drum, pounding, adrenaline sparking behind my eyes.

I can see the lake now, the water gleaming through the trees. I reach the edge of the forest, the campfire burning low in the distance, Noah and Cricket still asleep.

I'm almost there.

My legs stumble, but I don't fall. I reach out for an oak, about to step into the open, onto the shore of the lake—but a hand seizes my shoulder, an arm around my throat, yanking me back.

I let out a scream, a deep, terrified shout, echoing into the tall, tall pines.

And then everything goes dark.

SEVEN

I wake in a room.

Shadowy at first, but streams of dusty morning light break through thin slats in the windows, between wood boards that have been nailed into place.

The bottle of aspirin is gone from my coat pocket, but the worthless postcard remains, and I touch the back of my skull, wincing, my hair clotted with dried blood. They hit me over the head with something hard, a rock, the blunt end of a gun, and knocked me unconscious.

Slowly I push myself up from the floor.

My head spins, throbs, and I reach out for a wide table near one end of the room. There are other tables too, smaller ones with chairs pushed beneath them, running the length of the rectangular room. At the other end is a door.

I move quickly, my balance tilting wrongly to one side, little eruptions of light behind my eyes. I reach the door, hands against the wood, searching for the knob, but it's been sheared off, gone. I throw my shoulder against the door, but it makes my head pulse and scream, and the door doesn't budge. Not even a little.

It's locked, or barred by something on the other side.

My breathing jagged, I turn back to face the room. There are no objects inside, nothing I could use to pry free any of the boards over the windows. Still, I stagger to the nearest window and wedge my fingers between two boards, trying to pull them loose, but they only creak, refusing to give way.

No way out.

I sink onto the floor beneath the window and close my eyes. The pounding in my skull making me feel like I might faint, the room scattered with tiny pin drops of light.

I shouldn't have left our camp beside the lake.

I shouldn't have gone into the trees.

I was reckless, stupid, and regret slams into my chest. A sinking, sickening feeling. Like rot gathering on wet wood. I wish I could take it back, but it's too late now.

* ✹ *

Hours pass. Perhaps a full day.

I sleep strangely, curled up behind the large table, hidden in case someone comes.

And someone does come.

When the slivered light through the windows is dull and pale—a sunrise or sunset, I can't be sure which—a heavy sound echoes from the other side of the door. A moment later, it swings open, and a man steps into the room, silhouetted by the pastel light breaking around him.

The sickening fear presses against my ribs—whatever comes next probably won't be good. These men have been chasing me for days, killed August and many others, and now they finally have me, captive, with nowhere to run.

I stand up slowly, eyes darting from the man to the door behind him, but I stay behind the table, a barrier between myself and him. Yet it's hardly anything at all.

His boots against the wood floor echo up the walls of the room as he strides toward me, metal spurs *clank*ing. But before he even reaches me, I know who he is: the scar running lengthwise across his throat—a slit I now know was made by Noah. A wound that surely once ran red with blood.

Holt.

My pulse is electric in my veins, and he stops at the other side of the table, eyes blinking strangely at me as he smooths a hand across his dark, slick hair. Everything in its place. Tidy. Unsoiled: his face clean-shaven, white shirt pressed, each button neatly stitched one above the next. At his waist, the notched belt with two holsters—but no guns. Maybe it's meant as a sign that he doesn't intend to hurt me.

Yet.

He blinks, the odd angle of light through the windows streaming over his eyes: one bright blue, the other an insipid gray, as if a storm cloud has blown over it, muting all color, all vision. I'm certain he's blind in that eye.

Sick with consumption.

"Do you know where you are?" he asks through bared teeth, a flatness in his eyes now that almost looks like disinterest. As if I have summoned *him* here, a prisoner who has interrupted his day.

I don't reply.

Slowly, leisurely, he walks to one of the smaller tables, tapping a hand against the wood surface as if he's bored. As if he's playing a game he already knows he'll win. And for a half second I think he might turn and walk back for the door, deciding I'm not worth his time, and slip out into the pale light without another word. But then, like one of the Horaces' cats, whose fickle minds dart from one thing to the next, his gaze snaps back to me. Eyes fluttering, watchful. It wasn't disinterest I saw in his stare; it was patience. A careful tiptoe, a fortitude—he's a man who will take his time, until he gets exactly what he needs. "This is a schoolhouse," he says, cool and calm, answering his own question, as if he were giving me a lesson. "Before this town was abandoned, teachers would stand at that desk where you are now and instruct their students on literature and mathematics, science, and even art." He leans a hip against the small table, the soft leather of his belt giving way. "My own father was a teacher, for a time," he says, a flatness to his voice, without emotion, without anything at all, and I don't know where he's going with this. Why he's telling me any of it. "He stood in rooms just like this one, lecturing about our history." His good eye shivers, an unconscious clicking in his jaw.

"You see . . . ," he says slowly, to be sure I'm listening, that I hear the next words that leave his tensed lips. "The past is remembered by those who were there in the beginning, who saw what happened—" His dead eye widens like a raven, intent, refusing to blink.

He waits a moment—like he thinks I might know what he's about to say next, like I'm going to speak—but then he rolls his thin, pale mouth to the side, growing impatient with my silence, teeth sawing at the back—a sound I remember from the miners' camp when he stared down the barrel of Pa's gun, his teeth grating together. He exhales through his nose, quick and blunt. "And *your* ancestors were there, weren't they?"

I feel my jaw go slack, a ticking in my chest. But I don't say a word.

The scar at his throat seems to stretch wide, pale and dully pink, and I can see the impatience growing in his eyes, a twitch at the edge of his mouth. It sends chills down my flesh, being in the same room with him, feeling his eyes on me with nowhere to run. Without a rifle between us. He knows he has the upper hand, yet he's taking his time making his point.

He doesn't like to lose control. *Always in control. Even of himself.*

"I know more than you realize," he says now, tapping a finger to his temple, eyes unblinking as the next words slide between his teeth like spit and tobacco. "I have spent most of my life hunting you, living out here, in the filth of these out-of-the-way towns, trying to find any rumor, any witness or old tale about the last Astronomer who vanished years ago." He pushes out his lower jaw, the sickening sound of grinding teeth echoing in my ears. "Dead or hiding, no one had seen her," he says as if it were a puzzle, pieces scattered across the landscape. "And I always thought she would be old and ragged and barely alive when I found her, a woman I could easily break, easily get what I wanted from. And yet . . ." He raises a pointed eyebrow, a ruthless, bitter-edged smile taking shape on his lips. "Here *you* are."

His eyes grate down the length of my body, from my chin to my toes, as if he were cutting me open with a blade, and I feel my skin shiver, hating the calculating sharpness of his stare. My heart starts beating too fast.

I should have killed him, I think, remembering the feel of my finger against the trigger, how close I was. How easily I could have squeezed it back and let the rifle explode in my hands. A simple thing. And he would have bled out on the ground at my feet, in front of the miners' cabin. But I also know, I might have found myself dead shortly after—shot by one of his loyal, branded men.

"You are what I've been waiting for," he adds, voice slicked and awful, words drowned out by the thudding fear in my veins, growing louder.

I sway a little, my throat closing up, the bruise at the back of my skull pounding, and I want to close my eyes, want to sink to the floor, but I grip the edge of the desk to keep myself upright and conscious.

Holt tilts his head, like he can see that I'm struggling to keep from collapsing, and he straightens himself up, walking slowly toward me—as if he's in no great hurry—then presses both palms against the table separating us, his gray eye shuttering.

Every muscle in my body tightens—being this close to him, only a couple of feet away, hearing the tapping of his finger on the table, the scent of horses and sweat on his skin, makes the nerves beneath my flesh writhe and twist. I am trapped, with nowhere to run.

"Now . . . ," he says, releasing his hands from the table, scraping his eyes down to my throat—the soft skin, the place where the air quivers inside me. "I'm told there's something on your neck."

On reflex, I take a quick step back, my heels hitting the wall behind me.

He smiles, liking that I'm afraid, and he touches his hair again, smoothing it back around his ears, making sure not a strand has slipped out of place. *Always in control.* "I won't hurt you," he says, but there is an oiliness to his words. An ease to his lies—something he's well practiced at. Skilled, deft. "I just need to *see*." His gray eye shivers, winks, as if it's reminding him that he won't see anything through its clouded center—worthless now—an eye merely taking up space within his skull.

He moves around the desk, slowly at first, but when he's close enough, he snaps forward and grab the back of my head with his hand, pinching my temples until I buckle over. I let out a pathetic cry, then swallow it down. I don't want to give him the satisfaction of my pain.

He brushes the hair away from my neck, gentle, careful—and it makes me shudder in disgust—before he peers down at the marks. I can hear the heaviness of his breath, the deep rasp of air—dust in the lungs, dust on everything. He makes a sound, a pleased growl. And finally, satisfied, he releases his hand from me and I jerk back, pressing myself into the corner of the room.

He brushes his palms together, as if I'm covered in dirt and have soiled his clean skin. "I suspect—" he begins, grinding his jaw again. A habit he can't control. "—that the mark doesn't end on your neck, but is much larger, traveling the length of your body."

I wince. Hating that he's guessed the truth, that he's imagining the marks weaving down my spine—something only Noah has seen.

Still, I don't reply. I refuse.

Deliberately he moves back around the broad table to the other side, as if giving me my space—calming the wild animal that he's caged—then taps a finger on the wood surface again. He's unnaturally calm, in his movements and each word he speaks, but I wonder if there is a storm beneath the surface, a torment within his own mind, struggling to keep control. To seem as if he has all things within his grasp, no point losing his temper, better to portray a sense of calculated steadiness. He stares pensively down at his hands, thinking, and I can just make out the brand on his forearm beneath his rolled-up shirt—the starburst. "Throughout history—" he starts, as if he's about to share something that's only just occurred to him. "—there have always been easy ways of doing things, and harder ways." His one sharp blue eye clicks to mine, while his dead eye quivers strangely, out of sync with the other. "Let me assure you, the harder ways always amount to more pain. But I have no interest in harming you, in torturing you, however—" He lifts his hand from the desk, again touching his hair, sliding it across his forehead. "I'm also well practiced at it. Artful, you might say. You will tell me the truth . . . one way or another, and it will either be between painful, unnecessary screams, or seated comfortably, as if we are old friends. And I'd like to think we can both behave like old friends, wouldn't you agree?" His voice is cool and menacing. A perfect, sinister balance of both. And I hate it.

I clench my teeth—seeing how this will go, hearing it in the practiced calm of his voice: He is a man who gets what he wants, who won't stop until he does. He's come this far, killed countless people, and he'll push this to the very edge, until I talk, or until I'm dead. And maybe either is fine with him.

So I nod. I give him something he wants. A hint of compliance. Obedience. And it tastes like bile on my tongue.

"Good," he answers, nodding. "That's good." He walks to one of the windows, flattening his oiled hair against his temple. "Now," he begins again, as if it were a fresh start. "Are you the last Astronomer?"

I swallow, fear scraping at my windpipe—telling me not to give him the truth—but I have to give him something. And this one thing feels so small. "Yes."

His head swivels to face me, startled by the sound of my voice for the first time, the word carried up to the pitched ceiling. "Which means your mother must be dead?"

I breathe, feeling the cold wall behind me. "Yes."

He nods, like he senses I'm telling the truth. And he likes the rhythm of it, the back and forth, victim and tormentor, question and answer. "I'm sorry to hear that," he says, and his genuine tone makes me feel sick. I don't want his sympathy—I want to lunge forward and press my fingers into his eyes, one blue, one gray—I want to cause him pain. And when he drops to the floor, I will run, break down the door, and escape. But instead I stay quiet, obedient. *For now.* "Do you know what your tattoo means?" he asks.

I feel my rapid pulse at my throat, my hands curving into fists at my side. "It's the mark of the Astronomer," I say, because he already knows who I am.

One corner of his mouth lifts, an eerie half smirk. "But that's not all, is it?"

I keep my eyes on him, tracking every movement, afraid he'll come closer again, that he'll want to see the rest of the tattoo. "If you think I have a cure to the consumption," I say, "I don't."

He steps to the side of the table, circling me like a coyote hunting a rabbit. I want to shove past him, try to escape, but I'm certain he has a knife tucked somewhere in his belt, or at his ankle. He wouldn't come in here completely unarmed. "I know you don't have a cure," he answers, one eyebrow raised, a curious twist at the edge of his mouth. As if he knows something he's not saying.

Confused, I feel my mouth tuck down. "But you're a Theorist . . . ," I say. The man I saw at the market in Mill City, ringing the bell, shouted that *the cure is near!* And August told me that the men hunting me believed I had a cure. It's always been about a cure.

Holt's shoulders settle. "I've always loved that name—*Theorist.*" He smirks, a cruel turn of his lips. "It could mean anything, couldn't it? Someone who theorizes, ponders the yet unknown." He shakes his head now, lips falling flat. "Some might believe the Astronomer is a cure, that *you* are a cure. But that's not exactly right, is it?"

I narrow my gaze at him, keeping my teeth clamped shut.

"You're something else." He pushes out his lower jaw, and I think he's going to reach out for me, grab my neck, but his hands only tremble at his sides—resisting. "If we're lucky, you just might be our salvation." He bites against the words, breathing, and tilts his head to one side like he's cracking his neck. "But we both know it comes with risks. . . . We both know you might fail."

The room teeters softly, a flare of light catching through the window slats and glinting across my eyes. I press my palms to the wall behind me, using it to hold myself up. *He's lying,* I think. *He doesn't know the truth.*

"This surprises you," he says with a sliver of satisfaction. "You thought I was mindlessly chasing you, in search of a cure—" He lets out a sharp laugh, then snaps his mouth closed. "I know the stories too. As well as you."

How? I wonder, but don't dare ask. Don't dare utter a word. Instead I keep my eyes steady on his, refusing to let him see how scared I am.

"We are not so different from each other," he says. "We've both lost people to the sickness." His teeth tapping again, his head craned to one side. "We both want the same thing."

"We're not the same," I spit, unable to keep it in, the blood roaring in my ears.

And he smiles, revealing a full row of teeth, some broken—shattered from the relentless grinding. But then his mouth cuts into a hard, cruel line, eyes hooded, and when he says the next words, they are bitten through clenched teeth. "We can choose a different ending," he says now. "You and I. We might not be able to save everyone else, but we can save ourselves." He flashes me a look, eyebrows raised, like he thinks I'll see that he's right. That together, we can rewrite what's already been done.

But I tuck my mouth into a line, breathing through my nostrils, feeling more fury than fear. "Fuck you."

He watches me a moment, studying the lines of my face, the anger cut into every crease and slope of my mouth, before he turns to one of the windows, peering out—even though I'm certain he can't see anything through the narrow slats. "I know your tattoo is a map . . . ," he says calmly, his tone swinging from merciless to patient with a quick flutter of his gray eye. Now, at last, he's getting to the point. "Can you decipher it?"

I close my eyes, then open them again, blinking through the sparks in my vision, trying to keep the room from tilting. But I don't answer him.

I let the silence fall across the room.

I press myself into the corner—I won't answer any more questions. I won't tell him about my tattoo. He'll have to kill me first.

After a long moment, he lifts a hand into the air, letting a thin shaft of sunlight illuminate his palm, nails trimmed short, scrubbed clean, then exhales through his nostrils. "Did you know we are evolved from apes?" he asks coolly, dropping his arm back to his side. "Most people don't realize this, and sometimes I wonder if we're no better than animals, fighting each other for food and land, anything we think we deserve. But do you know what *we* have that apes don't?" He swivels back around, sliding his jaw left to right, not waiting for me to answer. "Language—the ability to discuss, debate, to use words to avoid pain." He cracks his knuckles against his palms, breathing in, then blowing out a long, irritated exhale. "But if you refuse to use this marvel of evolution, then I will treat you like an animal instead."

He gives me one last weighing look, like he's considering what he's going to do next—what torture or method of pain will be most useful—before he turns, teeth locked shut, then strides toward the door. I'm startled, watching him walk away—wondering if he's really leaving me alone. Maybe this is part of the game: leaving me in the dark of this room to consider if my secrets are really worth keeping. If I'm willing to endure pain, to keep them. He's going to let time sink heavily over me, until my own thoughts start to crack with doubt.

But before he reaches the door, he stops, glancing back at me. "I remember you . . . little lady," he says, using the name he called me back at the miners' camp when I pointed the rifle at his forehead. "From that little cabin up in the hills. You were with the tonic man." He presses his hands together as if in prayer. "If I had known then who you were . . . I would have taken you instead of the horse." He smirks, nodding to himself, remembering how close he was that day. Only a few feet away. He even offered the choice to Pa: me or Odie. "I would have killed to get to you." *You have killed,* I think, remembering the bodies hung from ropes in Fort Bell, remembering the barn. The screams of those inside. A twitch puckers his upper lip, becoming a snarl. A darkness sinking over his eyes. "You're more valuable to me than anything else. And now that I have you . . . I'll kill to keep you."

His words land like a stone—I am a prize, something to be snared and caged. A thing to wield power over.

He presses his hair flat against the nape of his neck, then spins around, walking down the center of the schoolhouse, and when he reaches the door, it swings wide, as if someone outside had been waiting for him.

Without another word, he slips out into the faint, dusty light—becoming only a shadow.

The door slams shut, and I sink to the floor. Temples pulsing. Feeling like I might cry. Might vomit.

When he returns . . . I know pain will be coming with him.

✳ ✳ ✳

Dust spills in through cracks in the windows, making patterns on the floorboards.

Wind tears against the roof, clapping the wood shingles, and I wonder if it's another dust storm sweeping over the town, turning the sunlight a dirty gray.

I wake to the sound of latches being slid free, and the door swinging open. I scramble to my feet.

But no one enters. Instead something is pushed inside.

They've left me a plate of beans and a single wheat cake, along with a cup of water. Starving, I drop to the floor: the cake is gone in one bite, the water in a single gulp.

I know it's only a matter of time until Holt returns. He'll come back, and he won't be so nice.

Voices echo beyond the walls of the schoolhouse. Horses stamp their hooves for hay and grain. But no one comes to the door. Holt doesn't return.

And the waiting, the not knowing, is the worst part. Time stretches out as the sun makes slats of light across the schoolhouse floor, a rough measure of day and night. I keep the plate they gave me, tuck it behind the broad desk to use as a weapon, while a nervous ache grows in my chest. I feel like a bird trapped in a box: injured, frightened, knowing my captors have no intention of setting me free.

I lift my hand into the air, imagining the constellations spinning above me, tracing them on the ceiling of the schoolhouse: Orion with its jagged band of bright stars, Rigel glimmering a blue white, Betelgeuse glowing a fiery red—a luminous supergiant that one day will turn supernova.

I rest my head against the wall, the bruise still a pulsing heat at the back of my skull. I need to sleep, but I'm too afraid to close my eyes in case Holt returns. I think about Cricket and Noah—when they woke in the morning beside the lake, the fire burnt low, and found me gone—did they think I slipped away on purpose, heading out on my own? Did they think I left them behind? Or did Holt and his men discover our camp beside the lake—have Noah and Cricket been captured just like me?

Are we all trapped? And no one is coming to save us.

The door swings wide suddenly, bringing with it a gust of sand and ruby sunlight, and a shadowed figure steps into the room.

Holt is back.

He strides up the center of the schoolhouse, hands looped around his wide belt—just as before, there are no guns in his holsters. Yet I suspect he has other ways of inflicting pain . . . and even death.

Pale streaks of evening light pour through the slatted boards, and he walks to one of the windows, light ricocheting off his face, his scar, the milky hue of his one gray eye. "You've eaten?" he asks, speaking to the sunlight. "They brought you breakfast?"

It's a simple question, one without repercussions. So I say "yes" from my place behind the large wood desk—the only barricade I have. Letting him know that I'm willing to talk.

He cranes his head to me and grins, pleased. He thinks we're getting somewhere.

Gray eye twitching, he brushes a hand down his dark, oiled hair. "Most of the people in this town are dead," he says, flicking his eyes back to me, like he's about to tell me a bedtime story, a tale to help me sleep—about the sick and the blind and the dying. "The rest," he continues, "fled because of the consumption. And now it's abandoned, a relic, useless really. Unless you need a place to hide out, to lock someone up until you get answers."

I think about the dust storm, and the night we spent in the old man's house. He'd warned us about the nearby town, how it had been quarantined because of sickness.

"Is this Mill City?" I ask.

Holt's eyes light up. "It is." And he releases his hand from his scalp, looking relaxed, easy, like we are both swapping stories now.

The brand on his forearm is just visible beneath his shirtsleeve, and I nod to it, thinking of the same mark on Noah's skin.

"Do you make all your men get that?"

At first he looks confused, but then his eyes drop to the red, fleshy mark—a starburst that's been scorched into his arm. "It ensures their loyalty," he says, running his thumb over it. "Once they've been branded a Theorist, they can never be anything else."

Unless you're Noah. Unless you escape and become the Architect—someone who protects me, instead of hunts me. Does Holt even know that Noah is still alive—the young boy who escaped that night into the woods, who nearly killed Holt when he ran a knife along his throat?

His jaw seems to be chewing over something, and his eyes drag from the brand on his forearm back up to me. "They're loyal," he goes on, "because they know I'm trying to save them."

I want to laugh; I want to tell him that he's full of shit. He's not saving anyone. He's killing people. But I bite the inside of my cheek, stuffing the words down.

"I'm trying to save you, too," he adds, darkness sweeping over the already-shadowed lines of his face. "I doubt either of us want to die like this"—he touches the splotchy skin below his gray, dead eye—"waiting for the sickness to eat away at our organs, our eyes, until we're rotting in the ground like all the rest."

A coldness blooms in my chest, a shiver of something right at the cusp of my thoughts.

"I know you're heading to the sea," he says. Eyes sharp like barbed wire. "You're escaping, leaving all this sickness and death."

My ears start to ring—*crackle, crackle, hiss.* "I don't know what you mean."

"Cut the shit!" he barks, the scar across his throat shivering when he swallows—an awful sight—and I jerk back, startled. He's been so calm—eerily, unnaturally calm—but now his temper flares across his miscolored eyes, and it feels like something inside him is starting to crack. "We both know what I mean—" he adds, baring his teeth. "The fact that you're here, no longer hiding, must mean that those stars are in alignment. The ones the Astronomer has been waiting for."

He knows. The back of my skull throbs. *He knows too much.* But how? I want to run, I want to sprint toward the door and pound my fist against the wood, but I know it won't open. And there's nowhere to hide in this narrow room. So I stand my ground, holding down the terror, not wanting him to see how frightened I am.

He strides around the side of the desk that separates us, and I square my shoulders to his. I'm starting to think he's the kind of man who respects that: someone who's unafraid, who stuffs down their weakness. It's the cowards who find themselves at the wrong end of his anger. "And your map—that mark cut into your flesh—is going to take us there." His teeth grind over the words, turning them to dust.

Instinctively I want to touch my neck, feel the comfort they bring. But I keep my hands at my sides, curling them into fists to keep from shaking. Keep every part of me from rattling.

"You can help us, Vega." His gray eye shutters quickly before opening again. "Tell me where the map leads."

In my mind, I trace the length of my tattoo, following the curve down my neck to my torso, spreading in starburst constellations, until it winds along my stomach to my right thigh, making a wandering path to my shin and the top of my foot. Several constellations linked together. And if I peered up at the sky tonight, in this late spring season, I could follow those same constellations, track them.

And they would lead me straight toward the setting sun. "East," I tell him, a partial lie.

But his mouth curls, irritation glinting in his eyes—he's losing his patience. "You know that's not enough. I need to be able to navigate. I need to know every point in the sky." There is a twitch at his temple, eyes fluttering rhythmically, out of time with each other. *He's sick.* Dying. This is why he's so desperate—he thinks I can save him before death reaches up inside his chest and strangles the air in his lungs.

When I don't answer, his eyes click away from me, and in one swift motion, he unsheathes a knife from the back of his belt—a place where I couldn't see it—and pulls it free. He taps it at his side, a sudden power in his hand. And I *know*, the back and forth of our discussion is now over. "I tried to make this easy on you," he spits now, jaw thrust forward. "We could have worked together." He lifts the knife so the blade is pointed at my chest, only an inch from my skin.

I shift uncomfortably, one hand pressed to the corner of the desk. I think about Noah, the blade he held to Holt's throat. I think about how close we each came to killing him. But failed.

My fingers twitch, eyes narrow.

The plate I hid is at my feet, tucked under the desk—I just need to bend down and grab it, swing it against his skull, and if I hit him hard enough, maybe he'll drop to the ground, knocked unconscious. *But then what?* I'll take the knife, use it to pry back the boards on the windows. Or I could threaten whoever is on the other side of the door, tell them that I'll kill Holt if they don't let me out. I'll use him as leverage. I'll get outside, and then I'll run.

"We all have roles here," he says, tapping the end of the knife against my chest. "Do you know what my role is, my talent?"

I meet his eyes but don't speak. My mind is thinking only of the plate—so close. I just need to reach for it, then stand back up and strike him in the skull. Hard.

"I know how to hunt people," he continues. "And get what I want." He lifts the blade toward my face, the tip of my nose. "And I've been hunting you for a very long time."

A sound stirs outside, shuffling footsteps, and Holt looks toward the door at the far end of the schoolhouse. *This is my chance.* I drop to the floor, reach for the plate—I have a good hold on it, firm, steady, and I rise back up—ready to swing it wide and strike Holt at his temple . . . when there is pain in my chest. A white-hot sharpness.

Holt has swung his gaze back to me and is shoving me away from the desk, one hand around my throat, while the knife is pressed to my chest bone—blood weeping to the surface.

I drop the plate and it clatters to the floor. *Shit.* Holt slams my head against the wall, a hard crack, and then the knife is at my throat, right where my heartbeat quivers in my veins. "Not sure what you intended to do with that." His voice is guttural, all the pleasantries gone from it. "But I see you're more than just a girl with a tattoo—you're willing to fight for what you want, and that's good. That's important."

He presses the knife harder, and I feel the warmth of blood dripping down my throat to my chest. He's broken through my skin. I suck in a breath. *Breathe, breathe. It's only a little blood. Not enough to kill me. Keep breathing.*

"Tell me how to read the map," he demands.

I exhale out through my nostrils, hot, terrified, but I stare into his one dead eye, refusing to answer.

He slides the blade higher, up to my chin. "Are you willing to die for it?" he asks. "Are you willing to bleed out on the floor like a gutted hog?"

I clench my jaw and lower my eyes on him. "You won't kill me," I say. "I'm the only one with the map. You need me."

His teeth tap together, then grind with a force that makes me wince. "Smart girl," he says, his face so close to mine that I can smell the oil in his slicked hair, the scent of tobacco and sweat on his sickly skin. He lowers the knife, and I pull in a quick breath before his hand grips my throat and yanks me back, forcing me to turn so my face is crushed against the wall. I don't know what he's going to do, but then I feel the cold blade of the knife again, making trails down the back of my neck, down my spine. The place where Noah touched my flesh with his fingertips in the lake. "But I could peel your skin back and cut out the marking." He says, an awful wetness to his words, like his mouth is hung open. "Maybe you'll die, bleed out. But if you survive, I suspect you'll start talking." He grates the blade up to my hairline, as if marking the path he will take, how much flesh he will remove. "And if you die, at least I'll have the constellation. And I'll find someone else to interpret it."

"There is no one else," I choke, swallowing hard, my voice barely audible. "I'm the only one, the last one." The blood is warm, still spilling down to my chest.

Holt digs the knife into my neck, and I realize he's going to do it—he's going to cut out my tattoo. "Tell me how to read it," he says one last time, his breath like fire against my ear.

My eyes stray past Holt's head to the open door behind him— *the open door*—where a layer of red evening sky is now visible, before

I flick my gaze back. "No," I say with hate in my throat, a sudden courage spiking behind my eyes. Because *he's* found me. "I'll never tell you, you piece of shit."

Air leaves Holt's lungs, a shuddering exhale—shocked by my defiance, shocked by something else. The whites of his eyes expand. The knife drops from his hand to the floor with a clatter. He releases his hold on me, pivoting around.

I swallow, *swallow*, touching my throat with my palms and gasping for air, trying to keep from collapsing to the floor.

And when I look up . . . Noah is standing on the other side of Holt, a knife thrust into Holt's side.

He found me.

The room vibrates, everything shaking back into focus, a slow, shimmering staccato as I draw in another breath.

Only a foot away, Noah shoves Holt back, against the wall where I had been pinned, and the knife in his hand drives in deeper, just below Holt's ribs.

I blink; I let out a trembling exhale.

But Holt is strangely silent, mouth hung open, soundless, while his eyes bore holes through Noah. A quiet fury. *The boy who almost killed him all those years ago.* The boy who is a traitor.

Noah presses the knife in deeper, his stare fixed on Holt, as if seeing his past in Holt's eyes, anger and fury mixed with something else, something I don't understand. "I should have done this long ago," Noah hisses.

Air escapes Holt's lips. "Traitor," he mutters. "You . . ." Blood drips from his mouth, stains his teeth, eyes turned huge and manic, staring back at Noah. ". . . betray me, for *her*." Holt's throat shivers, teeth pushed out. "This blood"—his eyes fall closed, then snap wide—"is yours."

At the far end of the room, in the open doorway, another figure appears. "Let's go!" Cricket shouts. "More men are coming."

Noah yanks the blade from Holt's abdomen, and Holt slides mutely to the floor. Gutted. "I'm not a Theorist anymore," Noah growls definitely, voice deep and hard and cut through with something that sounds like pain.

Bright, awful blood spreads across Holt's white shirt, dripping to the floor, pooling. His hand tries to find the wound. But there's too much blood. *A lake of it.*

Noah's gotten his revenge, and his eyes flash to me, hand reaching out, pulling me to him. "He cut you?" he asks, touching my neck gently, fingertips to my skin, trying to inspect the place where Holt's blade pierced my skin.

"I'm all right," I say quickly, not trying to be tough—I just don't feel any pain. Maybe it's the adrenaline, the pounding of my heart in my ears, but the blood hardening against my chest doesn't even feel like my own.

"Come on!" Cricket yells. "We have to go!"

Noah takes my hand, squeezes tight, and I flash one final look at Holt—his mouth sputtering open and closed, *open, closed,* like he's trying to speak, but his lungs have lost all air.

I turn to Noah, my own voice lost, the ringing in my ears too loud, and I nod. We sprint down the center of the schoolhouse, his green eyes wild with rage, while the knife in his other hand drips with Holt's blood.

✳ ✳ ✳

I hurry over the body lying in the dirt, just beyond the doorway—the man who'd been posted to keep guard—now dead. Slayed by Noah or Cricket. I barely look at him. I don't want to feel the guilt; I don't want to tally the number of people who've lost their lives because of me. Whether they deserved it or not.

Outside, I blink away from the evening sunlight, struggling to focus after being caged in the dark schoolhouse for days, prisms cutting across my vision. *I can't believe I'm outside. Can't believe I'm free.* Quickly I scan the unfamiliar town spread out before me, boarded up and abandoned, but Noah tugs against my hand—his warm palm pressed to mine. "You okay?" he asks, sensing my hesitation. I nod again, still unable to find any words, and he squeezes my hand tighter, an assurance that he's not letting go, then pulls me away from the body, from Holt now bleeding out inside the schoolhouse, and down a dusty, narrow alleyway.

I might be free of the schoolhouse, but we still have to get out of this town.

At the far end of the alley, between two slanted wood buildings, Cricket stops and looks back. Her breathing is quick, labored, and I see how much paler she's become—eyes lost of any color, skin waxy and damp. Like her body is both an unstoppable wildfire and a deep, winter cold she can't shake. She's sick, *really* sick.

She shouldn't have come; she shouldn't even be on her feet.

Behind us, shouts echo through the deserted town, footsteps thundering across the hard ground, men converging on the old schoolhouse. "This way," Cricket says, her teeth clenched so tightly, I worry they might crack, but we run down another row of buildings, the wind howling through open doorways and shattered windows.

We're nearly to the edge of town, only another block to go—I can see the dry, open landscape beyond—when we hear a series of footsteps pounding closer. *Too close.*

Cricket drives herself up against the wall of a single-story house, tucked into a thin stretch of shadows. Noah and I do the same, his hard chest pressing to mine, breathing in my ear, his heartbeat against my throat. The scent of him, of green and forest, almost makes tears well in my eyes. He is familiar in ways he shouldn't be. *He found me,* my mind repeats. He found me, and he's protecting me, like he swore he would. Like he promised.

And when I let my eyes flutter closed for the briefest of moments, feeling his heartbeat against my own chest, I realize that he reminds me of home.

A second passes, and the footsteps fade away, moving toward the schoolhouse—they haven't discovered where we are. Cricket blows out a raspy exhale, her lungs like sand, and peers around the corner of the house, watching.

"We have to get to that line of trees," Noah says, glancing across the barren stretch of land beyond the town.

Cricket nods. But she looks so weak, I'm not sure how much farther she can run. Her eyes glisten, mouth drawing in tight gulps of air like she can't ever get enough. Still, we break away from the corner of the house and sprint across the street to the last clot of buildings. We're almost free . . . when I see it.

A paddock filled with horses, only a couple of yards to our left.

And it's not just the horses—the crush of them all together, dust swirling around their heads—it's one horse in particular.

Odie.

She's among them, eyes wide, front hoof stamping the ground.

"Stop," I hiss to Noah, tugging against his arm. "Stop!"

He pivots around, eyes filled with tension, with adrenaline. "What's wrong?"

"Pa's horse, Odie. That's her." I point into the crowd of horses. "They took her before we reached Fort Bell."

"There's no time," Noah whispers, keeping his voice low, eyes darting back the way we came, looking for any sign of those men.

I shake my head at him. "I can't leave her." And I pull away from his hand, from his hard grasp, and run to the paddock. When I yank open the small gate, the horses clot together, kicking up more dust. But Odie's ears twitch forward and she stands still, trying to assess who I am—some deep memory fluttering forward in her mind. When I reach her, she lowers her head and pushes her flat face into my chest. "I found you," I whisper in a rush.

"We have to go," Noah urges behind me, standing at the gate, eyes flashing back to the center of town.

I grab a bridle left slung over a fencepost and secure it over Odie's head—there's no time for a saddle—and I lead her through the gate into the open. For a half second I consider grabbing two more horses, one for each of us, but it'll take too much time—securing two more bridles and two horses who might not be as agreeable as Odie. But I say quickly to Noah, "Leave the paddock open. If they don't have horses, they won't be able to come after us."

He nods, and several paces away, Cricket is standing at the back wall of an outbuilding, a toolshed maybe, looking like a ghost—her flesh so white, it seems almost transparent—but she peers back at us, shoulders wide. "Come on," she hisses, urgent, waving us past her.

Between the edge of town and a line of wind-blown trees in the distance lies a good two hundred yards of open scrub brush and no place to hide. We'll have to move fast. I draw in a tight, anxious breath, and the three of us sprint out into the open, away from the shelter and shadows of town—Odie trotting behind.

But when I glance back at Cricket, her gait is stilted, lumbering, like she's struggling to take in a breath, to swing her legs in front of her. I want to shout at her to move faster, but I'm afraid to say anything above a whisper. Those men have surely discovered the opened door into the schoolhouse, the body lying in the doorway, and Holt bleeding inside.

Now they'll be coming for us.

I tug Odie faster, toward a low gully ahead of us, where the ground drops away—probably a creek at one time. And beyond that, trees.

Safety.

We're only a few paces from the gully, and I feel the air quickening in my lungs, my skin tight against my bones, desperate to reach a low spot, out of sight from the town. *So close now.* My eyes find Cricket, and there is relief in them—she knows we're going to make it. A smile pulls at my lips, the certainty already pulsing through me. *Almost there.* Only a few steps now, we'll be—

Something moves behind Cricket.

A shadow.

A terrible, awful shadow.

My legs hitch beneath me, and I feel the seconds ticking past like raindrops on numb skin. At the edge of town . . . a figure comes into view.

They found us.

I feel my eyes widen, the air snatched from my lungs—and I catch the glint of metal reflecting beneath the wavy, all-seeing sun.

"He has a gun!" I shout, scrambling backward, stumbling on my own feet.

Cricket swivels, her motions slowed somehow, everything drawn out, time dulled into a few sluggish seconds. Her arm swings out, reaching for the knife at her waist. But the sound of a bullet leaving a chamber explodes in the air. Noah turns, reaching out for me, but it's Cricket who makes a strained, guttural sound. Cricket whose mouth is caught open; Cricket who sinks to her knees.

"No!" I scream, but the sound feels like a whimper, broken into pieces as soon as it hits the air.

More shouts echo from the town—*more men coming*—but Noah releases my hand, the sturdiness of his grasp vanished, and he runs back to Cricket, dropping to the ground.

My mind twists in on itself, terror making everything turn a blinding white, and I drop Odie's reins, leaving her where she stands, and scramble after Noah. My knees hit the dusty ground beside Cricket, and my eyes stutter in my skull, absorbing the sight.

Cricket lying on her back, head in the dirt. Cricket with her mouth half-open, trembling, *trembling, trembling.* Like she's trying to speak, *speak*, but can't find any of the words.

Cricket making a *terrible terrible terrible* wheezing sound.

Cricket with too much blood spilling from her torso. *Blood.* Oh god, there's *too* much blood. My eyes start to blur, but I blink, *blink*, force myself to focus. Heart crashing against my ribs, skin tight against my bones. I touch a hand to her chest, searching through the blood, finding the bullet hole. It's on the right side, not through her heart, but it's bleeding, weeping. Too much of it. *Everywhere.* It might have punctured a lung, air hissing from her throat, from the awful hole.

Too much blood . . .

Too much.

I press my palms to the wound, shaking with adrenaline. "We have to get her up," I say to Noah, my voice too high, too much panic on each word.

She's choking, coughing up blood—and it reminds me of Mom, the blood that heaved up from her broken, dying body.

Dying, dying.

"Cricket," Noah says, touching her face, trying to keep her eyes focused on him.

But they roll back in her skull, then snap back into focus. "Go," she somehow mutters, spitting up more blood. Choking on it.

I ignore her. "We can carry her," I say to Noah, nodding, *nodding.* Trying to convince him, convince myself. "Put her on Odie's back."

She coughs again, more blood dripping from her mouth. *Too much. Shit, there's too much.* Behind us, I can hear the men. Shouting, gathering, coming toward us. They want to take me alive—they won't risk firing another shot.

"Go," Cricket tries again, using her hand to push against my shoulder, and somehow she has enough strength to force me back onto my heels. Still some fight in her. Still stronger than most men.

Noah touches her face again, wiping away the blood, but it only makes it worse, spreads it across her cheekbone, along her bare scalp.

She nods up at him—words silently spoken between them. A language only they understand. He nods back, a solemn, terrible tilting of his chin, eyes dark. *An agreement.*

"No," I say to Noah, knowing what he's thinking, what's about to happen. "We can help her."

He shakes his head at me, tears against his lashes. But he says it anyway. "It's too late." A waver in his throat, in his trembling lips. His heart breaking right in front of me.

"It's not," I answer, heat and fear pushing against my eyes. *I can't let her die.* Not after August, not after everyone at the barn. They all die, everyone who tries to help me. They die—because of me. And I can't let it happen again. I wrap my hands around her shoulders, trying to pull her up. "Help me," I bark at Noah, spearing my eyes up to him.

But his gaze whirls back to the edge of town, where the men have stepped out into the open and are moving toward us. "We have to go."

More blood oozes from Cricket's chest, and I move my palms over the hole, pressing, keeping it bay. *We can save her!* my mind screams. "Please, Noah," I whimper, voice cracking. Time seems to stretch out briefly, the air soft and slow from my lips.

Noah releases his hands from her face, and stands up, towering over me—blocking out the dull evening sun. "Get up," he instructs. An order. A command—as if I were a soldier on a battlefield—but I refuse to hear.

I shake my head . . . even though I know, *I know*, there's no recovering from this. Even if we get her onto Odie's back and travel far away from here, toward the lake, she won't recover from this. She'll bleed out, slowly, painfully.

But my body is trembling, refusing to stand up, to walk away. She has risked her life twice now to save me—even for all the times I know she wanted to walk away—and now she's about to give her life because of me. Tears thread down my cheeks, awful little trails. I don't want her to die like this, bleeding out, in pain and afraid.

But her hand folds over mine, dirty fingernails and a calloused palm. Her chin quivers. "He'll protect you . . . no matter what—" She gasps for air, eyes pinching closed against the pain, and then they find me again, wide and watery and fearless. "He'll die for you—" she says. "But don't let him." She squeezes my hand so tight that it hurts, then lifts her head a fraction of an inch, looking me squarely, firmly, in the eyes. "You protect him . . . promise me."

I choke on the words I want to say, fear stiffening inside my chest like a fist. She loves him, I know. Loves him in ways that make my heart ache a little. In ways I don't fully understand. She would have gone with him to the edge of the world to protect him. And now she's asking me to do the same. She's asking me to not let him die. *But everyone near me dies.* Tears burns my cheeks, my heart so loud in my ears, it sounds like I'm underwater. But I squeeze her hand back and manage to nod, meeting her eyes dead-on, so she knows I'll keep this promise. Knows I won't let him die—this boy she loved.

She nods back, and without another word, she releases her hand from mine, a stubborn, fiery gleam in her eyes, then reaches for the knife at her waist.

Time cracks back into place, moving in fast-forward now. I release my palm from the hole in her chest, blood gushing to the surface. Spilling out.

I'm shaking, *shaking*. Noah reaches down, hoisting me up from the ground. "We have to go, now!" he says into my ear. I want to fight him—the guilt too much—I want to drop back down and brush the blood away from her mouth and wait for her to take her last, final breath—so she's not alone. So she isn't afraid. *Because this is my fault.* But Noah whispers, gently like he knows I'm near breaking, "Please, Vega." And I know we need to move. I need to keep my promise, because if we stay, they'll capture me and kill Noah. And I won't let him die here too, in this barren, nowhere stretch of land. Blood and choking back tears and too much pain in my chest.

Noah tugs me away from her, and I let him. We run, sprinting across the open plains, away from the deserted town. From Cricket. A shot is fired, then another, the echo vibrating through the still air, ripping past our heads. *Maybe they'll take me dead or alive after all.* As long as we don't get away. With the map still on my flesh.

My skull is a hammer, too much pain, too much blood on my skin, everywhere, and I wait for the next bullet to pierce my back, or Noah's, but our legs keep running, carrying us forward. We reach Odie, and Noah lands a hand against her rump, and she breaks away into a gallop, heading for the trees—her eyes wild, breath quick from her nostrils, ears flattened back.

At the low gully, we drop down into it, scrambling, adrenaline screaming in our veins, then climb up the other side. I want to look back; I want to peer over my shoulder and see if the men have reached Cricket. But I wait until we've staggered across the open patch of land between the gully and the line of trees, legs burning, and then we duck into the cover of the tree line.

Noah stops, his breathing like a storm, a gasp, then looks back.

The men are nearly to Cricket, and I feel like I can't breathe, like the trees are tilting above me, the sky splintering and breaking, *shattering* apart. I'm dizzy and I want to close my eyes, but instead I brace a hand against Odie's shoulder, who's stopped just inside the tree line, air still gusting from her nose, stamping her front foot, uneasy in the narrow thicket of trees, ears darting forward and then back like she might bolt again.

"She won't go down without a fight," Noah says under his breath, his voice thin, hardly there at all.

And he's right.

✳ ✳ ✳

Noah pushes me up onto Odie's back.

My hands fall to her mane, and I stare down at the blood on my palms, my fingertips—Cricket's blood. But there's more blood dried on my throat, smeared down my chest. Holt almost slit my throat, giving me a scar to match his own.

I gulp, I breathe, the air shaking around me, the trees swirling and fracturing above. I blink it away, everything numb and blotted out. I feel the weight of Noah climbing up behind me, folding his arms around my torso, keeping me in place—his hands gripping the reins—and we ride deeper into the trees.

As far from Mill City as we can get.

But *far* will never be far enough. *Cricket is dead.* Still, I don't let the sob break free from my throat. I hold it in tight. Because I don't deserve to cry; I don't deserve to hurt. This pain belongs to Noah, not me.

He doesn't speak as we travel through the forest, silent as a boy who's had everything taken from him. Everyone he loves.

Hours slip by, silence folding in around us, until we reach a ridge of rocks where a shallow stream knits itself through several large moss-covered boulders, before curving away into the forest to the west. We stop to drink, kneeling in the muddy bank to clean the blood from our skin.

We can't stay long. The men will be coming after us once they corral their horses.

And now they won't just want to capture me—the girl they've been chasing across miles of terrain—they'll want revenge for Holt.

I stare down at my reflection in the water, the pain surfacing again like a cold, musty shadow. But when I look to Noah, bent low, drinking from the stream—water spilling between his hands—I say nothing. There are no words anymore, nothing I can give him to set any of it right.

"We should keep moving," he says coldly, wiping his hands against his pant legs, but the thinness of his voice, the brokenhearted edge to each word, are sharpened nails against my own awful heart.

Wordlessly he helps me back atop Odie, and his loyalty feels like its own dagger—something I don't deserve. He's still here, with me, after everything that's happened.

Night comes, dark and starless, and Odie plods through the sparse woodland where the trees grow thin and tall, white trunks and small, pale green leaves beginning to turn golden. If we're lucky, the men will be a good hour or two behind us—the time it would take to track down their freed horses. To bury Holt, to come after us.

When light finally breaks across the landscape, we have trekked into unfamiliar terrain, the hills and distant mountains a strange, craggy silhouette—dense swaths of evergreens untouched by man, thick underbrush and grassy valleys where no path has been cut through the unaltered land. It feels as if we've ventured far past the known world.

Noah still doesn't speak—arms framing my torso, holding me to him—and I wonder if he's thinking this place isn't survivable. I wonder if he's thinking that my life wasn't worth Cricket losing hers—if he's regretting everything. I know I've caused him so much pain, immeasurable, deep and wretched. I want to tell him that I'd take it all back if I could, but there's no point speaking of impossible things, childish things, so I stay quiet—the wind biting at our backs, growing colder with each mile, yet we push on.

As if there is no other choice.

Sharp mountain air and clouded sky and Noah's compass taking us north.

We move by habit, his chest pressed to my back, his exhales always against my ear—making me shiver, making me want to sink closer, vanish in his arms, making me hate myself for what I've taken from him.

After another hour, my head lulled by the motion of Odie's footsteps beneath us, we reach a shallow creek, hardly any water bubbling down through its narrow channel. But, desperate, we fall to our knees and drink, pushing our faces into the cold. The rocks are slick, soggy with moss, and I dip my hair into the water, soaking it through and then coiling it down my back, letting it drip-dry over my shoulders. My body shivers, teeth rattling, but I welcome it, the feel of the cold mountain water against my skin and filling my stomach. I feel cleansed in some small way—the pain of my wounds, my hollowed-out insides, momentarily numbed.

"Look," I say, blinking, nodding to the other side of the creek where a low, mangy bush sags toward the water. "Blackberries."

We crash through the creek, pulling the berries from the thorny bush, then shoving them into our mouths. After my stomach begins to feel not so empty, I pocket several of the harder, not-quite-ripe berries, the ones that won't squish and flatten while we ride. I even carry a handful of berries back to Odie, and she nibbles them from my palm.

"We could camp here," I suggest quietly. "Beside the water."

Noah walks back across the creek, eyes scanning the wind-blown trees. "No. They'll need water too, and they'll stop here. We have to camp somewhere less hospitable."

✳ ✳ ✳

It's well after dark—two hours since we left the cold creek—when at last Noah finds a place he believes will be safe enough to rest for the night. It's unremarkable, no defining features, just a shallow place in the trees where we settle among the pine needles and dark soil.

He makes a small fire, just large enough to warm our hands, and we sit beside it like two thieves, desperate for its comfort. The silence expands around us, fills the quiet air, until it feels so big it hurts. We've barely spoken since fleeing Mill City. And I know time is running out, too many days wasted—we might not even reach the sea in time.

But for now, tonight, we need to sleep.

I rest my chin on my bent knees, the back of my skull no longer throbbing, the cut along my throat already starting to heal and scab over. "How did you find me?" I ask at last, words thin as winter ice, hardly even there. "How did you know where I was?"

Noah's hands are warming over the small flames, firelight shivering up his exposed arms—along the tattoos I trace with my eyes, the brand that marks him as a traitor. He is handsome in this light, and I long to stroke my fingers along his flesh, to be back in the lake with his body so close to mine. Before everything changed. I'd drift forward into his arms, water receding between us, and I'd press my mouth to his. I'd wrap my fingers around his torso and up his shoulder blades; I'd let myself kiss him until the night sky became a blur of unnamable starlight. I'd say "sorry" for all the things that hadn't yet happened. I wouldn't let go.

But I can't go back. And here we sit, beside a small campfire in a dark forest, with too much loss measured between us. And a look in his eyes like he'll never stare at me again like he did at the lake. Like all of that is gone now. The pain too massive inside him.

"I heard you scream," he says, still not looking at me. "I woke up, and you were gone from the campfire." He lowers his hands from the flames, nods a little, remembering. "I traced your footprints around the lake—then Cricket and I found the men's camp. We followed their tracks to Mill City."

"But how'd you know I was in the schoolhouse?"

"We didn't at first," he answers softly. "We watched the town for two days, waiting, then saw that the schoolhouse was the only building with someone posted guard out front."

He falls quiet, knowing how the story ends. How we ended up here. With Cricket choking on her own blood as we fled into the trees, looking back to see the first man reach her: He bent down to see if she was still alive, to check for a pulse, but her arm swung upward before he could even touch her—swift and quick—her broad hunting knife driving into his gut. He wailed like a child, and two more men approached, but her knife glinted in the air as she slashed their shins, their ribs, until at last, one of the men aimed a rifle, steadied it, and fired a single shot.

Cricket slumped back and went still.

It was a warrior's end. A hero's end. And now a thousand miles of distance rest between Noah and me, a loss that cannot be set right, settled in his eyes.

But he saved me, broke down the door of the schoolhouse and ripped Holt off me. He freed me from a room where I thought I'd die, Holt's knife cutting me apart.

"Do you think Holt's dead?" I ask.

"Maybe." Tension winds tight around his shoulders. "If he's not, he'll keep coming for us. But if he is, then his men will come for us anyway. They'll want retribution for his death." His eyes dim. "It's about honor now."

The air stiffens in my lungs. They won't ever stop hunting us. They'll track us all the way to the sea. It's not over.

Noah leans closer to the fire, poking at the coals with an elm stick, and sparks ignite upward, illuminating his face—a face that is marred by grief, a face I still want to touch. "What happened back there?" he asks, voice hollow, like an echo rising up from a deep, dark well. "With Holt. What did he say?"

I fold my arms around my knees, lowering my chin, the cold always there, never subsiding, even with the fire. "He asked about my tattoo."

The whites of Noah's eyes cut over to me.

"He wanted me to tell him how to read it, how to navigate by the stars."

"Did you?"

I lift my chin from my knees. "No." I remember the feel of the blade against my neck, the threat of it, the cold, sharp point nearly breaking my skin. "He said he was going to cut it out if I didn't tell him." I pull my lips in, hating the memory. Wanting to scrub it out, never think of it again. "But you came . . . before he could."

Silence burns the air between us—he saved my life, but Cricket gave hers in return—until his eyes graze mine. "What happens when we reach the sea?"

The question feels dangerous, too many old stories woven together, too much to unravel. The truth hidden somewhere underneath it all. I remember when he said that August only ever told him the *way* to the sea, nothing else. None of the reasons. None of the choices our ancestors made to lead us here. He said August didn't want him to know everything—the burden was too great.

And now I do the same.

Picking around the truth, giving him only enough to calm the questions in his mind. But careful not to reveal the rest—the things that Mom said were meant only for me.

I find Tova and Llitha, hovering bright and clear well above the trees. "See those two stars?" I say, pointing up to the eastern sky. "They're sister stars, caught in the same orbit." Noah tilts his gaze but doesn't speak. "For the last hundred years, they weren't visible in our sky. They were too far away. But now—" The words feel vulnerable, and I'm afraid he will hear the crack of fear in my voice. "They're finally near enough to see—our orbit and theirs have finally swung on the same axis. It's a rare event, and won't happen again for another hundred years." I dip my eyes back to the fire, a static pulse in my eardrums. "It's why I left the valley," I tell him. "Those two shimmering stars are the reason I came to find the Architect—find *you*. And now we have to reach the sea before they move away, out of alignment."

Noah breathes, and the sky expands. He breathes, and I feel unanchored in every deep exhale.

"How long do we have?" he asks.

"Not sure. I've lost track of the days. But—" I flash another look at the sister stars, trying to remember all the reasons why I'm here. The reasons why I need to keep going. "I'd say we only have a handful of days left."

"And if we don't get to the sea in time?"

My mouth falls, doubt nagging at my bones. "Then we wait another hundred years."

He shoots me a look.

"If we don't reach it," I say, "then in a hundred years our descendants will have to try all over again." And in truth, we won't make it another hundred years.

There won't be anyone left.

Noah narrows his eyes on me—impossibly green, sorrowfully green, crush-me-into-a-hundred-pieces-of-glass green. It hurts to feel his eyes on me, knowing I've taken so much from him.

A river of silence grows heavy between us, and my heart clobbers my chest, my mind remembering the moment when I saw him striding down the center of the schoolhouse, his eyes focused only on me, a fury in him I've never seen before. Determination and anger burning across his skin. He tore Holt away from me, knife burrowed into Holt's side, then took my hand in his, a tremor in his fingertips, like he thought he might have been too late, like he had feared he would find me already dead. There was relief in his eyes, and something else: a different kind of pain. And I remember what Holt said to him just before Noah pulled the knife from his gut.

You . . . betray me, for her.

I had thought he meant the kind of betrayal from a traitor, because Noah fled the Theorists years ago. But there was something else in his words. A hidden meaning. And the next thing he said seemed to make no sense.

"What did Holt mean," I ask, "when he said, *This blood is yours?*"

Noah's mouth parts, a soft exhale releasing into the night, and his eyes tip up to the sky. For a moment, he looks like a boy who's lost more than I even know. Who is breaking right in front of me. "I wasn't just a member of the Theorists, a soldier like most of Holt's men," he says. "I was going to be their leader one day."

I swallow and my stomach clenches.

"Holt was grooming me to lead, to command his men." Noah's eyes fall to me, jaw flexing, his dark skin somehow even darker in the firelight, in the waves of shadows and light. "I betrayed him when I left, when I escaped and never came back."

The heat from the fire suddenly feels like too much, and I brush my hands up my arms, narrowing my eyes on Noah, trying to see what else is there. What tiny secrets hide beneath his twilight skin. "Holt could've just found someone else," I say. "It didn't have to be you." But I hear the doubt in my own voice.

Noah's gaze darkens, bottom lip pulled tight, and he removes

SHEA ERNSHAW

the elm stick from the fire, digging it into the dirt at his feet. "I grew up as a Theorist, Vega. I was always one of them, born into it." He breathes, a pain in his eyes, as if each word is costing him something, a part of his skin shed, a piece of his heart broken. "I was destined for it."

He shifts his eyes to me, like he thinks I already know, like I should be able to see it in his face. The truth. Always there. Always right in front of me. If I had only looked—*really looked*. But I need to hear him say it, need the word to leave his parted lips, even though my head is already pinwheeling, the trees seeming to tilt too far toward the ground, the sky set upside down. *Everything made wrong.*

"I tried to kill him when I left the Theorists," he says, a waver in his voice, every part of him hating the thought that is about to become words, resisting, his voice catching against his teeth. "I tried to kill my own father."

I suck in a breath, my jaw clamping down. I touch the ground with my palms, needing the hard soil to steady me, but afraid to look away from Noah, afraid the words he just spoke will split him apart. Break us both.

"Noah," I say gently, his name slipping out, carried on an exhale. But how do I say the thoughts rioting in my mind—how do I knit all of it together?

Holt is Noah's father.

And although Noah tried to kill Holt when he fled the Theorists, he might have just killed him for good inside the schoolhouse. And he did it for me. *He chose me, over his own father.*

The air is gone from my lungs.

Words gone from my throat.

The hurt growing inside Noah is too big to be eased by anything I might say.

The campfire throws sparks up into the sky, and a moment stalls between us, as if we're both trying to gather together the missing parts of our pasts, the secrets we each keep. Noah rubs a hand across his neck, another memory shivering through him. "After I left the Theorists' camp, after I cut my own father's throat, I didn't know where to go. Wells was dead, and I didn't know anything other than my life within the group." He releases a trembling breath, memories spiking through him now. "I spent a few cold nights outside," he goes on, keeping his eyes on mine, sinking in, letting them settle deeper and deeper into my skin. "I slept behind a blacksmith's shop in some no-name town, starving, but with a Theorist brand burned into my flesh, I knew no one would take me in. I wouldn't survive on my own."

He's telling me everything. Showing me the shadows he keeps tucked into his darkest corners. His secrets are mine now.

"I knew I had to find August. He was the only one who would take me in."

This catches me off guard. "You knew who August was?"

He nods, eyebrows tented, and digs the stick deeper into the soil. "He and my father were friends once. Best friends." He blows out a quick gust of air. "August even told my father some of the old stories, about the first Astronomer and the first Architect. He trusted my father, confided in him. And my father vowed to protect August, keep his stories secret. But all that changed when my mother died." Noah leans back from the fire, his features cast in shadow. I've never heard him mention his mom, and I can see the latent grief rising to the surface. "She was pregnant with me when she started showing signs of the sickness." Noah swallows, starts again. "My father begged August to help him. He thought if they could find the Astronomer, she would be able to find a cure for my mother. He believed the Astronomer could save her. But August refused, told him there was nothing that could be done.

"My mother died only a month after having me. The consumption took her quick."

Noah swallows and I want to touch his arm, his chest, his face. I want to wrap my arms around his strong shoulders and tell him how sorry I am. That I know the pain of losing a mother. That I know how wretched his hurt feels. But I worry he wants no sympathy from me. The girl, an *Astronomer*, whose family was partly blamed for his own mother's death. The girl who has caused him so much of the pain he feels. But now I understand how Holt knew so much— about me, about everything. Because at one time, August told him.

"My father blamed August for her death," he continues. "And he vowed to find the Astronomer himself, to save those who were left. He started gathering men to join his group; he started promising a cure for the consumption. Word spread fast, and soon they were tormenting anyone who they thought might know where the Astronomer was hiding. They were violent, and I saw my father murder countless people."

His hand tenses around the stick he still holds, and I try to imagine what it must have been like to be raised by a man like Holt, to grow up within the Theorist camps, and then to leave it all behind. To know it's not the life he wanted—*to end up like his father*. It would take courage to abandon everything you know, to risk death. And I think of the valley, the cabin, Mom's grave beside the river—I left everything behind too.

"It took me a while to find August," he continues. "Almost a month, but when I found him hiding in a farmhouse outside Lohaw, he didn't ask questions—he just took me in and promised to raise me as his own son. I was only fourteen at the time." He flashes me a look, as if to see my reaction, but I remain quiet, letting him finish. Letting him get it all out. "I've been with August for four years, hiding from my father, always on the road."

I try to imagine how he must have felt, hiding, afraid of what would happen if Holt and his men found him. Not only was he a traitor when he left, but he joined August—the very man who Holt blamed for his wife's death.

"After a year, August started preparing me, telling me stories about the Astronomer. About the stars. I would be the next Architect once he was gone. He taught me the way to the sea, so that I could take her there—take *you* there someday."

When he looks at me, I'm surprised to find a gentleness in his eyes—no hate or regret.

He has just told me the truth about who he is: every scarred, awful moment from his past, laid out across the dry ground for me to see. *His secrets are my secrets now.* And when I look into his cold, sad, beautiful eyes, I feel a swelling beneath my ribs unlike I've ever known before. Like some part of me is breaking and blooming all at once. A thud in my chest, a tremor in my veins.

My mother is dead, but Noah might have just killed his own father. To save me. We are both orphans in ways that should shatter us. Destroy us both. Yet we're trying to do what's right and see this through. Both bound by a past, a story that's already been written for us. We are both broken. And I need him now more than ever.

But first, I need to get the words out before they rot inside me. "I'm sorry—" I shake my head, pressing my hands against my knees, knowing it's not good enough. Not even close. "I'm sorry for your mother dying before you ever knew her. I'm sorry about your father, for what you've had to do, for yourself and for me. I'm sorry August died before he could tell you everything, tell you all the stories that my mom told me." I breathe—I force myself to keep going, my eyes buried in his. "I'm sorry I walked away from our camp that night and got caught by Holt's men, for making you come after me. I wish I could go back and undo what happened." Tears push against my eyelids, then break free, but I wipe them away quickly, knowing he doesn't want my tears. They aren't worth anything. "I'm sorry she—" I lift my eyes to him, start again. "I know you loved Cricket. . . . I know she was all you had left."

He drops the stick he had been using to prod the fire, onto the dirt beside him. "I did," he admits, his jaw a stiff, measured line. "We saved each other's lives many times." For a moment, he looks away, like he might stand up and walk away into the trees—unable to talk about this, to hear my useless apology. But then he says, "She knew you were worth dying for. She tracked those men to Mill City, to where they'd taken you—she was never going to leave you behind."

A line of traitorous tears thread down my cheeks.

But Noah levels his eyes on me. "It wasn't your fault," he says. "None of it. My mother died because she was sick; my father became a man with cruelty in his veins, a man I was afraid of, who I couldn't trust. August died protecting you, which is what he wanted, a promise he made to his father, and his father before him. It was an honorable death. A better death than giving up slowly to the sickness, without purpose. He died the way he wanted. And Cricket—" His voice catches, and he clamps his mouth shut, holding back the pain. "Those men killed her, not you," he says. "She knew you were important, and she did it for August, for me." His eyes glisten with tears and I want to touch him, feel his warm skin beneath my fingertips, but I'm too afraid. Afraid of what will happen in my unstable heart if I let myself be that close to him.

I think about what Holt said in the schoolhouse, how we all play roles. Maybe we were always moving toward each other—the Astronomer and the Architect—and sooner or later we would have ended up here. Paths diverging in a wood, a story that was told long ago. A story about us, already written.

An Astronomer and an Architect.

"Back at the water tower," Noah says, eyes bottomless, never looking away, "when you showed me the marks on your neck, I knew you were her and I knew I would stay with you until the end."

The air catches against my teeth.

His eyes rake over me as his hand lifts, fingertips finding my throat, resting lightly against the place where Holt pressed the blade, where a pink line now rests—not fully healed. My pulse drives at my temples, and he trails a path up to my jaw, into my tangled hair. I feel the heat expand in my chest, the ache I've been trying to suppress— the burning that turns me to shreds whenever he looks at me. "I knew then that you were her . . . the one I've been looking for in the faces of every girl I've ever met. In every town and outpost, I would scan the crowds, hoping I'd find you."

Blood swims in my veins. "You were looking for me?"

"Every day for the last three years." His hand slides to the back of my neck, resting softly against the mark. "When I was with the The-orists, we hunted you, following any rumor we heard about a sight-ing of the Astronomer. No matter how far away. But with August, I started *searching* for you." His river-deep eyes fall to my mouth, then back up. "I knew my father wouldn't stop hunting you. I had to find you before he did." He swallows, a half smile stealing across his lips. "But you found me."

I draw the cool night air into my lungs, I let my gaze sink into his, and I find something ancient in his eyes—as if they have seen many shores, the wisdom of others living inside him. Just like it lives inside me. "It feels like . . . we were always meant to find one another," I say, my heart knocking against my ribs.

His mouth parts a little, and I can see the question in his eyes. The same question in mine.

Air escapes my lips.

Please, I think. *Kiss me.* His eyes blink; his mouth parts like he's going to speak, tell me a story about our past, about every almost-missed moment that led us to each other, but instead . . .

He leans forward, so close that I can smell his campfire-pine scent. Feel his breath on my lips. Feel every time his skin almost grazed mine, the unmistakable longing in my chest, all the nights when I stared at him and wanted to feel him this close. I exhale, letting my lips fall open, searching for a word, for a thought, that is long gone.

And in that half blink, in the second before my thoughts can rise up again—he presses his mouth to mine. Warmth and need and everything else I've kept bottled up inside me, the ache I've tried to ignore, finally breaks across my skin.

His hand slides up the nape of my neck, back into my hair. Like he'll never let me go—never let anyone take me again. No blades pressed to my throat, no cages inside abandoned towns. My fingers find his chest, his collarbone, coiling around his shirt—the parts of him I've wanted to touch for too long—dragging him closer, and I feel the sky spinning wildly overhead, breaking apart. Shattering me.

He kisses me harder, desperate now, like he believes there is hope woven into the fibers of my bones. Like I will save him. Put him back together. All the days we've spent together, the long, cold nights with his body so close to mine, and now, at last, that terrible pain inside me has calmed. It has found the thing it needed all along.

Him.

He weaves his other hand around the back of my neck, over the mark branded there, and I kiss him, wanting more than just his mouth on mine, needing him to never let go, a burning pain growing inside my solar plexus, deep within my gut. The truth resting behind my eyelids: I've wanted to kiss him since the moment I saw him beneath the water tower. He frightened me then, his dark, rigid stance as he squinted through the glaring sun at me, the black tattoos winding up his arms. But I also couldn't bear for him to look away.

I needed the feel of his eyes on me, tearing me open, making me something else—a girl he's been searching for.

I slide my hand up his jaw, tracing every line, every freckle, like constellations on the map of *his* dark skin. We each have scars. Markers of our past. His flesh inked by the tattoos of a friend who's been lost, the starburst brand burned into his forearm from the Theorists he escaped. His teeth graze my bottom lip, my heart battering in my ribs. He kisses me like I am starlight and darkness and the wind through the valley trees: this boy who is the last Architect. He kisses me harder, fingers along my skull, and the buzzing fear writhing along my joints sinks into the background.

His hands trace the bones of my spine, his mouth parting against mine, *deeper, deeper*, and I think: we have finally found each other.

A story that was always already written. Needles and ink pressed into our flesh, moments that brought us here, to this campfire in the cold, shivering trees, far from home.

And with his fingers tracing my lips, my breath against his skin, I know I can't let myself need him. Want him. *Love* him.

Because in the end . . .

At the sea . . .

I will lose him.

URSA MAJOR, Alpha UMa
+61° 45' 03"

It was raining the night she saw it.

The sky was a blistered shade of orange after the storm, but when the clouds receded and the stars shone through with the kind of clarity only possible on cold, damp nights, she found the patch of horizon where no flecks of light glimmered from the dark.

A place where the sky—strangely—held no stars.

She swiveled her telescope to the north, marking the points where the shadow began, and the rest of the sky ended.

There was something up there: a vast, shivering blur of darkness. Hovering, suspended, where it shouldn't be.

She made notes onto paper, studied the books she kept on a wood shelf above her bed—about anomalies and star sequences and nebulas. Still, she couldn't be sure what it was. Only that it made her uneasy; it crept into her dreams.

Whatever it was, it shouldn't be there—a great bottomless depth of nothing. But each night, with every measurement and notation, she realized something else:

It was getting larger.

Leeching across the night sky, spreading like black ink dropped onto soft paper. But it wasn't just growing—it was getting closer.

Hour by hour, the darkness was filling up the sky.

Swelling. Widening.

Until eventually there would be no stars left.

EIGHT

A small town appears suddenly through the windswept evergreens. But it's hardly a town at all: only a two-story building that looks like an oversize farmhouse, painted a soft daffodil yellow with wood-framed windows; and two smaller structures built across the dry, dusty street. Three buildings in all.

It's more of an outpost than a town. Set down in a clearing between trees.

"Have you been through here before?" I ask Noah, my mouth still recalling the feel of his lips on mine last night, under the dark, *dark* sky. We slept for only an hour or two, before the sun began slanting through the trees, and we continued north, until at last reaching this unknown town.

He shakes his head. "No." But he stands up from the tree line where we're crouched, and takes a step into the wide green meadow that separates us from the town.

I stay back, holding Odie's reins. "What are you doing?" I whisper out at him.

"We can't keep going like this."

He's right, we've been traveling a full day since we camped in the trees. We haven't eaten a thing, or found fresh water. "But we'll be seen," I point out.

"Those men are at least a day behind us. We haven't seen any sign of them. And this town"—he nods across the meadow—"is probably just filled with homesteaders. We'll get water and food, then move on."

He holds out a hand to me, his skin like a river under the evening sun, and I take it, stepping into the open.

We cross the meadow, then follow a rough dirt road into town. Odie sniffs at the ground, looking for something edible, then blows out a breath. We could all use a meal, a long drink of water, and a full night's sleep. On either side of the road, the ground has been marked with wood stakes, numbers painted on each one. "What is it?" I ask.

"Plots of land. Where homes will be built."

The town is so new, not even the houses have been constructed yet.

At the large yellow building, we peer up at an ornate sign suspended above the wraparound porch: MAYBELLE HOTEL AND RESTAURANT.

Across the street sit the Maybelle Saloon and the Maybelle Barber Shop. Several horses are tied to the post in front of the saloon, and a man sits in a chair in front of the barber shop, thinning gray hair combed to one side, hands working over something—carving a piece of wood.

Noah walks up the porch of the hotel and pulls open the door.

I tie Odie to the railing, then look back up the road. I don't like this—leaving Odie in the open where she might be seen. Walking into an unfamiliar hotel.

But I follow Noah inside.

The air of the hotel smells strangely clean, like rose water and mint—somehow they've managed to keep out the dust. The walls are painted with tiny sunrise-blue flowers, and a love seat with newly stitched cushions sits just below a stairwell that winds its way up to a second floor. To the left, a wide doorway leads into another room with a dozen square tables, and metal coffee cups and folded napkins are set in front of each chair, awaiting customers who I suspect rarely come.

Not way out here. In these distant mountains.

I swivel my gaze to the right, scanning a narrow desk positioned between two large chairs. The place is unsettlingly quiet. Empty.

"Maybe it's not open for business," I say, spinning around to look back at the front door. Our escape, if we need to run.

Noah nods, taking a step closer to the desk, when footsteps echo from the second floor. Small and quick.

A woman appears, swishing down the stairwell in a pale violet dress with white lace along the collar. "Terribly sorry," she announces, bright-eyed and all teeth, light auburn hair combed back and pinned at the base of her neck. "Didn't hear you come in." She glides across the foyer and perches herself behind the desk, a regal figure, back straight as a pine board, smelling of honey and lavender. Like soap and freshly washed hair. "How many nights?" she asks, eyelids batting.

"We're just looking for something to eat," Noah answers, staring at the woman like she can't be trusted. But right now, I don't think he'd trust anyone. "And maybe some water for our horse."

The woman peers past us, craning her head to the window where

Odie is tied at the porch. "It's a long way to Maybelle without sup-plies," she says, lifting an eyebrow. "You come looking for gold?"

"No." Noah's voice is measured and precise, not wanting to offer up any more details than necessary. "Just passing through."

"Huh." Her eyes dim a little, the cheerfulness sinking from her pinked face. "Everyone who comes this way is looking to stake a claim along the Payutte Basin."

Noah rests a hand on the desk, giving her a somber look. "We lost everything in a river crossing," he lies.

"Oh no." The woman's eyebrows slope, sincerity in her gaze—a woman without motives beyond what sits plainly in front of us. "You two do look like you've spent a few nights out in the cold."

I smile at her, trying to seem calm, unafraid of standing in the foyer of a hotel in the middle of a small, unknown town. I try to keep my eyes from nervously flashing to the front window, watching for men on horseback riding up the dirt road.

"You must stay the night," she presses, eyes wide and hopeful. "I insist."

But Noah shakes his head. "We can't."

My ears start to ring. I turn and look out the window again, but there's still no one there. A part of me wants to believe they aren't following us, that they've given up. Maybe Noah was wrong when he said they'd keep coming for us. If Holt is dead, perhaps the men have disbanded, scattered like dust, no longer motivated to pursue us deeper into the wilderness where the towns become fewer and farther apart.

Maybe they won't want revenge after all.

But the ticking in my eardrums, the dryness in my throat,

makes me think they're still out there, getting closer. Always closer.

The woman frowns at us, pressing down the sides of her dress. "I don't get many married couples at the hotel. Mostly miners and ranchers out here." Her expression changes, turns warm again. "I'll give you a room at no charge." A smile tugs at her pinked cheekbones. "And I'll draw you both warm baths. You can pay me for dinner, but that's it."

I look to Noah. This woman thinks we're married.

"I'll have Tom lead your horse around back to the stable," she adds, nodding cheerfully, and I get the sense she's desperate to have *any* guests in the hotel, someone to fill the silent hallways, to cut through the quiet echo. "He'll give her grain and fresh water."

Noah's jaw pulses—he thinks this is a bad idea, staying longer than a few minutes. But we have to sleep somewhere, whether out in the cold, in the trees against the hard ground, or here in a hotel. And if Odie is hidden in a stable, she won't be spotted. Maybe we can risk it, just this one night. A bath that smells of honey and lavender—just like the woman—sounds so good, I could almost cry. A soft bed, a pillow, clean sheets. I crave it in a way I never thought I could crave anything.

I look to Noah, and he exhales—he knows I want to stay.

"Okay," he says, turning to the woman. "One night. Thank you."

The woman's entire face brightens. "Come," she says, waving us toward the stairs.

* ✳ *

The second floor of the hotel is painted in the same tiny blue tulips with cream-white doors along both sides of a long hallway. It's an odd contrast to the wilderness beyond the hotel walls. A land of dirt and harsh winds and cold, cold nights.

The woman moves with purpose down the hall, glancing at each door, as if deciding which room is suitable, then stops at one on the left, turning the knob and pushing the door wide.

She lets us inside, then plants her hands on her wide, full hips. "The bathroom is at the end of the hall—I'll draw the warm water."

She leaves us alone and I stand in the center of the room, an itch beneath my skin. I run my hands along the quilt, a white patchwork with lace stitched into the edges, while Noah goes to the window, pulling back the curtain to peer out onto the street. "They've already led Odie away." He lets the curtain fall back into place, removing his coat and placing it on the corner of the bed, then pushes up the sleeves of his shirt. "But we should be ready to go if we hear anyone ride into town."

I nod.

The woman appears back in the doorway, two towels in her arms. "Are you ready, miss?"

Noah nods at me. But I see the woman's eyes stall on him, his arms lined with dark tattoos, and a starburst brand sunk into his forearm—the mark of a Theorist.

I walk to the doorway and her gaze pulls away, smiling curtly at me; then she leads me down the hall. I count five doors, aside from our own, and in the last room is a shared bathroom, a wood-sealed tub waiting in the center, steam rising up from the water. The sight of it makes my chest flutter.

"I've set out a nightgown for you," she says. "An extra one I had in my closet. I'll wash your clothes tonight and have them ready for you in the morning."

"Thank you." It feels wrong taking so much from her—a free room for the night, a hot bath, and now she's lending out her clothes and offering to clean my dirty ones. "Is the hotel yours?"

At the tub, she pours in the last bucket of warm water—heated on a fire somewhere downstairs, I imagine—her face turning pink from the steam, the fleshy part of her hip leaning against the edge of the tub. "My husband and I built it a year ago. He was going to be the mayor of our small town, once it was large enough. He named it Maybelle, after me." Her blue eyes dampen, and she brushes back a wavy curl that's come loose from her pins. "He died three months back," she adds swiftly, clearing her throat. "It took him quick, only a week after he became ill."

"I'm so sorry." I hold the towel she gave me tight to my chest, eyes falling to the wood floor.

But Maybelle's gaze lifts, turns clouded, and for a moment I think she's seen the mark on my neck. Perhaps my hair shifted forward when I glanced to the floor, parted enough for her to spy the ink sunk into my flesh.

My eyes skip to the doorway—I could dart through it in three quick steps, I could shout for Noah to run. He won't hesitate; he won't ask me what's wrong. He knows that danger is always close. We will sprint out of the hotel and find Odie, then be in the woods before Maybelle has even made it down the stairs.

But her mouth tucks flat, and she crosses her soft arms, the white knobs of her elbows poking out from her rolled-up sleeves. "He's not really your husband, is he?" she asks, her tone curt—a woman who doesn't like to be lied to.

Again, my gaze skips to the door. If I tell her the truth, she might not let us stay. But the truth falls out anyway. "No."

"I saw the mark on his arm," she says, her sad, narrowed eyes showing a flicker of distrust—she's wary of me suddenly, of both Noah and me. "He's a Theorist," she adds. "He's dangerous. You shouldn't be traveling with him."

A new kind of panic spikes through my chest. "He's not dangerous."

"I can send word for the sheriff," she says quickly, moving toward me. "He's a day's ride over at the next town, but he can be here tomorrow. If you're in trouble, you don't have to stay with that boy."

"No," I tell her sharply, shaking my head, hoping she sees the seriousness in my eyes—the fear that she might do something to force Noah and me apart, the thought like a cold blade separating my rib cage. "He's not dangerous, and he's not a Theorist—not anymore. The mark is from many years ago." I move closer to her, pleading, needing her to believe me. "He's saved me many times," I add. "He's kept me safe."

Her soft blue eyes narrow to points. "Were you a Theorist too?"

I scowl, shaking my head again. "No. Of course not."

"Because I saw the mark on your neck, when I came for you in the room. It looks like a tattoo. Like . . ." Her voice fades, chin tilted slightly to one side, like she's trying to place it, make sense of what she saw. "It looked like the night sky."

My throat is a fist, narrowing, suffocating. "It's nothing," I say, brushing a hand quickly across my neck, like I could wipe it away—only dirt and sweat. Nothing more. Nothing that means anything.

"I've seen the posters," she says now, blinking once, twice, her features tugged into a strange, unreadable line. "I know what it is."

Panic grips my stomach, the ever-present fear, pushed up, heaving, twisting against my thoughts. *Turn for the door,* my head screams. *Shout for Noah. Run. Run.*

"You're her," she says, a twitch at her left eye. "The one they've been looking for. The one who reads the stars." She steps toward me, peering, like she wants to see me closer, like she wants to reach out a sharp hand for me and pull me to her. Trapped.

Run. Don't let her get any closer.

"You're the Astronomer."

My feet inch backward. Only a couple more steps and I'll be at the door. I'll drop the towel, and I won't look back.

My heart pounds in my ears. I flash a look behind me, then back to her. But her face has changed. Her jaw untightens, and I think I see tears forming in her eyes. She lifts a palm to me. "I'm sorry, I—" She swallows, clears her throat. "I've heard rumors, but I didn't think you were real." Warmth reaches her face now, softness, her ears tugging down. "I think it's terrible how they've hunted you. How they torture people they think might know where you are. They hung a rancher a few miles from here when he refused to let them search his hay shed. They thought he knew something that he didn't." Her shoulders drop, and my heart settles only a little. *A little.* "Those Theorists come through here every month, they take half of what I make at the hotel, and threaten to burn the town if I don't pay." The wrinkles around her eyes make her seem older suddenly, too much heartache over the years wearing her down to the bone. "I won't hurt you," she says finally. "Or tell anyone you're here." Her eyes falter, and she swallows tightly. "My husband always said that you might save us. That you were the cure." She nods to herself, drawing in her lower lip. And I think she's going to ask me if it's true, ask for some cure I can't give—like the old man at the house where we took refuge after the storm. But instead she says, "I hope it's true. I hope that wherever you're headed, you set things right."

She wipes at her eyes, taking in a deep breath—like she's steeling herself, pushing down the pain—then she bends down, picking up the empty bucket from the floor, and slips past me. But from the hall, she pauses, looking back. "You're safe here. I want you to know that." A small smile edges across her mouth, kind, genuine, hiding nothing. "Get yourself washed up, and I'll bring dinner to your room."

My body is thrumming nervously, and I stay beside the door, listening as her footsteps move down the hall. I tap a finger against the wood—maybe I should still run back to the room, tell Noah we need to leave . . . but I stay and slow my breathing. Something inside me trusts her, believes her. Not everyone in this world can be bad. Not everyone beyond the valley will hunt me, *hurt* me.

She's taking a risk, letting us stay here, but she has reason to hate the Theorists: they steal from her; they kill her neighbors. I want to believe we are safe here, for just tonight. *I want to think she will keep us safe.* Keep our secret. Because she is a woman who knows loss as much as anyone. And I could see the pain of it in her eyes, the cavern of loss that makes holes so large in people you can't miss it.

Hiding us here is redemption for her.

It's something she needs to do: for her husband, for every person she's known who's been tormented and murdered by them.

She won't turn us in.

I release my hand from the door and undress swiftly, slipping into the bath. Warm water pools in all the shallow places of my body, the relief almost enough to make me cry, and briefly I let my throbbing head rest back against the hard edge of the tub. I could fall asleep; I could close my eyes and forget where I am and how I got here; I could let a daydream fool me into thinking I'm back in the valley and there's nothing to fear. But instead I wash my hair quickly, then hurry out of the bath.

I don't want to risk staying in too long, where I can't hear what's happening outside, where I'm too far from Noah.

Back in our room, Noah is standing at the window, curtain pulled back, keeping watch. My wet hair is coiled over my shoulder; the clean cotton nightgown that Maybelle left for me is a size too big, hanging from my frame, and when Noah turns, his eyes fall over me. Green *green green*, like he can see right through the thin white fabric, not just to my skin, my constellations, but to *me*, who hides beneath my flesh. He blinks, and for a second he looks like he's going to say something but can't find his voice. He looks almost in pain. Nervous. Lost in a swarm of his thoughts.

Heat pricks at my cheeks, and I tug at the waist of the nightgown.

"You look—" he starts, then changes his mind. Loses the words. His lip tugs at the corner, like he might smile, then forces it down. A fire roars inside me. An itch to be closer to him. *Closer*, always closer. But finally he clears his throat, snaps his eyes back into place. "She brought food." He nods to the wood dresser where two plates sit waiting, each filled with sweet-smelling biscuits and seasoned beans and fresh apple slices. And a pitcher of water.

I walk to the dresser, touching one of the apple slices, my mouth watering. "She knows who I am," I say before taking a single bite.

Noah's eyes cut to the door, then back to me. "Let's go," he says in a rush, reaching for his coat on the bed.

But I lift a hand to him. "She's not going to say anything."

"We can't be sure. We need to go."

I drop my hand from the plate and walk toward him, letting my vision settle on the coolness of his eyes. "It's okay," I assure him, resting a hand against his chest, feeling the rapid thud of his heart beneath his shirt. *Thump, thump,* his heartbeat like a wild creature ready to bolt. "She hates the Theorists," I say quickly. "Hates what they've done. And I trust her. She won't say anything."

I can tell he doesn't want to risk it; he wants to escape out into the woods, away from this town. But I don't pull my hand away, and we're so close that I could rise on my tiptoes and press my lips to his, kiss away the fear and the doubt, make him understand. I could kiss him and we'd lose ourselves, forget where we are, forget why we're running. And pretend there's nothing outside these walls hunting us. "Noah," I say, and his eyes hook into mine. "Trust me. We can stay here tonight."

He touches my chin, my jaw, nodding. "Okay."

It hurts being this close to him, a twisted, impossible feeling in the core of my chest, a gnawing like bone against bone, like time tumbles away from me, summer becoming winter becoming spring again. I could lose myself in this room, alone with him, with his fingertips against my skin.

But my stomach grumbles, desperate for food, and I pull my hand away from his chest. Not allowing myself to slip into his arms. "You can take a bath," I say softly, sensing he doesn't want me to be alone. "I'll be all right."

He lowers his hand from my face, watching me a moment, time slowed again, before reluctantly leaving the room and making his way down to the waiting bath.

I sit at the edge of the bed and eat so quickly that my stomach aches, then walk to the window, watching the street for approaching horses, for any sign of the men. But the town is quiet, not even a dog barking. It'll be easy to hear if anyone rides into town; it'll disturb the very fibers of this sleepy, out-of-the-way settlement. But in that silence is another sound: a ringing in my ears.

It's always there now, a low vibration rattling the curves of my skull, making my skin shiver and itch. *It's getting worse*. But I won't say anything to Noah—I don't want him to know how bad it is. I don't want him to worry. There's nothing to be done, anyway—but get to the sea before it's too late.

I lay a palm against the glass, watching as the sky loses its color, dipping into night. But I can still see the fractured edges, the buzzing, and up beyond the pines is the dark patch of sky—swallowing up every point of light.

It's larger now, the shadow closer than it should be.

Mom's warning ripples through my thoughts: *The sky is unstable. And soon there'll be only darkness.*

Noah appears in the doorway, hair wet, wearing gray linen pants that Maybelle must have given him—that were surely her husband's. But his chest is bare, still damp from the bath, and my eyes can't help but trace the lines of his tattoos, the silver ring hanging from a chain around his neck. He is made of nothing but lean, hardened muscle: a boy who fights, who runs, who *survives*. He has trained for this, and it shows in the rigid slope of his shoulders, his stomach like stone.

Eyes that meet mine . . . too deep, too filled with something that almost looks like need.

I blink my eyes away, air caught in my throat—not allowing myself to feel the pulsing ache in my lowest ribs—and I move away from the window, not telling him about the shadow. About any of it.

He walks to the dresser, eats one of the biscuits, then checks the window—neither of us able to feel completely safe. "I'll sleep on the floor," he says, an edge to his voice, like he doesn't want to make me uncomfortable—sharing a soft bed in this room all alone. He removes a pillow from the bed, then finds an extra blanket in the dresser, making a place for himself on the hard floor. I want to tell him no, that he can sleep beside me, but I feel strange saying it, awkward somehow, so I climb into the bed alone—beneath white sheets that smell of mint, burying my head in the pillow, toes curling against the clean fabric. For a moment, I try to imagine I'm back in the valley, warm in my bed, that Mom is still alive and nothing has changed.

Noah blows out the single candle on the bedside table, and I slide deeper into the blankets, but it feels odd, unnatural, after so many nights sleeping outside against the hard ground, with the wind always close, and Noah beside me.

The hotel walls settle around us, a quiet that feels too thin.

"Tell me one of your stories," he says from his makeshift bed on the floor, voice like winter snow, like a night sky. "About the first Astronomer."

Back at the lake, I told him I saw stories in the stars. But when he asked what they were, I only gave him the vaguest of answers. Afraid to say too much. Now, though, I want to give him something more—a part of me. Of who I am. "The first Astronomer," I begin, "was the one who charted the night sky, and gave names to the constellations that didn't yet have them."

Even though it feels odd to say the story aloud—to share something that only existed between Mom and me—the words are effortless, streaming from my lips as easy as an exhale.

"What happened to her?" Noah asks in the beat of silence.

"She died in the valley long ago."

"Alone?"

I imagine the tattoos that lined her skin, a woman who had marks just like mine—except she branded the ink into her own flesh, made a map of herself. "She wasn't always alone," I say, my voice a whisper in the quiet room. "She fell in love once." The word feels like electricity on my tongue: *love.*

I wait for Noah to say something, but he only listens, like I'm telling him a bedtime story—except these stories are true.

"She met a man who loved her as much as she loved him. But they couldn't be together. So he left her, and she spent her life in the valley alone."

"Why?"

I roll onto my side, facing the edge of the bed, where I can just barely see Noah on the floor. "It was a sacrifice," I tell him. "They did it for those of us who would come later."

Noah's expression pinches flat, like he doesn't fully understand. "It's a terrible ending to their story. Never seeing each other again."

"It's only a small part of a bigger story—the Astronomer's story—and now it continues with me. And l have to see it to the end."

There is an odd heaviness to his exhale—like he knows we're

marching toward something, the unknown, unwritten part of our story. "How will it end?" he asks, voice so deep it reminds me of the slow-moving river in autumn.

I let one side of my mouth pull down. "We won't know until we get to the sea."

The air feels still, a motionless quiet, thoughts stirring through both our minds. Beating hearts and sorrow and courage all churned up inside us.

"Who was he?" Noah asks after a long silence. "The man she fell in love with?"

Particles of light scatter across my eyes, and I take a deep breath, pushing them away. August never had a chance to tell Noah all the old stories—maybe he was afraid to tell him everything, after what happened with Holt. Maybe he wanted to be sure he could trust Noah before he gave up all the secrets, just in case Noah returned to his father. Just in case Noah betrayed him. Or maybe he didn't want to burden him with the truth. The only thing that truly mattered was knowing the way to the sea. Better not to know the rest, be weighted by the truth of it all.

But Noah is still here. *With me*. And I want to give him this one small thing.

"The first Astronomer fell in love with the first Architect," I say, flashing my eyes to Noah, his dark hair longer than it was when I first met him, grown out, his eyes like drops of morning dew. I could easily drown and never come back up. "They were together in the beginning," I tell him, giving him the truth. I slide my hand under my head, propping myself up. "She studied the sky while he built things, homes and towns and settlements." I think of how simple their love was in the beginning. When they had nothing to fear. It was a love without risk or threat of death.

Noah tilts his chin, looking up at me. And I think of the parallels linking my life with the first Astronomer. She and I both stared into the eyes of a boy who would protect us, who would know the way to the sea, who uprooted us from everything we thought we knew. Who made us feel alive, hearts beating like wings, stomach whirling each time their fingers grazed our skin.

It feels as if the past has bound me to this moment. Brought me here. To Noah.

I reach out my arm toward the edge of the bed, wishing I could touch him, wishing I could breathe him into my lungs and know for sure that no matter what happens, no matter what we find at the end of all this, I won't lose him. But I know it's a stupid thought. *It's a lie.* So I sit up from the bed, pulling the quilt around me, then slide my feet to the cold wood floor.

"What's wrong?" he asks, pushing up to his forearms, bare chest exposed.

"I can't sleep on my own," I say. "In that bed." I crave the hard ground now, the thump of Noah's heartbeat in my ears, the warmth from his body, the closeness of him beside me. His skin against mine. We've spent so many nights lying together in the cold—now it feels like the only way I could ever sleep.

I sink onto the floor and curl myself into the curve of his chest, skin and cotton sheets and breath in deep, weary lungs. He slides his arms carefully around me, along my torso, and I close my eyes, listening to the familiar rhythm of his breathing. *I need to make this last.* Hold on to this singular moment before it's gone. "Back at the water tower," I say, a memory skipping through me, "when I said my name, you flinched. Like you knew it."

I feel his breath against my hair, his sun-warmed forehead and lips so close, I could kiss the features of his face, let my lips trail over his skin so he never slips away. "I knew it was the name of a star," he says softly, each word gliding over my flesh. "August taught me a few of the constellations. And when you said your name, I knew you were her."

He lifts his hand and touches my temple, brushing the hair away—the girl he had been looking for, waiting for, in every town he visited. And now I am folded in his arms. He touches my lips and I close my eyes, wanting to keep this moment, grab it and pull it down from the sky, making it mine. But I know it won't last. It will be taken from me just like everything else.

His dark eyelashes blink, watching me, and I hate the space between us. The treacherous air, the divide. I don't take another breath, I don't bother—I let my mouth hover over his, running my fingers across his collarbone, pressing into the black ink that spirals over muscle and bone. He is a boy who wears the ring of the Architect around his neck, a boy I was worried I'd never find. But now that I have, I want him more than ever. He exhales deeply and looks at me with more emotion than I'm able to understand. "Vega—" he says in a rush, and then he crushes his mouth to mine.

He feels like a dream that has split and bled into the real world. He is warm, faraway nights; he is a story knitted into the stars. He makes me feel shattered and put back together; he is more than I have words to describe. Heat climbs up behind my eyes, and tears break over my eyelids, because I'm afraid. Afraid I'll lose him, afraid of what will happen in *the end*. Afraid this might be the last night I will feel his mouth on my skin, kissing my chin, my neck, like I'm the last and only thing he will ever need.

It's a feeling I never understood until now. A thing I don't want to lose.

A feeling that's so dangerous—it might destroy me.

Noah breathes into my hair, and I kiss his neck below his ear. Now I know what it feels like to want something so bad that it's a blade inside you, digging deeper, until someone comes along and pulls it out. "I'm afraid," I admit, whispering against his skin.

"Of what?" His voice is low, careful, like he already knows the answer.

I dig my fingers into his chest, trying to draw him closer. "Of tomorrow."

He runs his mouth along my neck, back to my lips. "I know." He kisses me again, harder, like he could imprint himself onto my flesh and our tattoos will become one. Like he could protect me from everything that hunts me outside these walls. Like he will never let me go.

But he doesn't know the hurt that awaits us. And I hate the secret I keep inside me, that I keep from him.

I trace a finger along the small scar on his chin, mapping it, trying to blot out my own thoughts, crush them into the background. Noah pulls his mouth away, eyes staring into mine, sensing the fear that pumps inside me. In both of us.

"I won't let them hurt you," he says, a promise, a devotion. An oath. His hands glide along my back, my spine, along the geometry of my flesh, a tremble in his fingertips, shaking slightly. But then there is pressure in his touch, pulling the white nightgown upward, over my thighs, my waist, my head, until I am bare beneath him. Only my tattoos covering my skin.

He kisses me, lets his mouth flutter against mine, reshaping itself, and I make a small sound against his lips, the need heavy in me now. I need him closer. I need him to drown out everything else. His muscled shoulders are tensed above me, the ring suspended from his neck grazing my chest, breath against my mouth. I kiss him again. *Again.* Again. Bringing him to me. Pressing his body against mine.

I need his hands against my flesh, and they find me, tracing every line, every star where it curves along my abdomen, down my thigh. A map beneath his fingertips. I kiss his throat, where his breath quivers. I touch the starburst brand on his forearm, kissing it too, this boy who was once a Theorist. A traitor. Who protects me now, who I know will stay with me until the end. *Until I leave him. And he won't understand.* My fingers find his lips, tracing their perfect shape, and I kiss him, needing all of him. Begging him not to let go, not ever. Not for anything.

His heart is beating through his chest, harder than when we ran from the schoolhouse, and he touches parts of me that no one ever has. He kisses me, and I feel myself shivering beneath him, shattering, digging my fingers into his flesh, into his tattoos—his past woven across his body. Both of us marked. Both of us still alive. And when my breath gusts against his ear, sweat and heat and tears, I feel like a girl broken apart and put back together.

I feel like starlight splintered into dust.

I close my eyes, feeling tangled up in him, stilled, and he settles onto his back, pulling me to him, as close as I can get—like this close will never be close enough. He places a soft kiss on my forehead, his fingers brushing away my hair, straying across my temple.

I rest my head against his chest, his heartbeat pulsing beneath his ribs, feeling the dreamy lull of sleep tugging at me. But I don't close my eyes. I think of the promise I made to Cricket, to keep Noah safe. We have each made promises to protect the other. To keep each other alive. But what's worse: death, or leaving this boy I might love?

Love.

Because lying to him might break me worse than anything so far.

* * *

I press my fingers against his warm chest, along the silver chain around his neck, touching the Architect's ring, tracing the constellation Circinus etched into the metal, while he drifts into his dreams. I peer across the room to the window where the moon is rising against the horizon, the sky severed into two sections, two halves. One filled with stars. The other without.

I hate the sight of it. What it means.

That this, here with Noah, won't last.

I want to close my eyes and make it untrue—I want all the stories that Mom told me to be a lie. But her words find me, cutting through my daydream. "It's the dead part of the sky," she said, a grim slant, a lump in her throat. "Where no light can survive."

She'd been studying it for years, swiveling her telescope into the deepest center of the shadow, charting it, trying to understand what her mother before her never did. Until the night, late in autumn, a hint of snow blowing down from the valley walls, when she called me down to the river, her eyes intent, wild like the fox who sometimes chased crickets up near the toolshed. She adjusted the rings of the telescope, then nodded. "Look," she said, and when I peered through the layered glass, cut at just the right angle, I saw the very edge of the shadow in the sky, where it nudged against a star. And there, in that brief place where they met, the star was erupting in ribbons of light.

"What is it?" I asked, pulling my face away.

"It's swallowing up the star," she told me, a light in her eyes, in her voice, the excitement of discovery.

"Why?"

She craned her head up to the sky, looking at the shadow with her bare eyes, her expression changing, tugging together into a frown. "Because it's a black hole."

I stared at her, then bent to peer through the telescope again, catching the last of the star's streaky light before it vanished.

"It happens so fast," she said, a somber edge in her voice. "It's why I never noticed it before, never caught it right as it was happening. But it's been eating up stars all around it. And the closer it gets, the easier it is to catch it when it happens."

"Closer?" I asked, a tremor working its way up from my toes, a bone-deep knowing.

She touched the telescope gently with her hand, lowering her eyes to me. "It's moving closer, Vega." A sudden seriousness in her voice. And I didn't need her to explain what that meant, because I already knew enough about the stars, about the sky, about anomalies like black holes.

"How long before it reaches us?" I asked matter-of-factly.

She lifted a shoulder, cut her eyes back to the sky again. "Not sure. I need to keep charting it, measure how quick it's expanding.

But—" Her words broke off and she wiped at her temple, avoiding the next thing she would say. Delaying it. But finally it found its way out of her mouth. "Eventually it will fill our entire sky."

"And then it will be too late," I finished for her.

She nodded, a grim cut to her eyes, and she wrapped her arms around me, pulling me to her. But I lifted my head. "What about the sister stars?" I asked. "What if they don't appear in time?"

Air left her nostrils, and she turned her gaze to the east. "We have to hope that they do. Otherwise . . ."

I pulled back from her, looking up at the dark half of the sky, at the black hole. "We won't survive."

This is what I don't tell Noah, what I keep locked away in the cage of my chest. I let him sleep, lungs rising softly, mouth parted. Because the weight of it is too big. And there is still hope in him—a light like flint in his eyes. And I don't want to rip that away. Because the end is a monstrous thing, smudging out the sky—an end that won't be like a fairy tale or bedtime story. It'll be broken skies and broken us, and nothing left.

It's the thing that not only blots out half the horizon, but it's also making us sick.

Mom said it was the *dark matter*, the stuff between stars—tiny, unseen flecks of dust, imperceptible. It spreads outward from black holes like pollen from a honeysuckle tree caught in October winds. And each day that the black hole inches closer, more dark matter rains down on us, making us sicker, weaker. Making our ears ring and our vision spark.

The dark matter has been breaking apart our bodies, disintegrating us bit by bit.

It's been there all along.

The consumption was never contagious, never spread from person to person. It starts seeping into our bodies from the moment we're born—we breathe it in, our air saturated with it—shredding us apart. Killing us.

We bury the dead, calling it *consumption*, a word we know. We understand.

But this is something else.

Not a disease, not a thing passed from one person to another. This filters down from our skies and kills us slowly. Until eventually it will take everything.

Mom always said that the anomaly held more mysteries than answers, a thing that was difficult to describe. To identify.

But what she knew for sure was . . .

This is how we all die.

SCORPIUS, *Alpha Scorpii*
–26° 25' 55"

No one believed her.

The first Astronomer had found a shadow that eclipsed part of the night sky, a feature of the stars she had never seen before. It terrified her worse than the sickness, worse than the burning in her ears that was always there now, that felt like it was punching tiny holes in her skull.

The others thought her foolish, mad, her mind swollen with ideas that could not be proved, could not be made true, no matter how much she pleaded for them to see.

They were too worried about the crops, the consumption that sunk into their bones, the graves they dug behind their homes, and the dust that sometimes choked out the sky. If the consumption didn't kill them all, then starvation would.

But the Astronomer sensed there was something else to fear.

A thing bigger than all the others.

She rarely slept anymore, just peered up at the night sky making notes, hands shaking from the weariness in her bones. She measured and charted—the only thing she knew how to do—she made coordinates where stars had once been, but now were gobbled up by the dark.

She felt alone. Fear wound tight around her tired, sleepless skull.

Until the day a man strode up the long, dusty drive . . . and knocked on the door of her home.

NINE

Morning comes too soon with pale light sneaking through the curtained window, warming the floorboards, the quilt, and my hands where they lie against Noah's bare chest—sun on clean, freckled skin, nails no longer packed with dirt. But I sit upright, gasping for air—as if I was drowning.

I dreamed of the ocean, the brutal, savage sea—and I wipe at my face, brushing away the choking memory.

Noah still sleeps, lips stirring with each breath, no worried creases edging his eyes, no tensed jaw—I don't want to wake him, because I know it won't last. But his arm stirs, sliding across the quilt as if he's searching for me in his sleep. As if I am familiar to him now.

Even though I have lied to him.

Even though I keep things buried inside me—the truth Mom always said was ours to bear, and no one else's.

He is still a moment, looking at me with sleepy emerald eyes, before his gaze flicks to the window, the sun pouring into the room. "It's late," he says, sitting upright. The blankets fall away from him, revealing the tattoos woven across his chest, looping over his collarbone and up his neck. Some look like coiled monsters, others just lines of black along his rib bones, and it makes me want to touch him again. Pull him close and press my mouth to his, sink back into the blankets, and forget the world outside.

But a knock comes at the door, a soft *rap rap rap*. Noah jumps up from the floor. And the calm I had felt is torn away.

The thing we fear will find us, it always does.

Noah opens the door a crack, his back pressed against the wall, ready for whoever's on the other side. But there's no one. He crouches down and retrieves something from the hallway floor, then closes the door again. In his arms, he holds a stack of our cleaned clothes, and something else.

"What is it?" I ask, rising from the floor.

"She left a canteen of water, and food." He sets the clothes onto the bed, and unwraps the cloth to reveal four corn cakes and a bundle of dried fruit—apples and pears.

Quickly Noah pulls on his clothes, his boots, and his canvas coat, then walks to the window and looks out at the street. I feel the change in the air before he speaks, before I even see the muscles along his neck tighten. "We need to go."

I reach for my clothes, yanking my shirt over my head.

We stayed too long. Slept in. Pretending we could be safe for just a few more moments.

"There's horses on the street, ones I don't recognize. They weren't there last night."

A door slams downstairs, followed by voices rising up the stairwell. Noah's eyes dart over to me, and we both go still.

They are men's voices, joined suddenly by Maybelle's—they're asking her something, words muffled at first, but then I make it out:

They're asking about two people on the road. *They're asking about us.*

"It's them," I hiss, and Noah grabs the package of food, tucking it into his coat pocket. I had thought we were safe—I had thought Maybelle wouldn't turn us in—but I was wrong. She must have sent word during the night that a traitor Theorist and the Astronomer were asleep in her hotel, trusting and foolish and unarmed. She lied, keeping us here long enough for the Theorists to reach her small town.

I hurry to the door and press my ear to the wood, my heart slamming against my ribs. *They found us.* I hear the shuffling of boots, and I wait to hear Maybelle tell them we're right at the top of the stairs, pinned inside a room.

"They arrived last night," she says, voice echoing up the stairwell.

I flash a look to Noah, where he's still peering out the window. We could escape through the window and down the side of the hotel, but it faces the street, and we'd drop from the roof right onto the porch, where they'd see us.

Still, Noah unlocks the window, tries pushing it up, but it doesn't even move an inch.

"—but they left," I hear Maybelle say now, and my eyes cut back to the door. I'm surprised, certain I misheard. "Took off early this morning on horseback. Didn't even pay for their room," she adds for good measure, maybe to make her story sound true. Like she's just as eager to see us apprehended. "Headed south, I think."

A rising feeling of relief presses against my rib cage, and I let out a shaky breath. She didn't turn us in. She didn't send for them after all. They tracked us here, on their own.

She kept her word.

The men speak swiftly, too low to hear, and then there are more footsteps, followed by the sound of the door opening again as they retreat outside.

Noah steps back from the window so he won't be seen.

My heart is beating too fast; I feel trapped in this room. I cross to Noah, softly so my feet don't make a sound, and I squint out into the daylight. There are five men, and five horses tied to the railing in front of the hotel. I expect them to mount their horses and ride on up through town, searching for our trail. But they hesitate. I realize Maybelle is on the porch, still speaking to them. I can just make out the top of her head, dark wavy hair stirring in the morning breeze, but I can't hear what she's saying.

One of the men tips his hat to her, and I see that he's bent slightly forward—as if in pain.

"It's Holt," I whisper. *He's still alive.*

Hope—the only thing we have left now—drains out of me.

Impossibly, beyond all reason—he's alive.

A man Noah has tried to kill twice. *His own father.* I touch Noah's shoulder, certain that a tangled storm of emotions is raging through him. He didn't murder his father after all—the guilt surely eased. Yet it means that the danger is closer than ever.

It means that Holt won't stop. And the panic slides up my spine.

Noah glances at me, his face a river of tension, but he only nods. This isn't the time to discuss what it means, how his heart is surely a piston beneath his ribs. We have to get out of here. Through the glass, I can hear Holt speaking to his men—low words I can't pick apart—but then they turn away from the hotel, crossing the dusty street to climb the steps of the saloon, disappearing inside.

The breath is still climbing up from my lungs, when there's a tap at the door.

Noah's eyes flash to me, and he puts a finger to his lips, so I stay beside the window. "It's Maybelle," a voice whispers from the other side. "A group of Theorists are looking for you, but I told them to let their horses rest and get a drink across the street, that it was on me."

Noah opens the door a crack.

"There's a fire escape off the bathroom," she says swiftly, her blue eyes darting down the hall. "It leads to the back of the hotel. You won't be seen."

In the bathroom, Maybelle slides open the squat little window, revealing a wood ladder down the backside of the hotel. Noah swings himself through and vanishes below the edge of the window. "Thank you for helping us," I say to Maybelle.

She grabs something from one of the bathroom cabinets—a wool blanket with a pale green stripe along the edge—holding it out to me. "To keep you warm," she says. "You'll find your horse in the stable, just south." I tuck the blanket under my arm and meet her eyes one last time—this woman who gave us a free place to stay and clean clothes and food for the road. She nods back at me, just before I slip out through the window.

Noah and I land on the hard-packed ground below, then run along the outer edge of town until we reach the stable, ducking inside where the scent of straw and manure is thick. Aside from a few horses standing sleepily in stalls, flies buzzing near their large eyes, it's deserted.

We find Odie, freeing her from the stall and slipping a bridle over her head. Noah pushes me up onto her back, and we're galloping out of the stable in less than three minutes, sprinting into the nearest line of trees.

We need to get far away from this town, ride until nightfall, until we can no longer see the way.

We'll sleep outside; we'll feel the itch always at our backs of those men not far behind.

But we'll keep moving.

Because the shadow in the sky is getting closer—the twin stars drifting away—and I can feel the story of the last Astronomer being written along my skin with each mile we cross, a fate I can't escape.

TEN

The air is cold. Barbed.

We trek into higher elevations, into a clot of steep hills. Noah's arms are braced around my ribs—his hands held tight to the leather reins—while his warm breath is at my neck, the wool blanket from Maybelle wrapped over both of us, the only thing keeping the cold from breaking through our skin. Our small shelter. Like it's enough to keep out all the dark things. All the death.

Odie picks her way through the sloping, rocky terrain, sure-footed, the oaks around us grown short and lopsided in the sharp northern winds. My ears vibrate, eyes flashing upward where the shadow has smeared out too much of the sky. More than yesterday. Or the day before.

But finally the sky begins to brighten—golden and rust with the sunrise—and the trees thin, turn to nothing.

Ahead of us, I see what's to come: a wide row of mountains.

Noah pulls Odie to a stop, eyeing the steep slope ahead of us.

"There must be a way around," I say. Maybe if we travel east or west for a short distance, we'll find a shallower, easier route over these jagged, snow-draped peaks.

Noah slips a hand into his coat pocket and pulls out the compass, holding it flat in his palm. His mouth tenses into a line. "North is straight ahead." He places the compass back into his pocket. "August always said I'd have to pass over a mountain range. There's no other way."

Snow starts to fall. Fat white clouds pushing across the sky.

"We'll get to the first slope," he says, voice beside my ear. "Then camp."

He urges Odie on, and we cut over a barren, treeless stretch of low hills toward the cold mountains. There is no place to hide, no shelter from the wind. It lashes at our backs, then changes direction without warning to sting and cut into our faces.

When I squint through the wind, I see only blowing snow and the sheer rock of the mountains growing closer. This is a place for the dead. For the doomed.

Maybe that's what we are.

Just after nightfall—my hands trembling in my coat pockets, eyes dry from the endless wind—we reach the base of the mountains and Noah finds a low overhang in the rock, a place where we're able to tuck our bodies in just enough to keep the wind from our faces. But there's no timber for a fire, no way to keep warm, so he wraps his arms around me and I lie with my face tucked into the hollow of his neck, shivering, while Odie stands with her back to the wind.

We don't speak. Not enough warmth in our throats for words. Only closed eyelids and shallow breaths now. All that's left of us.

✳ ✳ ✳

My eyes open—tiny snowflakes on my lashes, at the ends of my hair. But the sky is still gray, a carpet of low, swirling clouds, as if the sun hasn't risen at all.

A snowstorm has burrowed itself against the mountains and shows no sign of letting up. "Are you okay?" Noah asks, so close he could lay his lips on my temple, press himself to me, and we could stay this way until the cold pulled the last of the warmth from our bones. But I nod, mouth too numb to speak, and he runs his hands up my arms to warm me. "Odie can't come with us any farther," he says. "It's too steep. She won't make it."

I lift my head, a tremble at the back of my teeth. "No."

"We don't have a choice."

He pushes himself up from our little shelter beneath the rock, leaving the blanket around my shoulders, and starts removing the bridle from Odie's head.

"We can't leave her on her own," I snap, my voice brittle and cracked.

He rubs a hand down her forelock to her soft nose. "She'll be okay," he assures. "Horses know their way home."

"But she doesn't have a home."

Noah places the bridle on the ground, in the snow—leaving it there. "She'll probably find your pa, eventually."

I don't want to go on without her, not after I've found her again. But I also know he's right, she won't make it through this snow—it's too deep, too dangerous for her—so I stand up, keeping the blanket wrapped over my shoulders, and lay my palm against Odie's neck. I breathe in her damp, woolly scent—knowing I have to let her go. I think of the farmhouse and the apple orchard. Maybe she'll find her way back there: the memory of those trees, the soft, grassy land, will be enough to draw her there. "Okay."

I release my hand from her face, and she stands a moment, ears pointed forward, confused, but then slowly she starts moving back down the slope toward the trees in the distance.

I fight the rising tears. Not just for Odie, but for everything we're leaving behind. This feels like the point of no return. A divide inside me—the past laid out behind us, dotted with blood and scars and things I can't take back, while the future is a storm cloud ahead, a terrifying wall of snow and cold.

Noah wraps his hand through mine, squeezing—*not letting go*, just like he promised—and we start up the steep, rocky route between two mountain peaks, feet sinking into the fresh layer of snow, lungs heaving in the cold, awful air.

Noah makes a trail through the snow ahead of me, and I think of nothing else except keeping him within view, not losing sight of his silhouette in the gusting wind ripping down the mountainside. Every few yards, he glances back to make sure I'm still there—that I haven't collapsed or slipped down the steep terrain.

At a low spot, he stops, pulling out his compass to make sure we're still heading north; then we push on again. The wind is fanged, brutal, freezing the drops of moisture on my eyelashes, turning them to ice. I've never tasted air this cold, swallowed and felt it burn. The numbness in my hands and feet starts slowly, a tingling that becomes a stinging pain.

And then no feeling at all.

At last we reach a sheer stone wall, and Noah has to hoist me up over it, making me stand on his shoulders so he can push me up to the top of the ledge, before scrambling up himself.

On the other side, I place my hands over my eyes to block the wind, and look out at a landscape dotted with more mountains, and I think: *We're not going to make it.*

"Are you sure we're going the right way?" I ask, turning my face away from the wind.

He nods and says, "Not much farther."

But he can't know for sure. He just doesn't want me to look back.

Despair is a thing that sneaks up slowly, tendrils threading into your thoughts until you can hear nothing else. *We're going to die out here,* my mind begins to repeat, a loop that won't stop. And too soon, the sky grows dark, the moon hidden behind clouds, making it impossible to tell the hour. We sink down beside a boulder, away from the wind, but we don't sleep. We sit with knees drawn up, the blanket over our heads, and we shake. We eat the last of the corn cakes and dried fruit that Maybelle gave us. Noah cups my hands in his and blows warm air to keep the numbness at bay. I rest my head against his shoulder, then touch the chain around his neck, pulling the silver ring free from his coat. He watches me silently, lets me hold the ring between my fingers. I can't see the stars through the storm above us, but tracing the tiny constellation etched into his ring soothes me, makes me feel not so lost in these mountains.

"Do you know what your ring means?" My voice is cracked, teeth chattering.

Noah is quiet, and I wonder if he heard me over the wind, or if the cold has sapped his ability to speak. But then he says softly, "It's a constellation. Circinus."

I nod, and smile a little. August told him this much. "Do you know what *Circinus* means?"

He leans closer to me, shaking his head, and runs his hands up my arms to keep them warm.

"It's the draftsman's compass," I say gently. "A tool used by

Architects. The constellation Circinus was named after it." I can picture the string of stars resting in the night sky, faint, distant, but unique in their parallel pattern. "The first Architect wore the ring as a symbol, an emblem of who he was."

I run my thumb over the ring. "It was a way for the Astronomer to find the Architect," I say, peering up into his eyes, a hook tugging in the center of my ribs, always wanting to be closer to him. "It was a way to find you." He takes my hands in his, holding them to his chest, then bends close to kiss me, his lips lingering softly against mine, as if he could stall time, and for a moment, the cold feels a million miles away. But when his mouth lifts, the icy air finds me again. I tuck my head closer into his chest, as close as I can get, listening to the thrum of his heart, and he continues to blow warm air into my palms, rubbing his hands up my arms, folding himself around me. He does this all night.

And still, it feels like my body is shutting down. The cold finding its way in.

✳ ✳ ✳

The wind stops with the morning sunrise—an eerie calm.

Noah pushes the blanket away from our heads, snow sloughing away, and everything is coated in a frosty white, the sun winking off the perfect layer—not a single cloud above us.

The storm has passed.

Noah looks to me, his deep woodland eyes reminding me of the forest we left behind, the feel of the ground beneath us, the scent of moss always in my nose. I crave it now. Anything other than snow. "Can you feel your feet?" he asks, glancing at my boots.

"Barely."

"We'll get warm once we start moving again."

I know this is only partially true, because the cold is always there, relentless. But I stand, wincing away from the bright sun reflecting off the snow. "We're out of food, Noah," I remind him. "And we don't have much water left."

He scrubs a hand down his face, blinking out at the mountain range that seems to have no end. "I know."

I follow his gaze out over the sharp, serrated mountains draped in sunlit snow. It's beautiful, a place that few have likely ever seen, and I know these mountains might kill us, but there's no turning back now. It's too late for that. Noah breathes, and it's as if a wind is inside him, passing through his lungs with each inhale. He brushes the hair away from my face and helps me up.

We move quickly now, without the sharp wind always at our throats. But I can feel my skin burning beneath the bright sun, winking off the snow. I sweat—and I am cold, all at once.

It takes half a day to scale the steepest point, and when I reach the top, Noah is staring out at something. "What is it?" I ask, afraid to hear the answer, afraid to see another endless series of jagged mountain peaks. Certain we might never find our way out of this cold.

But when I lift my eyes, sucking in the thin mountain air, I let out a small gasp. . . .

We've reached the edge of the mountain range.

Stretched out before us is a black-sand beach, with an ocean that falls away against the horizon. My eyes well with tears, and a lump expands in my ribs—I feel like I might drop to my knees.

We found the end.

We've come to the sea.

TAURUS, *Alpha Tauri*
+16° 30' 33"

He made the long walk up the driveway to her small home, built just outside of town.

He had heard in Fort Bell about the Astronomer who saw something in the sky, who talked of things that were surely a madness of the mind, a symptom of the sickness that couldn't possibly be true.

The man knocked on her door, a curious slant between his brows, and he asked her what she saw. The Astronomer led him out to the quiet, grassy place near the pines, and they sat under the night sky, where he listened to her talk of the stars, of the constellations she was sketching onto paper so they wouldn't be forgotten, and he felt a sureness in his ribs he had never known before.

Night after night, he visited her home, and they stayed awake until the sun crept up over the row of pines. She taught him how to chart the sky and pointed to constellations that still had not been named.

They didn't mean to fall in love. It was a symptom of something greater—greater than the crackling ache in their ears or the twitch in the center of their eyes. This feeling took hold inside them, a soft, gentle coiling of the heart, a buzzing they couldn't ignore.

They spent two months this way, together, marking the stars, talking of theories and possibilities. But none of it mattered, because there was no cure for the sickness, no remedy.

No way to save themselves. Except one.

But they would need to wait . . . wait for the twin stars to appear in the east.

And in the waiting, the Astronomer would need to hide.

She would go where no one would find her, where time would slip over her, decades, generations, until she would become a rumor, a story talked about and almost forgotten, a woman who was lost.

Alone.

Because only the Architect knew the way to the sea, and that made him just as valuable, just as hunted. Together, the Astronomer and the Architect were dangerous.

The Astronomer began marking her skin with ink, tattoos to chart a course—a map, *a way*—while the Architect had a ring forged by a blacksmith in Fort Bell, stamping the constellation Circinus into the metal—a symbol of the draftsman's compass.

Each with their own marks, their own tokens, they hoped that the generations who came after them would be able to find one another.

They sacrificed themselves, kissing one last time beneath a half-waning moon, the Architect holding her close, the pain of letting her go almost too much. But they didn't have a choice.

They said goodbye.

And the Astronomer watched the Architect walk over the ridge and out into the plains, before she, too, turned and began her march to the west, to look for a place far from the other towns and colonies. Far from everything. She walked for days, until she came upon a valley where a river carved its way through the rock cliff. She would build a small, quiet life. Where she would teach her daughter—now growing in her belly—to map the stars.

She would stay hidden.

And when the child was born, she would teach her of responsibility. Teach her to stay in the valley, safe. Teach her to wait for the sister stars to appear, and then maybe they would be saved.

ELEVEN

The wind carries scents of aged wood and salt before our feet have even reached the beach.

We pick our way through sawtooth rocks, descending the mountains quickly, before finally stepping onto the black-sand beach. The softness beneath my boots is such a relief, tears spill down my cheeks, and a smile edges across my lips.

We made it.

"August said this place is called Turnback Beach," Noah says, lifting a hand over his eyes, the shrill cry of birds carried on the wind as they circle over the foaming sea.

I breathe in the salty air, clouds sitting low and somber over us, burdened by moisture. It will rain soon. "Why?"

"Because anyone who makes it this far should turn back and go home. He said this is the end of the continent. There's nothing beyond this." Noah squints through the mist rising off the water, eyes glassy, as if recalling the few stories that August told him over the years—stories passed from one Architect to the next—the passage he might someday take to get here with the Astronomer at his side. I can almost see the years of waiting in his eyes.

Waiting for me.

And now we've arrived, standing on the beach that I've tried to imagine in my mind for most of my life. A place I struggled to believe I'd truly reach someday.

Our feet make watery depressions in the sand, a path from the spiky mountains to the edge of the sea, where the waves are sliding foamy and slick across the black sand. But the ocean is not docile, a gentle rolling. The tide—a thing my mother described to me in one of her many lessons—lashes against the beach, waves crashing violently several yards out, a great explosion of sound, before they push up onto the shore.

Noah squints out at the heaving, tossing sea, a weariness in his eyes—all the miles we've traveled cut into his face. "What now?"

I scan the water's edge, but there's nothing here. "There's supposed to be a ship," I mutter under my breath, something I haven't said aloud until now. A part of the story that Mom told, that I've kept all to myself.

But maybe we're too late. Maybe too much time has passed, generations, a hundred years. Anything could have happened in that time. It could have long ago drifted away or sunk in the violent waters.

"A ship?" Noah repeats, stepping closer to the sea, the water sliding up across his boots. "Could it be out there?" He points across the ocean to where a rocky formation—a small island—sits just offshore against the stormy sky. "Hidden on the other side?"

I squint through the mist. "Maybe. But how do we reach it?"

Noah's jaw tenses, not liking the answer he's about to give. "We swim."

Gray-spotted seagulls sit perched atop the jagged rocks at the center of the island, then dive out over the water, hunting for fish, while waves thunder against the beach, exploding when they hit the sand. I try to imagine a way through without drowning. But this sea is nothing like the river back in the valley—the predictable flow of the water always moving in one direction.

"But the water's too dangerous right now," he adds. "We should wait until low tide, for the waves to settle."

"We might not have time." I flash a look at the mountain ridge behind us, knowing Holt might not be far behind. Knowing the sky above is breaking apart—the darkness above looking too close, filling up too much of the horizon. A smear of black where there should be gray-blue sky.

I skim my gaze back to the sea, wishing there was another way.

Noah's eyes darken, water on his lashes. "Vega," he says, nodding behind me.

I hesitate, unsure what he's trying to say with his half-lidded eyes, a crease forming between his brows, but then I turn, and through the heavy fog and gray clouds, a man is moving up the shoreline.

A shadow through the misting rain.

I blink, certain it's only a trick of the dull light. But then two more figures appear. A third, a fourth, coming into view, encircling us.

They already made it over the mountains to the beach.

Holt and his men have found us.

✳ ✳ ✳

Fear is like a rope around my ribs. Cinching tight.

"I was beginning to wonder if you two died in those mountains,"

321

Holt says, striding toward me, hands hooked at his belt, gaze leveled in the damp wind.

I watch as four other men encircle us—including Samuel, greasy hair and twitching fingers and a wad of tobacco in his lip. Beside me, Noah's shoulders draw back, and I know he's calculating how many of them he could hold off if he had to, perhaps one or two before they overpowered him. It might be enough for me to get away, but I won't leave him.

I shoot him a look and shake my head only a fraction of an inch. *Don't do it,* I say with my eyes.

"But now here we all are," Holt muses, a pleased, buoyant quality to his voice. "The Astronomer, and"—his mismatched eyes cut to Noah—"and my own disloyal son, who tried to kill me . . . more than once." For a moment, Holt looks like he's going to move toward Noah, wrap his hands around Noah's throat, and end it quick. Be done with it. But then his eyes swivel toward the sea. "I've waited a long time to see this place." He pauses, then flashes Noah a look over his shoulder, his gray, clouded eye wincing—beneath his shirt is surely a bandage and a deep wound where Noah's knife cut into his torso. He's still alive, but he's in pain, and I wonder if he's been taking the pills he stole from my coat. "August never told me how to get here—he didn't trust me enough."

I sense Noah wanting to speak, say some sharp-tongued thing, but he resists. Still, I can feel the tension tightening in the damp air, closing around us, and I worry what will happen next—Holt and Noah, all the betrayal and blood spilled between them, and now they're standing only a few feet apart.

"I understand why you did it," Holt says now, jaw pushed out too far as if it's on a lever, made of wood and wires, instead of bone. He moves toward Noah and reaches out like he's going to touch Noah's face—a father wanting to feel his son after all these years—but Noah shoves his hand away, little pulses erupting at his temples. I can see the fury inside Noah, coiled tight; he wants to lunge at Holt. But still, he holds his ground. "I know August has turned you against me," Holt continues, shaking his head, tapping his teeth together. As if it were so simple.

I try to imagine Holt as a father, caring for a young son. Tenderness and reading bedtime stories. I try to see Noah in Holt's face. In his eyes. But he's not there—no part of him remains in his father's features. Maybe Noah looks more like his mother. Yet there is fury in both of them. Anger and revenge. A duty, a loyalty to what they believe in, a fight they will see to the end, no matter what. Even if it kills them both.

Noah's stare cuts into Holt, his hands fisting at his sides. "I left you because I hated what you'd become, not because of August." His shoulders tense. "I left on my own."

For a second, Holt actually looks confused, hurt, an ache in his eyes, but then his features harden again. "Your mother died of the sickness."

"I know," Noah answers swiftly, as if he doesn't like being reminded of her death. I want to touch his hand, comfort him, but I don't dare move. Afraid to draw attention to myself, afraid that they'll force us apart.

"Then help me," Holt replies, both of his eyebrows raised, rain streaming over his perfectly combed hair, down the hollow shape of his jaw. "I'm dying just like her, like so many others," he admits, and he rolls his neck to the side, as if he's holding back the pain of the sickness working through his joints, and the pain of the deep gash at his side. "But we can leave this place."

I look to Noah, unsure what he's thinking. What thoughts are crashing through his mind. I know this must be painful for him, hearing his father say these things, cracking open old wounds he thought he'd left behind. All of it being torn wide. And another part of me wonders, *worries*, that Noah might feel some old loyalty, looking into the eyes of his father, hearing his words. Maybe he will agree, he will see that his father might be right, and turn against me.

But Noah glares back at his father. "I won't help you," he spits, the muscles along his neck tensing, a look of disbelief in his eyes. "I'll never be what you wanted me to be—I was loyal to you for too long. I hurt people because of you, because you asked me to. But I knew it was wrong even then." He meets his father's eyes. "You tried to turn me into something I wasn't, a monster like you. But now"—Noah's hands flex, and I can feel the anger rising from his skin, see the torment in his shadowed eyes—"I know what you really are." His mouth curls in disgust. "And I was always stronger than you. Even when you thought I was weak." He exhales but doesn't blink, doesn't flinch his eyes away. "And I'll kill you eventually."

Holt takes a swift step toward Noah. "You *were* weak. It's why you left. And now . . ." He cuts his eyes over to me. "You're protecting *her*, over your own family."

Holt makes a sudden move toward me, but Noah jerks in front of him, blocking him before his hands can claw into me. "Don't touch her!"

The look in Holt's eyes changes, turns almost feral, and I think he finally understands how deep his son's betrayal goes. That there is nothing he can say to convince him, to bring him back—Noah will protect *me* until the very end. His loyalty to his father is long gone, broken like glass dropped into a fire. Not even a flicker remains.

Holt curls his upper lip and cracks his neck to the side, taking a step back away from me, toward the sea, then pivoting back to face us. "You could have led the Theorists, you could have been something, something powerful." His mouth puckers down in disappointment, a son with so much potential wasted, and his eyes flash to Noah's forearm, like he's imagining the starburst brand that's hidden there. The mark of a Theorist. "But instead you chose her." His mouth twitches, and he touches his lower ribs—the place where Noah shoved his blade into his flesh—air gusting from his nostrils.

Noah reaches out, hand finding mine, and he pulls me closer to him. As if to show where his devotion now lies. That he will risk death, his father's own blade, to keep me safe.

"You never were good at following orders," Holt says now, a snarl puckering his upper lip. "Too defiant, like your mother."

"It's not defiance," Noah barks. "I just wasn't a murderer like you."

Holt laughs, baring his broken teeth. "No, but you'd try to kill your own father. Twice."

Rain begins to fall heavier, spitting from the sky, and I can feel the change in Noah's shoulder against mine, the tension coiled down every muscle—if Holt even tries to come toward me, Noah will stop him. He'll fight back . . . until they kill him. "And I'd do it again," Noah says with such grit in his voice that a chill runs down my spine.

Holt takes two quick steps toward Noah, his shoulders rolled back, a look in his eyes like he's lost all restraint, and he raises his arm, as if he's about to hit his own son, drive his fist into Noah's skull. But Noah lifts his chest and steps forward too, willing his father to throw the first punch. Urging him to start a fight that Noah will finish. Because although they are the same height, Noah is undeniably stronger, younger, the muscles in his arms and shoulders flexing in anticipation, itching to end it with his father once and for all.

But Holt must see that he's outmatched, outweighed, and with a deep, unhealed wound in his ribs, it wouldn't take much for Noah to knock him to the ground, to end his life before Samuel and his other men had a chance to pull Noah off. Holt taps his front teeth together and makes a sound of irritation from his throat. "I trained you well," he says, licking his front teeth. "Never back down from a fight."

Noah doesn't reply, just stands his ground. And I hate that it's come to this, hate that he must face his father and be willing to kill him. I hate that I brought him here, and that now he must defend me; I hate that we're not back at Maybelle's Hotel, his hands against my skin, breath against my ear, where I should have told him the truth. Should have told him everything, and then he could have decided if he still wanted to bring me here, to see it through.

But Holt clicks his gaze to me—past Noah—as if Noah is no longer an obstacle he's concerned with. No longer his son. *Nothing at all.* "Now, little lady . . . ," he says, calling me the name he spoke at the miners' camp when he stole Odie, when he thought I was simply the daughter of Pa. "You will get us out of this godforsaken place." The scar at his throat flutters, voice rattling up from the sick, dying cage of his chest, and he casts his eyes out to the sea. "Tell me where it is?"

I breathe in the rain, feel it dampen my throat. I don't answer him.

The smirk on his lips disappears. "No more silence," he barks, a cruelness finding his eyes. "We're past that now. Tell me where the ship is."

"I don't know," I answer coldly, clenching on the words.

He laughs, a quick sound. But his eyes are dark, darker than the sky, darker than I remember from the schoolhouse. Death is waiting inside him—rotting, sneaky. Not long now. "You're the Astronomer," he growls, as if he hates the sound of the word. "You know everything about this place. I bet you even know more than your *Architect* here." He no longer calls Noah his *son*, no longer looks at him as if they share the same blood. "I bet you've kept all your secrets from him, forced him to bring you here, and now you'll leave him. Quick as anything. As if he means nothing to you."

The bitter taste of anger expands in my throat. *No,* I think. *No, no, no.* And I feel Noah's eyes flick to me briefly—he doesn't understand, doesn't know what Holt's saying.

But I do.

And my head pounds, tilts, the guilt spiking up behind my eyes.

Holt's mouth peels up into a triumphant grin—he likes this, likes watching me twitch beneath the weight of his words. "He doesn't know that you came all this way, and all along you planned to leave him, does he?" His smile only widens, and I know now that August told Holt more than he had time to tell Noah. Holt knows more than I ever wanted to believe. And the knowing makes him dangerous. "She lied to you," he says, turning to Noah, dead eye winking out of time with the other. Wanting his son to see that he never should have trusted me. That I will betray him just as he betrayed his own father. "She used you to get here, and then she planned to save herself."

"That's not true." I clench my teeth. And Noah's eyes swing to me again, looking for answers, looking for me to deny it, but I can't meet his stare.

I never wanted it to happen like this, never wanted to reach the end, the sea, and feel my heart cracking wide at the thought of leaving Noah behind. I wanted to tell him the truth—*myself*. But now there's no time.

"Tell me," Holt demands now, eyes skipping back to me, an impatient edge to his voice—like he's grown tired of his own games. "Tell me where the ship is."

I hold down the breath in my lungs, feel my chest heaving with the pressure, and without meaning to, without thinking, my eyes flick out to the sea.

To the small, rocky island in the distance.

Holt's gaze follows mine, and a smirk rises from his lips. "Good." He nods and takes a step closer to me—as if I belonged to him, as if he could snatch me from Noah whenever he wanted. Quick and sharp.

But I press myself against Noah, my heartbeat against his side. Knowing that if I'm pulled from him, it will feel like being pulled from my own body, pulled from my own beating heart.

Holt grins, as if he's watching a frightened animal skitter away from his grasp, and I hate the feel of his dark, grisly eyes on me, the awful slant of his mouth as he bites down, grinding against his teeth, and nods to one of the men behind us. I don't even have time to turn, to react, before there are hands on my shoulder, yanking me backward, out of Noah's grasp.

"Don't fucking touch her!" Noah shouts, turning in an instant and ripping Samuel's hands free from me and shoving him back. Samuel staggers a moment, stunned, then reaches for the knife at his waist, dark eyes suddenly leveled on Noah.

"Stop," Holt commands, flashing Samuel a warning look. Samuel hesitates, anger cutting across his face, before re-sheathing his blade and spitting onto the sand at his feet. Noah steps in front of me, a hand at my waist, ready to fight, his eyes darting to the other men.

"We all want the same thing," Holt says now, a calmness to his voice I don't like, and he wheels his gaze back to me. Yet I know what he says isn't true. He wants to save himself, only himself. *But I'm trying to save everyone.* A knot binds in my stomach, and I tilt my eyes up, the watery sky shimmering at the edges, along the rim of the atmosphere.

We're running out of time.

"You're going to swim out there," Holt says, blowing out an irritated gust of air, and points a finger out to the island, waves crashing against the shore.

Sparks lick at my vision as I stare through the rain at the rocky island. "I don't know if it's out there," I say truthfully, meeting his eyes, needing him to believe me. "It might have sunk, or washed away with the tide. It's probably long gone."

"Bullshit." Holt lifts his chin, the red puckered skin of the scar on his neck almost looking like an open wound, and I cringe, imagining blood gushing from it, a wide cut stretched ear to ear. *He's unwilling to die.* "It's still out there," he says, a certainty to his voice, a desperation. It's something he needs to believe to give meaning to all the awful things he's done. To bring meaning to his wife's death, to losing his son to August. "It might be hidden, but it's still there. I know it." His gray eye, the same color as the flat, razed skyline, blinks against the wet air. "You're going to swim out to it, and find it."

"No," Noah interrupts, stepping closer to Holt. "She'll drown."

One side of Holt's mouth inches upward into an amused, animal-like grin, and he cranes his head up to the rainy sky. "If she does, then maybe it was fated in the stars." But his words are scoffing, doubtful. "Isn't that what you believe?" His eyes fall to me. "That your story has already been foretold?"

I don't answer him.

"You believe your ancestors knew this day would come." Rage curls his upper lip, and the wind blows water up from the sea, pelting our faces.

Noah's chest rises stiffly, and I know he doesn't understand what his father is saying. I know he's starting to see that I have kept things from him, more than I want to admit. Even to myself.

"But your ancestors could have left this place long ago," Holt says, running his tongue along his broken teeth. "But instead they stayed and let us all suffer. Let us die."

"They didn't have a choice," I sputter, feeling like I'm choking on my own words. I flick my eyes to the sea, the horizon marred by clouds, broken by shafts of strange light—the shadow above us churning against the atmosphere. The anomaly has grown, gotten closer, and it makes the air buzz strangely, my ears ringing even louder.

"They always had a choice," Holt answers, dragging a palm down the side of his slick hair where the wind has stirred it loose. "They waited a hundred years . . . for nothing."

"They sacrificed themselves so we could live," I say, a rattle in my throat.

Holt shifts forward, licking his lips, like he's struggling to keep the fury from boiling up inside him. To maintain control. "They sacrificed all of us," he counters, each word blunt, jaw stuck out. "They made the choice for us. Only the Astronomer could navigate the stars, and only the Architect knew where the ship was hidden." His eyes vibrate. "They kept it secret, while the rest of us died."

I keep my mouth shut, anger burning behind my eyes. *He's wrong,* I think. *Wrong about all of it.* But we're wasting too much time. Again, I feel Noah's eyes scrape over to me, too many questions in his stare. The missing pieces, the things he still doesn't understand.

Holt points a finger at his gray, dead eye, and it blinks as if of its own command. "I won't die here," he says, repeating what he told me at the schoolhouse. "We've waited a hundred years, and I'm leaving this place—for good." He touches his ribs, pain briefly cut into his face, before he lowers his hand. "You will swim out to that island and find the ship."

My pulse rises in my throat, erratic, and I glance through the rain to the island—a watery outline, the sea still thundering against the shore—and I try to imagine swimming through the tossing waves, my lungs burning, seawater spilling down my throat. I imagine the feel of the cold water pulling me down, *down*, into the deep, until—

"I'll do it—" another voice says. My heart stops, eyes slipping to Noah. "I'll swim to the island."

For a moment, Holt goes silent, jaw cleaving left and then right, staring at Noah like he's trying to decide who he'd rather see drown—who he'd rather watch die. His traitor son or me. But I already know the answer. And after a long, cruel pause, he shakes his head. "No. Only she can do it." He steps even closer, peering past Noah, right into my eyes. "Only the Astronomer will know what to do." He tilts his head, patience gone. "You're going to swim out to that island and find the ship," he says tightly. "Now."

I open my mouth to speak, to tell him again that I don't think there's anything out there—that the ship is surely long gone—but Holt snaps a hand out and grabs my arm. Squeezing. In an instant, Noah lunges forward, trying to push Holt back, to protect me, but at the same moment, two of the other men are on him, yanking Noah away. Samuel forces Noah's arms behind his back, twisting, causing a sharp wince of pain to tighten across Noah's face.

"No!" I cry out. "Stop!"

Holt calmly brushes his damp hair back from his face, then pinches his fingers around my forearm, digging into my flesh. "You've made this harder on yourself than it needs to be." He gives a quick nod to the two men holding Noah, and Samuel pulls a knife from his belt, pressing it to Noah's throat. A flicker of satisfaction catches in Samuel's eyes—he's wanted to do this since the moment Noah shoved him away from me, and now the glint of the blade digs into Noah's flesh.

"Please, don't!" I yell, trying to move toward him, but Holt only hardens his grip on me. My jaw aches, pulsing in my skull, and above us, the sky is heavy with moisture, a weight that I can feel pressing down.

But Noah's eyes find mine, the green in them suddenly like stone, like they're made of the dark sand beneath our feet, and he's pleading with me not to fight. *To stay put.*

"You will swim out there—" Holt demands, pointing at the choppy, thunderous sea. Waves pounding against the shore. "Or I'll kill him." His eyes break over to Noah, mashing his teeth together. "And if you think I won't kill my own son, you'll find out how wrong you are."

A swirling, sickening dread tears through my entire body, twisting around my chest.

"No," Noah replies, tugging against the two men, but the blade is only pressed tighter to his throat, turning the skin red, nearly slicing through. He doesn't want me going into the sea, risking my life for him, when the tide will surely kill me.

"I guess we'll find out if she's a strong swimmer," Holt says, glancing in Noah's direction, then back to me. "I'll send one of my men with you, to make sure you don't try to leave on the ship on your own—although I suspect you won't leave your Architect to die. And if you drown while swimming out there, I'll kill him. If the man I send to the island with you ends up dead for any reason, I'll kill him. If anything happens other than you finding the ship, I'll kill your Architect. Understand?"

Noah shakes his head, eyes pleading with me. "You can't swim out there," he says, voice stifled by the pressure of the blade at his throat.

Tears gather in my eyes. The pain in my chest, in my crackling ears, is like a thousand bricks, and I don't know what to do.

But Noah yanks an arm free from Samuel, swiveling around,

and lands a blow against his face. Samuel stumbles back, holding a hand over his bleeding nose, spitting the wad of tobacco to the ground, while the other man tries to grab Noah's arm. Noah ducks, his knuckles colliding with the man's ribs, then another blow to his jaw. The man drops to the ground, gasping. But the two others who had been standing closest to me dart forward, grabbing Noah around the neck and dragging him backward, forcing him into a headlock. Samuel swipes at the blood dripping down his face, then retrieves the knife where it had fallen to the sand, holding it to Noah's throat so tightly, I'm sure it's going to puncture his skin and bleed him out right here. "You done?" Samuel asks.

And Noah stops struggling.

His eyes pinned on me.

Tears streak down my cheeks, and I step away from Holt, slowly, and for some reason he allows me to go. Maybe he knows I'm not a threat, knows there's nothing I can do. My heart is thudding in time with my breathing, and I move toward Noah—I know I can't fend off these men, I know I'm not strong enough to fight any of them. But gently I touch the shoulder of the man who's standing in front of Noah. He flinches, spins around like he's ready to fight, then lowers his arm. I just need to reach Noah, touch him, make him understand. Because I know now, Holt has taken away any choice I thought I had.

I step closer to Noah, and the men let me. Even Holt doesn't speak, doesn't try to stop me—they sense something in my eyes, a calm settled over my entire body, a strange, sparkly quality in the salt air. I move slowly, as if I'm already swimming in the sea.

"Noah," I say quietly. His eyes are wild, and a single trail of blood drips down his throat where the blade has begun to dig into the skin. His chest is rising rapidly with each breath, his heart a battering ram against his ribs. "I'll be okay," I say. I reach forward and touch my hand to his chest, over his heart. Samuel and the other men have fallen still; even Holt is quiet, watching me.

"You can't go out there," he chokes. "You'll drown."

I smile softly up at him, feeling his heart clatter beneath my palm. "Don't fight them," I whisper. "Or they'll kill you." I think of my promise to Cricket, the vow I made to keep him safe. This is me keeping that promise. When we fled the barn, when Noah touched my skin at the lake, when we kissed beside the bonfire, and he pulled me to him on the floor of our room inside Maybelle's Hotel, I told myself I couldn't love him. I told myself it would hurt too bad if I did. But now . . . it's too late. And I might love him anyway. The rain spills over us, and for a moment it's all I hear, raindrops on skin, on hair, on the sand at our feet. I can't let him die—I won't let it end like this. "I'll be right back," I say, my voice a breeze in my throat, like a spell set loose into the storm. I release my palm from his chest, my insides breaking, *shattering open*, and turn away—but he reaches out and grabs my hand, pulling me back to him, crushing his lips to mine. His fingertips find the back of my neck, and my palms dig into his collarbone while the blade is still pressed to his shivering throat. And for a half second, it feels like goodbye. Like it's the last time his skin will touch mine.

"Don't die," he says against my mouth, letting his lips linger a moment more.

I nod up at him, making no promises, then slip away from his grasp and turn toward the sea. "I'm ready," I say to Holt.

I undress down to my underwear, feeling Noah's eyes on me, knowing the anger churning in his gut, in his chest. He hates that I'm standing in the cold, in the rain, my flesh exposed—skin that he has touched, drawn close, his breath in my ear. He hates that I'm entering the water alone, and there's nothing he can do to stop me.

That he can't *protect* me. Not this time.

I lift my chin to the sky, feeling the hum along the curves of my skull. A knowing that is marrow-deep. *This is what I'm meant to do.* It was rooted in me at birth. I would travel to the sea, to this beach. I will finish what the first Astronomer started. This knowing is greater than the fear. Greater than the eyes watching me.

I leave my clothes in a pile on the sand, the air strangely electric—unnatural—a white-hot prick along my flesh, tugging at the hairs of my arms.

The sky is darker than it should be, a smear of inky black. The shadow so close, it's stealing all light.

But I move toward the water and wade out into the shallows.

* ✳ *

Waves break against my shins, my knees, the water swelling up around my torso until I'm forced to swim. My body crashes through the surf, and the man who Holt sent with me is a few yards behind, his thinning, light blond hair slicked across his forehead, doe eyes wider than moons. He's terrified to be wading into the deep after me, and I think there's a good chance he won't survive the swim.

A surge of waves rolls toward me, and I gulp in the damp air before sinking below the water and paddling beneath them—my heartbeat roars, salt water blurring my vision. I take one quick inhale before the next series of waves rises over my head, and I duck back beneath the water, kicking hard against the force of the current trying to push me back to shore. It's nothing like swimming in the river—a steady flow of water dragging me downstream—this is a turbulent storm of water, smashing into me with every stroke.

When I come up for air again, I've only made it halfway to the island—my legs and arms already going numb from the cold. Exhausted, I look back to the beach, at the figures standing beneath the clouded sky, watching. If I give up and let the sea carry me back, if I crawl up onto the sand, defeated—Holt will kill Noah.

So I turn back toward the island. I don't have a choice; I have to keep going. I kick forward, slipping beneath the surface—I hold my breath for as long as I can, knowing I need to stay beneath the waves if I'm going to make it past the surging tide. My lungs strain, desperate for air, the panic starting to beat against my chest, but I force myself to kick even harder, using my arms to pull me forward. And when my lungs begin to burn, I finally rise to the surface, gasping for air . . . and I've made it past the worst of the waves.

But I can hardly feel my feet, my hands white and aching from the cold.

I swim hard, the last few yards, and when I reach the shore of the island, I pull myself free of the ocean and flop onto my back on the slick rocks. I suck in air, blinking up at the gray, gray sky. Relief and adrenaline pumping down my veins.

I made it.

I didn't drown.

But I think I hear a voice over the waves. Blinking through the film of salt water still in my eyes, I see Holt at the shore, right at the edge of the water, shouting—maybe to see if I'm still alive, but I can't hear what he's saying.

The light-haired man is still in the water, but he's made it past the worst of the waves, and he's swimming slowly toward the island, eyes wide, hands swinging pathetically over his head, gasping. Like he's never swum before in his life. I push myself up, bare feet slipping on the wet rocks, my legs like liquid, and start up the rocky slope of the island.

It's even smaller than it looked from the beach. Only a dot of rocks and sand rising up from the shallow sea. I hurry down to the far shoreline, squinting out to the gray sea, but there's no ship. Nothing bobbing in the water, rocked by the waves. Nothing half-sunk on the rocks, not even remnants shattered apart long ago and washed ashore—there is only rain and sea and sideways wind. The ground feels odd beneath me, hard to describe, but I stagger over clumps of seaweed and stones, up to the center of the island, turning in a circle, hoping for something. Anything I can give to Holt, prove to him that I tried.

But the island is barren, no hint of the stories my mother told to me.

And I start to wonder, to worry, if it was all lies. If none of it was true.

Or maybe the stories became muddied over the years, distorted by time, until the Astronomer's tales were knitted together by folklore and fantasy, losing the history of what truly happened. I press my palms to my eyes, holding back the anger and fear. They will kill Noah. Then me. But it won't matter, because without the ship—we'll all be dead soon anyway.

I need to find something.

I glance back to the water, the man almost to the shallows, and I start back down toward the far shore. I will circle the island again; I will look for anything left, pieces of a shipwreck to prove it was here. I clamor over the slick rocks, rain streaming over my face, stomping over a strange hollow place in the soil, and almost reach the water's edge when I pause and look back.

It's the same hollow spot I felt before. An oddity in the ground.

I climb back up, stomping my foot against the soil until I find it again. An unnatural echo beneath my feet, like I'm standing atop an empty water barrel.

I drop to my knees, quickly brushing away the sand with my palms, clearing the rocks and bits of broken shells, *hoping* I might find the destroyed remains of something. I lift up a large stone and toss it aside, scraping at the ground, panic swimming through my veins.

There has to be something here. I need there to be.

I pry up more rocks, fingernails packed with wet sand, eyes stinging from the salt water and tears clouding my vision, when my hand touches something smooth.

Not a rock.

Something else.

Man-made.

I suck in a breath, hope like a drum in my ears, and shove away more soil and stones, uncovering a peculiar, flat, solid layer beneath the sand. Smoother than any river rock. Cold and slick. I run my palms over it, trying to make sense of its size, what lies beneath . . . but I already know what it is.

Near my left knee, I find a handle, a rectangle of bent metal. I try pulling it upward, but it doesn't budge.

The light-haired man finally staggers up from the shore, breathing heavy, cursing, then buckles over to heave up deep exhales of salt water. "Help me," I shout down to him.

I point to the handle and he lifts his head, swaying a little like he's on a teetering ship.

"I think it's a door," I say. "But it's too heavy—I can't lift it."

He looks like he might be sick again, but he keeps it down, and together we wrap both our wet hands around the handle and pull. At first nothing happens, but on our second tug, I can hear the low moan as the door gives way, and after another hard yank, we're able to pull it open. Like a cave being exhumed. The hinges creak and shake, but the door swings wide, resting diagonal with the sky. The man blinks at me, confused, having no idea what this is.

But I know.

I peer down into the darkness below, the hull of a ship hidden in the belly of this island. But with the sky thick and overcast, there's not enough sunlight to illuminate the hole. My hand feels down inside, and my fingers find the rung of a ladder.

The man glances from the hole to me, uncertainty cut into his features, but I swing my legs over the edge and feel for the top rung. "Keep the door open," I say up to him.

He only manages a nod.

I slip my body through the opening, my feet finding the ladder, and slowly scale down into the dark. It feels like entering a tomb, a cavernous, echoey space untouched by time.

I climb down six feet, then twelve, until I finally reach the bottom, and my feet land on a smooth, level surface. Not the uneven rock you'd expect if this was an actual cave. There is no light, so I take a few cautious steps forward, hands reaching in front of me.

The space is empty, the echo of my footsteps ringing in my ears, and the structure around me moans, a long, labored settling. My lungs catch, holding in air, *listening*. I almost call out into the dark, ask if anyone is there, but then the sound quiets.

With my fingers twitching in the cold, I wave them in front of me, inching forward—afraid of what I'll feel, what I'll find—when my right foot meets with something solid.

A table.

I move closer, squinting, trying to see, and run my palm over the surface.

A ripple of light shivers across my vision, and I yank my hand back.

My breathing is a rasp and a sputter in my throat. Mom told me what I'd find inside the ship, described it to me as best as she could, but it's another thing entirely to see it for myself. To face something so unfamiliar that it's hard to describe.

I glance back up at the open hatch in the ceiling, knowing that my escape is close if I need it, then slide my gaze back to the table. My fingers shake, from the cold, from what I'm about to do, but I reach forward and touch the glowing table, and light erupts from its center. Not like candlelight—flickering and uneven. This light glows softly from all corners, pale and muted, and it illuminates the rest of the space around me. The walls are dark and curved, smooth, and the light also reveals something else.

The table is a map . . . of the stars.

Not like the maps that Mom used to draw in our cabin, flat and dull.

This one hovers, as if suspended on the surface of a perfectly still pond. Except there is no water at all. Only air and humming waves of light.

I've never seen anything like it.

"What's down there?" the man calls through the opening above.

I swallow, emotion gripping my throat—too many thoughts mashed together. "I found it," I yell back to him, hoping he'll signal to Holt back on the shore, buy myself some time, so they'll keep Noah alive. *Just a little more time.*

"Hurry up!" he shouts back. "There's a bad storm blowing in."

It's not a storm, I think. It's the anomaly.

But I ignore him and lower my eyes back to the map. I recognize most of the constellations, Pyxis and Perseus, Leo Minor and Indus, and I'm able to orient the formations. It takes me a moment, but finally I spot the Lyra constellation, and the brightest star in the array—Vega. The very star I was named after, and the star that is the northernmost point of my tattoo—inked into my neck, just below my hairline.

My hand hovers over the mirrored Lyra constellation on the table, my finger settling on the point of light that is Vega. The star on the hovering map instantly changes color, from a soft white to a solid black.

I pull my hand away, startled. My ears start to ring again, a nervous fluttering inside my ribs. I hesitate. Once I enter the constellation marked on my body onto the map in front of me, there's no going back. The map will mark the coordinates, the way, the route to the other place.

But . . . there was never any going back. Always forward. And this map is the last point of no return. The last stop, charted by my ancestors.

"What the hell are you doing down there?" the man yells. "If you're just stalling, I'll tell Holt to kill him."

I swallow down the tightness in my throat. "I just need a minute."

Mom's words tremble in my mind. *The stars belong to you now.* She was giving me not just the sky but a responsibility. She was giving me the stories of the first Astronomer, a past I would bear, one that is being written as I lean forward and touch the rest of the stars in the Lyra constellation, and each one blinks from pale to black. My eyes scan the map, finding Hercules, the many-starred constellation that trails down my spine and around my ribs. I press each point of light, watching them all turn dark. I do the same for Corona Borealis, to the Virgo constellation, until the tattoo on my skin ends at Lorvus on my right foot—a constellation that depicts a raven. I touch each star on the glowing map, linking them, until I reach the last two—the brightest—Tova and Llitha. *Binary stars*, Mom called them. Two suns caught in one another's orbit, with a single planet spinning on an axis around them both.

At last I let out a shuddering exhale, and take in the expanse of the hovering, layered map before me, with a series of stars now darkened, connected, mirroring the same stars on my skin.

The coordinates have been set. A route made.

I draw in a cold breath, and from some distant place below me, I hear a soft hum. A buzzing from deep within the belly of the ship as if a wind were being stirred up through an open window. The map flickers slightly, and then the hum grows louder, followed by a subtle shaking.

I've awoken it, after a hundred years of rest. It finally stirs.

A flare of light catches my eye. Across the dimly lit room, a door appears, lit from the other side. With my ears ringing, I cross the room, sensing that the space is much larger than I can see—much wider and deeper and cavernous. A place that I could lose myself in, so I keep glancing back, orienting myself to the glowing table, and the shaft of soft light from the opening in the ceiling. But as I get closer to the door, I already understand what it is, what is waiting for me.

Mom explained how I would need to find a smaller room within the larger ship. So small, it would only be large enough to fit a single person. A room that was more important than all the others within the ship.

When I reach the narrow door, it slides open on its own, light pouring out from the small space waiting on the other side. I edge closer, peering into the compact room, where a single metal chair is fastened against the wall, and a panel of glass to the left is illuminated. Within the glass, the map of my tattoo is already hovering, points of light connected.

The constellations I entered on the large table are somehow linked to the panel in this smaller room. *A lifeboat*, Mom called it. And at the bottom of the panel, below the map, is a blinking white light. There are no words, just a pulsing, shivering glow.

But I sense its meaning—I understand its purpose.

Once I press the button, the *lifeboat* will move, it will break free of the larger ship, and follow the course I've set.

Nervous adrenaline climbs up from my toes, rushing down every vein, throbbing in my eardrums. *This is it.* What I was always meant to do. But everything is more complicated now. Because of Noah. If I press the button, I will fulfill the final chapter of my story, the moment my ancestors had planned for, waited for, sacrificed everything for. But if I press the button, I will be leaving Noah behind.

And leaving him behind means letting Holt kill him.

I close my eyes and scratch my hands through my tangled hair. This is why I didn't want to let myself tumble into the endless, impossible, heart-cracking need of his eyes. Why I tried to ignore it, push it away. But then his fingertips touched my skin, my lips, and I let this reckless, stupid thing happen. I let my heart spill out into his hands, messy and burdened and dangerous.

And now he will die if I leave him behind.

So I cross back through the dark, shadowed room, past the table, to the ladder. My hands are cold, numb, and they slip off the first rung—still soaked from my swim. My body begins to tremble—a delayed reaction, the adrenaline wearing off. But I grab the ladder again and manage to pull myself up, legs shaking. At the top, the man doesn't even help me over the edge; he's distracted, staring out at the ocean.

Once I've pulled myself free of the dark hole, I sink onto my stomach, breathing, shivering. "I did it," I say, teeth clacking together from the cold. "I did what he wanted. I found the ship. Tell Holt to let Noah go."

I lift my head, but the man isn't even listening—his eyes are trained out at the sea, where the waves have grown larger, thrashing against the side of the island. I peer up at the drowned sky, thick with rain, and the air is swarmed with tiny sparks.

Like thousands of fireflies caught in the downpour.

I turn my gaze to the beach, where two men are dragging Noah closer to the water, like they're preparing to slit his throat and dump him into the sea. "Tell them!" I shout at the man, but he's still not listening—his eyes caught on the churning sea, as if it both frightens him and has caught him in a dizzying daydream.

On shaking legs, I push myself up, the cold sunk into my bones, my entire body soaked, then start down to the shoreline. "I did what you asked!" I shout, hands cupped around my mouth. I think I hear one of the men yell something back, but it's lost to the wind. If I can't hear them, then they can't hear me.

I don't want to sink back into the icy water—I don't want to battle the waves back to shore—but there's no other way.

I have to swim back.

I have to leave the ship behind.

I take a step into the cold seawater, my body already shaking, and I wade out into the deep, just as the rain stops falling.

Just as everything becomes strangely stilled. I crane my head up, blinking, squinting . . . my mind reorganizing itself, trying to understand.

Every drop of water sits suspended in midair, caught, motionless, the wind no longer at my neck.

Something that shouldn't be happening . . . is happening.

✶ ✳ ✶

I swallow down seawater, choking when I come up for air, the ocean more violent now. But the current pushes me forward, waves crashing over my back, and I find myself crawling up onto the sand much quicker than it took me to swim out to the island.

I stand on the shore, buckled over, wet hair in my eyes, cough-ing, *coughing*. Trying to keep from collapsing completely.

"What the hell did you do?" Holt asks a few feet away, his eyes flashing across the skyline.

The buzzing static in the air makes the hair on my neck rise on end, my eardrums hiss, and I try to keep my eyes from blinking closed—wanting to sink onto the sand and coil myself into a shiv-ering ball. I grind my teeth to keep them from chattering, knowing that this isn't a storm gathering over the sea—this is the sky breaking apart. Disintegrating. Crumbling open, and there's no stopping it.

The rain begins to rise back upward . . . back into the clouds.

Wrong. *All wrong.*

But the clouds themselves have started to evaporate, and the sky is a carpet of black. Leaving only a splatter of starlight, like paint flicked from a brush.

"I didn't do this," I say to Holt. *This* . . . is the black hole. It's spreading like a giant hand over the stars, sweeping them up in its path. *This* is the anomaly shredding through our atmosphere.

It's finally reached the upper edge of our planet, and now there's no time left.

We came too late. I got here too late.

Holt's face has gone slack as he watches the sky fracture apart. And behind him, his men look just as startled. Samuel—a black eye already blooming where Noah punched him—even reaches a hand forward, brushing through the drops of rain that rise upward in the wrong direction.

Back, back into the sky.

I drag myself upright, the air in front of me swarmed with little sparks, droplets flecked with colors like a rainbow. Watery and translucent. A rumbling fear vibrates up from the bottom of my stomach. The anomaly is here. My eyes find Noah, the blade of the knife still at his throat, but he's watching me—the only one whose gaze isn't tilted to the sky.

We're out of time.

I scrape my wet hair back from my face, finding my clothes where I left them in the sand, and quickly yank on my shirt, my pants, and shove my wet feet into my boots.

I have to get Noah free . . . but there is a sound behind me, a strange rush of water, the pull of a current like a river spilling over rocks. And when I turn, my mouth falls open as I watch the ocean retreat back from the shore.

The cold, violent mass of churning water is being pulled away from the beach, like a low tide, except happening all at once—a roar of water being sucked back, *back*, away from us.

I hadn't imagined this . . . that the ground and sky would turn themselves inside out. That my lungs would feel like blades with every breath I drew in.

There's no time. It's all happening quickly now.

Out at the island, the man has finally entered the water and started swimming back toward shore—the waves crash over him, but the tide is moving the wrong way. It's no longer pushing him toward the beach, it's drawing him back. *Back, back,* just like the sea. His head dips below the water line, once, twice, and through the silvery moisture hanging in the air, I can see the panic in his eyes. He knows he's not going to make it. His mouth falls open, like he's going to yell something, ask for help, but I never hear any sound leave his throat.

Maybe it's pulled out with the wind, or maybe the words never leave his mouth, because the water is moving too fast now—he's pulled past the island, out into the deep, stormy sea. He becomes a small dot in the churning waves, like a tiny, floating beetle, and when he slips below the water line again . . . it's for the last time.

He doesn't reappear.

A brick-hard weight lands in my gut—*that could have been me.* If I had left the island a moment later, if I hadn't swum hard enough.

The man is gone.

The ocean is being sucked out, revealing the barren, rocky bottom of the sea—leaving small tide pools in the sand, and wriggling, stranded fish who flop onto their glistening sides, searching for the water, now long gone.

But it reveals something else.

The island where I stood only moments ago, where I slipped down into the hole, is not an island at all.

As the water recedes, sand and rock spilling away, the base of the island is exposed, but it's not made of reef or stones—it's a smooth structure of metal.

A ship.

Silver-sided and domed near the top. A behemoth.

"There it is," Holt says, his voice almost a shudder—not shocked, but amazed to see the thing he's surely tried to imagine in his mind. Yet never seen until now. He wipes the rain from his forehead and steps closer to the receding shoreline, his miscolored eyes focused on the sleeping giant resting on the bottom of the ocean.

The ship we have both been trying to find, now visible. Only hidden by rocks and sand over time, obscured to look like an island.

The wind picks up; the sky shivers like thousands of bees swarming over the beach.

I look to Noah again, his eyes reminding me of the sky: stormy and cloud-knotted.

The two men who'd been holding Noah drop their arms, the knife lowered—too distracted by the rain lifting up into the sky, the silver ship perched on the seafloor with barnacles growing along its belly.

But Holt finally snaps his eyes to me, sensing my movement. "Did you turn it on?" he asks, the whites of his eyes too wide. "Did you find the map inside?"

I stare back at him, not wanting to tell him anything, but knowing that Noah and I aren't free of him yet. "Yes," I say, voice toneless.

A glimmer appears in his eyes, a dark wistfulness, like he senses how close he is—to finally escaping the sickness that's taken half his sight, that's killing him. But before he can start across the seafloor . . . the sky releases a loud *crack*. Like a massive piece of wood splitting in two. Like thunder ripping through my bones.

The beach shakes beneath us, so violently that I'm certain the ground will open up. Death from above and below. The men beside Noah wobble, terror in their eyes, while Holt lifts his palms, as if beckoning down the sky. "What the hell is happening?"

He might know some of the history of our ancestors—he might know more than most, told to him by August—but he's not an Astronomer. He hasn't spent every night of his life peering up at the stars, watching as we slipped closer and closer toward the dark, bottomless orb in the sky. He doesn't know that the shadow—the thing that shimmers in the early dawn hours when it slants through the atmosphere just right—is finally right over top of us, cresting the horizon. And now the rain is being pulled up into the sky, the ocean yanked back by the force of the black hole's gravity. All of it disintegrating. And I suspect, there's only minutes left before . . . we're next.

The air crackles, sizzles, in my eardrums.

No time left.

My eyes flash to Noah, then out toward the ship. There is pain in his eyes—not the kind made from the blade of a knife, but from watching me swim out across the sea while he was forced to do nothing. Helpless. But he nods back at me, understanding. And in the next second, I swallow down a damp, jagged breath, and we both bolt away from the beach, heading out toward the sea.

Toward the ship.

TWELVE

The ocean has abandoned the seafloor, drawn well past the ship, past the place where the ground slopes away.

Noah and I run, the air static against my skin, while he keeps glancing up at the bleak, shivering sky, watching as the last of the rain is pulled up through the atmosphere. "Hurry," I say, reaching back to grab his hand and pulling him after me.

We don't have time, my head repeats in a screaming loop.

We cross the exposed bottom of the sea, where water had churned and heaved only moments ago, but now we scramble over rocks and sharp reef.

But through the rush of the wind, I hear Holt's voice behind us. "Go after them!"

Yet when I look back, none of the men are in pursuit. Two of them have even begun retreating up the beach, away from the ocean, terrified of whatever is happening to the sky and the sea—*what will soon happen to all of us.*

We reach the front edge of the ship, and using the clumps of reef and rock and barnacles, we pull ourselves up its sleek side. Near the top, Noah heaves me over the edge, and I stand on what had once looked like an island but now is partly flat, the sand washed away, only a few rocks remaining.

"What's happening?" Noah asks when he pulls himself up, looking out at the ocean where the water has slid farther back than I can even see. Only tide pools remain. Small pockets of water and sea life. A strange, horrifying sight. "What is this?"

My lungs feel tight, head pounding. "The shadow in our sky is a black hole," I tell him, the wind capturing my voice and carrying it away, up into the dark mass above. The truth—the thing that Mom said was too big for anyone else to carry, the thing that would only make others hunt us with a desperation that would make even the valley unsafe—finally released from my chest. "It's killing us," I say. "It's always been killing us, moving closer to our planet every year, every hour, making us sick."

Creases form between Noah's eyebrows. "But what is this?" His eyes flash down to the silver, gleaming ship.

"It's . . ." I force myself to take a breath, knowledge threading through the very center of my bones. ". . . the ship our ancestors arrived on." He only blinks at me, needing more, needing to understand, while the sky rips open above us. "They came from up there," I say, pointing into the writhing dark. "From a planet . . . called Earth." This is what August never told him, or maybe August didn't know—maybe the stories were lost to the Architect long ago. Altered and forgotten, as stories tend to do over time.

"I don't understand," he replies, his dark hair stirring across his forehead, over his eyes, making him look like he's caught in the eye of a peculiar storm. Waves of light dancing across his face. "What happens now?"

A rumbling of too many emotions hardens in my throat. "We have to leave," I urge. "Before the darkness swallows up everything."

"How?" The wind is a scream now, and I can barely hear him.

"We don't have time," I answer. "We have to get into the ship. The lifeboat is only meant to hold one person, but I think we'll both fit. We have to try." I remember Mom describing the ship to me, sketching its outline into the soft dirt beside the river. *There's only room for one,* she would say. *This is what you were born to do—only you can go, only you will know the way.* I always knew I'd be leaving Noah behind once we reached the sea—just like Holt said. Just like Mom foretold. It's been destined from the beginning, since the first Astronomer began marking her skin with a map. But I'd hoped I would be able to come back for him, for Pa, and all the others. That there'd be time to save everyone. But now . . . the sky is splintering and there's no time left. *We got here too late.* And I have to find a way to bring him with me.

Noah shakes his head. "What the hell is a lifeboat?"

A storm stirs inside me and above me. "The other colony," I shout over the wind. "The lifeboat will take us to the other colony."

"Where?" His eyes are clouded over, and there is something in them I haven't seen before—hesitation, doubt, like he's realizing how much I've kept from him.

I reach forward and grab his hand, then lift my eyes to the sky. "To another planet, orbiting two twin suns." The two twin suns I first saw in the valley, the sister stars that set everything in motion. Stars that will only be in alignment with us for a short time—close enough to reach. "But if we don't go now, it'll be too late."

Time has run out, and now Noah and I stand on a wrecked ship with the sky twitching and cracking. But if we leave now, maybe, *maybe*, we can still reach the other colony, the other planet, and return in time to save the others. Before the black hole—thundering and swirling above—destroys everything.

This is what I was always meant to do, what every Astronomer before me has been waiting for, what Mom has taught me. But now it all ends with me. I will be the one.

I look to Noah, needing him to say something, but his eyelashes are stilled, drops of mist caught mid-fall, and his mouth is cut into an uncertain line—like he's not sure he believes any of it. "You knew this all along?" His voice is ice, evaporating in the air. "You knew, and you never told me?"

These words hurt me more than anything else, daggers through my chest. "I should have," I admit, dropping my eyes, all the guilt I kept stuffed down, rising up inside me. All the things I didn't say. "I should have told you everything." I swallow, but the air rises in my lungs again. "I'm sorry. But I need you to trust me now."

He stares at me, and the wind slides between us, a torrent, a violent upending of ground and sky. Yet at the rim of his eyes is a hint of light, and I can see in him the boy who rescued me from the schoolhouse when Holt was about to cut me open, the boy who dragged me through a dust storm and kicked through the wall of a barn just to keep me safe. The boy who has kissed me with such need and hunger in his eyes, I thought it might destroy us both. The boy I know now that I love. "Okay," he says, nodding, meeting my eyes. "Let's go."

My heart is already pounding in my ears, and his words send a ripple of relief straight into my chest. Together we kneel down and yank open the hatch in one swift motion.

I can hear the hum of the ship below, the low buzzing of energy like lightning when it charges the air. My body shivers, convulsions that make it hard to breathe, to think. The last of the light empties from the sky, all the stars swallowed up.

But there is another light growing, a rush of it, crackling and bursting overhead, like lightning catching on the remaining drops of moisture in the air. Filling the sky with tiny eruptions of light.

Noah touches my hand, and the feel of his skin settles me, his eyes finding mine—stark and pinpointed—like he's witnessing tiny particles of dark matter smashing through my retinas, disintegrating my cells, breaking me wide open for him to see. I glance back to shore one last time, where I can no longer see Holt or any of the men. Maybe they've retreated back up the beach toward the mountains, toward their homes—days away from here—that they'll likely never reach in time. The black hole will swallow up the planet before then, pulling it into the black hole's dark center and likely crushing it, or stretching it out flat until there's nothing left.

My ears crackle and burn, a pressure in my chest I've never felt before. Above us, the sky turns an odd hue of black, dull somehow, but also slit through with ribbons of light as the last of the stars are gobbled up.

I turn, eyes stalling briefly out on the empty ocean floor, when I see it.

A wall—just like the dust storm that overtook us when we crossed the dry farmland—but this one is made of seawater.

Every thought inside me sinks into my stomach, and I feel my eyes expand.

All of the water that had been sucked out is now . . . surging back inland. A great rising tide. "It's coming back!" I shout over the wind and thrumming air. "The ocean—it's coming back in."

The black hole is tipping everything off-balance and inside out—the tide and gravity—none of it behaving as it should.

"Get inside," Noah shouts, and I reach a foot down through the hatch, finding the top rung of the ladder. Noah is right above me, about to step inside, when there is a hand at his throat, an arm wrapping around him, yanking him back. *Back, back.*

"No!" I shout, but the sound is lost just as quickly.

Holt is dragging Noah away from the hatch, away from me. But I scramble back up the ladder, onto the surface of the ship, and run toward them.

Noah's hands are grasping, trying to reach his father behind him, push him off. But they're both moving back, toward the edge of the ship, feet slipping on the wet surface. The wind rips over the ship, coiling my hair upward, and when they're only a foot away from the abrupt edge, Holt stops, pivoting so that Noah is balanced right on the precipice, the ground dropping away beneath him, down to the barren seafloor below.

"Holt!" I shout.

He turns, glances over his shoulder at me. "I only need *you* alive," he yells. "This traitor has done his part, led us here." He won't even call him his son anymore, and I realize he was right when he said he'd kill Noah. There is only hate and greed left inside him now. His son is only in the way.

The air feels charged, little pinpricks in my lungs as the temperature drops, turns impossibly cold—the atmosphere evaporating. "No!" I plead, lifting my hands toward him, as if I could reach for

Noah and keep him from falling over the edge. "There's still time—if you let me leave now, I can reach the other colony and come back with their ship, and there'll be enough room to save everyone. No one has to die."

Holt bares his teeth, an ominous grin, a twitch in his dead eye. "You know it's too late for that," he says, nodding up to the sky.

But I shake my head. *I don't believe that.* I can't let myself believe it. "We can try," I beg, just wanting him to release Noah. I won't watch him die like this. I made a promise, and Cricket's words hiss in my ear, in my bones. But my own words are there too: *I love him.*

And I can't lose him.

My eyes flash out to the sea—the wall of water only a hundred yards out, seventy-five, fifty. It's taller than the tallest pine, a steep, snarling mountain of water, churning, crashing, violent, as if a surge of anger has been bottled up inside it.

"Please!" I scream over the increasing wind, everything inside me breaking, tears scattering across my cheeks, absorbed with the rain, the sky erupting, sizzling with a darkness that feels like light. Feels like fire. Feels like death.

Feels like the end.

"Vega!" a voice shouts, Noah twisting so his gaze finds mine. "Run!" he says. "Get inside."

But I won't. I refuse to leave him—I knew it would come to this, didn't I? It's why I didn't want to let myself love him. Afraid that in the end, I would lose him, one way or another.

I step closer, both of them teetering too far on the edge—my lungs burning, ears shrieking like my eardrums are about to burst. Noah's eyes widen, seeing something.

Everything slows.

I shift my head, following his gaze, and see . . .

Noah thrusts his elbow back, into his father's ribs—the place where the knife tore him open only days earlier—and Holt drops to the ground, nearly slipping off the edge. He's buckled over, hand to his side, wheezing. But Noah wheels his eyes back to me. "Run, Vega! Now!"

I turn, but it's too late—the wave slams into the ship, a sudden crack.

My legs give out and I hit the metal surface, palms splayed open. The ship screeches, moans like a monster come alive, the wall of water pushing it across the ocean floor, breaking apart the jagged reef. The vibration passes through my hands, my arms, through my bones.

I try to grab on to something, but the ship is churning with the waves, grating against the seafloor, and the force of it is pushing me farther away from the opening. My eyes flash to the hatch, then behind me, finding Noah climbing to his feet, staggering toward me—away from Holt, who's clawing at the ship, searching for something to keep him from sliding off the edge.

Noah's mouth opens and he yells something, but his words are drowned out by the rain, the screaming sky, the ship grinding across the seafloor.

He's still yelling, pointing to the hatch. And I know I need to move. My body no longer feels like my own, but I stagger upright, take a step, then hit the ground again. My left hand finds a craggy piece of coral grown onto the roof of the ship, and I dig my fingers into it, gasping for air, but my lungs seize against the cold wind, my fingers going numb where they cling to the ship. I glance back and see Noah still inching closer, eyes squinting away from the wind, but Holt has gotten to his feet and is moving toward him.

"Noah!" I scream, but still there is no sound. Everything numbed, edges blurred. The last of the moisture clinging to the air. I try to stand again, but I'm tossed onto my left side, my shoulder slamming down hard against the ship, sending a spike of pain through my chest. Far below, the ocean heaves, no longer moving with the steady rhythm of the tide—it swirls and tosses waves in every direction. Jolting the ship one way and then another, making it impossible to keep my footing. Noah is almost to me, reaching out an arm—like he's going to hoist me up and haul me to the hatch.

But I see what's coming before he does.

Holt staggers a moment, blood now visibly soaking through his shirt, dripping to his feet, but he lunges at Noah, and they are both knocked sideways onto the ship.

Father and son. Trying to kill each other.

I try to breathe, but everything spins; every inhale burns. The hatch is only a few paces away, but Noah is being dragged back, both men sliding as the ship lurches one way and then another, Noah with a hand gripped around Holt's ankle. There is a sudden grinding beneath us as the ship is thrust up onto the shore, moving toward the wall of mountains, the sea still foaming, pushing, colliding.

No time. There's no time left.

I look up, just as Holt turns and lands a blow against Noah's face with the heel of his boot. Hard. Noah slumps back, unmoving. "Noah!" I think I yell, or maybe it's only in my head. All sound, all time, lost now.

Holt drags himself to his feet, bleeding, leaving his son in a heap at the edge of the ship, and he takes a few shaky steps, then starts toward me. Toward the hatch.

No no no.

The air shivers around me, a loud *crack* breaks the atmosphere, a strange cacophony of hums, and I can feel the cold in the air become like ice. Only seconds now. My heart drives against my ribs. I get to my feet, eyes locked on the hatch ahead of me. *I have to move.* I take a step, fall, then push myself up again. I scramble over the coral and rocks cemented to the ship—a hundred years while it sat beneath the sea—and I'm nearly to the hatch, only a foot away, when I hear a voice—distant, tugged away from a cold, weak throat. "Vega!" Noah's yelling. "Go!"

I turn, time spun out, *stretched out*, then snapping back. I feel the spray of the sea on my face, and my eyes find him, as if by memory, as if by fate—eyes seeking the other, needing, *meant*. The breath in my throat is ice. And Noah looks at me across the thick cloud of moisture and shivering light. He stares at me as he gets to his feet, blood dripping from his nose, and moves toward Holt. But I sense something in his eyes that I don't like. Words hidden there, words he won't say aloud. Because it's too late for that now.

Seconds unwinding. No time.

I blink, *blink, blink,* and see Noah edging up behind Holt. He's going to stop him from reaching me, from reaching the ship. He'll *protect me, no matter what.* Like he said he would. Even now. Even when the sky turns to watercolors of light. And I want to scream at him, knowing what he's going to do.

But he reaches Holt and nods at me—the same words in his

eyes, the ones I want to ignore: *I'm sorry*, they say—just before he yanks an arm around Holt's throat and drags him back, back . . . away from me. No sound leaves Holt's mouth, but his eyes are domes about to burst, unblinking. The air gone from his lungs, like it's gone from mine.

No. Not like this.

I claw my way to the hatch, hooking a hand down inside, onto the ladder, and I turn, looking back . . . where Noah still has his arms pinched around Holt, squeezing, not letting go, not for anything. The ship heaves one last time, tips too far to one side, and I meet Noah's eyes—river green, sunrise green, my-heart-screaming-in-my-chest green. "No!" I shout.

But he shakes his head, and his mouth parts, saying something to the wind, to me—it looks like words I never thought I'd see anyone say. Little words, tiny and lost to the tottering sky. *I love you.* And then, his faraway eyes blink, arm choked around Holt's throat—his father, his enemy—he's finally going to end it, once and for all. A smile finds his eyes, *finds me*, the last shiver of warmth in them . . . just before he slips over the edge of the ship.

And is gone.

A scream rises in my ears, a wailing cry—a sound that is coming from some dark place inside my gut. I feel myself shatter, every bone and fiber disintegrating apart.

I feel my skin peel open, baring the last of me, the awful, worthless pieces that are left.

The air is a swarm of bees in my ears, my eyes starting to lose their sight, a blackness seeping over my vision. I don't even feel myself tumble down the ladder, landing on my side. I barely feel my feet slipping across the smooth floor, staggering through the door and into the chair in the tiny room. Tears cascade down my cheeks, but I feel my palm slam against the blinking light. I feel the jolting around me, the little room—the lifeboat—breaking free from the destroyed ship that's grinding across the beach. I feel my body sinking against the chair beneath me as if my limbs are worthless, bones turned to water.

I feel everything being ripped away from me.

Destroyed, drowned.

Taken.

Cruelly, awfully.

The walls of the lifeboat change. They aren't walls at all, they're windows—and below, I can see the ocean, the ship suspended beneath me, then getting farther, *farther*, away. I close my eyes, and I swear I can hear Noah's heartbeat thudding in my ears, feel every exhale of his lungs, every lift and shudder of his eyelids. It all becomes a drum against my skull. *He is the only thing I hear.* All that's left.

No drops of salt water on my skin.

No dark matter breaking me open.

There is only air rushing into my ears . . . and I am drifting between stars. Slipping up beyond the horizon, beyond the atmosphere, where I can see it all. The black hole like a massive orb, darkness spilling into it and around it, reflective and shimmering with all the stars it's eaten, blinking their final gasps. And our planet, our tiny home, is moving closer to it, nearly at the apex—the point of no return. Only seconds now, until it's swallowed up. Leaving nothing in its wake, no ripple of what had been—a planet, once rested here, perched at the edge of a galaxy.

I was too late.

My head *thuds, thuds*.

This isn't how it was supposed to happen; this isn't what my ancestors had planned. They thought there'd be more time—once the sister stars appeared, and the other colony's planet was finally close enough for the lifeboat to reach. *You will be the first to leave,* Mom would explain, looking me in the eyes when she said it, making sure I understood. *You will reach the other colony, and you will return with their ship. You will gather the rest of us. You*—she would touch my face—*will save us.*

But she got one thing wrong: The black hole choking out half our sky was closer than she realized. She thought I'd have time before it swallowed up our sky, our planet.

Instead I reached the ship too late. And I've saved no one.

Only myself.

A broken girl who's lost everything. *Everyone she loved.* An Astronomer who was supposed to fix it all—*the* cure—a hundred years of waiting.

But it was for nothing.

And I failed.

Tears stream down my face—worthless, vile tears. I am made of water and bone-cracking, unspeakable, immeasurable pain. I am nothing now. Only a memory of Noah—tipping over the edge of the ship, pulling his father with him, ensuring that Holt wouldn't reach me, wouldn't stop me. He sacrificed himself so I could live. But I don't want any of it.

Through the windows, through the salty, unbearable blur of tears, I watch as I spin farther away—from Noah, from the hurt in his eyes—and the sky turns a deeper blue, a deep black, stars and particles of light beginning to peek out from the dark. But behind me, the black hole is amassing, my planet draped in shadow, a flickering, vibrating wave, and then finally . . . I hold my breath, wanting to look away, yet I force myself to watch—I need to see it happen, I owe them that, I owe *him*—a witness to the end.

Observing the last final seconds before it all—

In a sudden, unremarkable flash, the planet seems to quiver, vibrate, and then . . . without a sound, without a crash or a whimper or a scream . . . it's gone. Vanished.

Slipped into the precipice of the shadow, and blinked out.

Noah is gone and I want to rip out my own heart; I want to go back and tumble over the side of the ship into the sea with him. I want to press my palms to my eyes until everything goes black with death.

I want none of what I have: this tiny one-man ship spit out into the night sky, air in my treacherous lungs, blood in this broken body. Thoughts in my worthless, shattered mind.

I only want one thing.

One fucking thing.

Him.

The first Architect said goodbye to the woman he loved—knowing he would never see her again. He walked toward the setting sun, where the northern mountains concealed a ship half-sunk in the sea, off the shore of a black-sand beach.

Only he knew its location, only he knew where the ship crashed into the sea—because only he stayed aboard when the Artemis broke through the atmosphere and careened toward their new planet. The other colonists had been ordered to evacuate, flee in escape pods that would scatter across the continent below. But the Architect stayed aboard, trying to keep the ship from breaking apart on impact. He had been a helmsman during their journey across the stars, but once they landed, like most of the crew, they would take on other roles. He would help to build towns, construct a framework for their new life.

But when the ship crashed into the sea, he nearly didn't make it ashore—the ocean more violent than any he'd known back on Earth. But he was alive. And when he looked back at the ship that almost looked like an island, he knew, over time, the tide would push sand and rocks over its slick metal exterior. The sea would begin to swallow it up. In time, it would be lost.

Forgotten.

He strode across a series of snowy mountains, three days in the cold and wind, before he reached a forest. And several more days before he found anyone else alive.

It was months before the towns began to sprout up from the soil, homes being built, lives taking shape. They were a colony meant to drive stakes into the ground for communities and towns that would eventually be built, to study the surrounding landscape and the stars in their new solar system. They each came with different roles, tasks to be performed—farmers and teachers and carpenters.

But when the sickness started rising up inside them, when they began burying their dead in the unfamiliar soil, they knew they were the unlucky ones. They had arrived on a planet with an illness that would eventually wipe them out.

The Astronomer knew how to chart paths across the night sky; she knew the way to the second colony who had settled on a planet not far from their own. They could leave this planet, travel to the *other place*—where perhaps no one was sick. But their ship had been wrecked on impact—no longer able to leave their atmosphere.

Yet there was hope.

The Architect had remained on the ship when it crashed—his lifeboat, his escape pod, was unused. Still attached to the ship. And it could be used to flee the planet.

But it was never built to travel long distances. Only meant as a last resort. If the other colony—in its solar system with its two suns—swung close enough, the escape pod might be able to reach it.

The Astronomer charted the sky; she measured and made formulations. And she knew they would have to wait. It would be a hundred years before the other colony's orbit swung close enough to their own. Close enough that the escape pod could reach their planet.

They, the originals, would never leave this planet. By sickness or something else.

But they could save others, their descendants, the ones who would be born later. They could sacrifice themselves and hope that enough of them would survive long enough to see the sister stars come into alignment, and then, one person—the Astronomer—could go get help. Hope that the other colony's ship was still intact. Hope that they could come back and save the rest.

Help would come. A cure for the consumption would come—by escaping the planet. But it wouldn't arrive for another hundred years.

The Astronomer and the Architect agreed—they would keep the location of the ship hidden, they would hide the map to the other colony. They would keep it all safe.

So they said goodbye, to protect those who would come later, to protect the hope that they could be saved. The Astronomer hid herself in the valley, while the Architect kept to the roads, never settling anywhere for long.

But even if a hundred years should pass, the route to the ship would be taught, the knowledge passed down. Each new Architect would be told the path through the mountains to where a ship sat beneath the sea, waiting.

So when the sister stars appeared, and the other colony was close enough to reach . . .

The Architect would know the way. But the Astronomer was the map, the key.

Only together could they leave.

THIRTEEN

The small ship, the *lifeboat*—as Mom called it—spears through the dark, whirling past shimmering starlight in the distance. But I feel nothing. I'm as hollow as a spring seed after the birds have torn it apart.

Fragments of a broken girl. Damaged by what I left behind.

My arms sag at my sides, eyelids heavy, wanting to close and never open again.

Our planet held so much promise when our ancestors—the colonists—first arrived. With dark soil and more water than the planet they were fleeing. And most important, air they could breathe: nitrogen, oxygen, carbon dioxide. The perfect measure of sustainable life. A rare planet, similar to their own. They were the ones who volunteered—doctors, carpenters, metal workers, astronomers and architects, meant to build towns and colonies and crops—they were pioneers, homesteaders who set out into this bleak, cold frontier with a ship stockpiled with seeds for crops, livestock for farms, even weapons, everything they'd need to begin again. They made the journey into the darkness, to the very edge of their known galaxy.

But they weren't the only ones.

Two ships left their home planet, two hopeful colonies sent to two life-sustaining planets on far ends of a galaxy. In case one of them was too hostile, unsurvivable. But my ancestors got the shit luck of landing on the bad planet, the one with a sickness. An illness that would kill us slowly. Eventually.

The first colonists didn't know their new planet hovered so dangerously close to a black bottomless hole that was swallowing up the sky, a whorling silent mass that emanated too much dark matter from its dark, dark center to sustain life on the planet for long. And it would only get worse, year after year, as the black hole drifted closer, gobbling up all light in its path, until our bodies were comprised of more dark matter than anything else.

They didn't know that the shadow in the sky was to blame.

So the first Astronomer and the first Architect made a plan.

But I reached the ship too late . . . and now I wish I'd never left. I should have been the one to stay, to die, to sacrifice myself. It should be Noah on this ship—someone brave, someone who can survive. I hate myself for it: all the little moments I can't take back like blades carving me open, peeling back my flesh, just like Holt wanted to do at the schoolhouse. But in the end, Noah killed Holt, *his own father*. He died protecting me, as he always said he would.

And I broke my promise to Cricket.

Now . . . I'm the only one left, the rot inside me more than I can bear. I close my eyes, but I don't dream. There's no hope left for dreams, for thoughts beyond the smooth, silver walls of this cell. I wake, and I stare numbly out at the dark: the beautiful, wretched galaxy that I should love. I should trace the stars' formations on the glass, study how they shift as I move past them, an expanding kaleidoscope of starlight.

But I feel nothing.

Only the ache that twists around my heart, pinching, cracked wide in my chest.

I've lost everything.

My ears ring, then fall quiet. The pulsing at my temples disappears. The subtle nagging of pain that has always lived inside me dulls and softens, until it's hardly there at all.

The black hole that was making us sick is now slipping away behind me.

Hours pass.

I start to wonder if this lifeboat will make it to the other colony. Maybe the first Astronomer got it wrong, the calculations—maybe the other planet is much too far away, and I will die out here, among the stars.

A death I deserve.

A part of me wants it—begs for it. This metal coffin.

I slide my hands into my pockets and feel for the flat piece of paper, pulling it out. I hold it curved in my trembling palm, my finger tracing the shape of the Eiffel Tower, and it feels suddenly ridiculous, useless. A thing I have kept because I thought it reminded me of Mom. But it's an image of a place I've never seen, and never will. I wish instead, I had a postcard of the valley, of the cabin and the river. Of Noah, the evening we swam in the lake and he touched my lips. The night we lay together on the floor of our room inside the hotel, his frame hovering over me, fingers tracing the marks on my flesh. I want to hold these moments in my palm. I want to go back and live them again.

In the end, I found Noah. But I wish I'd had him from the start.

I loved him too late.

I let the postcard fall from my fingertips to the floor, worthless, and I pinch my eyes closed, letting myself cry.

Letting the wretched pain heave through me.

Pain and *pain* and nothing else.

I wake suddenly, sitting up, hands pressing to the window, and call out, "Noah!" Tears stain my cheeks, the grief waking up inside me, the last moments before Noah yanked Holt over the edge, finding me even in my sleep.

But all around me, the ship begins to make a strange whirring sound, like a windmill turning too fast in a spring gust.

I pull myself up straight, wiping at my eyes—the hunger and thirst a deep, clawed ache, a thing I can no longer ignore. But out beyond the dark, something is drawing closer.

A planet. Round and unnaturally teal blue, a storm of white clouds blurring over a third of the surface.

The *other place*.

The tiny ship vibrates as I get closer, rattling through the upper atmosphere, plunging, falling. *Crashing*. Maybe it'll end like this. Quick and fiery and blunt.

The sky is an amber color, two like-sized suns hovering against the blue horizon—Tova and Llitha. When I peer down, against the glass, there is more blue than anything else, a shivering, pulsing ocean. With a dozen tiny dots of land.

The ship begins to jolt, a heavy vibration, and I clamp my teeth down against it, lowering myself back against the seat and securing the straps over my chest. I'll either die or I won't. Either means nothing to me now.

The shaking clatters my skull so violently that I'm sure I'm going to lose consciousness, everything whipping by too fast.

I press my palms to my ears and let out a sound—a guttural cry—knowing my body is about to be broken apart.

I suck in my last breath of air.

I pinch my eyes closed.

I wait for the end.

But . . .

. . . the vibration stops.

Followed by a long, strange lull.

I can feel the change in air pressure, like my ears want to pop, shatter. I press my head to the wall, hands clutching the armrests, eyes pinched closed so tightly that flares of light spark across my vision . . . just before I feel the ground slam beneath me.

And then nothing.

A soft hum sputters out from somewhere in the small ship, followed by silence.

Quiet.

I hate the quiet, the aliveness of my body, *still breathing*. I sit for a moment, not wanting to open my eyes, refusing to believe that I made it. That the grief isn't the only thing pulsing through me.

Reluctantly I drag myself up, fingers gripping the edge of the window, and look out at a blue-white sky. A pale, shivering sea. And soft, wavering sunlight.

Tears try to break over my eyelids again, but my body is too numb. Too desperate for water, for *him*.

I stare out at the foreign landscape, little mounds of earth rising up in the distance.

Islands.

But they're not rocky and battered by ocean waves. They're blanketed in white sand, beaches glistening against the sunlight.

I breathe, I stuff down the hurt—*down down down*—and turn the metal bar keeping the door locked in place, pushing it outward. The air instantly smells different: a sweet saltiness, like a flower I've never known before, like late-spring evenings. It's the wrong scent—I want dark, clouded skies and deep, unending rain. I want a world that feels like the unbearable weight in my chest.

But I pull myself out onto the roof of the little ship, head reeling, dizzy, like I'm caught in an impossible, horrible dream where everyone is dead and I'm the only one left alive.

With a hand over my eyes to block the brightness of two suns, I squint out across a perfect, turquoise sea where the lifeboat now bobs at the surface. The water reflects the blue, blue sky, and it's beautiful. *So beautiful.* A soft, warm quality of light draped over everything. I hold out my palm, and even my own skin looks different, glistening, like morning dew in the garden, back in the valley.

A sob shutters from my lips.

I don't want to be alone, the only one to witness this place: crystal water and dazzling sunlight and air that smells of floral, sun-kissed skin. I want him to see it too.

I want his fingers coiled in mine, his mouth against my lips, knowing we made it. We survived.

But when I close my eyes and open them again, none of it's true. And I'm still alone.

Alone.

No other ships rest in the distance, no structures on the islands.

No colony. Maybe Mom was wrong; maybe the first Astronomer was wrong. *Maybe this is the wrong planet.* Maybe the colonists died shortly after they arrived—sick just like us. Their bodies scattered across the islands, skeletons now, picked apart.

I rake my hands through my hair. This isn't how it should have happened. This is all wrong. "No," I mutter to myself. "No, *No.*" My knees give out, and I sink to the surface of the ship, but through the painful beating of my heart in my chest, I hear a ripple of water breaking against the ship.

I drop my hands, listening, certain I'm wrong. *Only the wind.* But when I turn, glancing behind me, I see it:

A boat moving toward me.

Long, narrow. Like it's been carved from the trunk of a tree. And inside sit three people—skin dark, golden hands moving oars seamlessly through the blue-green water.

All the air leaves me. All my thoughts spill out into nothing. And I weep. Tears pour down my cheeks, a long, endless cascade of pain.

"Hello?" one of them calls up to me, standing at the bow of the boat.

Mom was right.

* ✳ *

I sit with my knees drawn to my chest inside a small domed structure—a house—with a roof made of strange wooden slats, built around a tree growing green spiky fruit that sags heavy from its limbs. My palms brush across the floor beneath me, a carpet of leafy green fronds woven together, and a woman brings me a wood cup filled with the nectar of the green spiky fruit—it tastes like a not-quite-ripe pear blossom. But it eases my thirst, and even makes me a little sleepy.

I don't want to sleep, though, because when I wake, I'll have to remember it all over again.

"You came from the other colony?" The woman's voice is smooth and careful, her long hair plaited down her shoulder with shells knitted along her scalp. She's the same woman who stood at the bow of the small boat, then helped me down from the ship and brought me to her half-moon shaped island.

She sits on the woven green floor across from me, knees tucked under her, with a pale, thin dress draped like petals across her legs, the fabric bleached white from the sun.

"Yes," I answer her, voice dry, and I take another drink.

"But only you?"

My eyes fall to the floor, tracing the tightly knitted pattern of the leaves. The words are a fist in my chest. I may never say them aloud again.

But she nods, like she understands. "How many others were at your colony?" she asks, long, pale eyelashes fluttering against her soft, freckled skin.

I lift my gaze, trying to see something familiar in her: a woman who is descended from the same people as me, those who left their home planet long ago to settle on two new ones. She carries the same origin, the same blood. Yet she feels wholly unknown, another being entirely. A woman who was born on a planet made of mostly water—bodies shaped by the salty sea and two bright suns—who spent a hundred years on this newly colonized land, making a life, while we spent our time, on our planet, dying. Just trying to survive.

"There were thousands," I say. "But not now."

Her mouth tucks down, her elaborate braids swaying across her shoulders. A row of freckles dot her cheeks. She's beautiful, but there is something in her eyes, a ruthlessness, like she could leap forward and end my life quickly if she wanted. Arms strong and scarred in places.

She leans over and places a palm against my head, as if she were anointing me, blessing my grief-ruptured mind. The pressure makes me feel tired, safe, and she doesn't ask any more questions. She folds a blanket over my shoulders and urges me to rest, to close my eyes. I resist at first, afraid to dream, but then my eyes tumble closed— unable to fight her calming voice, the nectar from the tree blurring out all sounds—and in the hours that pass, sleep becomes the only thing I crave.

It sinks over me like a starless sky, dark and endless, and I pull the blanket up over my eyes, drifting into the nothing.

Someone comes, a plate of food set in front of me, but I push it away and close my eyes again. I hear worried voices whispering around me, but it all means nothing. Each word trickling into my ears is like a hooked knife, pulling me back, reminding me of everything I've lost. I am adrift, homeless, motherless. All the people I love—gone. So I sink deeper into my dreams, willing the stars to take me, to rip the air from my lungs so I may never wake again.

I want to disappear.

Become only air and light, barely a memory of the girl I was.

I don't want to be here.

And in the darkest hours of night, in the pain cracking through my skull, a voice tiptoes up from the shadows, a wind in my ears that becomes solid words: *The stars belong to you now, Vega*. I wince, trying to force the voice away. But it grows louder. *You can't go back*. It's my mother's voice, not real, and I try to sink deeper into my dreams, but she finds me again. *Wake up, Vega*. No, I feel my thoughts repeat. No. I don't want this. I don't want to be here. *You can't go back*, she says again, her voice a smile in my ears. *Vega. Wake up*.

My eyes snap wide, my throat so dry, I can't swallow. I gasp, sucking in a jagged rasp of air. I try to blink, but it's too dark, and then there is a hand on my shoulder, and something is pressed into my palm. A cup. I drink desperately, letting the liquid rush down into my stomach. It's cool, tasteless water—not the nectar the woman gave me before. She refills the cup, then hands it to me again, and I finish it in one gulp. Sweat pricks my upper lip, my palms, and I let the blanket fall away from my shoulders.

"Sorrow is like a serpent that coils around the heart," the woman says, and a soft glow appears from the far side of the room. Not a candle but something else—the woman holds a jar filled with water, and inside are small swimming creatures, round with long gossamer tentacles, and they emanate a warm glow from their pale white bellies. This is her light. Her way of seeing in the dark. And she places the jar on the floor between us. "The serpent might never leave your chest," she continues. "But it will loosen its grip over time."

Each word is a dull echo, barely reaching my mind.

She places a round, waxy fruit in my palm, green and speckled with seeds. I eat and it warms my insides; it removes the hollowness in my stomach. And after I've drunk some more, sunlight begins to peer through the slats in the wood roof. The woman shows me a small bathroom at the back of her house, which is mostly just a room at the far side of the tree with a hole dug into the ground. When I return, she folds me into the blanket again and brushes her cold hands across my forehead, whispering words with each stroke of her fingertips, as if she is wiping away the hurt. Whispering spells against my skin. But when I lie down to sleep again, my head no longer thumps with the pain—it only lives in my chest now.

A day passes, maybe two, and when my eyes flutter open, the light is pale and gentle through the ceiling. Somewhere between sunrise or sunset. I push myself up and see that I'm alone in the small house. I sit for a moment, staring down at my palms, as if I might find answers in my hands, in the fingers that once pressed to Noah's flesh, that once swam in the river. I want answers I won't find.

The woman appears in the doorway, her aqua eyes meeting mine, and she steps inside, bringing me a cup of water, then sinking onto the floor in front of me. "You have slept a long time," she says gently.

I want to tell her that time doesn't mean a thing to me anymore. I could sleep for a thousand years and it wouldn't be enough to heal what has happened.

She lets me drink, lets the minutes pass between us, and then her thin eyebrows turn down at the corners. "The others want to know what happened on your planet. Why you are the only one left?"

I grip the cup in my palms, squeezing, needing it to keep the sob from rising in my throat. "There was a shadow in our sky," I manage, barely louder than a whisper.

She tilts her head, examining me.

"It was a black hole." I clear my throat, looking to the small thatched door of the house, longing for fresh air, but knowing that if I step outside, nothing will look or smell as it should. Nothing familiar. So I stay put. "There's no one left."

She taps her fingers against her strong thigh, lips puckering, then leans forward. "You came on one of the escape pods," she says. "You had a map." Her blue eyes narrow on me. "Are you the Astronomer?"

I should feel a glimmer of something, hearing her say the name, yet it no longer feels like mine. A title I left behind, a girl who is destroyed now. But I nod my head, keeping my mouth flat.

She stands, walking to the door of her home and looking out at the sea. "Our Astronomer died many generations ago. He drowned." Her eyes swivel back to me. "We've lost much of the knowledge of the sky."

A soft wind stirs through the doorway, bringing with it the scent of fruit and sand and sea air.

"The shadow in your sky," she goes on. "We see one too, at night, after the suns have dipped into the ocean."

My eyebrows lift, an itch at the back of my neck—an old feeling, a curiosity rising inside me—the part of me that breathes starlight, that longs to understand their patterns. The part of me that isn't dead just yet. "Show me."

She takes me by the hand and leads me outside, where the air is warm and gentle, blowing up from the sea. We stand on the shore of her tiny island, my boots sinking into the pale sand, and it isn't long before the twin suns begin to slip past their horizon, the light dusky and muted. The two other people who had been in the boat with the woman when they found me—a man and a woman, both tall and lean with long waves of dark auburn hair—are pulling in nets from the shallows, each filled with strange, hard-shelled creatures that they place into a round woven basket.

When the last of the sunlight peels away into the night, the sky is a flurry of starlight, patterns and constellations I don't recognize. Everything out of order. Bright points of light I've never seen before, collections of stars clotted together that make no sense. It's a new sky, unmapped, uncharted. But the woman points a finger up to our left, to a place beyond the swaying treetops, where the sky is a small stain of black. No stars blinking. No light breaking through.

The black hole that I escaped is crossing through the galaxy, swallowing everything up, and soon it will reach this planet too.

"Is it the same as your shadow?" she asks.

I nod, memories snapping through me, of the moments just before the end. The erupting sky and crackling air and my body vibrating like I was going to shatter into pieces. "It's the same," I tell her.

"Every year it gets larger," she says, an edge to her voice. Like she already senses what it means. "How long do we have?"

I lower my eyes. "I'm not sure," I tell her honestly. "Years, probably. But your people will start getting sick before it ever reaches this planet. You will start losing your eyesight, your hearing, and then you will all begin dying."

She blinks at me, the dark sky in her eyes, weighing my words. "Then we have to leave before that happens."

I turn away from the shadow, unable to look at the thing that took everything from me, knowing that I haven't escaped it yet, that it's still coming for me. It should make me afraid, or angry, but instead I want to sink onto the sand and lie on my back and wait for it to come.

The woman touches my shoulder. "Thank you," she says, nodding. But I'm unable to look at her.

"I know you lost people you loved." She lowers her hand, gazing back up at the shadow. "But you made it here, and you'll save many people who would have died if you hadn't come."

I look at her now. "Where is your ship?"

"A day's sail from here, to the west. Near the rock island where we travel once a year for the founder's celebration."

I turn so I'm facing her, pale starlight casting across the strong features of her face. "But where will you go?"

"I don't know." The light dims in her eyes. "Without an Astronomer, we can't chart a course. But"—her mouth relaxes as she touches the braided strands of her hair—"we have all the maps from our Astronomer, before he died. Everything he recorded, all his notes. I can show you."

I want to tell her *no*. Tell her I'm not that girl anymore, that I just want to lie here and wait for the end.

But I also know . . .

I thought my story was over—the end nothing like I thought it would be. But maybe I haven't reached the end quite yet.

"Okay," I tell her.

✳ ✳ ✳

I sleep in the woman's home.

We eat fish and a brown, citrus-tasting nut crushed into a paste, and she tells me her name—Palona. I sleep and don't dream, and I'm grateful for it.

In the morning, Palona takes me in her narrow boat across the bay to another island, where several homes just like hers are built around trees at the shore. She tells me that the green spiky fruit growing on the trees keep the biting insects away, so they build their homes nestled against the trunks, they make fires in hollows in the sand to cook their fish, and they bathe in a freshwater stream that spills down from a mountain two islands away.

The boat slides ashore, and we make our way across the warm white sand to a small grass-sided structure situated by itself on the jagged point of the island, away from the others. "He was a private man," she tells me, her skin gleaming like copper in the shaft of sunlight through the door opening. "He preferred to be alone, to study the sky. And he never joined us for gatherings or the half-moon feasts."

Inside, I find that it's nothing like Palona's home. The Astronomer's dwelling is littered with slats of wood, constellations painted on each one in bright blue ink. There is a table against the trunk of the tree, with rolled sheets of thick paper littering the top. I see no bed, unless it's buried beneath the mess he's left behind.

Palona leaves me, and I stand in the center of his home, feeling like I might cry. I've lost too much, the numbness like an ocean that will never recede. A pain that will never be dulled. And I don't want any of this, to be here on this planet with these people. To pretend as if I can help them.

To start again.

I walk to the opening in the door and look out at the glistening sea, at the dozen islands I can see in the distance. These people have made a life here—a good life, it seems—but just like me, they will have to leave it behind. The twin suns arch across the sky, one a hint of blue, the other a duller orange than our own sun back on the planet I left behind.

I've lost everything.

The heartache like a tectonic shifting in my bones, rearranging who I used to be.

But as if by habit, a thing I know so well that it's unavoidable, I turn and walk back into the Astronomer's home. I sift through the scrolls of paper on his desk; I unearth a bed where more scrolls have been hidden underneath. I try to orient my place in the cosmos by studying his maps, learning the points of light he witnessed in their sky and charted during every season. I do it to distract my mind, to dull the minutes, the hours, that have become a thud in my skull. I do what I know: study the sky.

Their Astronomer might not have been a social man, but he was thorough, and every falling star, every flickering planet in their solar system, was meticulously recorded and marked. He left me a roadmap to follow, bread crumbs in every star he wrote down. He even has a telescope, but it's much more detailed, more elaborate, than Mom's. He did not make it himself. His telescope arrived with his ancestors on the ship, intact. Unlike the first Astronomer on my planet, whose telescope was lost when our ship tore through the atmosphere and crashed.

I also find notes about the shadow in their sky—but it was still only a small smear against the atmosphere when he made mention of it. He speculated what it might be, *a black hole*. But clearly he didn't share this with the others before his death. Maybe he thought it was so far away, it would never reach them, pass right on by, only grazing their outer solar system.

The day turns to evening, and Palona brings me cooked white fish and green fruit. But I eat alone, a wax candle burning on the desk while I read through a stack of detailed papers on the orbit of their tiny moon, so small that it hardly creates a tide in their calm waters. I press a finger to the space between my eyes. There's so much—and not enough.

And I don't know if there's enough fight left in me to do what they need: to find another planet like this one, survivable, habitable. A *Goldilocks planet*, Mom called it. A place so rare and perfect, it's nearly impossible to find. One that they can chart a course to. But I feel too battered. I need time, rest, to burrow myself in the dark of my mind and let myself grieve.

They think I'm a savior, but I'm too broken to be any good to anyone.

I push my half-finished plate away, the hunger replaced by an old, ever-present ache.

But within that pain, tucked inside it, is another feeling. One I remember from the valley, just before Mom died, a pulse just beneath the center of my ribs: a responsibility.

A role I might not want, but one I've been handed all the same.

I rest my cheek on the desk, staring across the Astronomer's cramped home, at stacks of paper and wood slats and scraps of tree fronds. The desk wobbles beneath me, uneven on the woven grass floor. I tilt my gaze and notice something beneath one of the legs. A notebook, placed there to balance the table, keep it level. I prop up the desk and pull it free, flipping it open in my lap.

At first, it looks just like all the other notebooks written by the Astronomer, detailed logs of star patterns and declinations. But several pages in, he begins writing about something else.

Black holes.

He questions their origin, their movement through our galaxy. And he even poses a theory: Perhaps a planet could pass through one . . . and survive. Stretched thin, time made long and perilous, but on the other side, all might be restored.

I sink onto the grass floor, reading through the pages quickly, the candlelight making fractured patterns across the paper. At the top of a page near the back, reads: *Black Hole Exploration.* And below it, he has written out a calculation to define the celestial place where a black hole begins and ends.

If a planet was to survive passing through one, he had determined a way to calculate where it might be spit back out into some far region of the universe.

The breath drops into my stomach, and a torch ignites in my chest, followed by the rush of unstoppable tears. I stand quickly, clutching the notebook, and scramble out the small doorway. A bonfire is burning several yards down the beach, a dozen people gathered around it, eating, talking, laughing voices bouncing up to the night sky. I stop short, not moving toward them—a gnawing in my chest at seeing so many people, unaware of what I've lost, of what they, too, might lose—but one of the figures rises, noticing me, and strides across the beach.

Palona's hair spins outward in the soft wind, and when she reaches me, she lowers her eyes to my face, an impossible aqua color in the moonlight. "What is it?" She already senses the gravity in my eyes.

"I think I know where we need to go."

She watches me, giving me the space, the time, to continue.

"It's nearly impossible to find another planet like this one," I say, glancing out to the motionless water. "Or like the one I came from. One that will sustain life. It's why we traveled so far from Earth. But I think—" I clear my throat. "I think your Astronomer found another way. We don't need to find a new planet, we just need to find mine."

Her flaxen eyebrows tuck together. "I don't understand."

"If your Astronomer was right, then there's a chance my planet survived going through the black hole. It might be out there somewhere, tossed out the other end into some distant part of the universe." A smile steals across my lips, a rumble in my chest that feels dangerously like hope. "The people on my planet were sick because of the black hole. Too much dark matter was pouring through our atmosphere, but now that it's passed through the center of the shadow, and out the other side, there shouldn't be any dark matter left. The planet should be inhabitable . . . livable."

She is quiet for a time, the night breeze stirring her long braids. "What about your people?"

The smile fades from my lips, quick as water. "Your Astronomer didn't think they could survive." My throat wants to close up, the hurt pulsing behind my eyes. But I continue. "But if the planet is still there, if we can find it, then—"

"It's our only chance," she finishes, swaying her eyes up to the sky, finding the blur of black on the horizon—the shadow—the anomaly moving through our galaxy, tearing apart solar systems. Death, inching closer, *closer*.

"But how will we find it?" she asks.

"Your Astronomer figured out a formula, a calculation, a way to determine the black hole's end point as long as you know the starting point."

"And you know the starting point?"

I turn, lifting my hair from my neck, letting her see the tattoo I've spent my life keeping hidden. "It's inked onto my skin," I say, the words coming out breathless, like I can't get them out fast enough. Because I know the declinations of my home planet better than I know the valley. I know the exact point in the sky where the black hole swallowed it up, the exact place where everyone I loved perished.

Palona nods, a light in her eyes, a dangerous glimmer of excitement. "We'll hold a gathering in the morning, tell people what's coming. We'll start preparing the ship."

✳ ✳ ✳

My name—Vega—means *dweller in the meadow*. But it also means something else: it's the name of our star, our sun, on the planet where our ancestors landed a hundred years ago. A planet that was swallowed up by a black hole.

Palona leaves me on the beach to bring in the last of their fishing nets, and I stay, lying on my back in the sand, overcome with a feeling I can't begin to describe. I count the stars as they appear in the watery sky—constellations that are nothing like the ones I've spent my life memorizing. Formations that have no meaning.

But somewhere out there, I hope . . . our planet has survived. And maybe, somehow, *impossibly*, Noah has too. And all the rest.

My fingers dig down into the sand, and the sea slides up onto the beach over my legs, then retreats back down again, displacing sand and driftwood and rocks. Displacing me, in the endless pattern of stars. I am a girl on a planet where she doesn't belong.

I squeeze my eyes shut, and in the farthest back of my mind, in the deepest hollow of my broken, split-apart chest, some part of me needs to believe—needs to dream. If he didn't drown, if our planet made it through and out the other side, if there's a chance my people weren't broken apart when they slid through the dark, lightless center of the black hole . . . then I will search for him, all of them.

I swing my gaze upward, force my eyelids back, and look up at the altered sky. If our lives are stories written in the stars . . . then I will find him again. Just like before.

The Astronomer and the Architect, fated like Perseus and Andromeda.

I will map the sky and make new marks on my skin—black ink to chart the way. I will find Noah. Just like I was always meant to. My path woven into the starlight, braided into my bones, just like every woman before me.

Our story is not done yet.

Acknowledgments

I wrote this book at the end of 2019, not knowing how much the world would change in the months that followed, or how eerily poignant this story would feel by the time of its publication. And yet, here we are.

There are countless people to thank who helped bring this book to life. Firstly, thank you to my husband, Sky, who talked through the elements of this story with me when I was drafting it over the course of a single month—the fastest I've ever written a novel. This book wouldn't be what it is without you.

Thank you to Nicole Ellul for going on another adventure with me! A big thanks to Justin Chanda for giving my stories a home. Thank you, Kendra Levin, for all that you do. Thank you to the whole team at Simon & Schuster BFYR: Katrina Grover, Clare McGlade, Sara Berko, Hilary Zarycky, Christy Noh, Nicole Russo. Thank you, Lauren Castner, for getting my books into new readers' hands. Thank you, Mitch Thorpe, for your enthusiasm and organization. Thank you, Sarah Creech and Jim Tierney, for the magical, star-adorned cover. Many of you work behind the scenes, and I hope readers will see your names and remember them, because you all make books possible. I am indebted to each of you.

Thank you to Jess Regel for encouraging all my absurd story ideas. A big thanks to my publicist, Kristin Dwyer, for being my second brain. Thank you, Jenny Meyer and Heidi Gall. Thanks to

Jody Hotchkiss for your wisdom. To Leo Teti, thank you for your endless enthusiasm.

But mostly, thank you to those of you who made it to the end of the book and took the time to read these acknowledgments. Your love of stories and imagination give me hope that humankind is filled with more goodness and possibility than what we often see in the news. Keep looking up. Keep dreaming. The world is bigger than we know.